# GULAG

## SEAN FLANNERY

CHARTER BOOKS, NEW YORK

GULAG

A Charter Book / published by arrangement with
the author

PRINTING HISTORY
Charter edition / February 1987

ISBN: 0-441-30598-9

Charter Books are published by The Berkley Publishing Group,
200 Madison Avenue, New York, New York 10016.
PRINTED IN THE UNITED STATES OF AMERICA

This book is for Laurie

M.I.C.E., which stands for Money, Ideology, Compromise, and Ego.

*An old CIA acronym*
*for why spies defect.*

When the sheath is broken, you cannot hide the sword.

*An old Russian proverb.*

*Gulag* is a Russian acronym for Chief Administration of Corrective Labor Camps.

# I

# THE INVESTIGATION

Moscow was decked out for the Winter Festival, New Year's Eve only six days away. The theater season was in full swing, circuses from a dozen of the republics were in town, and the gigantic Luzhniki Stadium had opened in Carnival on Wednesday.

The dark gray Zhiguli sedan came around the corner onto Duzhinik Street, doused its lights, and stopped on the east side of the Moscow Zoo. Two men got out, one very tall and lean, nearly cadaverous. The other, slightly shorter but much huskier, was the deputy chief of the KGB's Second Chief Directorate's First Department. Both men were wrapped in thick, fur-lined parkas. They hurried across the street to the zoo entrance where they listened to the surveillance team who had followed Bertonelli from the American embassy two blocks away. The surveillance was routine, though this night it was only happenstance that they picked up his trail. Bertonelli, who worked for the embassy as a trade mission specialist, was in fact the number two man in charge of Central Intelligence Agency activities in Moscow. In the year he had been here, he'd been watched carefully, though from time to time he did manage to elude his surveillants. The relief team driving over to the embassy had been early. They spotted Bertonelli emerging from the apartment building connecting with the embassy, and followed him. They reported he had entered the zoo an hour earlier, on foot. With a Soviet citizen, whom he'd met across the street.

The deputy chief was less concerned about the Russian than he was with Bertonelli. He had worked for months to get something concrete on the American spy. Enough to call for

3

his expulsion from the Soviet Union. This now tonight seemed tailor-made.

Two trucks ground their way up from the Lubyanka, the noise loud in the quiet street. They parked down the block. Quietly, a dozen uniformed troops jumped down from each truck, formed up at attention, and their officer, a young KGB lieutenant, dog-trotted up the middle of the street. It was intensely cold, well below zero centigrade, too cold for snow.

The KGB was divided into four chief directorates and seven subdirectorates. The deputy chief was number three in command of the department within one of the major directorates that was charged with subverting foreign diplomats, and denying them any unapproved contact with Soviet citizens.

"Major Kostikov." The young lieutenant, green piping on his uniform, saluted, coming to attention in front of the deputy chief.

"You will not move until I give the word. I want no bloodbath here," Valeri Kostikov snapped. He looked beyond the lieutenant to his troops.

"Yes, sir." There was little love lost between Kostikov and the lieutenant who was technically under the command of the unnumbered Border Guard Directorate, on rotation here to Moscow.

"Disperse your troops around the park perimeter. I want every possible exit covered," Valeri said. "Do it now!"

"Sir!"

Contrary to regulation, Valeri carried a Western weapon, an Italian-made Beretta .380. It was a small-caliber automatic. He liked it for its accuracy, its compactness, and its elegance. He pulled it from his pocket and checked to make sure a shell was in the chamber and the safety was on. Bertonelli was a dangerous man. The so far unidentified Russian was an unknown factor. He wanted no slipups.

"Perhaps you were too hard on the snotnose," the tall thin man, Shevchenko, said contemptuously.

"They're used to it." Valeri pocketed his gun. The Border Guard troops were dog-trotting both ways up the street, the first of them disappearing around the far corner onto Zvenigorod Highway. Traffic had been blocked off in the vicinity of the zoo. It had all happened very fast in response to the call from the primary surveillance team. Maybe this time there would be enough hard evidence to send Bertonelli home. This time there would be no mistakes. This time Valeri would supervise the operation himself. Directly. Behind him, the bells in the Kremlin towers each sounded once, signifying the hour. Elsewhere across the great city parties were in full swing. May Day was for the worker; V-E Day was for the Veteran; the Great October Revolution Day, November 7, was for the patriot; but the Winter Festival—which lasted twelve days from December 25 through January 5—was for the Russian spirit, which loved a sloppy, drunken party. The Militia was very busy in this season.

"No one else is in the zoo?" Valeri asked. "No one followed them inside?"

"No, sir," Lipasov, the thick-shouldered surveillance team chief said. "That is, none of our people are inside. There may be park maintenance staff."

"No heroes here tonight, Valerik," Shevchenko said. "I'm going in with you." Shevchenko was Valeri's chief of staff. They got along well with each other, and Valeri had a great deal of respect for the other's abilities and judgment.

"We'll split up inside. I would very much like to hear what they're saying. We need hard evidence, Mikhail, do you understand?"

"Perfectly. But no heroes. Your father would never forgive me. Bertonelli is a very hard man."

"One we will do well to be rid of."

Shevchenko checked his weapon, a standard-issue 7.65mm TK automatic, as Lipasov unlocked the gate. Valeri stepped inside, the odor of zoo animals suddenly assailing his nostrils. This was a maintenance gate. A narrow paved path led into the park. Hulking dark buildings rose above the trees, which were bare now in winter. Bertonelli and the Russian had come this way. They had not left. They were still here. Discussing what? State secrets?

The gate closed with a soft click, and Shevchenko was right behind him.

"We'll stay off the path," Valeri said without looking back. "You go right, I'll take left."

Shevchenko had his weapon out. Valeri looked into the older man's eyes. "I want no bodies, Mikhail. This is no *mokrie dela*. No cowboys and Indians."

"Nor will I be dogmeat, Valerik." Shevchenko stepped off

the path and a moment or two later was lost in the darkness toward the interior of the park.

Valeri waited a few seconds longer, then stepped off the path and worked his way through the bare trees and well-tended bushes along the perimeter stone wall.

A lion or some other large animal roared in the distance to the right. The big cats were mostly kept inside at this time of year. Perhaps it had been a bear. Valeri angled away from the wall, catching glimpses of a fountain or some statuary marking the wider thoroughfares in the system of paths. He came to a tall fence of iron bars that enclosed a yard of dirt and rock. Three trees, each with only a couple of limbs from which hung old rubber tires on chains, cast shadows from several strong overhead lights.

It had been a very long time since the deputy chief had been in a zoo. Even as a youngster they had made him sad. The first had been Leningrad, before his fifth birthday. He couldn't really remember it, but his mother, before she died, told him that he had cried for days afterward. She had been sensitive too. Neither of them liked anything caged.

A stray gust of wind rattled one of the metal reflectors on the lights, startling Valeri, and he spun around reaching for his gun until he realized what it was. It was so quiet here in the park. He'd been home when the call came. Listening to music, sipping champagne, the apartment warm and comfortable. He wished for a cigarette now, but the odor of tobacco would surely give him away.

Valeri skirted the lights, hesitating before he crossed the paths, watching and listening both ways from the shadows, then silently slipping across behind the large trees, keeping the lines of hedges between himself and the openings.

Across Gruzinskaya from the park a large domed building rose up above the others. It housed the planetarium, the one place near the zoo he had loved. Red, green, and blue lights bathed the curved roof. It was a place of promise. Twenty years ago his father had taken him to meet the stocky peasant cosmonaut Yuri Gagarin. In Washington he had met John Glenn, Jr. He liked Gagarin better, though he had seen the similarities of character.

The night had turned really cold. Valeri could see his breath thick in the dim light. Why the zoo? he asked himself as he kept moving. Why had they selected this place to meet?

Why not a warm apartment somewhere? Why not GUM, the big department store, during the day when there were crowds? A written message could easily have been passed without detection. Why here in this isolation?

The zoo was divided roughly in two, east to west, by a broad tiled walkway along which were ice-cream vendors, souvenir shops, rest rooms, and park benches. This was the place, especially in the summer, where most of the pedestrian traffic converged. Zookeepers came up and down this main thoroughfare pushing large handcarts laden with buckets of meat or feed for the animals. Children ran after the carts each day to watch the feeding. It was the ferocious noise, the roaring and growling and snapping they loved. Better than the cinema, because here it was real.

Valeri hesitated at the edge of the path, behind a short iron fence. Only every fourth stanchion light was working, lending a soft, mottled effect to the open area. Off to the right, just beyond a stand that sold *kvas*, whitefish, and potatoes and vinegar at sidewalk tables, Valeri spotted two figures in the shadows.

For a long moment he stood stock-still, but then the two moved out of sight beyond the pavilion, and Valeri jumped over the low fence. It was about a hundred meters to the outdoor restaurant, and he raced as silently as he could on the balls of his feet, keeping his eyes glued to the corner of the building around which they had disappeared, lest they return and spot him.

He reached the turnstile gate to the tables on which the chairs had been piled and leaped over it without slowing, threading his way to the face of the building, the openings at the counters all closed up now with wooden shutters. His heart was pounding, his breath ragged. He wasn't used to the exercise.

The paint on the building was chipped and peeling, and Valeri smelled something that he could not immediately identify. As he moved closer to the corner he thought it was coming from inside the pavilion. Something sweet, such as sugar water, perhaps lemonade. There were no sounds. He got to the end of the building, when he heard a voice speaking Russian, but with a heavy American accent. He froze, all at once realizing what he had smelled. It was cologne. American after-shave lotion.

Quickly he pulled off his gloves, stuffed them in his pocket, and withdrew his gun. The voice stopped. He listened a moment or two longer, then took a deep breath and stepped around the corner.

"KGB—you're under arrest!" he shouted.

A short squat man in a long dark overcoat was just turning around. Beyond him a much taller man in a Militia uniform disappeared around the corner.

"Fuck your mother," the squat man spat in Russian.

Valeri got the momentary impression of a very large handgun coming around, when he fired twice, both shots catching the short man in the chest, driving him backward, his arms flying out, his gun dropping, and a grunt escaping from his lips.

Garbage cans crashed at the rear of the building, and the other man swore in English.

Valeri leaped over the downed Russian, whose legs were violently twitching, his heels pounding the frozen ground, and skidded recklessly around the corner.

"Stop! KGB!" he shouted at the back of the figure crossing the playground.

Valeri stooped down into a crouch, bringing the Beretta up in both hands in the approved shooter's stance, and squeezed off a shot just as the man disappeared into a copse of trees.

"Shit," he snarled. He had been wide by a kilometer.

A shrill whistle blew back toward the main entrance as Valeri raced across the playground and crashed through the brush in the direction the other man had gone. It was Bertonelli. There was no doubt of it in his mind. But he had been wearing a Militia uniform. The surveillance team had said nothing about that. What the hell had happened here?

The trees gave way to a hill that children used for tobogganing when there was enough snow. It rose up past the bear cages. Valeri stopped a moment before he exposed himself to the open ground in time to see a flash of movement at the crest. It was impossible for anyone to be that fast, he thought, stepping away from the trees.

He bent into the hill, his legs driving like pistons, his feet slipping on the thin snow and frozen grass beneath. He fell, scrambled back to his feet, and topped the rise.

More whistles were blowing behind him, and he could hear

several men shouting. He thought he heard Shevchenko calling his name somewhere off to the north, but he wasn't sure.

A broad path led left and right; a large building housing the aviary was straight across. Valeri hesitated again. It was Bertonelli. He was caught in the park. Where would he go? He had to have had a plan.

More whistles blew off to the left, and he turned that way. Below was the Presnensky Street exit. Just around the corner, barely a block and a half away, was the American embassy. Militia uniform! Motherless whore, it was brilliant!

Valeri spun on his heel and raced down the path, his feet flying, his stride too broad.

Several of the uniformed Border Guard were hurrying up the path from the gate.

"Stop him!" Valeri shouted. "KGB! Stop him!"

The troops pulled up short, confused for a moment, their weapons trained on the rapidly approaching figure.

"You stupid bastards, he's getting away!" Valeri shouted. He slipped on a patch of ice and fell headlong on his outthrust elbows, pain jarring his shoulders and numbing his fingers.

He scrambled to his feet. He was all out of breath, and his side ached. He thought he had broken a rib in the fall. The Border Guard troops were blocking the path. They were all staring at him. It didn't matter. It was too late. He took a tentative step forward, but then stopped.

Shevchenko was coming over the hill past the aviary, others were hurrying up the path from beyond the bear cages, and still more whistles blew in the distance. Russians did love to make a fuss.

"Who has gotten away, sir?" one of the troops asked respectfully.

"A tall man," Valeri said. "In a Militia uniform."

"There were shots."

Valeri shook his head in disgust. They were farm boys, but it was he who had made the mistake. He had warned them that there was to be no shooting. No mistakes, and he had bungled it. He had the experience. He had been taught by the very best. Yet in the end his pride had overcome good common sense. The Border Guard soldiers were worried that they had done something wrong. Well, let them worry, Valeri thought.

"You may stand down," he said. "This operation is over."

"Are you all right?" Shevchenko puffed, out of breath. He had run clear across the zoo.

Valeri pocketed his Beretta and gestured back the way he had come. "I shot our fellow citizen. But Bertonelli got away. He was wearing a Militia uniform, an unfortunate circumstance we did not foresee."

Shevchenko looked at the troops. "They let him pass?"

The young lieutenant arrived with two more troops. "There was shooting," he said.

"Your people may stand down, Lieutenant. Thank you for your kind assistance."

"What has happened, sir?"

"Go make your report. You are finished here," Valeri snapped.

The lieutenant was brash. He was losing face in front of his men. "May I remind you, sir, that this was a cooperative effort."

"You may not . . ." Valeri growled, but Shevchenko stepped between them.

"There are many excellent opportunities for the right young man with the Northern Missile Defense Command. Perhaps a word in your favor, Comrade Lieutenant?"

The lieutenant, chastised, saluted, turned stiffly on his heel, and screamed at his troops. "What are you gawking at? You heard the man, we're done here!"

"Was it Bertonelli?" Shevchenko asked as they watched the lieutenant and his troops march in close order down the hill.

"I think so," Valeri said. "He got hold of a Militia uniform from somewhere. Not too difficult, actually. And he just waltzed out the gate."

"He's a sharp bastard. Are you really all right?"

"I'll live," Valeri said. He and Shevchenko followed the paths the long way back down to the pavilion where the squat Russian lay on his back, his eyes open, steam rising from the blood that had poured out of his chest.

"Do we know him?" Shevchenko asked, stepping around the body. It was clear the man was dead.

"I don't think so." Valeri carefully opened the dead man's coat and extracted his wallet, which contained a KGB identification card and party booklet.

"What do you know," Shevchenko said.

Valeri looked up. Shevchenko was holding a very large handgun in his gloved hand. He recognized it immediately as a Graz Burya. The "Enforcer." The KGB Department Viktor's weapon of choice for assassination. Had they stumbled on an executive-action operation? he wondered. Had Bertonelli been marked for elimination? Had he been lured here to the zoo so that he could be killed?

The card identified the man as Rotislav Yefimovich Okulov . . . Colonel Okulov.

"KGB?" Shevchenko asked softly as if the trees had ears.

Again Valeri looked up and nodded. "Colonel Okulov."

"Was he here to rid us of Bertonelli?" Shevchenko asked. He was upset.

Valeri got stiffly to his feet. He shook his head. "Listen to me, Mikhail. They were together here in the zoo for at least an hour. If it was going to happen, it would have happened much sooner." He shook his head again. "I identified myself, but this one was ready to shoot me. He is no friend of the Soviet Union. I can guarantee it."

"A traitor, Valerik?"

"It would appear so."

"Fuck," Shevchenko said. "This is going to be a very long day."

It was not unusual. Or at least it was not surprising to Valeri. Bertonelli's specialty was turning intelligence service operators. He had done it in Chile, in Berlin, and a few years ago in New York. There was never any proof, of course. Had there been, the American would never have been allowed into the Soviet Union. But the rumor had it that a platinum American Express credit card had done the trick. Bertonelli had passed the card to a Soviet KGB officer working out of the United Nations under cover as a diplomat. The poor fool had gone on a spending spree, and in the end three credit bureaus and a dozen credit collection agencies had pestered the man to such an extent that his only recourse was to turn to the Americans for money.

There was nothing else in the dead man's pockets other than a few rubles and kopecks, a comb, a package of pipe tobacco, and a well-worn Danish-made pipe. But no matches or lighter. It was odd.

"I'll stay with him," Shevchenko volunteered.

Valeri pocketed Okulov's identification, and the big gun.

"I'll send the Technical Operations van along with the pathologist. Stick with the body. I want you to watch the autopsy."

"Shit," Shevchenko swore. "He was shot to death. By you, Valerik."

"I want to know if there is any evidence of alcohol or drugs in his bloodstream."

Shevchenko shrugged sheepishly. "Bertonelli could have fucked him up."

"Exactly. And watch yourself, Mikhail. If he wasn't working alone, there'll be a cover-up."

"Thanks for nothing."

Valeri let himself out of the zoo through the main gate as the Border Guard trucks were roaring around the corner. He briefly explained to the surveillance team what had happened, and ordered them to stand by at the gate for the van and the doctor. Across the street he got into his car, started the engine with some difficulty, and as it was warming up he radioed control at the Lubyanka Center, identifying himself and requesting a Technical Operations van and the pathologist, all in code. He was Hammerhead Three, the van was Pushkin One through Seven, and the pathologist was Look See. This was something new since the Americans had begun monitoring KGB spot communications on a twenty-four-hour basis.

He drove way, across the Zvenigorod Highway, traffic already beginning to flow again, though it was mostly taxis, back toward the inner circle along Kudrinskaya Street. Steam rose from the manhole covers in the middle of the streets, and an ice haze had formed around the street lights. Tonight would break temperature records. Coming around the corner within sight of the Kalinina Prospekt, he pulled into a courtyard beside a five-story yellow brick building that looked like a warehouse but in fact housed the Second Chief Directorate's Department One. The guard at the gate recognized him and swung open the barrier so that he could drive through without stopping. He parked in the back and took the elevator up to the fourth floor.

Department One was a huge operation charged with keeping track of U.S. and Latin American diplomats in Moscow. Besides a chief and two deputies, the staff included fifty officers, a corps of reservists, recruiters, and agent handlers, as well as three hundred professional surveillants on perma-

nent loan from the Surveillance Directorate. Because of his
education and his background, which included a number of
years in Washington, D.C., Valeri was in charge of the U.S.
operation. In the basement was a new IBM mainframe computer, and on the roof were dozens of communications antennae and dishes, all necessary in order to maintain a certain
order in the herculean task.

The "Wild West," as the facility was called, never slept.
It was one of the busiest operations within the entire KGB.
Nevertheless, Valeri was surprised to see the chief of the
entire directorate, a tall, massive man with a Georgian face
and the Order of Lenin medal hanging from the breast pocket
of his black suitcoat, waiting in the busy U.S. Situation
Room, over which Valeri's office looked.

"Ah, Valerik," the general said, putting down the glass of
tea he had been drinking.

"Good morning, Comrade General. I was not expecting
you," Valeri said.

The general laughed. They embraced warmly. General
Gennadi Demin was a close personal friend of Valeri's father.
He had been like an uncle.

"How is Tanya? Better?"

Valeri shrugged, a little hurt rising. "It is the same."

General Demin shook his massive head sadly. "You would
think the very best Soviet doctors . . . the very best in the
world . . ." He let it trail off.

The computer operators in the dimly lit blue room had not
failed to notice the affection the general held for Valeri. He
was well liked. But no one thought Valeri let the close
personal relationship, or his own privileged background, go
to his head. He was considered a very fair man, if a bit
zealous at times when he had a bone in his teeth.

"This business with our friend Anthony Bertonelli in the
zoo, of all places," the general said. "I understand there
were shots."

Close family friend or not, Valeri knew enough not to cross
the invisible line by wondering out loud how the general had
gotten the information so quickly. The man was incredible.

"They were my shots. I fired," Valeri said.

The general was startled. "You are not pulling my leg,
Valerik? This is very serious."

"I didn't shoot Bertonelli. It was a Russian."

"Is he dead?"

"Yes."

"What of Bertonelli?"

The half-dozen computer operators were busy with their work, but Valeri was certain they had overheard most of what had been said. He did not think it wise that they hear more.

"I think we should go up to my office, Comrade General," he said.

A momentary look of irritation crossed the general's face. He had the reputation of being an exceedingly hard man when he was crossed. Valeri had never actually seen the man lose his temper, but rumors were legion.

"Where is your chief of staff?"

"With the body. He is waiting for the Technical Operations van, and the pathologist. He will supervise the autopsy."

"Anyone else there?"

"The Border Guard troops have left. Only my two surveillance teams are still at the scene."

"Militia?"

"No, sir," Valeri said. "Excuse me, but I think it would be better if we went to my office."

"There is more?"

"Yes, Comrade General."

They went up the iron stairs to Valeri's office behind a tall glass window that afforded him a view of the entire Situation Room. He had had the place modified himself, with the general's approval, two years ago. It gave him a better sense of the hour to-hour happenings within his department. Best of all it had finally curtailed the Russian vice of procrastination among his staff. On the opposite wall was a large window that overlooked the rear courtyard and, beyond, the Museum of the Revolution.

"Now, my nephew, do not disappoint me," General Demin said. "Are you in trouble?"

"No, sir," Valeri replied, surprised at the general's remark. "But I believe I may need your advice."

They had not bothered to sit. They faced each other in front of Valeri's littered desk. A lot of books lined one inner wall. On the other was a map of the Soviet Union flanked by a dozen or more photographs of him, his mother and father, and his sister Lara in widely separated settings around the world. Always they were smiling.

"What happened to Bertonelli?" the general asked.

"Unfortunately, he managed to escape from the zoo. He was wearing a Militia uniform, though I have no idea, yet, how he got it. My people reported that he entered the zoo in ordinary civilian clothes."

"Yes?"

Quickly Valeri told the general every single thing that was said and done up to the point where he searched the Russian's body.

Valeri took the dead man's wallet from his pocket and handed it to the general. "He was armed with a Graz Burya."

The general opened the wallet and stared at the KGB identification card for a long time. Then he sagged. He turned and went to the outside window where he looked out over the city, a wistful set to his shoulders. It seemed as if he had received an unexpected blow.

"I am sorry, Comrade General, but did you know this man?"

"Of course. He worked for me."

This was terrible. Worse, it had the potential of becoming a disaster. Traitors did not betray their country on a whim, out of the clear blue sky. They did so after a long period of disintegration and corruption, signs of which were clearly recognizable to the able administrator. The supervisor of a man who defected was held accountable for his lack of vision, foresight, and observation. In turn, supervisors did not become lax in their duties overnight. It was a gradual but clearly foreseeable process. Woe be it to the administrator who failed to recognize such signs in his subordinate supervisor. And so it went. The list continued upward . . . only to a point, perhaps, but directorate chiefs were not above the ax.

"There now is no identification on the body," Valeri said. "Perhaps a very quiet investigation to assess the damage . . ."

General Demin spun around, his face livid with rage. "I forbid this talk!" he bellowed.

Valeri was taken aback.

"Do you hear me, Valerik? I forbid it!" General Demin glanced again at the ID card, then tossed the wallet down on Valeri's desk. He seemed to have grown half a meter in stature, though Valeri could see he was deeply shaken.

"Then my investigation—"

"Shall proceed as normal. But make no mistake about it, this is a very special case."

"Of course . . ."

"Of course nothing, nephew," the general said distantly. Then he came to himself. "Rotislav Okulov is not an ordinary name. I am surprised you did not recognize it."

Valeri racked his brain, but the name meant nothing to him. He shook his head.

"His father, now dead, was a member of the Presidium. His grandfather, Baron Okulov, was one of the very few czarists to successfully make the transition and survive the purges. They all were patriots, and exceedingly capable administrators. Leaders. Contributors to the Communist party. This Rotislav had an uncle who is a nuclear scientist, and a brother, I believe, serving on the Politburo staff. A very important family, which makes it all the more hurtful."

"Which means my investigation will be very quiet."

The general's eyes were pale. "We are a nation of laws, Valerik. One must not be swayed by important names. That was what 1917 was all about."

"I understand," Valeri said.

"On the other hand, a bad compromise is better than a good battle."

"What is important here, is Bertonelli. He is a devil. He must be removed."

General Demin put his finger to the side of his nose. "But with care, Valerik, and precision and, most definitely, with delicacy."

"May I come by later this morning for Okulov's file?"

The general thought a moment. "Better yet, I'll arrange for you to see his office. There may be something there. Some clue to his aberration."

"Won't questions be asked?"

"No," General Demin said flatly. He went to the door. "Give my regards to Tanya."

"Thank you," Valeri said, and the general left.

Alone in his office, Valeri pulled his files on Bertonelli and on Roland DeMille, the handsome career intelligence officer who was presently the CIA's chief of station in Moscow, and who presumably in the next few years would be elevated to deputy director of Operations back in Langley. DeMille's name was one of the more closely guarded secrets within the

KGB. His position was supposedly safe. In the clear. The Americans apparently did not yet know that the KGB had positively identified him for what he really was. Through a carefully engineered series of disinformation operations, under Valeri's direct supervision, his department had targeted Richard Scofield as the CIA chief of station. Scofield in fact was nothing more than an ordinary analyst. But the Americans were convinced by the ruse.

He looked for a pattern in DeMille's and Bertonelli's movements over the past six months or so, from the logs built up by his surveillance teams. Something that would indicate an operation to force the defection by Okulov. But there was nothing discernible. Except for Bertonelli's random disappearances (and then usually only for an hour or less each time until he was picked up again), there was little reason for anyone to suspect that such an important man as Okulov was the target of an operation.

At around four-thirty he telephoned the Technical Operations supervisor to ask if the van and pathologist had indeed been dispatched. He was assured that it had gone out and had already returned. A report would be forthcoming later in the day.

Next, he telephoned the forensics lab at the Lubyanka Center. It was a special direct number; nevertheless it rang twenty-five times before it was answered. Valeri identified himself and asked to speak to Captain Shevchenko, who would probably be in or near the autopsy room.

It was a full ten minutes before Shevchenko came on the line.

"I'm sorry, Valerik, but there is nothing to report as of yet."

"Has the autopsy already been performed?"

"They finished twenty minutes ago. Cause of death was massive destruction of the left ventricle of his heart, precipitated by a thirty-eight-caliber projectile." Shevchenko chuckled with the rough humor. "Your second shot punctured the bastard's right lung, but by then he was dead or dying."

"What about his bloodstream, Mikhail? Any evidence he was drugged?"

"There is one final gas chromatograph test to be completed, and another on the mass spectrometer, but both will have to wait until late this afternoon, I am told. Perhaps not until tomorrow. There was some vodka in the poor bastard's stomach, along with fish and potatoes, some caviar, and some black bread. Not a pretty sight or smell, I'm telling you, Valeri. But the doctor told me there was no outward evidence that the man was either drunk or drugged.''

"Anything else?" Valeri asked. "Anything at all?"

"Nothing. Have we found out anything about him yet?"

"Plenty," Valeri said. "Are you finished there?"

Shevchenko was sharp. He picked up on Valeri's curt answer. The walls did have ears. So did telephones. "I can see no reason to hang around here for the rest of the morning. They will send their reports to us in due time. You know how it is.''

If ever, Valeri finished the thought. "Go home and get some sleep now. Have Sasha fix you a big breakfast, and get back here by ten. There will be much work to do. Bring Lipasov and Votrin along with you." They were surveillance chiefs working Bertonelli.

"What about you?"

"I'm going home," Valeri said. He hung up, pulled on his coat, and locked up his office. Downstairs in the Situation Room, before he left he stopped at the night supervisor's desk. She was a young woman in her mid-twenties with an incredibly sharp mind, and a Western hairdo of which she was very proud.

"Good morning, Comrade Major," she said, looking up from the computer screen. Valeri suspected she was in love with him, from afar.

"If either Bertonelli or DeMille makes a move, I wish to be informed immediately. No delays."

"Of course. Will you be at home?"

"Yes."

The woman smiled. "Good night, then."

Again Valeri had trouble starting his car. When it finally caught he had to let it warm up for a long time before it would move. He drove home. His modern apartment was on the sixth floor of a new building in the Southwestern District in the Lenin Hills just off Gagarin Square, and barely two blocks from the Moscow River. The elevator was out of order again, so he had to trudge up the stairs. The lights were still burning in his living room, but the Tchaikovsky tape he had been listening to before he left had run out, the full reel still turning, its tail softly flapping.

"Tanya?" he shouted, slamming the door.

There was no answer. He threw off his coat and rushed into the bedroom. His wife lay curled in a fetal position on the floor beside the bed. She had had a seizure. The room smelled strongly of feces and urine. She was awake, her long black hair in disarray, the back of her white nightgown stained, tears streaming down her cheeks.

"You bastard," she croaked weakly.

Mindless of the dirtied gown, Valeri gathered her tiny, frail body into his arms and took her into the bathroom where he carefully undressed her, ran warm water in the tub, then gently set her down. She looked up at him, hate in her large dark eyes, as he peeled off his suit jacket, undid his tie, and pulled off his shirt. Then he began washing her, goosebumps standing up on her arms and shoulders, and the nipples on her tiny breasts erect.

"Oh, Tanya," he sighed. His heart was breaking, but there was nothing he could do.

Outraged, Roland DeMille, Moscow chief of station for CIA activities in the Soviet Union, paced back and forth behind his desk. He looked almost like a movie star, with his modishly long dark hair, graying at the temples, blue eyes, and good build, and he carried himself as if he were well aware of that. Most of his subordinates hated him, while his superiors loved him. He was the perfect Company man.

"I've spent eighteen months building Scofield as the mark. Building trust, building an atmosphere in which we can finally get something done. Some real work. And in this the ambassador has clearly given me his support." He stopped in mid-stride to look at Bertonelli who stood at the door. "In one night you've threatened to tear down everything I've done."

Bertonelli was a large man, with broad features and thick, muscular limbs. But he had the grace and economy of movement of a thirty-six-year-old who was a former college football star and who had, before his posting to Moscow as number two man behind DeMille, spent the better part of six months chasing around the mountains of Afghanistan. In another time or place, he thought, he would probably take DeMille apart.

"Kostikov couldn't have been sure it was me," he said.

DeMille's office was carpeted. A flashy, full-length oil portrait of his wife Stephanie hung over the porcelain-tiled fireplace across the narrow room from the single window covered with thick steel mesh. The mesh was tied to a white-noise transmitter that effectively blocked most types of electronic surveillance.

20

"He followed you to the zoo, didn't he?" DeMille's hands were shaking. "What does that tell you?"

"Kostikov was following the colonel. But even if they were on me, it wasn't a setup. They would have taken us immediately."

DeMille scowled. "They had him spotted as a defector, then."

"He wasn't trying to defect, Roland." Bertonelli was tired and still jumpy from the near encounter. This time the Russians had come uncomfortably close to finally nailing him. It would happen sooner or later, he thought, if he didn't quit screwing around.

"Then, traitor. I don't care which terminology."

The telephone on DeMille's desk burred softly. He turned in irritation and answered it. "Yes," he snapped, but then his entire attitude underwent an instant transformation. "Yes, Ambassador," he said civilly. He glanced at Bertonelli, then turned away.

Bertonelli lit a cigarette, then stared up at the painting of DeMille's wife. She looked like a piss ant, he thought. She was probably the perfect match for her career-climbing husband, though she had refused to come to the Soviet Union. At least in that Bertonelli couldn't blame her. He hated Russia and Russians. It was an attitude he had come to the hard way; in the field, in a dozen places from New York City to Afghanistan, from East Germany to Iran and back again. In his estimation, they were crude, stupid, plodding butchers who sent men up into space while persecuting factory workers and farmers for initiative. They were an incredibly cruel and heartless people (he'd seen countless examples with his own eyes) who produced chess masters and composers of world-class quality, while making it impossible for the unapproved artist to work or publish, let alone live. They were liars, all of them. Dirty people. Untrustworthy . . . there were many more defectors to the West than to the East. They had never honored a single treaty they'd ever signed . . . hell, he could go on and on.

". . . eight in the screened room would be fine, Mr. Ambassador," DeMille was saying. "And I couldn't agree with you more, sir. It *would* be best at this juncture to keep the need-to-know list to a minimum."

Bertonelli thought about other times and places. He had

pulled a lot of strings, twisted a lot of arms, called in a lot of favors to get here. Why? To get even? To strike a blow . . . ?

"Yes, sir, I do understand," DeMille said. He hung up the phone.

Bertonelli glanced at his watch. It was just five in the morning. "I'll have my briefing ready by eight."

"Just hold on, mister. Not so fast."

Bertonelli had turned. He understood that DeMille would try to cover himself now. Standard operating procedure. The chief of station was an expert at the game. Shit ran downhill, didn't it? If the Russians wanted to push it, this could easily become a major international incident. Heads would roll. But the chief of station was four hours behind. Bertonelli had had a head start.

"I've already queried Langley, Roland. The message went out at oh-two-thirty with a Flash designator."

DeMille was thunderstruck. He had been outmaneuvered, and he knew it. It showed on his face. Messages were passed back and forth between the embassy and either the State Department in Washington or CIA headquarters at Langley by encrypted high-speed burst transmissions bounced from a satellite. All, of course, were classified. In addition, each had its own designator; *Routine* for ordinary business, and *Most Urgent* for important business. Two remaining designators, very seldom used, were *Flash* for an item of extreme importance that demanded by its very nature an immediate reply with instructions, and *Lightning*, which had never been used, because it meant war was imminent.

"I hope this is a joke."

"No," Bertonelli said.

DeMille's eyes steadied. "I'm relieving you of duty, Tony. I want your briefing on this Okulov business by seven o'clock. I need some time to prepare myself for the ambassador. Then I want you to clear out your remaining project reports. I'd like that finished by noon. You will report to the deputy director of Operations in Langley—by the first available transportation—for your debriefing. I'll have your orders cut immediately."

"No."

"Don't make me put you under arrest."

Bertonelli had expected this possibility. He reached into his pocket and withdrew the flimsy of the Flash he had sent to Langley, and handed it to DeMille.

TOP SECRET

260530Z**************001A
FLASH

TO: LANGLEY DDO****F.Y.E.O.

FM: MOSCOW OPS****02

1. ON 22 DEC. 85 THIS OFFICER WAS APPROACHED BY A SOVIET CIT-IZEN WHO IDENTIFIED HIMSELF AS OKULOV, ROTISLAV YEFIMOVICH, TO SET UP A PRIVATE MEETING OF AN UNKNOWN NATURE XX
2. RE LOCAL RESEARCH, SUBJECT WAS IDENTIFIED AS KGB COLONEL IN CHARGE OF SECOND CHIEF DI-RECTORATE POLITICAL SECURITY SERVICE XX
3. UPON SUBSEQUENT CONFERENCE WITH C.O.S. IT WAS FELT SUCH A MEETING, IF HANDLED WITH CARE, COULD PRODUCE A WORTHWHILE PRODUCT XX
4. CLANDESTINE MEETING TOOK PLACE 26 DEC. 85 0100-0200 MOS-COW CIVIL TIME AT MOSCOW CITY ZOO XX
5. MEETING WAS BLOWN RPT MEET-ING WAS BLOWN XX OKULOV WAS SHOT, PRESUMABLY FATALLY XX MOSCOW OPS 02 MANAGED TO ES-

CAPE, BELIEVE WITHOUT POSITIVE ID OF SELF XX

6. OKULOV SAID ELEMENTS OF HIS GOVERNMENT WISH TO NEGOTIATE THE RETURN WITHOUT PREJUDICE OF AMERICAN(S) OF UNKNOWN NUMBER OR IDENTIFICATION PRESENTLY BEING HELD AT AN UNDISCLOSED LOCATION WITHIN THE SOVIET UNION XX

7. SUBJECT OFFERED TWO PROOFS NEITHER OF WHICH WERE OBTAINED BECAUSE OF THE PRECIPITOUS BREAKUP OF MEETING XX

8. EVALUATION: BELIEVE ID OF KGB OFFICER WHO SHOT OKULOV TO BE KOSTIKOV, MAJOR VALERI KONSTANTINOVICH, HEAD OF SECOND CHIEF DIRECTORATE, DEPARTMENT ONE XX BECAUSE OF NATURE OF MEETING BELIEVE SOME VALIDITY TO OKULOV REQUEST XX

9. QUERY: REQUEST IMMEDIATE ANALYSIS XX REQUEST LIST OF ALL AMERICANS CURRENTLY LISTED AS MISSING WITHIN THE SOVIET UNION XX REQUEST AUTHORIZATION TO PURSUE OPERATIONS FOR FURTHER INFORMATION XX

END FLASH
MOSCOW OPS∗∗∗∗02
260537Z
BTR

DeMille looked up and shook his head as if he were dealing with a small child who had done something naughty. "We have the list, Tony."

"Dopers. Two murderers. A lot of black-market types. He wasn't talking about them. He told me to look to Washington. He said he had . . . two proofs." Bertonelli could see the Russian in his mind's eye; pleading, begging. The sonofabitch! He hoped Okulov would rot in hell.

DeMille looked at the message flimsy again. He was smiling.

"Your reputation preceded you, Tony, you know. And to tell the truth, when I heard you were coming here I was dismayed. Chile, Afghanistan . . . even New York . . . those were your true battlegrounds. But here in Moscow the restrictions under which we operate, the constant surveillance, the tightrope we all walk every single day puts us in such a precarious balance that your methods would surely wreak havoc." DeMille shook his head. "Have you any idea what I'm saying? I even toyed with the idea of returning to Washington and having a chat with the DCI. Perhaps a mistake had been made, perhaps a policy change had been decided, perhaps I could change his mind. And let me tell you something else: Ambassador Scott shared my views. But in the end we followed orders. I could be wrong. It could not turn out half so badly as I feared."

Bertonelli didn't bother to reply. He'd heard it before, at a dozen other stations.

"But I was wrong, Tony. Dead wrong. You turned out to be very much worse than my most terrible nightmares."

"I'm sorry, but if I'm to get ready to brief the ambassador at eight, I'll have to get busy. I've a lot to do."

DeMille handed back the message flimsy, and Bertonelli turned on his heel and left the office.


The U.S. embassy was a couple of blocks east of the Moscow River at 19–23 Tchaikovsky Boulevard, more than a mile from Red Square. The building itself was a not-so-grand pile of yellow brick that had once served as an apartment building, and almost always was a disappointment for the first-time visitor. Soviet guards watched the front gate from the outside, while U.S. Marines stood their ceremonial posts within. The facility was divided into two sections: one housed the offices and various administrative functions; the other contained apartments for various embassy officials, as well as for guests.

DeMille's office was on the same floor as the ambassador's. Between the two was the screened room, which was one of the few places within the embassy that was absolutely clean of any sort of surveillance—electronic (including microwave), photographic, or audio. Bertonelli's office was on the third floor where most of the CIA's functions were performed, including the reading and translating of daily newspapers, periodicals, books, and the collating of information gathered from field agents and informants.

Bertonelli took the stairs down. Activity had increased quite a bit since he had gone upstairs. The clatter of typewriters was nearly constant. Richard Scofield, the analyst DeMille was presenting to the Russians as chief of station, was in the corridor. He was a scholarly-looking man in his mid-fifties who always wore wool tweed suits, winter or summer. He had come out of Harvard as a Russian studies expert who wanted to get closer to his subject for a few years. He was one of the few men in the embassy who actually enjoyed himself here.

"How did he take it?" Scofield asked, in his soft East Coast drawl.

"The man's a prick. What can I say?"

Scofield chuckled. "You are a never-ending source of amazement to me, Anthony."

"I'm going to need your help on this one, Richard."

"That's what I'm here for."

Bill Hobbs, the West Pointer on the staff as a military analyst, hobbled down the corridor carrying a thick bundle of Soviet newspapers and magazines, as well as a number of file folders. He had been wounded in Vietnam. A mortar round had taken off his right kneecap. Rather than sit out his career behind a desk at the Pentagon, he had taken a job with the Company. He'd been in the Soviet Union for five years. He was practically a fixture at the embassy. Everyone, including a lot of Russian friends, called him Uncle Bill.

"I thought Roland would have had you shot by now."

"Once in an evening is enough," Bertonelli said. "Did you resurrect Okulov for me?"

"Would that I could, kid. But I have a few tidbits we missed first time around."

They went into Bertonelli's office. It was a small room, without a window, dominated by a huge, square table. There were piles of books, files, maps, and documents lying everywhere. The only human touch was a photograph of his ex-wife JoAnn and their eleven-year-old daughter Cynthia on a file cabinet. The divorce had happened long enough ago that he seldom noticed his wife's face, only his daughter's.

"There wasn't enough time to dig out every last scrap, but we're working on it," Hobbs said. "But I came up with a pretty fair representation. Okulov was one sharp cookie, on his way up. He had all the right breaks, all the right connections, and there would have been nothing to stop him."

"That was my impression," Bertonelli said. "But Kostikov just blew him away."

"Maybe he was trying to defect, Tony," Scofield said thoughtfully.

"I didn't read it that way, dammit."

"Signals have been crossed before. Misrepresentations have been made. Don't you remember the business with Andre; Whatshisname in Geneva? He was listed as a second secretary to the Soviet mission there. In reality he was GRU. A major, I believe. It happened a couple of years ago during a United Nations conference. In any event, Andrei came up to one of our dips and said: 'I think Brezhnev stinks!' So what, the dip thought; Reagan ain't so hot either. It took the poor bastard three tries before he made our people realize he wanted to defect. He couldn't understand that we would think nothing of someone criticizing their leadership."

"It's possible, Richard, but he was a hell of a lot more specific than that," Bertonelli said after a pause. He'd smelled the other's sour odor moments before all hell broke loose. It had been a close call. Too damned close. He didn't like to think about it; it made him shiver. His mother used to say it was a sign that someone had walked over your grave.

"Can you be sure? I mean he was offering you two proofs but he never handed them over. Not during an entire sixty minutes of talk."

"He was skittish. Christ, he wanted assurances that once he turned over his information we wouldn't make a big coup out of it. He kept telling me it was all a big mistake."

"But he gave no hint what those two proofs constituted?"

"Not a thing," Bertonelli said. But then he wasn't being completely honest, was he. There was the look in the colonel's eyes. Unforgettable. It had been the nearest thing to stark terror Bertonelli had seen since Afghanistan. "If Kostikov hadn't shown up, we would have gotten to it. But there just wasn't time. I was promising him the moon. He wanted to hear it a few more times, I think."

"Well, let me tell you something about Okulov," Hobbs interjected. "He was big. About as close to Gorbachev himself as possible without actually being blood. He and his wife were frequent dinner guests of half the power of this country."

"But he was nothing more than a *sluzhba* . . . a political security officer."

"What better place for him," Scofield interrupted mildly. "He had all the rights and privileges he wanted, so he had no real need of rank. Hell, he was watching every important Russian in Moscow."

"But who watches the watchdog?" Hobbs mused. He had laid his bundle of papers on Bertonelli's table. A thin buff file folder lay on top of the pile.

Bertonelli picked it up and opened it. On a single typewritten sheet Okulov's background was summarized with references to source material. Hobbs had done a thorough job in an amazingly short time.

"An uncle, Stepanovich, is working on bombs at the Krasnodar Research Center, and a brother, Uri Vladimir, is chief secretary for Western research on the Central Committee's Politburo. Administrative Organs Department."

"He is married?"

"Very. Wife is Larissa Nechiporenko, whose parents were powers in the Mexico City embassy some years ago. Regular heroes of the USSR. Solid stock."

"Happily married?" Bertonelli wondered out loud.

Hobbs laughed, but Scofield looked up.

"Don't be thinking what I think you're thinking, Tony," the older man said. "This isn't New York."

"DeMille has already reminded me. But we're not simply going to let this slide."

"Langley might have something to say about it."

"Do you believe it's a disinformation plot, Richard?"

"It has all the earmarks of that, or a defection. Okulov himself discounted the thirteen Americans missing here, so who does that leave?"

"Uncle Bill?"

Hobbs shrugged. It was a habit of his whenever he felt he was going out on a limb. "I suspect it's a disinformation plot, perhaps in conjunction with their First Chief Directorate. Such interdepartmental efforts are rare but not unheard of. Probably aimed at you personally for the Invanovich business in New York."

"Kostikov isn't anyone's fool. Christ, he would have heard something about it. He has better connections than Okulov had. And no ax to grind."

"The sixty-four-dollar question," Scofield said softly. "But the next question is what are you going to do, Tony?"

One of the junior staffers from Communications stuck his head in the door. He was a pimply-faced kid just out of Kansas State University who'd always wanted to be a Marine.

"You've got an acknowledged receipt of your Flash, Mr. Bertonelli."

"Any message?"

The staffer shook his head. He looked glum. The bearer of bad news. "I'm sorry, sir, but it was classified Confidential, and designated Routine."

Bertonelli couldn't believe it. What the hell could they be thinking about back there? Scofield and Hobbs were looking at him, almost with pity.

"Is there anything else, sir?" the young man asked.

A thought came to Bertonelli. "Has Mr. DeMille's traffic gone out yet?"

"Just the one message, sir."

"Thanks," Bertonelli said, and the young man left.

"No need to ask what he sent," Hobbs said sardonically. "Or why."

Bertonelli went up to the screened room just at eight. The ambassador was like a captain of a ship at sea in his own embassy. He not only transmitted current U.S. policy to his host country, but he had a nearly absolute power over his staff. In theory, CIA chiefs of station worked for the Company, took their orders from the DCI, and therefore were autonomous. Only in theory. In practice the COS served at the pleasure of the ambassador. If they had no understanding of each other, if they could not get along well, the Agency had no recourse but to recall their man and put someone more agreeable in his place. One such transfer could be set down to an honest difference of views. More than one, however, and the hapless COS would spend the remainder of his career at Langley, sweating out his retirement. The ambassador, in turn, answered only to the Secretary of State and the President.

U.S. Ambassador to the Soviet Union Thomas Frederick Scott sat at the head of the long mahogany conference table in the screened room. His dress, as usual, was impeccable. He was freshly shaved, the odor of expensive cologne strong in the room. He wore a dark three-piece suit, a gold chain hanging across his vest lending him a particularly patrician air that morning.

DeMille sat at his right.

"Good morning, Anthony." Ambassador Scott motioned toward a chair. "Coffee?"

Bertonelli took a seat at the far end of the table. "No, thank you, sir." The room was barren except for the table, a half-dozen chairs, and a photograph of President Reagan on the wall. The fluorescent lights overhead hummed. They were a part of the electronic interference system. Venetian blinds, also part of the screening system, covered the single window that looked down upon a bleak courtyard at the rear of the embassy.

"This is a very disturbing business just now." Ambassador Scott delicately raised his coffee cup to his lips. His voice was soft, his eyes pale. He was sixty-four, but he radiated a youthful if somewhat reserved vitality. In more than one difficult negotiation the opposition across the bargaining table from him mistook his delicacy for weakness, and lost for it.

"I assume Roland has briefed you," Bertonelli said.

"I would like to hear your side of it."

"I believe Colonel Okulov was genuinely trying to pass some information of very great importance to us. I believe he was killed for his attempt."

The ambassador's gaze never wavered. "How did you come to have contact with this KGB colonel? A dangerous association, I would imagine, considering your position."

"There was a production at the Yermolova Theater on Gorky Street. He sought me out at the intermission in the lobby. We spoke briefly. He said he wanted to meet with me, in private, that he had something of extreme importance to discuss.''

"He identified himself?''

"Yes.''

"Tony came to me with his report that very evening,'' DeMille interjected. "I authorized the follow-up only if it could be done in the open . . . totally in the open.''

"Okulov had set the time and the place. There simply was no way of getting back to him with any degree of security,'' Bertonelli said.

"If you hadn't shown up, he would have made another try,'' DeMille snapped. "We covered that.''

"Excuse me, Ambassador, but that is a moot point, considering what Okulov was trying to tell me.''

"Which was?''

"That he had knowledge of a number of Americans being held within the Soviet Union. And that certain elements of his government wanted their repatriation, but only if it could be accomplished with some degree of security against retaliation.''

"Extraordinary,'' Ambassador Scott said. "But I don't understand. What sort of retaliation concerned him?''

"He never had a chance to say.''

"You believed he was sincere?''

"He said he had two proofs.''

The ambassador's left eyebrow rose. "Go on.''

"He never had a chance to give them to me,'' Bertonelli said.

"You do not believe the man was attempting to defect, or perhaps involve you in some sort of a disinformation plot? You believe, in actuality, there are some American citizens being held against their will within the Soviet Union? That is, other than the thirteen of whom we are aware?''

"I think it is a possibility.''

"Enough of a possibility that an investigation should be mounted, in view of the difficulty of such an endeavor, with its inherent dangers?''

Bertonelli was momentarily nonplussed. He had expected almost any other reaction from the ambassador.

"Yes, sir, I do.''

Ambassador Scott turned to DeMille. "What do you think, Roland?''

The COS shook his head. "It would be extremely dangerous to our position at this point." He glanced at Bertonelli, venom in his eyes. "But considering General Canfield's response, I don't know as if we have any real choice."

Bertonelli sat forward so fast, he nearly slipped off his chair. General Charles Canfield was the deputy director of the CIA.

"It came in at seven-thirty." DeMille passed the message flimsy down to Bertonelli.

```
TOP SECRET
261032Z*******002A
FLASH
TO: MOSCOW OPS 01
FM: LANGLEY DDCI

1. REF UR 001A THIS DATE PARA
9C REQUEST GRANTEDXX
2. ANALYSIS
REQUEST IMPOSSIBLE GIVEN LIM-
ITED NATURE OF INFORMATIONXX
3. LIST OF AMERICANS
CURRENTLY BELIEVED HELD WITH-
IN USSR REF UR FILE FC001721-
10-85Z13AAXX NO OTHER KNOWN DE-
TAINEESXX
4. SUGGEST PROCEED WITH EX-
TREME CAUTIONXX

END FLASH
LANGLEY DDCI
261033Z
BTR
```

Bertonelli looked up.

"How would you go about it, Anthony?" the ambassador asked.

"Valeri Kostikov, Mr. Ambassador. He is the key."

For days after one of her seizures there was an almost mystically translucent aura to Tanya. It was as if she had been transformed into a fragile porcelain doll, or a rare Fabergé egg with its hint that just beneath the surface were other wonders. This morning she wore her rabbit fur coat, its collar turned up around her tiny ears, the matching hat at the back of her head.

"I knew it was coming. After you'd left I found myself staring at the tape machine. The reels were going around and around and around." She looked at Valeri driving. He glanced at her. "There's a light behind one of the reels . . . the one on the right, I think. It kept blinking at me."

He could see her breath. It was very cold in the car. The Zhiguli's hearter had gone out again. Normally there would be points of color in her high, aristocratic cheeks, a rosy blush, but this morning she was pale.

"Why didn't you look away when you felt it starting?" he asked.

She turned her head and gazed out the window. They were passing the huge, ornately styled Byelorussian Railway Terminus with Vera Mukhina's monument to the writer Maxim Gorky rising between it and the metro next door. There was a lot of taxi traffic. A train would be departing soon. Pedestrians in fur hats and heavy overcoats and felt boots seemed to be everywhere. Something in the gay scene stirred Tanya.

"His real name was Aleksei Peshkov. Gorky's. Did you know that, Valerik?"

"Every schoolboy knows that. How do you feel this morning?"

She frowned. "Detached."

33

"Why didn't you look away when you felt it coming?" Valeri repeated his question. "This has happened before. You could have taken your medicine."

"I was writing poetry. I looked up . . ."

"I found you in the bedroom."

"I must have made it that far. *What reasons can there be for my life/so oddly shaped/so like the visage of some terrible apparition./ Looking out the window across the plane of my past/what hint of future/what harbinger of fates yet unknown.* I remember it. Does it sound good to you?"

"It's sad."

She reached out and touched his cheek with the back of her gloved hand. "Poor Valerik, desperately seeking a mother who isn't there."

"I'll stay with you at the Institute this morning."

She shook her head. "Or a lover who isn't there either, so instead he's the devoted party member wedded to his work."

"Stop it."

"Long live the Soviet people, builders of communism. Glory to work." Her weakened, reedy voice rose. A thin line of sweat had appeared on her upper lip. Her cheeks were hollow.

She looked away, her body seeming to shrink in the thick coat. Valeri studied her finely formed profile. He liked to think of her during their summers on the Black Sea beaches. Both of them were always tanned in those days like ancient Greek athletes, or swarthy, yellow-skinned Uzbeks. Their days were spent sunning near the water, their nights making love in their rooms. The fun had ended in Washington, D.C., where her seizures had begun. Grand mal, the doctors said, though none of them had found the cause, let alone the cure. Since then they had not returned to the Black Sea. Moscow at these times seemed like a nightmare, dark and dreadful.

"I would like to go away," she said, as if she had read his mind.

"Perhaps in the spring."

"I mean permanently. Even Leningrad would be better than this."

"The Institute is here."

"Comrade General Demin is here. Uncle Gennadi. Blood is thicker than water . . . only he's not blood. You're like an Italian. The Mafioso of Moscow."

There were no brothers or sisters. Only an elderly spinster aunt outside Leningrad. Her parents were killed in an airplane crash seven years ago. Her father, whom she adored, had been president of the Soviet Writer's Union. She got her literary talent from him. But she knew no one in the Union any longer. Besides, they were frightened of her because of her husband. Artists and the Komitet held mutually exclusive ideals.

A dozen children with their nurses were getting off the bus and trudging through the cold across the main courtyard when Valeri pulled up at the outpatient entrance of the Skifovsky Research Institute. The complex was located just beyond the Ministry of Agriculture building on Sadovaya Boulevard. The vast structure housed the Moscow Ambulance Service and Emergency Hospital as well as the Institute.

Tanya watched the poor crippled children for a moment, then got out of the car. She held there for a moment or two longer, as if she were afraid of leaving. "My poetry is sad, Valerik, because I am sad."

"I am sorry. Do you want me to come in with you?"

She shook her head. "I'll be here all day. They'll poke and prod and measure, and put their heads together and cluck like old ineffectual hens. And in the end even the great *Rodina* won't be able to do anything for me."

"We'll go to see Mikhail and Sasha tonight."

"No. I can't stand their children," she said, and she shut the car door, turned, and hobbled toward the Institute entrance, her unsteady gait that of a timid, weary sailor just home from the sea.

Tonic-clonic convulsions, her doctors called her seizures. Napoleon had them, he was told. So did Baudelaire, Mozart, Cellini, and Caesar. A curiously Western list, he thought; if you discounted Dostoevsky. But then every schoolboy knew about his epilepsy.

At the heart of Moscow, very near the Polytechnic Museum and the Bolshoi Theater, was the Lubyanka Center on Dzerzhinsky Square. The very large gray stone structure was divided into two areas. The low, squat section housed the prison for political dissidents. Across the courtyard, a nine-story addition built by German prisoners of war housed many of the KGB's functions. It was known simply as the "Center." There were other KGB installations in and around the city, most notably Valeri's warehouse near the American embassy and the new Foreign Operations Center—modeled very closely after the American CIA's Langley complex—outside the city along the Circumferential Highway, but the real work was done at Lubyanka.

Yuri Bondarev, General Demin's personal secretary, was seated at his desk talking softly into the telephone in the third-floor anteroom. He held up his hand for the deputy chief to wait. The door to the general's office was closed. A new photograph of Gorbachev had been hung on the wall.

Valeri stood just in front of the desk on the polished parquet floor. The walls were a pale green; the color was uniform throughout the Center. Only in the offices of the generals was there carpeting and a choice of paint. It was depressing.

Bondarev put down the telephone and looked up. "Yes?" A man in his mid-forties, he looked much older. He had the faintly disapproving air of a bureaucrat. He had been with the general for several years, so he tolerated Valeri, though he was fond of saying that there was no room in the Soviet Union for aristocrats.

"General Demin is expecting me this morning."

Bondarev glanced at his appointment book open in front of him. "He made no mention of it, Comrade Major. In any event, he is not here."

"When will he arrive?"

"I do not know."

"Where is he now? Home?"

"I don't know that, either." Bondarev barely suppressed a sneer.

"Then perhaps you can help me, Yuri Yakovlevich," Valeri snapped, purposely slurring the man's patronymic so that he would know his place.

The secretary stiffened. "The general left no instructions."

"I am here at his orders. Call him."

Something crossed Bondarev's features. It was the nearest thing to fear Valeri had ever witnessed in the normally collected man.

"I am sorry, Comrade Major, but I cannot do that."

"Why?"

"I don't know where he is. There is no answer at his apartment."

"Did you try his *dacha*?"

"It is the same."

Valeri glanced at his watch. It was nearly nine-thirty, long past the time General Demin normally arrived for work. But there was something else. He could see it in Bondarev's eyes.

"He was here this morning. Early."

The secretary nodded. "He was just leaving when I arrived."

"Yes? What did he say to you?"

Bondarev shook his head. "Nothing. Absolutely nothing. Not a word."

Back at his own desk, Valeri instructed the day duty officer to try to reach General Demin at his office, his home, and his *dacha* outside the city near the Istra River, and to keep trying until he was on the phone. Then he turned his thoughts to Anthony Bertonelli and Colonel Rotislav Okulov, two names he was having trouble connecting. If even half the speculations about the American were true, he was very good. But a *sluzhba* was simply not his kind of target. It was a puzzling exception.

Men of Bertonelli's ilk looked for the KGB or GRU officer with an ax to grind. The officer whose position would be improved outside the Soviet Union. A man who, for love or money or some ideological reason, was willing to trade his knowledge of organization, perhaps of military strategy, for a place in the West. Their names were legion, their reasons divers.

Oleg Bitov, living now in England, had once been the chief editor of the KGB *Gazette*. He skipped during the Venice Film Festival because he had expected a thaw in the treatment of writers after Brezhnev's death. When it didn't happen, he became disgruntled and defected.

KGB Major Stanislav Levchenko, who had been the Active Measures specialist at the Soviet Residency in Tokyo, defected because he had become disillusioned with what he called the corruption and hypocrisy around him.

Or, further back, Georgi Agabekov, who headed KGB operations for the entire Middle East, defected so that he could marry an English girl he had met in Istanbul.

Okulov was from a privileged family. He would have had nothing to gain by going over to the West, which meant Bertonelli had evidently found out something about the man, something so terrible that Okulov had been willing to meet with him at the zoo despite the great danger. That he had been aware of the extreme risk he was taking was evidenced by the fact that he had actually attempted to gun down a fellow KGB officer.

It simply could not have happened overnight. Bertonelli would have needed time to find his bit of dirt, and then to play Okulov like a fish at the end of a very fragile line that could break and whiplash at any moment.

In that direction lay three difficulties for Valeri. First: What information did Bertonelli possess that was so terrifying to Okulov that he would risk such a meeting? Second: What did Bertonelli hope to gain from the turning of a political security officer? And third: Why hadn't Okulov gone directly to General Demin after the very first attempt at contact? It would have been the perfect setup to force the American's ejection from the Soviet Union.

Just at ten, Shevchenko came upstairs with the square-shouldered Viktor Ivanovich Lipasov, who had been the relief team leader to spot Bertonelli coming from his bolt hole.

"Votrin will be late," Shevchenko told Valeri. "He's turning over the teams at the embassy."

"Has Bertonelli made a move?"

"No, but they're plenty busy over there, let me tell you, Valerik."

Shevchenko was very sharp. He had a storehouse of knowledge, and a vast list of informants, but he had a viewpoint curiously blind to the world outside of Moscow. Lipasov, like most surveillance team chiefs, was dull, a plodder. But when he was given a job he would stick with it until the end of time, if need be, providing it did not involve too much overtime. Oleg Dimitrivich Votrin, the other surveillance team chief assigned on rotation to watch Bertonelli, was much the same.

"We're going to do more than that," Valeri said. "This is no longer a passive operation of simple surveillance."

Shevchenko's eyes were shining. He loved a good fight. "We'll nail the bastard."

"Yes, but first I want to know what Okulov was doing in the zoo. I want to know what the hell he told Bertonelli."

"He was defecting."

"Perhaps. But let's take it from the top. I want an hour-by-hour accounting of every move Bertonelli has made since he entered the Soviet Union. Later this afternoon, with any luck, I'll have comrade Okulov's work logs. There just might be some points of comparison."

"Do we have a positive identification on the scumbag?" Shevchenko asked. "Do we know who he worked for?"

"He was a *sluzhba*. But armed."

Shevchenko slapped his leg in irritation. "Yuri said General Demin was here this morning. How'd he take it?"

"Not well. But it gets worse, Mikhail. A lot worse."

Lipasov's eyes went wide. Valeri watched him try to work it out. Political security officers almost never carried a weapon, especially not a big gun like a Graz Burya.

"You watched them go in together? As friends?" Valeri asked.

"Yes, sir. Colonel Okulov had the key. He unlocked the gate. But before they went in they shook hands."

"Which meant he might have been luring Bertonelli into the zoo to kill him after all," Shevchenko offered hopefully.

"It would have happened much sooner," Valeri disagreed. "But I think he was in fear of his life. I think he went to that meeting with the understanding that Bertonelli is a dangerous man, and that something could have happened."

"A defection, then?"

Valeri shrugged.

"Bertonelli must have been expecting trouble as well," Lipasov said.

"Because of the Militia uniform?"

"Yes, sir, and I think I know how he did it."

"He wasn't carrying a bag, or a bundle?" Valeri asked.

"Nothing, just his long overcoat. It came to me just now that the overcoat was the same length as a Militia overcoat. I remember he wore gray trousers. The same as the Militia."

"He turned it inside out."

"Yes, sir. The cap and belt were in his pocket. It was dark; so no one would have noticed he wasn't wearing boots."

"Very good work, Viktor," Valeri praised him. "So both of them have grave doubts. One carries a gun, the other has a way out of the park."

"Which means Comrade Okulov approached Bertonelli, not the other way around," Shevchenko said.

"How do you see that, Mikhail?"

"It's easy. If Bertonelli had set up the meeting, he would have made damned sure it was safe. There would have been fallbacks. A lot of shuffling around. Instead he leaves the embassy, walks directly to the zoo where he shakes hands with Okulov, and in they go. But Bertonelli, suspecting some sort of a trap, prepares himself a means of escape even if all hell breaks loose."

"That makes sense," Valeri said. "So Comrade Okulov approaches Bertonelli with a message: one o'clock at the zoo; come alone. It must have driven Bertonelli crazy trying to figure out what Okulov was up to."

"He must have suspected a defection," Lipasov suggested.

"On that basis alone I don't think Bertonelli would have put himself out on a limb. Not for an ordinary political security officer."

"Okulov could have had something specific for him," Shevchenko said. "Something very important."

"He offered him a bit of the meat?" Valeri mused out loud. It was the same conclusion he had come to.

"But Bertonelli is very good," Lipasov said.

"One of the best."

"He was worried enough about the meeting to arrange the Militia uniform. But he went to the meeting just the same. Not simply on Comrade Okulov's word."

"Exactly," Valeri said, smiling. "He offered the American something very specific. A fact, perhaps. A document."

"There was nothing on his body," Shevchenko said.

Okulov's pockets had contained a pipe and tobacco but no matches or lighter. That oddity was beginning to make some sense to Valeri.

"How thoroughly did the Technical Operations boys search the area?" he asked.

"Not at all, Valerik. They photographed the body, then carted it away. There was no reason to search . . ." Shevchenko stopped in mid-sentence. "Fuck. He was carrying something with him. He could have dropped it when you shot him."

"Or he could have already passed it to Bertonelli," Valeri said. He was still thinking about the matches.

Votrin came up the iron stairs and entered the office. He

was a wiry little man with a head far too large for his body. He looked like a poorly done caricature of an angry Siberian. But he was one of the very best shadow men Valeri had ever seen. He knew all the tradecraft on tailing there was to know. His one desire was to someday be stationed overseas, preferably in Washington or New York. He simply could not understand that it would never happen. In Russia he was one of the crowd, if a little odd; in the States he would stand out like a sore thumb.

"They're a bunch of Armenians, grumbling about the cold," he complained.

"Has Bertonelli made a move?" Valeri asked.

"No, sir, but Scofield left half an hour ago. I put two people on him."

"How reliable are they?"

"They might be spotted, but they're all right. They won't lose anyone. They wouldn't dare."

Valeri handed Lipasov the surveillance logs he had gathered on Bertonelli. "You two may have to do some legwork to fill in the blanks. As soon as I come up with Okulov's work logs I'll get them to you. Meanwhile, I want Bertonelli watched. Put a team on his apartment around the clock."

Lipasov took the bulky files. Valeri flipped open his Rolodex—one of the very few in existence in Moscow, a present from his sister—and picked out a number for a friend at Technical Operations. He wrote the name and number on a piece of paper and gave it to Lipasov.

"Anatoli Myshko. One of the best second-story men in all of Russia."

"Sir?" Lipasov asked. Shevchenko was grinning; he knew what was coming.

"I have a feeling our friend Bertonelli will be camping at the embassy for a bit. Especially if we make our presence outside the door known. Tonight, with Myshko's help, you are going to make a very thorough search of his apartment. I want it taken apart piece by piece."

"He'll know we've been there."

"Fine," Valeri said.

"If we find something?"

"If it has anything to do with Okulov, put it back. Don't take it."

Lipasov and Votrin were both thoroughly confused, but

they knew enough not to question such an emphatic order. They left.

"How about a cognac now, Valerik?" Shevchenko said.

"It's not even eleven in the morning."

Shevchenko grinned crookedly. "Sasha was too lazy to get me breakfast, and anyway I can't stand bad news on an empty stomach."

"It's worse than you think," Valeri said. He took a bottle of cognac and two glasses from his bottom drawer, and poured them both a drink.

Shevchenko raised his glass, a sudden, serious expression in his eyes. "First, to Tanya."

Valeri's breath caught. "She called?"

"Sasha talked to her just before I left. Around nine-thirty. She said she was at the Institute. Said she was sorry about tonight, but she didn't mean anything by it."

Valeri started to put his glass down, but then drank instead, and poured himself another. Shevchenko quickly downed his and held out his glass for a refill.

"She had another seizure last night. I found her on the floor when I got home."

"Why can't they fix her?" Shevchenko muttered.

"She said she was writing poetry again just before it happened. She remembered it. Even recited some for me this morning. It was quite good. But very sad." Valeri shook his head. "She called me a bastard." He looked up. "There was real hate in her eyes, Mikhail. But of that she had no memory."

"You're healthy. Perhaps she resents it."

"She wants to get out of here. Permanently. She talked about moving to Leningrad."

"A pretty city, but there are too many fag artists and hooligans up there," Shevchenko said. Moscow was his town. He drank. "What did she mean, Valerik, that she was sorry for tonight?"

Shevchenko was a model communist. He attended doctrinaire meetings, he was the block captain for his apartment complex, he was a Komsomol junior leader, he was married to a good (if somewhat hairy) woman of solid Russian stock, and best of all he had seven children. It was a source of amazement to Valeri how he could feed them all. Shevchenko's children, ranging in age from six months to eleven years, all adored their father at the top of their lungs. And he loved them with the fierce pride of a father who wasn't supposed to sire even one child. As a young man, one of his testicles had been badly damaged by mumps. At the very best of times, Shevchenko's children were barely tolerable for an outsider to the tiny, cramped five-room apartment. Tanya loved them, but she knew her condition well enough to know she could not have stood up to their onslaught so soon after a seizure. Valeri couldn't think of any way of telling that to Shevchenko without hurting his feelings.

"I don't know."

Shevchenko shrugged it off. "Sasha said she sounded all in. The kids would have been too much for her. Maybe I'll take them to the circus on Sunday. Might calm them down."

Valeri dialed the extension for his day duty officer. "Any luck finding General Demin?"

"No, sir. But I left word with Lieutenant Bondarev."

"Keep trying, would you?"

"Yes, sir."

It wasn't like General Demin to disappear. Especially not in the midst of such a delicate yet potentially explosive situation. The news about Colonel Okulov had hit him pretty hard. But Valeri would have suspected some action from the general. He had expected to see a lot of activity at the Center this morning.

He took Okulov's Graz Burya out of his desk drawer, and handed it to Shevchenko.

"Tell me what you notice about this weapon, Mikhail."

Shevchenko put down his drink and studied the big handgun for a long moment. Opening the breech, looking down the barrel, turning it over. Then his eyes lit up. "It has a serial number."

"What does that tell you?"

"It was meant for an internal affair. It was never meant to leave the country. Those guns have no serial numbers."

Valeri nodded. "A Department Viktor weapon with a serial number. Curious to say the least. But traceable. Someone must have a record on the gun."

"Maybe he lifted it," Shevchenko suggested.

"I don't think he'd have to do that."

"Now the bad news?"

Valeri nodded and poured them both another drink. "Comrade Colonel Okulov was a very important man, Mikhail. His uncle is a nuclear scientist, and his brother works for the Politburo. Even his wife is a somebody.''

"Did he go sour? Was he trading dirty laundry?''

"They were guests at the Gorbachev *dacha*. Very influential.''

Shevchenko's eyes were bright. "We don't belong on this one, Valerik. Let's send it back to—''

"General Demin?''

Shevchenko looked at the telephone. "Whom you cannot reach.''

"Which needn't deter us. We'll find out what Okulov was doing in the zoo at one in the morning with an American CIA spy.''

"The dirty sonofabitch.''

Valeri looked at his watch. It was just past eleven. "I want you to go home, have some lunch, then change into your uniform and take the gun over to the Center. Make a formal request for a trace. Date of issue, purpose for issue, and to whom issued.''

"What if they ask me how I got the gun?''

"Refer them to me . . .'' Valeri stopped. "Better yet, refer them to General Demin. Personally.''

Shevchenko finished his drink, pocketed the gun, and got up. "What do you think he was doing there in the zoo with Bertonelli?''

"I haven't the faintest idea, Mikhail.''

After Shevchenko left, Valeri spent the next hour and a half going through the daily surveillance logs with the duty operator and chief computer officer. At the present time the department was monitoring, in one way or another, the activities of more than one hundred Americans living and working in Moscow. A number of them were stationed at the U.S. embassy, but quite a few were American businessmen.

Every visitor from the West was considered an enemy in the current political climate. It was a known fact that tourists returning from the Soviet Union were questioned by the U.S. State Department. Each bit of information gleaned in this way was added to a mass of data that the CIA was very expert at collecting, collating, and analyzing. It was their specialty.

Those Americans who lived in the Soviet Union were even more dangerous because their knowledge ran deeper and approached more sensitive areas. Prima facie they were spies.

When he was finished he got his car and drove over to the zoo entrance on Bolshaya Gruzinskaya, parking just off Vosstaniya Plaza and walking the half a block back.

Despite the subzero weather there were a lot of pedestrians out and around, their breath like steam engines in the early afternoon. This was Winter Festival. Everyone seemed happy, drunk, or both. Huge banners had been placed above the zoo gates, proclaiming Father Winter's reign.

He paid four kopecks at the turnstile and went in, joining the throng heading down the main thoroughfare that led back into the zoo. In the afternoon on weekends, and all during the Winter Festival, there were special shows for children. The zoo closed at five.

A lot of people were seated at the pavilion, eating and drinking, apparently mindless of the cold. Children were playing on the swings and bars beyond. Near the restaurant turnstile an old man was playing the violin, the ancient Russian melody barely recognizable. Valeri thought it incredible that any music could be made in this cold, but the old man was a Gypsy. As Valeri walked by, the man looked up nervously, then scooped up his hat into which a few listeners had thrown an assortment of coins and hurried off. Parasitism, a wonderfully catchall phrase. Valeri had wanted to tell the old man not to bother leaving. But then the Militia would have rousted him sooner or later.

Valeri went around to the side of the pavilion building, when a thick-waisted man came out of a rear door, carrying a heavy garbage can. Their eyes met for just a moment, but then the worker set the can down with the others, turned, and went back inside. The animals were not the only captives here in the zoo. The man had had the haunted look of one who might recently have returned from prison, or perhaps ten years of external exile; glad to be back in Moscow, but frightened he might be sent away again.

There was still a little frozen blood on the snow where Okulov had fallen. The incident had certainly not been publicized, so it was a safe bet that very few people at the zoo could have any idea that a man had been killed here. The blood could have been anything: drippings from animal feed, perhaps.

The Technical Operations team had not searched for anything around the body because they had not been told to search.

There was a better than even chance that whatever Okulov had offered to Bertonelli had already been passed by the time Valeri had arrived. There was also a very strong likelihood that the only thing passed were words. Still, there was the business of the matches. It was not neat, or tidy, and it bothered Valeri.

He stood there, staring at the blood spots, listening to the cries of the children, crisp and sharp in the cold, listening to the occasional roar of some large animal farther up the hill. He decided it was a bear. The music would have been nice, but the Gypsy was a captive of his own spirit. Despite the czarist purges, despite Stalin's attempt to eliminate the peasant, and despite the new education and rules against parasitism, the Gypsy survived.

No one had expected Okulov to be here. The team had followed Bertonelli to the gate where the two of them shook hands. Possibly Okulov had passed something to the American at that point. But that wouldn't be consistent with their subsequent meeting, which had lasted an hour, and perhaps would have gone on much longer if it hadn't been broken up.

Okulov had the key. It was he who unlocked the gate, and they slipped inside. Arm in arm? Had they strolled along the paths, past the animals in their cages? Past the silent fountains, the mute statuary? Had they chatted as old friends? Or was their meeting more furtive? Fraught with the danger inherent in such an extraordinary get-together: a high-ranking, well-placed political officer and the number two American spy in all of Moscow.

Valeri tried to put himself in Okulov's position. The meeting had been arranged in advance. Okulov certainly knew who and exactly what Bertonelli was. He knew the man was dangerous, so he had armed himself with a big gun. They met at the gate entrance, which meant Okulov had spent some thought on this place, enough thought so that he had come up with the gate key. They spoke briefly. *"Were you followed?"* Okulov might have asked. Once assurances had been given, they had shaken hands. To seal a bargain? And then they had slipped into the park, closed and locked the gate.

At that point they were secure. They were out of sight of any chance passerby on the street. At that point they could have conducted their little business, slipped back out the gate, and disappeared.

But no, they had moved away from the gate, going deep within the zoo. Why?

Valeri turned and looked toward the main thoroughfare, a lot of people still streaming by. No one was paying him any attention.

They had come this far into the park on Bertonelli's suggestion. He had been wearing his inside-out Militia uniform. He was afraid of something. He wanted several choices for his escape. He did not want to be cornered near a single gate.

So they had moved. Here they stopped to conduct their business. Had Okulov been asking for something? Some assurances? Was that why they had spent such an extraordinary amount of time together?

Bertonelli would have given his assurances. And finally satisfied, Okulov might have started to hand over his bit of material, his teaser. Proof of his sincerity.

By that time Valeri was hiding just around the corner. He could hear them talking. And he could smell Bertonelli's after-shave lotion. Curious, he thought, but Americans almost always had the same smell: soap, after-shave lotion (or, on women, perfume), and dry-cleaning fluid. Americans were ultraconscious of personal odors. It was their national mania.

Valeri raised his arm and sniffed his coat sleeve. Cabbage? Cigarette smoke? Vodka? Sweat? He couldn't smell anything. But his odors were his own; he lived with them twenty-four hours a day. He had smelled Bertonelli. Had the American smelled him?

He moved a few paces forward so that he was standing next to the blood spots, facing toward the rear of the pavilion. Okulov stood here, talking, when for whatever reason Bertonelli became spooked.

The American bolted. Okulov pulled out his gun and turned.

Valeri did the same now, an imaginary gun in his right hand.

Both shots caught Okulov in the chest, driving him backward. His hands flew out with the force of the double impact. He dropped his gun from his right hand. Valeri glanced in that direction. The few inches of snow had been trampled down by Shevchenko, who had picked up the weapon, and by the Technical Operations people who had come to fetch the body.

He turned the other way, the snow just as dirty, just as trampled down.

If Okulov had had anything in his left hand—say, a book of matches—he would have dropped them as well. They might not have fallen as far as the gun. But such a small object might have gone unnoticed in the dark. It might have been trampled under the snow.

The logic was thin. A thousand-to-one against it being so. Where were the matches, then? If Bertonelli had already received them, wouldn't he have left?

Valeri moved on a few feet away from the blood spots, and pushed at the snow with the toe of his shoe. Technical Operations would have the entire area scraped clear of snow and thoroughly searched within an hour or so. His own people could do it in about the same amount of time, perhaps with less precision but certainly with more enthusiasm.

He glanced back at the blood spots, then traced a probable trajectory with his eye that ended in a circle about three meters in diameter. Starting from the center, and working in an outward spiral, he began pushing at the snow first with his feet, then on his haunches with his gloved fingers.

Twenty minutes later he uncovered a book of matches, plain cover crushed and dirty, obviously stepped on, trampled into the snow and dirt but still dry because of the cold.

Straightening up, Valeri opened the matchbook. Half the paper matches were missing. Inside the cover were eight numbers, handwritten in pencil. 17573360. Colonel Okulov's offering. Valeri stared at the numbers for a long time, trying to make some sense of them. In Moscow, telephone numbers consisted of only seven digits. The Lubyanka number, for instance, was 246–17–01. The U.S. embassy was 252-00-11.

Then he had it. The number Okulov had intended for Bertonelli was 175-73-36. When he reached that number he was to ask for, or dial, the 0. The last digit was an extension. For whom?

Gorky Street was a broad modern boulevard that ran generally north from the Moskva Hotel up toward Kalinina Prospekt. In the old days it was called Tverskaya Street, and was a narrow, twisted lane lined with wooden houses. All that was gone, replaced by modern shops and hotels, including the National and the relatively new, twenty-one-story Intourist.

There was a lot of traffic as Valeri pulled up in front of the Central Telegraph Office and parked in a loading zone. His car had KGB plates. It would not be bothered even though Militia had quotas for everything, including parking tickets.

A large illuminated world globe rotated slowly on its axis in front of the semicircular main entrance. Inside, individual telephone kiosks were lined up against two walls of the vast main lobby. A broad stairway with thick, polished aluminum banisters rose dramatically to the mezzanine on the second floor. A young girl wearing too much makeup and a fuzzy Angora sweater sat behind the information counter. She was not particularly impressed by Valeri's KGB identification. Valeri figured she probably had a boyfriend in the Service who bought her things at the foreign exchange store, and who taught her insolence.

"I'll have to call my supervisor, Comrade Major," she said languidly. "We don't handle the reverse directories from this desk."

The girl called someone on her telephone. Even though Valeri was barely a meter away from her, he could not make out what she was saying. She looked up at him and nodded, then hung up.

"You may go upstairs. Supervisor Zelenev's office is the second door to the right."

Valeri unbuttoned his coat as he went up the stairs. A short balding man with thick glasses had just stepped onto the mezzanine walkway from the second office. He was smiling nervously.

"Major Kostikov, come in, come in," he said.

Valeri preceded the man into his large, brightly colored modern office.

"How can I help State Security?" the supervisor asked, hurrying behind his desk.

Valeri gave him the telephone number, leaving off the last zero. "I'd like it matched to a name and address."

"Of course you could have simply telephoned your request."

"This is an investigation of some importance, Comrade Zelenev. I will not be forgetting those who helped me. Or those who did not."

The little man jumped. "Of course, of course," he said. He had jotted down the number on a note pad. He picked up his phone and dialed an extension. "I need a reverse on the following number."

While he waited, Valeri glanced out the window that looked down on the vault of the lobby. Outside he could see the gigantic globe. It would have been so much simpler to drive back to his office and telephone his request. It was done frequently. He hadn't given it any thought, though. He had merely driven here instead.

The supervisor was writing something down on the pad. "Yes, thank you. I have it." He hung up.

Valeri turned back.

"It is not a city number, as I suspected."

"You have a name?"

"Well, yes and no, Comrade Major. The number belonged to a Novikov, Vladimir I., well out on Dmitrovskoye Road. Here, I have the address."

"A private number?" Valeri asked. Perhaps the final digit hadn't been an extension. Perhaps it had simply been some sort of a code. A recognition signal.

"What once was a house, presumably. However, the number is no longer in service."

"You're certain?"

Zelenev nodded.

"Have there been any other requests such as mine for that particular number?"

The supervisor managed a slight obsequious smile. "I anticipated that, Comrade Major. But no, there has been no activity associated with that number for more than two years. Since its discontinuance from service."

Novikov. The name wasn't familiar to Valeri. But what was Okulov doing walking around with a discontinued number jotted on the inside of a matchbook cover? Unless the plan was for Bertonelli to discover Novikov's name, and go out there.

Downstairs in the lobby, Valeri telephoned his office. General Demin had still not been located, nor had Shevchenko returned. The surveillance team had reported that the American Scofield had gone to GUM, the department store, where he had looked through the children's clothing section and then had returned to the embassy. Bertonelli had still not moved.

Leaving his car where it was, he walked back the block or so to the Intourist Hotel with its dozen bars, restaurants, and cafe's. He picked the small second-floor cafeteria that looked down on busy Gorky Street, selected a fish stew, bread and butter, and a glass of beer, and took his tray back to a small table by the windows. From where he sat he could see his car parked up the street, traffic flowing past it. A Militia car cruised slowly by, but did not stop.

Tanya and he used to come here often just after the hotel had been built. She said it reminded her of New York or Paris, because of the foreigners. If it was a Saturday, after their lunch they would go window-shopping, unless it was raining, or snowing very hard. In that case they would sometimes go down to the Kremlin where they would wander through the museums. She especially liked the Armory with its nine halls. In number three was a collection of eighteenth- and nineteenth-century jewelry, and in six an exhibition of the czars' thrones. For days afterward she would dream about princes and princesses. A very uncommunist fantasy, she would admit, but fun nevertheless.

The doctors said her seizures came whenever she forgot to take her medication. They had a lot of arguments about it. Valeri suspected she used her illness to punish him. They had spent five years in overseas postings. First Paris, then New York, and finally Washington, D.C. Afterward she had never seemed able to settle down in Moscow. For her, the city had become drab and uninteresting. With the deaths of her parents, what little resistance that she possessed to her illness had gone out of her. Perhaps Mikhail was right, Valeri thought. Perhaps she hated him because of his health, and because of the isolation his position brought her. KGB officers were rarely able to socialize with anyone other than fellow officers. He often wondered if it was the reason American CIA officers had such a high rate of divorce.

He finished his stew and beer and got out of the cafeteria, which had suddenly become a very depressing place to him. All the way back to his car he wondered if Tanya would be spending the night in the Institute. It had happened before. He found himself wishing she would. He thought it might be difficult facing her tonight.

He drove out past the Hippodrome, cutting through Petrovskiy Park near the Dynamo Stadium, which was decked out for Winter Festival, picking up Dmitrovskoye Road, dirty snow piled up along the ditches.

Vladimir I. Novikov had at one time been quite an important figure, judging by the ruins of the very large *dacha* set back from a lovely small lake.

There was no telling how long ago the place had burned down, or what had caused the fire, just by looking. But it was a fair guess it had happened at least two years ago, when the telephone went out of service. The ruins had been picked over but had not been bulldozed. Whoever Novikov had been, he was no longer important. The property was simply too valuable to remain fallow.

There was nothing here. Unless Okulov had planned this as another meeting place. That speculation seemed far-fetched. Bertonelli would have had to have gone through too much effort to find it. It wasn't practical.

Valeri gave up, and drove back into the city, the winter sun already low in the west. It would be dark before six.

Shevchenko showed up well after three, his KGB uniform neatly pressed, the bill of his cap and his boots highly polished. He looked frustrated. "I hope you had better luck than I did," he said, slumping down into a chair.

"Possibly. A telephone number for a burned-down *dacha* by a lake. And another name for us to check."

"What are you talking about? Did General Demin call?"

"No. He still doesn't answer."

"I saw him at the Center. He and his fag secretary were coming down the third-floor corridor. Passed me right by without even seeing me."

"Good."

Valeri dialed the general's office direct. Bondarev answered on the second ring.

"This is Major Kostikov. I'll speak to the general, now that he's back."

"I believe he is in conference, Comrade Major," Bondarev said smoothly.

"Tell him who it is. I'll wait."

"Ask him about the gun," Shevchenko said, sitting up.

Valeri put his hand over the mouthpiece. "They didn't tell you anything over there?"

"Not a thing. Thanked me for returning State Security property. Promised they would take my request under advisement. And when I insisted, like you said I should, they promised they would send their report to General Demin this afternoon, the prick teasers."

General Demin came on. "I am sorry, Valerik, but I am busy at the moment. Is there something I can help you with quickly?" It didn't sound like him.

"Excuse me, sir, but I came this morning to look at Colonel Okulov's office."

"That's all been taken care of. Believe me when I tell you, it is a tragic situation."

"I don't understand—"

General Demin cut him off. "Nothing to understand, let me tell you. The poor bastard was guilty of nothing more than misjudgment. And it got him killed. Really, a tragedy. If he had only come to me, or had he liaised with you, he would be alive today. Of course this will not reflect on your record. I don't want you to worry about that. Your actions were perfectly justified. I expressed that in no uncertain terms to Comrade Chairman Chernetsov. And he agreed with me fully. On all counts."

Valeri was stunned. He didn't know what to say. General Demin sounded as if he were speaking lines for a radio drama. He wasn't merely saying the words, he was acting them.

"How is Tanya? I understand she had a relapse last night."

"She is at the Institute," Valeri said. His capacity for surprise was becoming jaded.

"I know. Please, as soon as she is up to it, I want the two of you over for dinner. Perhaps even this weekend. Can you come?"

"Yes, sir. of course. She'll be happy to see you."

"It's been too long, Valerik. Entirely too long. Now I must get back. It never ends. Live a hundred years, learn a hundred years, still you die a fool."

"Am I to understand that the Okulov case is closed?"

"What case? What is this?" General Demin snapped. "There never was a case, as you put it. It was all a terrible misunderstanding. I wouldn't want you to spread such rumors."

"He was meeting Bertonelli in the zoo. Am I to understand that he was working a disinformation operation on the American? I think I should have been informed."

"Yes, of course you should have been informed. I made that quite clear as well. We can't have independent operations getting in the way of serious work. My point exactly. Counterproductive."

"Then I would like to see that report. I will need it if I am to be effective against Bertonelli."

Valeri suspected he was putting himself out on a very dangerous limb. But something was going on here that didn't feel right.

"I'll see if it can be arranged," General Demin growled. "Is there anything else?"

"Colonel Okulov was carrying a gun. I have requested a report on it, which will be sent to your office."

"When it arrives I will personally review the facts and pass them on to you without delay."

"Thank you."

General Demin hesitated. "Never forget who you are, Valerik, or what you represent. It is important."

"I have the name of a possible third party. Possibly an intermediary. I found a matchbook that Colonel Okulov dropped in the zoo, on which he had written a telephone number."

"Who is this man?"

"His name is Vladimir I. Novikov. Does it mean anything to you?"

"Never heard of him. Have you found him? Is he in custody?"

"No, sir. I found his *dacha* . . . or what once was a *dacha* outside the city. It burned down some time ago. The telephone number went out of service two years ago."

"I don't understand what this means. You say you have a telephone number for a telephone that no longer exists, that may have once belonged to a Vladimir Novikov whom you cannot find. What has this to do with Colonel Okulov? Were those matches on his body? You didn't mention them when we spoke this morning."

"No."

"Then what in heaven's name are you talking about? Fear has big eyes, Valerik. Are you seeing too much?"

"I searched Colonel Okulov's body. He carried a pipe and tobacco, but no matches or lighter. I thought it strange, so I went back to the zoo where I found them near where the body fell."

"So, there were fingerprints on the matchbook? Was Okulov's name written somewhere? Did you see the matches fall from his pocket? Or is it possible that the matches weren't his? Perhaps Bertonelli dropped them. Perhaps someone else dropped them. Talk to me. Tell me what evidence you've gathered."

"Nothing ties the matches to Okulov other than their proximity to his body and the fact that he was a smoker but had no means to light his pipe."

"I'm sorry, but that is not enough. Colonel Okulov is dead, but I promise you—I give you my personal assurances—that you will be spared any unpleasantness. You were doing your duty, even if you were somewhat overzealous. We cannot punish you for such zeal. In fact it is commendable. But Colonel Okulov was a patriot from a family at least as good as your own, certainly with more highly placed friends than even your father or I can count as our own. Make no mistake, Okulov was not breaking the law by meeting with Bertonelli. On the contrary, he died in the service of a grateful nation."

"I don't understand . . ."

"Let me go on. You had no way of knowing, when your people followed Bertonelli to the zoo, what might be happening. It is very unusual for an American to be wandering around the streets of Moscow at that hour of the night, even if it is Winter Festival. I know that you have been after Bertonelli from the moment he set foot in Moscow. This morning your very words to me were that Bertonelli is a devil, and must be removed. When you have a job to do you get it done. But remember, please, my words to you. Your investigation must proceed with care, Valerik, and precision and, most definitely, with delicacy. I'll send you the reports as soon as I see them, merely to satisfy your curiosity. But then this investigation of Colonel Okulov will stop. You will concentrate your efforts on Bertonelli."

"What if my investigation brings me back to Okulov?"

"I cannot see how that is possible."

"What if it happens?"

The general chuckled. It was the most natural expression he had heard the man use in this entire conversation.

"Then I will have been wrong. You will have made a fool of an old man. Please, nephew, stick with your surveillance of Bertonelli and leave the cloak-and-dagger work to Department Viktor."

Valeri had been backed neatly into a corner. If he so much as asked another question, he would be accused of setting out to make a fool of his superior, one of the most heinous crimes in the Soviet Union. Sloth was counterproductive; ridicule was heresy.

"You're correct, of course, Comrade General," Valeri said.

"I know I am, Valerik. But it is understandable. You're simply having a reaction to the shooting death of a comrade in the service, and of course to Tanya's illness. She telephoned me from the Institute a short while ago. Asked me to convince you to move her to Leningrad."

"I'm sorry . . ."

"Don't apologize. I spoke with her doctor afterward. She was on medication. He said such reactions are normal. Perhaps you should call your father. He might be able to spare Lara for a week or so. I'm sure she would enjoy coming back to Moscow for a visit. She could help with Tanya."

"They don't get along."

General Demin sighed deeply. "I am sorry, nephew, but truly I must go now. If there is anything I can do to help, anything at all . . . perhaps a different hospital . . ."

"Thank you."

"Perhaps we will see you over the weekend."

"Yes, sir," Valeri said, and he hung up. He was depressed, and exasperated.

"I didn't like the sound of that," Shevchenko said. He had unbuttoned his uniform blouse. His shirt beneath was dirty; there were grease stains on the collar.

"Colonel Okulov is a hero of the state, Mikhail. It seems I shot the wrong man."

"If he was such a hero, why did he try to gun you down? And what's this about a matchbook?"

"It probably didn't belong to Okulov."

"Bertonelli?"

Valeri explained how and where he found the matchbook, his efforts at the Central Telegraph Office, and his fruitless trip out to the ruins of the *dacha*.

"So we run a check on this Novikov."

"No, Mikhail, didn't you hear me? Okulov is a hero. We are not to interfere with his memory."

"But the matchbook belonged to Bertonelli. You said so yourself."

"General Demin was adamant."

Shevchenko smiled wanly. "It is a good thing, being simply a captain. A second in command. The responsibility falls like water off a duck's back."

A snatch of Tanya's very sad poem came to Valeri. *What harbinger of fates yet unknown.* "Bertonelli is our target."

"Meanwhile, I could find out about Novikov. It wouldn't be difficult. Perhaps I could take a few of those Ukrainian boys out there with me. They like to get their hands dirty. We might get lucky." Shevchenko got to his feet.

Valeri jotted down the number on Dmitrovskoye Road and handed it to Shevchenko, who stuffed it in his pocket and left without a word.

Alone, Valeri sat back and lit a cigarette. He had a fair idea what had happened this morning. The news that Colonel Okulov had been shot to death got to someone influential who called General Demin on the carpet. *Stop the investigation now,* he had been told. Before too many people were embarrassed.

But that line of thinking led him to two areas of speculation, at once intriguing as well as disturbing. If Okulov had indeed been attempting to defect, no one wanted that news to get out. It wouldn't set well. A highly placed influential man with nearly all the advantages and privileges the system could provide simply could not give it up for the decadence of the

West, specifically the United States. The fact that America
wasn't any more decadent than any other nation (faster-paced
and more undisciplined, perhaps) didn't mean a thing. The
Russian mind could never be understood there. No one in the
West had suffered through the centuries like the Russians. No
one in the West had written the music, or the poetry, because
of it. Suffering played no real part in the Western spirit. A
Russian would simply languish there. If a man defected, by
definition, he was mentally unbalanced. If Okulov was attempting to defect, therefore, how much of his insanity had
infected other high-ranking party members with whom he had
associated? Too many questions would be raised.

However, if Okulov had been running a disinformation plot
against Bertonelli, why hadn't it been cleared with Valeri's
own department, or with General Demin? That was the usual
procedure. Okulov had pulled his gun. That single fact stood
out above all others. Combined with General Demin's insis-
tence that Okulov was a hero of the state, it made for some
puzzling difficulties.

Okulov was an influential name. The colonel had had more
friends than even General Demin or Valeri's own father, who
commanded the entire Northern Missile Defense Command.
General Demin had issued a clear warning on the telephone,
but had he foreshadowed his admonition earlier that morning?

An old proverb came to Valeri: The Russian is clever, but
it comes slowly—all the way from the back of his head. Was
he being dense by not heeding the signs?

Sergei Zabaton, the night duty officer, came up early to
review the overnight assignments. Like Shevchenko, he was
one of the good ones who seemed to relish work. He was also
discreet. Valeri had him look up what information he could
on Okulov in the service directories without ringing any bells
over at the Center. Ten minutes later he was back with a brief
dossier, which included the colonel's address.

The sun was nothing more than a blood red ball reflecting
off the upper-story windows of the modern apartment block
on Kalinina Prospekt. There were five buildings, each twenty-
three stories, each with 280 apartments, on the right-hand
cluster beyond Arbatskaya Plaza. The ground floor and first
floor of each building contained shops: the Malachite Box

jewelry store, the Ivuska Café, a drugstore, the Melodiya record shop, and the Sireny, for perfumes, among others. A separate, much smaller building housed the Dom Knigi—House of Books—which was the largest bookstore in all of the Soviet Union. Attached to the bookstore was the October Cinema, and a large bakery.

This street, along with Kutuzov Prospekt nearby, were the showplaces of Soviet Russia. Only important people lived here—Politburo members, ministers of state, high-ranking KGB officers. This was the region of privilege, of class, of *kulturny*. There were a lot of people out and about, and every second automobile, it seemed, was a sleek Zil limousine. All the women were either Western-looking and svelte, or short and dumpy with fur collars on their expensive but not very stylish cloth coats.

Valeri made his way up the broad sidewalk, past the movie theater, and entered the third building in the cluster. A sour-faced guard in a splendid uniform stopped him at the elevators. He felt shabby next to the guard. A woman leading a toy poodle passed. Her perfume was so heavy he almost gagged.

"I've come to see Madame Okulov," Valeri said, showing his ID. It seemed strange in his ears to use such formal address. But he had a feeling it would be correct here. The guard didn't seem to notice. The stringent security measures were common in this type of building. Even a KGB officer didn't carry much weight.

"Have you an appointment, Comrade Major?"

"No."

"I will just telephone . . ."

"That won't be necessary," Valeri said.

"This is a restricted-access building, Comrade—"

"Use the telephone, but call General Demin. I have his number for you," Valeri said sharply. He had seen this sort of thing in New York, and especially among doormen in Paris. It was something new to Moscow.

Confronted with this sort of challenge, the doorman seemed a little less certain. Valeri decided to make it easier for the man. He stepped a little closer.

"Listen, there has been a tragedy in the Okulov family. I was sent to bring the wife the news. It concerns the colonel. Very sad, let me assure you. Terrible."

The security guard clucked knowingly. Now he was on

familiar territory. "In Moscow they ring the bells often, Comrade . . ."

"But not for dinner," Valeri finished for him. "It will be better this way, for her."

"You'll just have to sign in, then, Major."

"Naturally," Valeri said, full of bonhomie, moving to the small desk. The open pages went back for at least two days. No one else had signed in to visit the Okulovs. But that meant little. Ordinary visitors—generals, businessmen, politicians— would not be required to sign their names.

Valeri took the elevator up to the twentieth floor. The corridor was narrow but carpeted. There were paintings by well-known Russian artists flanked by light sconces at regular intervals. The Okulov apartment was halfway down the hall. He knocked on the door.

Larissa Okulov came as a complete surprise to Valeri. The man he had shot to death in the zoo had been the typical Russian: squat, barrel-chested, square-headed with heavy Slavic features. His wife was tall, with long, jet-black hair, expressive eyes, thick, moist lips, and probably a willowy figure. She was dressed in a floor-length caftan of silk beneath a sleeveless bright red brocaded coat. A silver sash was cinched at her narrow waist. Her teeth were straight and beautifully white. Her bearing was regal. She was a beauty in every sense of the word, with class.

"Should I know you, comrade . . . ?" she asked, her self-assured voice soft, mellifluous.

Valeri was smitten. He fumbled for his identification and showed it to her. "Larissa Okulov?" he asked, sounding a lot more official than he wanted.

She smiled and nodded. "To what do I owe the pleasure of your visit, Comrade Major?"

It had been nearly eighteen hours since her husband had been shot to death, but Valeri did not think she had been told. He was sure he would have seen it in her eyes. But her expression was clear, if somewhat amused. There was a hardness there, too, he suspected.

"I am sorry, but I came here to talk to you about your husband."

"Has he done something wrong? Is that why you are here?"

A strand of hair was caught at the corner of her mouth. She

looked to be no more than thirty. Valeri remembered Okulov's age as forty-two. He had come here to tell her that he was sorry about her husband. A fool's errand considering her social position, and General Demin's warning. Suddenly he had no idea what he would say to her.

"He didn't come home last night. Is that it? Has something finally happened to him?"

"No one has telephoned you today?"

"No. Should they have?"

Valeri felt absolutely rotten. Guilty. He had shot her husband to death, and here he was, sniffing after the wife. But he had to say something.

"He may be missing. I'm sorry."

"Missing? What do you mean? Has he run off?"

Valeri was astonished. Had Okulov intended to defect after all, leaving his wife behind? It wouldn't be the first time such a thing had happened. But from the way she talked, did she suspect that just such a thing was likely?

"I don't know, Madame Okulov. He did not show up at his office this morning. I would very much like to find out what he has been doing for the past few days. Perhaps it would give me a clue . . ."

"You're trying to help, I understand," she said, the slightest hint of amusement in her eyes.

"It may not be possible," he said lamely.

"But then again it may." She took his arm and drew him inside.

The apartment was very large and modern, with thick carpeting, mirrors on one wall, and what appeared to be a Picasso over a very long snow-white couch. Valeri had seen apartments like this in New York, but never here in Moscow.

"This is nice . . ."

"May I take your coat, Major?"

"I won't be staying long. Could you tell me where you think your husband might be?"

"Is this an offical investigation? Should I be telling you . . . anything?"

"It's all right, believe me."

She smiled. "I suspect it is. You look like the honest, hard-working type. Are you sure I cannot take your coat?"

Valeri was impressed. She had just been told by a KGB major that her husband was missing, and yet she affected an air of half-amused indifference. Or was he being naïve, he wondered.

"You must be here after clues, then, Major. But what sort?" she asked. "Secret notes? Hideaways . . . ?"

"Did he say anything to you during the past few days about his plans?"

She shrugged and shook her head. "No. Nothing specific, I'm afraid, but when I've never cared enough to pay attention, you see. I went through all of that when I was a little girl. let me tell you an amusing story. I spent the first twelve years of my life in Mexico City. My father and mother both worked for the Service. They were the very best field operatives in all of Latin America. Between the two of them they took over the entire embassy. My father used to take my brother and me into the Referentura, to show us off, he said. But it was really to show himself off. He was the *Sovyetskaya koloniya*—you know, the one in charge of preserving the security of the Soviet Colony. My mother even used to work as a maid at embassy parties. We couldn't have outside help. Everyone had to pitch in. A lot of drunken confidences could be overheard that way. My father's downfall came when he decided it was time to take over Mexico. So don't come here and tell me about your little investigation. You see, I have been there."

Valeri decided that she was exactly what Tanya pretended to be: Western. This one had the stories, the veneer, and the indifference, while Russian tragedy dripped from Tanya's every pore.

"You don't believe me," she said, laughing. She turned, her caftan flaring, giving him a glimpse of her ankles and bare feet. Her toenails were manicured and painted red.

At a white enameled sideboard that held an ice bucket, she poured two glasses of white wine and brought them over. She handed one to Valeri.

"Do you enjoy wine, Comrade Major Kostikov?"

Valeri took it. "Not if it's too sour."

She laughed again, the sound musical. "Ever the true Russian. But you've been places too, haven't you. I can see it in your eyes, you know."

"New York. Washington."

"Ah, the States. I've not been there. Only Mexico City, and then last year, Paris."

"I was stationed in Paris."

"Then we have something in common. Quaint."

She was making fun of him. Valeri's ears got warm. Whatever relationship she had shared with her husband, he suspected it wasn't close. He set his wine down on the low coffee table.

"You don't like it?"

"Does the name Vladimir Novikov mean anything to you?"

"No. Should it?"

"Your husband apparently knew him."

"My husband knows a lot of people he hasn't bothered to introduce." She drank half her wine. "Look around, Major. Look at me. I'm his little showpiece, hadn't you guessed?" Bitterness had crept into her voice.

"Maybe he mentioned the name."

"No."

"Does the name Bertonelli mean anything to you?"

Something flashed in her eyes. But briefly, just for a split second, and then it was gone. But Valeri had seen it.

"No," she said. "Should I know him as well? An Italian?"

"An American."

She shrugged again.

Something she had said earlier suddenly stuck in his head, though he no longer thought she would be of much help.

"You mentioned something about secret notes, and hideaways."

She laughed with pure delight. "That's really very banal, Major."

"You don't care?"

"I wouldn't care if he was dead."

"Did he beat you?"

She laughed again. "I would have killed him had he tried." She inclined her head coquettishly. "You're shocked?"

"Did he bring his work home with him? Lately?"

"Never."

"You said hideaways."

"What man doesn't have them?"

"Plural?"

"It was the one thing about him that I could never fault. He was a virile bastard. Of course he had his privacy."

"Here in Moscow?"

Larissa Okulov turned, went back to the sideboard, and filled her glass. "Don't be boorish. Leave now, please."

"Here in Moscow?" Valeri repeated his question sternly.

She shrugged. "Yes."

"Where? Have you the addresses?"

She turned around. "Can't you leave me alone?"

"I think you'd better tell me."

"I don't . . . know," she faltered. "I didn't follow him to the whore's apartment."

Valeri waited. She had lost some of her aplomb.

"I only know of two apartments. One is way out on Leningradsky Prospekt, before it turns into Volokolamskoye Highway. It's a plain white building. Very tall. Still under construction. I didn't ask the cab driver to stop."

"There is a second?"

"Closer in the city near the Kazan station."

"Near the post office? On the square?"

"Around the corner. A yellow brick building. Three or four floors, I think."

"You don't have the number?"

"No," she said, She shook her head. "No. Please leave."

On the way down in the elevator Valeri couldn't take his thoughts away from her face, from her eyes. She had had absolutely no reaction to the name Novikov. But she knew Bertonelli's name. He was certain of it.


Valeri spoke with Dr. Dmitri Klimov at the Skifovsky Institute.

"Last night she was writing poetry. It was at least as good as some of the other things she's done, but it was different. It contained real sadness. The thing that bothered me most was that she remembered what she had written well enough to recite some of it back to me this morning. Yet she claims to have no recollection of calling me a bastard, or of hating me so fiercely. It was too selective. She told me she wanted to leave Moscow. She spoke about Leningrad with more urgency than ever. It's as if she were winding down. But on purpose. Three days ago I found a vial of her medicine floating in the toilet. I think she had tried to flush it down, but it got caught and came back up. And then this morning she called General Demin. From here at the Institute."

Klimov, who had studied at the Menninger Clinic in Topeka, Kansas, adding psychiatry to his neurological training, was a fairly young man. He was the Soviet Union's expert on epilepsy and headed a huge research staff. He was bony, with huge liquid eyes.

"Her poetry comes from her soul—it's quite common among epileptics—and only natural that she should have total recall. But she doesn't hate you. Not really."

"It was in her eyes."

Klimov nodded. "At that moment, perhaps, she did hate you. But believe me, it was nothing more than a momentary transference of her own anxiety. She was ashamed that her own body had once again betrayed her. In her state, a self-defense mechanism came to the forefront of her mind. You appeared, and her fear was transferred to hate, and directed at you. The organism, true unto itself, will survive."

Klimov was nervous in Valeri's presence. He had taken Tanya as a special case and had become genuinely interested in her. Yet for about two years after he had returned from the United States, he had been harassed by the KGB and by his colleagues who said he practiced magic. He was a Jew.

"What can you do for her?"

Klimov spread his hands. "There is no scar tissue on her brain. We can't find any chemical imbalance, nor are her seizures musicogenic . . . though at times, with certain music, we do see the typical spike-dome on her electroencephalogram."

"You can't do a thing."

"Her medicine will control her seizures. Except for very rare occurrences, they should never happen."

"But she refuses to take her medicine."

"She's unhappy."

Valeri could see a statue of a woman clothed only in a robe off her shoulder, perched atop a tall, thin column in the rear of the courtyard. She looked cold.

"What should I do?"

"I want to keep her tonight, perhaps over the weekend. We have just received a new CAT scan machine. The latest technology. Perhaps there's a lesion we missed during an earlier examination."

"I meant in the long run. Should I move her to Leningrad?"

"No."

"Then, what?"

Klimov sighed deeply, and turned around to look out the window. "I'm sorry, but I simply do not know. Somewhere locked very deep within her brain two functions have somehow gone terribly wrong. One is physical, the other psychic. I haven't been able to reach either."

Valeri thought he was listening to a witch doctor. He got up and left the office.

Tanya's room was two floors up the west wing. It was dinner time. Food carts were passing up and down the halls, odors of fish and borshch and tea with lemon mixed with the vaguely sour hospital smells. The nurses' station was busy. It was also medication time.

She was in a six-bed ward. She sat propped up with two pillows, writing something on a legal-size yellow tablet, her head bent low, the tip of her tongue sticking out of the corner of her mouth.

Valeri stood in the doorway watching her for a long time, a lump in his throat. She seemed unaware of anything around her, totally at peace with herself and her environment. Four of the other five beds were occupied by old people; sparse gray hair, sunken gums, veined, wrinkled skin, palsied hands. Tanya looked like a rose in a manure field among them.

The tall aluminum dinner cart came along as Valeri turned and hurried down the hall. He took the elevator to the parking area, got his car started, and then sat there, his hands tightly gripping the wheel as tears slipped silently down his cheeks.

# 5

A lot of the U.S. embassy people were going home to their apartments around the city and across the covered walkway to the residential section.

Overall there was a mood of gaiety and lightness because Winter Festival was one Russian celebration where no one minded who you were or where you were from, whether Washington or even Langley (whose cautions at times bordered on the paranoid). And the Militia took the attitude that all Russian drunks were the same—no threat to the state or anyone else other than themselves.

Bertonelli brought Laurie Morgan, the archives clerk, back to the library table at which he had been working for the past three hours and showed her what material he had been able to gather on Valeri Kostikov. She was blonde, with blue eyes, pretty teeth, and a pert nose. Bertonelli wondered why she had buried herself there. The basement was damp and cold. She wore a bulky sweater that didn't do much to hide her figure.

"The word is you're out," she said.

"Where'd you hear that?" Bertonelli smiled.

"Around." She shrugged. "I don't know if I'll be able to help you."

"Look, Kostikov was stationed in New York, and then Washington. Records were kept. I want them. You can clear it with DeMille if you'd like."

"Oh, I will, believe me."

DeMille was very powerful, especially since he had the support of the ambassador. But Bertonelli wondered if any of them could think beyond their petty grievances. "Find out what you can for me," he said, and he left.

*   *   *

There were vending machines in the first-floor dayroom. Bertonelli stopped on the way up to get himself a ham and cheese sandwich and a Coke, then took the back stairs up to his third-floor office. Wyatt Grant was just coming down the corridor from Hobbs's office. He was an undistinguished-looking man of medium height, medium build, with pale blue eyes. He carried a small leather bag over his shoulder, his coat unbuttoned, his fur hat in his hand. He had evidently just come in.

"Where's Posman?" Bertonelli asked.

"Parked in front of Kostikov's apartment."

"Any trouble?"

"Piece of cake. He didn't look over his shoulder once. Not during the entire day."

They went into Bertonelli's office. Grant unslung his leather bag and took off his coat while Bertonelli put a fresh cassette in his tape recorder and switched it on.

"Our boy has been pretty busy." Grant looked at his watch. "I'm due to relieve Ralph at oh-two hundred. He'll return at oh-seven hundred. We don't think Kostikov will be moving until then.

"Did he go back to the zoo?"

Grant looked up and grinned. "He sure did, just like you said he would. We couldn't get close to him, though. He was over beside the pavilion, exactly where you thought he might be. But it was too damned open for us to get close."

"So you got nothing?"

"Oh, no. Cost us five rubles, but it was enough to convince the worst-smelling old Gypsy you've ever had the misfortune to get downwind of, to swing around and take a peek. I think he picked up a week's worth of dinner from the garbage cans behind the snack bar."

"Go ahead."

"He said our man was doing all sorts of weird things back there. Dancing around, playing cowboys and Indians. And then he dug around in the snow for about half an hour. Picked up something. The Gypsy couldn't rightly say for sure what it might have been, but he thought it might have been a book of matches."

"Matches?"

Grant shrugged. He was a man unique in that he apparently

made no judgments. He called himself "pure and simple, a sensory animal. What I sees, you gets." He was a Texan.

*Okulov had fiddled with a pipe. He had loaded it, but then he had put it back unlit in his pocket. Bertonelli had thought it odd at the time, because Okulov had had a book of matches in his left hand. One of the two proofs?*

"Start at the top, would you, Wyatt? Where'd you pick him up?"

Grant opened his leather bag and pulled out the tiny Polaroid camera, along with a folder filled with a dozen photographs. The film was very small, less than 35mm finished size. The camera had been developed by the CIA through the Polaroid Land Company. It took high-speed color photographs with a development time of under ten seconds. Each camera cost the government twenty-five thousand dollars. The film sold for a hundred fifty dollars a ten-exposure pack.

He spread the photographs on Bertonelli's desk, and they both leaned over them.

"Do you want it step by step?"

"Details later, just give me the high points for now."

"He wasn't home by the time we got over there—his car was gone—so we went directly to the Warehouse and hung around until ten when he finally showed up."

"Alone?"

Grant nodded, pointing to the first photograph, which showed Kostikov in his Zhiguli arriving at the Warehouse just a few blocks from the U.S. embassy. It was a profile view of his head and shoulders, but it was clearly Kostikov.

"Any sense of where he might have been?"

"No."

"Go on."

"He was in there for quite a while, and when he came out we followed him over to the zoo. He parked on a side street just off Vosstaniya Plaza and walked the half a block back to the Bolshaya Gruzinskaya entrance, paid his money, and went in. We caught up with him about halfway to the pavilion, where he scared off the Gypsy. I took a quick pass while Ralph bought the old man, then we backed off and waited where we could watch the main sidewalk."

"He picked up the matchbook, then what?" Bertonelli asked.

Grant pointed to the next three photographs, one showing

Kostikov heading toward the zoo exit, apparently in a big hurry. The next two shots showed him parking in a loading zone in front of a large building, and going in. A world globe was visible in the background.

"Central Telegraph Office?"

"Right," Grant said. "He talked to the gal with the big tits at the information desk, then went upstairs to the mezzanine office of Nikolai A. Zelenev, where he remained for something under four minutes."

Bertonelli looked up in real amazement.

Grant smiled deprecatingly. "Afterward he went over to the Intourist Hotel where he had lunch in the second-floor cafeteria. Ralph baby-sat while I went back and made a pass. Zelenev had stepped out of his office, leaving his door open. I read his nameplate. He's a directory supervisor."

Bertonelli sat back. "A directory supervisor. As in telephone directory?"

"We'll see what we can dig up first thing in the morning."

*Kostikov picks up a book of matches at the zoo, then heads straight for the Central Telegraph Office where he speaks with a directory supervisor. One of Okulov's proofs was a telephone number.*

"He didn't go back to his office. He went someplace else. An apartment—" Bertonelli cut it off. He spotted a photograph of what appeared to be the burned-out remains of a house or some other building. There were a lot of trees in the background. It was in the country. "A *dacha*?"

"Bingo," Grant said, stabbing a finger at the photo. "He hightailed it out of town on the Dmitrovskoye Road. We had to hang a long ways back, so we nearly lost him. Picked him up as he was turning down a dirt road."

"Anything else there?"

Grant shook his head. "Not a thing. Just the burned-out *dacha*. He didn't stick around long. Went straight back to his office. Mikhail Shevchenko, his chief of staff, showed up in uniform after three, then left about an hour later. About four-thirty Kostikov came out again and headed over to a fancy apartment building on Kalinina Prospekt."

"Colonel Okulov's apartment?"

"Our boy gets around."

"Amazing. He blows the man away and then heads over to see his wife."

"We couldn't get inside. I didn't think we should force it. Damned near like Fort Knox over there."

"How long was he there?"

"Half an hour, maybe less, from the time he entered the building until he came out."

There were photos of Kostikov arriving and leaving the luxury apartment building. The next showed a large building Bertonelli didn't recognize.

"The Skifovsky Institute. His wife apparently is an epileptic."

Mention had been made of it in Kostikov's file. Bertonelli hadn't thought anything of it until now. "Has she been hospitalized?"

Grant nodded. "We got inside with no problem. His wife is under the care of Dr. Dmitri Klimov. According to a *babushka* on the second floor, he's the Soviet Union's leading expert on epilepsy. Ralph followed him upstairs. Wife's in the west wing."

"Did he pick her up?"

"He went home alone."

"Hasn't moved since?"

"No."

Bertonelli opened his file on Kostikov. He found a photograph and very brief dossier on his wife, whose name was Tanya Alexandrovna. Her father had been president of the Soviet Writers' Union at one time. A shirttail relation to Boris Pasternak. He and his wife were both dead. There was an old photograph of her, but it was of very poor quality. It showed a woman in her late twenties, apparently, with pretty, delicate features. No beauty, but not the typical Russian flat-faced woman.

Kostikov. He was the key. Somehow Bertonelli knew he was going to have to get to the major. But first he was going to have to get the man's attention.

It was past eight o'clock. Bertonelli told a story to Richard Scofield, the embassy's political analyst.

"Two months after I was stationed in Afghanistan I was dropped at night outside Khanabad, about forty miles south of the Soviet border. That's just above the Hindu Kush range. Really rugged country. In normal times there's not a lot of activity up there, even though the town has a population of more than thirty thousand. It was winter, and cold enough to freeze the balls off a brass monkey. The absolute poverty is something you simply cannot believe unless you are actually there. And even then you feel as if you're in a dream. I brought along a musette bag filled with cans of beef stew, packages of raw rice, and tea. They wouldn't touch the stew—it smelled tainted to them—but the rice was okay and they loved the tea. The Russians were coming down in their big Sikorskys, laying down what we figured was something like Agent Orange, a big-time defoliant, in preparation for an all-out breakthrough. They were playing around the Khyber Pass to the south, and the Shibar to the east, connecting Kabul with the north. At any rate, I was supposed to go in, make contact with the rebel forces, and document Soviet chemical warfare. Back home they needed hard evidence to present to the U.N. They bounced me around town, house to house—I don't think any of them could have afforded to put me up for more than a day or two—until a major breakthrough was supposed to occur farther to the north. The Russians were sending half a division down from their staging area on the border at Pyandzh. Took three days to haul our asses up there, and by then we were too late. The Russians had come and gone. Big raid, lots of casualties. We came in on horseback about seven in the morning, sunrise, with a lot of smoke and some real rigid sights. Never forgot that part because it marked the beginning of the end for me there. There was a small mountain village within spitting distance of the Soviet border. Not more than a couple of hundred people, probably less. The Russians had flattened the place. Yet it had no strategic value. No need to have done what they did. There were bodies everywhere. On the narrow road leading in they were stacked like cordwood, stiff as year-old steaks in the deepfreeze. Funny thing, though . . . all the men had been shot to death, while the women and girl children had all—and I mean *all*—been raped and then cut to pieces with knives, or clubbed to hamburger. I didn't really want to see that, you know. I was looking for signs of chemical warfare, and what I found was the great Russian spirit: if you can fuck over your fellow man, do it! But if it's a woman or child, why not have a little pleasure while you're at it. Animals. That was the last time I ever thought straight on the subject.''

Scofield, who had been accused of being soft, at times, on the Russians, did not seem especially impressed with the story. Still, Bertonelli had a lot of respect for the man. DeMille was nothing more than a distant and ineffective irritation to Scofield, who enjoyed the autonomy that Bertonelli could only wish for.

"It's war," Scofield said mildly.

"They were ignorant, half-starved peasants, for chrissakes! They never had a chance."

"Need I mention My Lai?"

Bertonelli was perched on the edge of a chair in Scofield's office. The window behind the desk was dark. It all reminded him of a fifties science-fiction movie in which the scientist was in love with his horrible creation. Scofield had become so close to his subject, he was no longer objective. The room had a musty, closed-in odor, and was filled with Soviet journals and newsletters. Scofield knew a lot of dissidents, as well as Moscow State University and museum people here and in Leningrad.

"So we all make mistakes, I'll grant you that. But My Lai was plastered all over the newspapers and television. It went to a court of law."

"Did it?"

"Yes, it did," Bertonelli said. "There is a difference."

Scofield nodded. "Granted. But it brings us back to you. Something is on your mind, Tony. And why is it that I think it might be something particularly nasty."

"Valeri Petrovich Kostikov is a patriot."

"From what I gather."

"Let me tell you something, Richard. Have you any idea why the Russians have invaded Afghanistan?"

"Well, I think I have a fair idea."

"Afghanistan is a country composed of tribal groups, the most predominant of which are the Durani. According to them they are descended from the Jews taken into captivity in Babylon six hundred years before Christ. They still call themselves *Ben-i-Israel*—Sons of Israel."

"I think it has more to do with the strategic value of the country. Real estate."

"I'm talking about their degree of barbarity. They hate the Jews. It's a national sport."

"You don't like Russians very much."

"No."

Scofield was a reasonable man, but at times he was an evangelist when it came to Russians. As long as he was being presented as the chief of Moscow station he was treated with a great deal of respect. He enjoyed the limelight. He was afraid Bertonelli was going to ruin it for him. "Have you decided why Kostikov was following Okulov in the first place?"

"His people were at the Yermolova. Probably picked us up. Figured Okulov for a defection."

"Okulov told you he had the support of certain elements of his government. They tried once to approach you, they'll try again."

"Not with Kostikov sneaking around."

Scofield threw up his hands in exasperation. "You're playing a dangerous game, Tony. What the hell do you think you're going to do?"

"I don't think you want to hear it."

"Then why did you come in here and tell me that bullshit story about Afghanistan?"

Bertonelli stood up. "It wasn't bullshit, Richard. Kostikov's wife is an epileptic."

"I saw Hobbs's file."

"What can we do for her?"

"I can't believe this . . ."

"What can we offer him?"

"The best clinics for that are right here in Moscow."

"There's nothing we can do for her in the States that's impossible for her to get in the Soviet Union? Mayo Clinic? Bethesda Naval Medical Center?"

Scofield smoked a pipe. His teeth were yellowed; three of them were bowed slightly outward on the left side of his mouth from where he held the stem. It made Bertonelli think about Okulov and his pipe . . . and the matches. "Don't be a bastard. Leave his wife out of this."

Bertonelli wondered how far the man would go to stop him. DeMille wouldn't give a damn. What was there left? "Okulov said there were Americans being held somewhere in Russia."

Scofield started to object, but Bertonelli held him off.

"Makes you wonder, doesn't it, just how they're being

treated. Maybe they're Jews. Maybe they're women or children."

"Save me the histrionics. You were being fished. Admit it, for Christ's sake."

"Maybe," Bertonelli said at the door. "Maybe not. Thing is, I can't get those poor Afghan bastards out of my mind. You know, I wake up in the middle of the night smelling the rotting corpses." He shook his head. "You should have seen them, Richard. Really, you should have."

After a day of being cooped up in the embassy, Bertonelli was in a dangerous mood. He grabbed his hat and parka from his office. Before he left he idly fingered the Militia epaulets at the shoulders of his inside-out overcoat. He thought about an old Russian proverb that the old man on the border had told him. Adi Bamianani was his name. He had a lot of amusement about what was happening to his country, though Bertonelli expected it was gallows humor. *Make yourself into a sheep, and you'll meet a wolf nearby.*

Bertonelli had made himself into an Afghan. He would never forget the gut-wrenching fear that had traveled with him every hour he was there.

He went downstairs to the dayroom. Grant was there alone, reading the *New York Times* and finishing a cup of coffee.

"Heading out?"

"I thought I'd go home and get a couple of hours sleep. How about you, Mr. Bertonelli?"

"Give me a lift?"

Grant smiled. "They've got you spotted. But if you don't mind riding in the trunk . . ."

"Wouldn't travel any other way."

Out back in the courtyard, Bertonelli folded his bulky frame into the small trunk of the pool-issue Toyota Celica.

"Any place special?"

"Whatever looks clear a couple of blocks from my apartment."

"Yes, sir." Grant closed the trunk.

Bertonelli could feel Grant getting into the car. The door slammed, the engine started, and the car moved away. They stopped at the gate, and then accelerated up Tchaikovsky Boulevard toward the river. It was very cold in the trunk. The spare wheel dug into Bertonelli's shoulder, and he could smell the exhaust. It seemed to take forever. The car slowed and stopped, then started again several times, until it seemed as if they were climbing a hill, the engine laboring.

At last they stopped. The car door opened and seconds later the trunk lid opened.

Bertonelli had to have help out of the trunk; his legs were so stiff he could hardly stand alone. They were parked beside a broad roadway. It took Bertonelli several seconds to get his bearings. Below, the city of Moscow was spread out in a profusion of white and violet lights, the red star atop the Kremlin the only real point of brilliant color in the night. Behind them, farther up the hill, was the Lenin Hills lookout tower, bathed in lights. They were less than two blocks from Bertonelli's apartment building in Moscow's Southwestern District, and barely a mile from Kostikov's. Just below was the Chinese embassy, and behind and above was the Olympic Village. It was extremely cold.

"Will you be all right from here?" Grant asked.

"I'll manage."

A train whistle blew somewhere in the distance. It sounded lonely. Foreign.

"I think I should tell you something," Grant said. He seemed embarrassed.

"Not if it's going to get you into trouble." Bertonelli had a fair idea what was coming.

"Shit. Mr. DeMille wants to know everything you're doing. He wants duplicates of all my reports. He wants to know everything you say."

"He's chief of station."

"I know, but without you knowing about it. He has the entire embassy focused on you."

"Then I'll have to watch my step."

"He wants you out of here. He and Mr. Scofield. I heard them talking . . ."

"Keep your nose clean, Wyatt. Just do your job, and when the big fall comes you'll turn out okay."

Grant looked away. It was clear he wanted to say more, but he thought better of it. "I thought it would be a lot different here."

"I didn't," Bertonelli said. He clapped the man on the shoulder. "Thanks for the ride." He hunched up his coat collar and crossed the street. He didn't bother turning around when the car started up, but he waved as it passed him and turned the corner at the end of the block, its taillights winking.

During the day there was a lot of traffic here. Moscow State University was nearby. A lot of the buildings were old, Byzantine, or Gothic, but mostly well kept up. Bertonelli thought that Moscow was a city of great contrasts. There was a lot wider disparity between the classes than the Russians wanted to admit. Ayn Rand had called it the aristocracy of pull. He knew better. Nothing had changed since the czars. Fear was the motivator that pushed the Russians into a dull, plodding inefficiency that erupted in fits of incredible barbarity at unpredictable intervals. Boredom. It drove them all crazy. The drab sameness of everything was maddening.

He had lied to Grant. He too had thought Moscow would be different than this. The Okulov meeting was the first real excitement he'd had since he had been assigned to Moscow. Until now he had done little more than eavesdrop at parties, listen to news broadcasts, and read technical journals. In May he had gone with Hobbs to watch the big military parade on Red Square, where the two of them had cataloged the hardware and the pecking order of the government leaders on the reviewing stand. There were a couple of surprises, but nothing that would start anyone's heart pumping. Nothing there.

The DDO had once called him a cowboy, but his wife, before their divorce, had called him a bully, which was curiously hurtful. As a kid he endured names. He was the dago with worn corduroy trousers. *How does an Italian helicopter start? With a guinea . . . guinea . . . guinea . . . wop-wop-wop-wop.* The only people lower on the totem pole were the Hunkies from Raleigh Street. He'd never been a bully.

He remembered, though, when he was a kid just after the war, maybe in the early fifties, before his old man got lung cancer and died. They used to go down to the North Pole bar. The kids would be playing the bowling machine and drinking Nesbitt orange pop or creme soda, while his old man and his buddy, Nick Blotti, would sit at the long, tall bar drinking Fitgers beer. They would be laughing by two in the afternoon about how they had to beat their wives and kids, just to keep 'em in line. A man works all his life, and what does he get? Shit! All their talk in those days was rhetorical. No one had to

listen to anyone else because everyone was saying the same
things.

But they weren't bullies. They were passionate. JoAnn
used to laugh when he tried to explain it, so he stopped trying
about the same time he stopped trying everything else with
her.

His apartment was on the eighth floor of a never completed
twelve-story building that stood alone in the center of a small
parklike field of tall grasses and sparse birch trees. The
parking lot was in the back, but there was no rear entrance.
The building was exclusively for foreigners, so everyone had
to pass the Militia man in his box at the front door.

Bertonelli approached from above and behind, slipping
through the trees down the shallow hill that emptied into a far
corner of the parking lot.

He knew all the cars that would normally be there at that
time of night. Even so, he would never have picked out the
battered Moskva sedan parked close to the rear of the apartment building, except he noticed the glow of a cigarette. He
pulled up short. Someone was seated behind the wheel. Smoking. Waiting. For what?

Bertonelli glanced up at his apartment. A light shone from
the living room window. He had left no lights burning. The
bastards.

Keeping low, he skirted the edge of the parking lot, darting
out of the trees and crouching behind the cars as he ran. He
worked his way around to the rear of the Moskva, then
crawled very carefully around to the driver's side.

He reached up, grabbed the door handle, yanked the door
open, and rose up.

The thick-shouldered Russian turned in surprise as Bertonelli
grabbed a handful of his coat and pulled him out of the car.

Both of them sprawled back on the pavement, but Bertonelli
had the advantage. He hammered two quick blows to the
man's face, the Russian's head bouncing off the frozen as-
phalt, his nose splitting and erupting in blood, his eyes
fluttering.

Bertonelli hit him savagely a third time, and the Russian
went slack, his arms falling to his sides, his breath whistling
through his battered nose.

The Russian was armed with a 7.65mm TK automatic. In
his breast pocket was a KGB identification booklet. His name

was Viktor Ivanovich Lipasov. Second Chief Directorate. The Warehouse.

"Sonofabitch," Bertonelli swore softly. He wasn't winded, but his heart was hammering.

They had come to search his apartment. This one was their front man. But what the hell were they looking for? There was nothing up there. He wasn't foolish enough to keep sensitive material outside the embassy. They would know that.

It made him mad. He was being harassed. Unless Kostikov was a lot sharper than he had given the man credit for being. Had Kostikov made him at the zoo after all? It would explain why they were here tonight of all nights.

Bertonelli got up and heaved the unconscious Lipasov back into the car and closed the door. He picked up his hat, which had fallen off, straightened his coat, and went around to the front entrance.

The Militia guard in his box nearly fell off his stool as Bertonelli strode by him and barged into the lobby. The elevator was on the eighth floor. He punched the button for it, and as it started down, he went to the stairwell and took the stairs up two at a time.

The stairwell smelled of cement dust. For the first two flights there were no railings. The building was six years old; the railings would come someday. In the meantime you just had to be careful. All the way up he kept thinking that he should back off, that he should leave this alone. Kostikov could sign the order and have him on a plane out of here so goddamned fast his head would swim. Or he could be arrested and thrown in prison for beating up an officer of State Security who was merely doing his lawful job. By the time his release could be secured through diplomatic channels a lot could happen.

He also thought that he should have taken the Russian's gun. His own was locked up in the safe in his office at the embassy. It was strictly against regulations to run around Moscow armed, unless very specific instructions came from the director of the Central Intelligence Agency himself, and only then in an emergency with the ambassador's full knowledge and consent.

Bertonelli reached the eighth floor. He was winded. He

eased open the steel fire door and looked out into the corridor. It was empty.

He could see the elevator indicator at the end of the hallway. The car was on the ground floor. He stepped back and looked up the stairs, holding himself very still so that he could listen for a noise from above—a scuffling of shoe leather, anything. But the stairwell was silent.

In the corridor Bertonelli walked softly on the balls of his feet to the elevator. He punched the button, and when the car started back up, he went to his apartment door where he stopped to listen. There were no sounds from within.

He took out his key, unlocked the door, and pushed it open with his toe. The apartment was dark. The Militia guard downstairs had telephoned up and warned them. But they had not taken the elevator down, nor were they on the stairs.

"Who's in here?" he called.

He reached inside and flipped on the light. The apartment was an incredible mess. From where he stood just within the doorway, he could see that the couch and two chairs had been turned over and cut apart, upholstery material spread all over the place. The big rug had been pulled up and shoved into a corner, pictures had been taken down off the walls and their backings torn off, even the wallpaper had been ripped from the walls. It was a first-class search. One in which no one gave a damn who knew about it. It was a typical KGB trick of intimidation.

A door opened and someone ran down the corridor.

Bertonelli spun around and stepped out in time to see two men, one of them short, the other much taller and huskier, reach the stairwell door and tear it open.

"Hey, you!" he shouted.

The door banged shut with a hollow echo behind them. Bertonelli turned the other way and raced back to the elevator, just as the door was sliding open. He punched the close-door button, and the button for the ground floor. With maddening slowness the door closed, and the car started back down.

If the Militia guard had come into the lobby, it might be better. Bertonelli figured he could start yelling "Thief!" and keep yelling it until the poor man would have to do something about it. At least make a halfhearted attempt to mollify the American by demanding to see the intruders' identification.

Yet he hoped the man had been instructed not to interfere.
If that were the case, Bertonelli would get his message across
to Kostikov loud and clear.

The car reached the ground floor, and even before the door
was halfway open, he had slipped out into the lobby which,
like the eighth-floor corridor, was deserted. He raced back to
the stairwell door, opened it, and stepped inside. The two
Russians were coming down. He could hear them still two
floors up, as he hurriedly ducked beneath the cast concrete
steps.

The floor was extremely dirty. The space smelled like dog
shit. One of the regular Militia guards had a dog. Bertonelli
figured the man probably brought the animal in here to do its
business as a joke. Just a little shit on the Americans.

He was being a damned fool. There were two of them, and
they were probably armed. When the big guy out in the car
came around, he was going to be mad.

They were on the last course of stairs, just overhead. But
they had slowed down, apparently convinced they had not
been pursued.

Bertonelli stepped out from beneath the stairs and straightened up just as the shorter of the two men started to open the
door. Their coats were peppered with plaster dust from tear-
ing the wallpaper off the walls.

"Are you looking for me?" Bertonelli's voice boomed in
the stairwell.

Both Russians jumped so hard it was almost comical. They
turned around, the shorter one reaching inside his breast
pocket. His head seemed too large for his body.

Bertonelli held out his hands. "You'd better have a good
reason for shooting me, comrades," he said in Russian. "I'm
not armed."

They both looked at Bertonelli, an expression of consternation frozen on their faces. They had not expected this.

"What were you doing in my apartment?"

"I don't know what you're talking about," the short one
murmured.

"There is a recording device in the ceiling light fixture of
my apartment."

The tall one instinctively glanced up the stairs. Bertonelli
laughed. It was so obvious.

"We were visiting a friend. It is all. We will go now," the other one said. He reached for the door and started to open it.

"I know about the matches, and the telephone number," Bertonelli blurted.

A flat, deadly expression came into the short man's eyes. This one could do some damage, Bertonelli figured. The other one was nothing more than a technician. He had the look. He would not stomach a fight.

"I don't know what you are speaking of."

"Comrade Major Kostikov knows," Bertonelli said slowly and distinctly. He wanted no mistake made because of his less than perfect Russian.

"Yes, and what does this mean?"

"I suggest you tell that to no one but Major Kostikov."

The two Russians looked at each other, then back to Bertonelli. "Perhaps you will come with us now."

Bertonelli dropped his arms and bunched up his fists as he stepped back.

The short one's eyes widened in surprise. He shook his head, then turned and pulled open the door.

"Crazy fucking American," one of them said and then they were gone.

Bertonelli's muscles were tight. Alone, he relaxed, and let out the breath he had been holding. Round one, he thought.

The wind had begun to blow. The building groaned menacingly. There was a Winter Festival party upstairs. It sounded as if they were having a good time. Valeri figured by morning they'd all be sorry they'd stayed so late.

He lay on the couch, the living room too hot although there were a lot of cold drafts from the imperfectly fitted windows. After he had fixed himself some supper, he had taken a bath and then had tried to go into the bedroom. But it hadn't worked. He had lain on top of the covers with his clothes on, but he couldn't blot out a mental picture of Tanya. She was there with him. Disapproving. So he had come out to the living room where he had tried to get some rest. He looked at his watch. It was past two in the morning. He supposed he had gotten some sleep. He couldn't remember passing midnight. Twice he had almost gotten up to telephone his office about Bertonelli. He couldn't get the American out of his mind. The man had a lot of arrogance, but Valeri wondered how he was sleeping tonight after being shot at. Both times he had lain back. In the morning, he told himself.

General Demin's about-face was worrisome, as was his warning. Yet there were so many unanswered questions, not the least of which was Larissa Okulov. He felt as if he were a boulder in a swift-moving stream, caught for the moment but on the verge of being dislodged and ground to pebbles in the gathering maelstrom.


Khabarovsk was quite a large Siberian city of half a million population. Built on three hills well north of Vladivostok, each defining a different district, it lay on the river that all

Russians called "Little Father Amur," but which the Chinese more appropriately called the Black Dragon because of its fearsome reputation. The city was young, less than a century old, but even younger in a lot of its garish architecture because of the severe damage done to it during the Revolution.

As Valeri slept his telephone rang. It was his father, General Konstantin Illyich Kostikov, commander of the Northern Missile Defense Command based at Khabarovsk.

"I'm sorry I'm calling so early, Valerik, but I leave within the hour on an inspection tour."

"Dada," Valeri mumbled, half awake. The apartment was dark except for a light in the kitchen. He leaned his forehead against the cool wall.

General Kostikov chuckled. "Is Tanya back from the hospital yet? Or are you alone?"

Valeri opened his eyes and fumbled for a cigarette. "Dr. Klimov wants to keep her for the weekend. Are you all right, sir? Is everything okay?"

"Do you want Lara with you? She said she would be happy to come to Moscow to help out. There is some shopping she would like to do, and she wants to see Winter Festival again."

"I don't think so."

"No. I suppose not. But Klimov is an asshole. I could arrange for you to take her to the United States. The Mayo Clinic?"

"Dr. Klimov is the best there is, Father. Tanya trusts him."

"I'm taking my leave soon. Lara and I thought we might go down to Yalta. Take the big house we used to have. It's still available. You and Tanya could join us."

"That would be fine. When?"

"Soon. Perhaps in the spring. March?"

"I could use the rest."

"We all could. Listen, Valerik, Uncle Gennadi telephoned. He is very worried about you."

Valeri took a deep drag on his cigarette, drawing the acrid smoke into his lungs. It gave him heartburn. His lips seemed thick, his nose plugged and his eyes scratchy. He always felt this way when he didn't have enough sleep. "He shouldn't be."

"Well, he is. And frankly, after what he told me, so am I. Lara has her own theories."

"I'm sure she does."

"For once I have to agree with her. In this day and age no one expects a son to follow in his father's footsteps. The sons, especially, have to make their own way. Carve their own mark."

"What are you talking about?"

"You have nothing to prove, believe me. Just do your job. Don't try so hard to make yourself into a hero."

"I don't understand." Valeri wondered why he was making his father work so hard when it was so perfectly clear what had happened. It had been this way since his mother died, however. Valeri didn't think he knew how to change. Neither of them did. His father wanted a son to emulate him, a son he could guide and shape and mold in his own image. Valeri refused, had always refused, always going off in his own direction instead. There was nothing left for his father (in his own defense) to do other than try to shame his son into it.

"Don't be so goddamned obtuse. I can't blame you. But I called to help."

"Yes, sir."

The line was quiet except for the hiss and pop of the imperfect connection. The sun would be up in Khabarovsk by now. The big missile silos were farther east toward the Sea of Japan, but the city itself was very near the Manchurian border. There were a lot of nervous Russians in the mean, industrial town.

"They want to promote me next year."

"Congratulations, Father."

"Lara and I would have to move back to Moscow. It would be good for us to be a family again."

"Like the old days."

His father laughed again. "You're a bastard, Valerik," he said.

Valeri had to smile. "Technically not very accurate, I think. At least I hope not. But I am a service brat."

"That's Washington rubbing off on you. Is this Bertonelli all that important to you?"

"He is a very dangerous man."

"They all are. But I wonder how much risk you are willing to take to rid yourself of him. Isolate him, yes, I can understand that. All I have to do is watch the radar screens and await my orders. The rest is simple. But for you there are a lot of variables. Kill the fox, but don't tear down the chicken coop in the process.''

Comrade Okulov. General Demin had telephoned with his concern, and his father, a good and loyal friend, was following up. The implication was, however, that if Valeri continued to make waves, it could adversely affect his father's promotion. Or, he wondered, was he reading too much into this call? Was he being a realist, or a cynic?

''What else did Uncle Gennadi tell you?''

''This is for your own good.''

''Did he mention Rotislav Okulov? Did he tell you that the man was most likely a traitor?''

''Listen to me, son, what do you think you know? Have you got all the answers there in Moscow? Is it all so clear to you?''

''Nothing is clear to me.''

''No, I suspect not. But you are missing the most important principle of all. You must follow the orders of your superiors. I do. Uncle Gennadi does. Even Comrade Chairman Chernetsov takes his orders from Gorbachev himself. Now *there* are two real heroes. Modern men.''

''What am I missing?''

''Ah-hah. He asks, so it must be coming clear even to him. In a field of wheat only the stalk whose head is empty of grain stands above the rest.''

''Okulov must have been very important. Did you know his wife was beautiful?''

''Valerik . . .''

''He tried to kill me when I came upon their little meeting. One in the morning in the middle of the zoo. The American wore a Militia uniform. The meeting had been prearranged. It must have been planned for quite a long time; Okulov actually had a key to one of the maintenance gates. They met, shook hands, and he let the American inside. They talked for an hour. What do you suppose they talked about, Father, that has Uncle Gennadi so upset?''

''Did you actually hear what they were saying?''

''No. But Okulov dropped a book of matches on which he had written a number . . . a telephone number for Vladimir Novikov.''

"Gennadi spoke of this name. He believes it is a fabrication. Novikov is nothing."

"He told you that?"

"He told me you were playing a dangerous game."

"Going after traitors?"

"Disobeying a superior officer! He called me as an old family friend."

"Then you want me to stand down?"

"I want you to do your job, Valerik. Is that so difficult?"

"I spoke with Comrade Okulov's wife. As I said, a very beautiful woman. She hated her husband."

"It is none of your business."

"Oh, but it is. It is exactly within the charter of my department. But perhaps Comrade General Demin will fire me if I continue my investigation. Do you suppose he might do that, Father? Or perhaps he might even have me sent into external exile. It would kill Tanya."

"I don't understand you."

"I think you do. But did you call me to lure me to the States with Tanya, or did you call to invite us to Khabarovsk?"

"I don't see—"

"My job is catching spies. American spies, or Russian spies. It does not matter in the end, except that I am very good at it."

The line was quiet again. Valeri could visualize his father holding the telephone to his ear, a stern expression in his deep-set eyes, his high forehead wrinkled in consternation. From as early as Valeri could remember, it had always been this way between them. They argued about everything. During their better times together, his father would boast that he was merely training his son to be a master of debate in a world where the syllogism was mightier than the sword. During the worst of times, his father would complain bitterly that somehow genetics was to blame: Valeri was the *daughter* he had always wanted—intelligent, sensitive, good-looking—while Lara with her tough, pragmatic soul was the *son* he should have had. Fate had played them all a cruel trick. It didn't make any of them happy.

Valeri stubbed out his cigarette. He was extremely weary. "Tell me to quit and I will. Tanya and I will come to visit you and Lara. From there we can fly to Tokyo, and then on to the States. I'll be gone at least a month, probably much longer. By the time I get back a lot of things will be different."

"Valerik?"

"Yes, sir?"

"In March, definitely we'll take the house in Yalta. We can be a family again."

"Thank you."

"Uncle Gennadi says you are having supper with him over the weekend. Say hello for Lara and me. It's been too long."


Valeri went to his office where he had a glass of tea in a silver-handled holder as he stared at the many photographs of his family. Smiling faces. Happy faces. At peace, at least outwardly. But there were few photographs of his mother, who had been a frail, lovely woman with translucent skin and silken hair. She had been camera shy for some reason, and after her death Valeri had locked away most of the pictures of her. He could not bear to look at them very often. It reminded him too sharply of his loss. Like Tanya, she had hated the drab, closed-in feeling of Moscow, and she had dreamed of Paris and London. Yet the Russian spirit surrounded her like the halo of a saint on an icon, totally natural and integral to her being.

Valeri had taken orders all of his life. Some men chafed under organization. But he thrived on it. He had been brought up to respect his superiors. To respect the greater will and wisdom of the state. The collective mentality was greater than the sum of its parts. It was the secret of the great Soviet.

Bertonelli was a devil. But he believed in his country, and he was here with a job to do. In that, at least, Valeri had respect for the man. On the other hand, Okulov had been a traitor. He had worked for nothing but destruction.

What had he told Bertonelli to lure the American to the zoo? Who was Vladimir Novikov? And who had gotten to General Demin? Valeri had skirted the main issue all day long. Even now, after the call from his father, he hesitated to give it a conscious thought. Yet like any notion born intuitively, it had a life of its own.

Okulov had offered something to Bertonelli. There was no doubt of it in Valeri's mind. Whatever it was, it scared the hell out of General Demin. Frightened him so badly that he

ordered the investigation called off. Something, once the
Americans had it, that would be harmful, perhaps even disas-
trous to the Soviet Union.

Valeri thought that General Demin's almost frantic efforts
to stop the investigation must mean whatever knowledge
Okulov had offered had not already been passed. What was
it? Why were they trying to hide it from him? And how could
they be certain Bertonelli didn't know, or at least suspect?

He knew that he should back down. But Okulov and
Bertonelli had made contact. They were in league together.
There was the chance, after all, that Bertonelli *did* know. It
made Valeri's ears warm to think what little bits of dirt
Bertonelli would be passing back to Langley. The Americans
loved to laugh at Russians. When he was stationed in the
States he had seen a rerun of the movie *The Russians Are
Coming! The Russians Are Coming!* It still embarrassed him
to think about how Soviet soldiers had been portrayed.

Valeri threw his glass against the wall, tea splashing across
the big USSR map. He turned and looked out the window.
An ice fog had formed. It looked very cold. He felt so
damned impotent. He felt as if he were a man who had come
upon a terrible road accident and didn't know a thing about
first aid. He wanted to help, but he feared that any move he
might make would be fatal.

He had three leads for now. Novikov. Okulov's wife. And
the two apartments she said her husband had maintained.

There was work to be done. Not all of it pleasant, or even
popular, but it was necessary.

Fainna Skvorstov, the attractive night supervisor, appeared
at the doorway out of breath, her cheeks flushed.

"I heard a crash," she said, not sure if she should come all
the way in.

Valeri looked around. "I spilled the tea."

She glanced at the spreading stain on the map, and at the
shards of glass on the floor, and nodded uncertainly. "I'll get
something to clean it up, Major . . ."

"No. Come in and shut the door."

She hesitated.

"Yes, it's all right, there is something I would like you to
do for me. It will be illegal, certainly dangerous, and possibly
it could cost you your job, but I need it."

She smiled and came the rest of the way in. Valeri noticed

that her print dress was far too thin for winter weather, and she wore no slip. Her hairdo was attractive.

Lipasov and Votrin came in early. Valeri took them down the block and around the corner to a cafeteria across the street from the State Conservatory of Music. It was a half hour before the place opened, but Valeri knew the old couple who ran it, and they let him in.

He ordered a bottle of vodka, some black bread and butter, and hard-boiled eggs with mustard. It was like lunch for them because they had been up most of the night.

"Fuck your mother, I didn't know what happened," Lipasov said. "He was suddenly there, that's all."

Lipasov's face was swollen and red. His left eye was closed, and a butterfly bandage had been placed across his slit nose. He held himself erect as if something were broken inside.

"You're sure it was Bertonelli?"

"I'll never forget that face," Lipasov said with much feeling and, Valeri feared, a lot of anxiety.

"Myshko said he would have to file a report," Votrin volunteered.

"His right, certainly. Did you find anything?"

"There was nothing there, Major. Not a thing. Just his clothes. The place was sterile."

"No trouble getting in?"

"None. It was easy. When the guard called to say that Bertonelli was on the way up, we got the hell out of there and went next door. The apartment was empty."

Lipasov looked up. "I was on the ground, and the next thing I knew I woke up in the car with Oleg and Myshko hovering over me."

There was something else, though. Valeri had felt it the moment they had walked into his office. Something that frightened them even more than Lipasov's shame. He poured them both another vodka.

"I'm like you," Valeri said. "I want to get rid of that bastard. And now it seems as if we have enough to do it. But there's something I'm thinking. Something better."

Votrin's eyes were shining. Lipasov looked toward the door almost as if he expected someone to come in. There was no one else in the cafeteria but them.

"He's making fun of us, you know. He turned Colonel Okulov, and now he's making fools of us."

Lipasov's jaws tightened; his knuckles turned white where he was holding his glass. Valeri reached out and touched the man's hand.

"Easy. There's another way."

"The sonofabitch thinks he owns Moscow," Lipasov said through clenched teeth.

Valeri forced himself to smile. "Not for long, Viktor Ivanovich. But when he falls I want to make it big, and important."

Lipasov was a lifeguard during the summer at the Dynamo Stadium indoor pool. Two years ago he had saved a mother and small child from drowning. They'd clung together and were going down for the last time when Lipasov dove in and dragged them to the shallow end of the huge pool. His picture and heroic story had been published on the front page not of *Trud*, but of *Pravda*, the Central Committee's newspaper. It gave him a dangerously inflated opinion of himself, but no one minded. Everyone was happy for him.

"He said something about matches, and about a telephone number," Votrin said. "Excuse me, but we had no idea what he was talking about."

Valeri sat back in his wooden chair all of a sudden, the slats groaning under his weight. Bertonelli knew about Novikov! Evidently Okulov had spoken the number out loud. He had read it off his matchbook.

There was a bead of sweat on Lipasov's upper lip. He carefully wiped it off. "What are we to do?"

Valeri lit a cigarette. He was trying to slow himself way down. He wanted to run off in all directions. He wanted to pull Bertonelli in right now. It would not be terribly difficult, given enough troops, enough organization. But he held himself in check. There was more here.

"What else did he say?"

Votrin shook his head. "We came down the stairs, and there he was, waiting for us. I damned near shot him. He said you would know about the matches and the telephone number. His exact words were: 'Tell that to no one but Major Kostikov.' "

"Extraordinary."

"He threatened us . . . Myshko and me."

"He had a gun?"

"No, sir. With his fists."

"He was ready to fight you?"

"Yes, sir."

Valeri drank some vodka. There was little doubt that Bertonelli understood what was happening better than Valeri did. The sonofabitch might think he owned Moscow, but Valeri knew better.

"How did he get out of the embassy unnoticed?"

Votrin shrugged. "No way of knowing for sure. We talked about this before. He probably went out in the trunk of a car. We need more informants inside."

"That's always the problem, isn't it," Valeri said. "Is someone watching his apartment now?"

Lipasov nodded. "I'd like just one hour with the bastard over at the Center. Hell, twenty minutes."

"Let us bring him in, Comrade Major," Votrin said.

"Not yet."

"We have enough to arrest him . . ."

"That's not enough. He'd wriggle out of it somehow. Besides, he knows something that we don't. And I'll be damned if I'm going to be like the country bride on her wedding night."

Votrin and Lipasov had no idea what he was talking about, but it didn't matter.

"Are you two up to a little more legwork this morning? I know you're tired . . ."

"What is it?" Lipasov asked. He had a real grudge now. It gave him a lot of energy.

"This is going to be illegal."

Both of them grinned.

"Colonel Okulov maintained two apartments here in the city in addition to the one on Kalinina Prospekt. I want to know where they are."

"Was he meeting Bertonelli there?" Lipasov asked, leaning forward. He held his vodka glass cradled in both hands.

"I don't know. But I want you to find them. All I have for you to go on is that one was out on Leningradsky Prospekt just before Volokolamskoye Highway. A plain white, tall building. And the other is around the corner from the main post office, near the Kazan Station. A three- or four-story yellow brick building. The apartments are probably not in his name, and under no circumstances do I want a fuss made.''

"Comrade Major, do you want us to search them?''

"It's not necessary. I want you to find out where these two apartments are located, that's all.''

Lipasov and Votrin looked at each other, nodded, then finished their vodka and left.

A few minutes later Valeri paid his bill and walked back to his office. Shevchenko had just arrived. He was upstairs in the operations room sipping a cup of tea. He looked worn out. They went up to Valeri's office.

"If there's anything out at Novikov's *dacha*, it's not worth a damn,'' Shevchenko said.

"What did you find?''

"Not a thing, Valerik.''

"Anything of Novikov himself?''

"He died in that fire, that's all. Worked as a civil engineer.''

Valeri laughed. "Civil engineers do not own *dachas*.''

"He did. It may have been in his parents' name. The father has something to do with the UPDK.''

"The diplomatic corps?''

"Presumably. But is it worth following up?''

"It may be, Mikhail. Listen, I spoke with Okulov's wife. A real looker, let me tell you.''

Shevchenko's eyes were bright. He loved a soap opera if it had pretty girls.

"Do you think there is a connection between him and Novikov's father? Is that what we've been missing?''

"It's possible.''

"I don't even know if he's alive.''

"It would be interesting to know what he's up to.''

"He could be the conduit.''

"Mikhail, with them you will have to be careful. They don't take kindly to interference.''

"He may even be out of the country at this very moment.''

"Intriguing,'' Valeri said.

"This could be tied to a network of thieves and spies with Bertonelli as the grand master.''

"Spies, I should think, Mikhail, not thieves.''

\* \* \*

When Shevchenko was gone, Fainna Skvorstov came up. She had been due to go home several hours ago, but she had remained to finish the assignment Valeri had given her. She looked tired, though if anything Valeri thought it made her seem more attractive somehow. She laid a file on his desk.

"Any trouble?"

She shook her head. "None. Stepanovich V. Okulov, the uncle, is deputy chief of research at Krasnodar. The brother, Uri Vladimir Okulov, is the chief secretary of Western research for the Administrative Organs Department of the Politburo."

Valeri opened the file folder. A brief dossier on each man was accompanied by several photographs that had obviously been taken off the computer. The uncle was an old man, with long white hair, reminiscent of a Georgian Albert Einstein. The brother was much younger, with the wire-rimmed glasses, the slicked-back hair, and the pinched expression of the typical bureaucrat. Both were party members in good standing, and both maintained extremely high security clearances. The uncle's travel was restricted to the Soviet Union itself, while the brother had an unlimited travel status.

Whatever Okulov had been trying to do—defect to the States or merely pass information to Bertonelli—the brother could very well be involved. A high-ranking official within the Politburo staff, Uri Vladimir would know the strings to pull. It raised some intriguing questions.

Through the remainder of the morning Valeri worked on surveillance reports, though he found it difficult to concentrate on what he was doing.

A circus parade of clowns and Gypsies and bears was snaking down Kalinina Prospekt in gaily painted trucks, wagons, and funny-looking little goat-pulled carts.

A lot of people had gathered to watch the show, especially to watch the bears that shambled along the street like huge stuffed animals. Little children cried out from their fathers' shoulders, and drunks seemed to be on every corner.

Valeri found a parking spot across from Larissa Okulov's apartment building and settled down to wait. The woman had not been informed her husband was dead. But the name Bertonelli had meant something to her. He was sure of it. He wondered if she had known about the meeting, and he wondered if she had reported the appearance of a KGB officer on her doorstep. It would go a long way in explaining General Demin's sudden reversal.

For a time as Valeri sat there, he let his mind wander back and forth from the mysterious Novikov, to Okulov's apartments, and finally back to General Demin's warning and his father's strange telephone call. If he were smart he would back off. Certainly he had no business involving his staff in something so potentially dangerous. Yet he could not let it go. He was not built that way. Whatever the reasons for the meeting between Okulov and Bertonelli, Valeri would find them.

It was well after two before he spotted Larissa Okulov, dressed in a black fur coat and matching hat, step out of her apartment building, cross the broad courtyard, and walk down the long steps toward him.

The parade was long gone, and traffic had returned to normal. Valeri tossed out his cigarette as he watched her. She stopped at the curb. She seemed to be waiting for someone.

Moments later a Zil limousine pulled up, the rear door opened, and a small, very thin man stepped out. He greeted her and then helped her into the car.

Valeri flipped open the Okulov dossier that Fainna had bootlegged for him, and picked out the photograph of Uri Vladimir Okulov.

The man turned before he followed Larissa into the car, giving Valeri a clear glimpse of his face. It was Uri Vladimir. There was no doubt of it. A high-ranking official of the Politburo staff here. He was dressed in black, as was Larissa. And even from this distance, Valeri could tell that neither of them was happy.

# 7

Traffic was heavy on Tchaikovsky Boulevard. Lumbering trucks, trolley buses, and cabs competed with a surprising number of automobiles, most of which were fairly clean. It was against the law in Moscow to drive a dirty car.

From a third floor window of the American embassy, Bertonelli watched the flow as he thought about last night. He was treading on very dangerous territory. The Soviets now had sufficient grounds for his arrest. A little voice in the back of his head kept telling him to back off, walk away from this, break clean. But he could not. Willfulness, his parents said, and his father tried to beat it out of him. Stubbornness, JoAnn said, and she had divorced him.

He turned back to Bill Hobbs, who had invited him into his office for a little chat. A bottle of whiskey and two glasses were set up on the desk.

"Let me give you a piece of advice," Hobbs told him, handing up one of the glasses. "With Okulov you were playing with fire. But with Major Kostikov, from what I know of the man, you're dealing with a nuclear explosion. The Russians want you out of Moscow, and so does DeMille. Let me tell you, there wouldn't be any tears shed at your funeral."

Bertonelli tossed his whiskey back. Hobbs had been in Moscow for a long time. He had come to understand the Russians. He knew practically everyone worth knowing, and he seemed to get along with all of them. Yet the reports he generated on the Soviet military establishment were considered by the Pentagon to be nothing short of insightful. He understood the *kollektiv* mind, yet he had not been tainted by his close association, as had Scofield. Bertonelli had a lot of respect for him.

"What should I do? Leave it?"

"The last thing anyone wants is for you to upset the apple cart. But if Colonel Okulov was telling the truth and there indeed are Americans being held—Americans that the Russians now want to release—we can't simply forget about them. In that, everyone agrees with you."

Hobbs drank his whiskey and poured them both another.

"What are you saying to me?" Bertonelli asked. He was tired. He hadn't gotten much sleep in the past couple of days. From being shot at to confronting the KGB at his apartment building tended to make the nights too short.

"Tony, in the five years I've been here I've not heard so much as a hint of it. Neither has Scofield nor DeMille nor anyone else."

Okulov had offered two proofs, one of which was the telephone number of a burned-out *dacha* outside the city. And the second, Bertonelli hoped, Kostikov would provide for him. If the Russians did indeed want to repatriate the Americans they were holding, then Kostikov should be willing to cooperate.

"Why wouldn't the Soviets simply kill them and bury the evidence?" Hobbs asked. "Have you asked yourself that?"

"Gorbachev is a moderate. They're talking détente again."

"What do you think such a revelation would do to détente? Blow it into the toilet, that's what. Reagan would have a field day. It would prove everything he's ever said about the Soviets."

"He's right, Uncle Bill."

"Yes, he is. But they've got ten thousand warheads just like we do. Which changes the game. Which means we can't make them go away. Which means for better or for worse, we live with the bastards. Which means we talk with them. Because when the shooting starts it won't make shit how many unknown Americans are being held in the Soviet Union, or how many Soviet defectors were given asylum in the United States."

"Maybe the're a bunch of druggies, or black marketeers. Gorbachev could make points for being the great humanitarian."

"Why now? Why did Okulov pick you at this particular moment to make his announcement? I think if you can figure that out, you will go a long way toward proving whether or not their move was a disinformation plot, or the real McCoy. And, Tony, they're masters of the game. Even you can't imagine.''

Grant had left a note that the burned-out *dacha* had belonged to Vladimir I. Novikov, an engineer who had apparently died in the blaze two years ago. In the afternoon Bertonelli went downstairs to see Laurie Morgan in archives. It was rumored that she and DeMille had a thing going, so she was no less cold to Bertonelli than before. But she did search her records for reference to the engineer, coming up with nothing. Novikov may have existed, but he was a nonperson as far as concerned U.S. embassy files. Up in communications Bertonelli sent a brief query to Langley, though he didn't think they'd come up with anything either. He was getting the feeling that perhaps Novikov the man wasn't the key as much as the *dacha* itself. Or perhaps the telephone number held some coded message.

Back in his office he closed his door to make sure he wouldn't be disturbed for a little while, then he removed the seal from his office safe and opened it. For just a moment he hesitated, but then he took out his Smith & Wesson snub-nosed .38, loaded it, then screwed the short silencer cylinder on the end of the barrel, and stuffed it in his pocket. There was no telling how Kostikov was going to react in the next twenty-four hours. But Bertonelli wasn't going to be caught short again.

He grabbed his coat, then took the elevator down to the first floor where he stopped by the consul general's office, which was the section within the embassy organization to which he was technically assigned. U.S. embassies were controlled by the Chief of Mission (whose title was Ambassador), aided by the Deputy Chief of Mission (who was the chargé d'affaires when the ambassador was absent). Below them were the four sections: Political, Economic, Administrative, and Consular affairs. As chief of station for CIA activities, DeMille was listed on the roster as special assistant to the ambassador. As number two CIA man in the embassy, Bertonelli was listed as special assistant to the consul general, Carson Ayers, an old-school Harvard graduate, career diplomat.

''You've got that mean look I've come to worry so much

about," Ayers said when Bertonelli came into his office. The consul general was a man in his mid-fifties, with an absolutely bald head and laugh wrinkles around his eyes. "We missed you at the staff meeting this morning."

"I was cleaning my apartment. You can't believe the mess."

Ayers grinned. "Ah, the life of a bachelor. Did you have a party?"

"Something like that."

Bertonelli glanced out at the busy outer office, which was fronted by a long service counter, then closed the door.

A lot of Soviet citizens worked within the embassy, some of them here in the Consular section that kept track of Americans living and working within the Soviet Union.

"Can we talk?"

Ayers's expression became serious. He nodded. "Scuttlebutt is that you and Roland had another falling out, but that Ambassador Scott backed you this time."

"I need some information, Carson."

"Don't tell me you're actually going to occupy your Trojan desk?"

Bertonelli had to smile. He shook his head. "Nothing as drastic as all that. What I need is the name of someone working or studying here in Moscow. An American."

"A double agent?"

"Not even anything as dramatic as that. I'm looking for the name of a medical doctor."

"There are several of them here in Moscow at the moment. Study grants. Research exchange programs. Do you have his name, or will I have to guess?"

"I need to assume an identity for about an hour, maybe less. It wouldn't have to hold up to much scrutiny, but I would like a legitimate name."

The consul general sat back in his chair and eyed Bertonelli with obvious distaste. "I don't think you would get much cooperation if you asked."

"I hadn't intended on asking, Carson. Nor would I be asking you if it wasn't terribly important."

Ayers made a bridge of his fingers and closed his eyes. His tie was knotted correctly but his vest was unbuttoned, and his jacket hung over the back of his chair.

"I could ask you to go through channels, but that would

simply put me in the middle of your squabble. The hell of it is, I like you." He opened his eyes. "But I don't trust you any farther than I could throw the Kremlin."

"I'll explain the entire thing to you if you want."

Ayers waved him off. "Absolutely not." He rummaged through some papers on his desk, coming up with a letter on heavy beige letterhead. "It just happens you're in luck. Dr. Clinton Moore. Left yesterday afternoon to go back to the States. I know, because I personally handled the details. University of Minnesota, neurology. He's on a study grant here. University of Moscow."

"An intern?"

"He's teaching them, from what I understand."

"How long has he been here?"

"Less than two months. Will he do? Or shouldn't I even ask that?"

"He'll do," Bertonelli said. He went to the door.

"On second thought, I'm not so sure I should have done that," Ayers said. "Are you going to create trouble for the poor bastard?"

"No," Bertonelli said. He left.

It was well after four o'clock and already the streetlights were coming on by the time Bertonelli had done his background reading in Archives, had made one telephone call, and had driven over to the Skifovsky Institute on Sadovaya Boulevard. The complex, which had once been a palace for princes, was fronted by a semicircular row of Doric columns through which the wind-driven snow blew in fitful gusts. At the rear was the Moscow Ambulance Service. The east wing held the hospital, and the west the research institute that had been named after a famous Russian surgeon.

Bertonelli entered the west wing and was directed to the fourth-floor office of Dr. Dmitri Klimov, who turned out to be a tiny, intense-looking dark man who walked with a pronounced limp. To Bertonelli he seemed sad yet somewhat bemused. But Bertonelli could not imagine a happy Jew in Russia. The KGB had hounded the doctor for years.

"You're Dr. Moore. You telephoned?"

"I appreciate you seeing me on such short notice."

"You work with Dr. Sverdlov at the university?"

"Yes, I do. A good man."

"I understood that you had left Moscow."

"Not until tomorrow. There was a problem with my flight," Bertonelli said. Evidently Dr. Klimov had checked on him as he supposed the man would.

"I see," Dr. Klimov said, gesturing Bertonelli to a chair. The office was quite large by Russian standards with a lovely oriental rug, an American Indian painting on one wall, books on two others, and a large window overlooking a statue in a rear courtyard along the fourth. "I see. Well, you weren't specific in your call. What exactly was it you wanted to see me about?"

"Tanya Kostikov."

Dr. Klimov had seated himself behind his desk. A sudden wary look came to his eyes as he studied Bertonelli. "What is your interest in this case?"

"Her husband, Major Kostikov, came to see me this morning, asking for a second opinion. I promised nothing. I would not normally interfere . . . but he was quite insistent."

"He came to you?" Dr. Klimov asked sharply. "How did he come to find your name? This is interesting."

Bertonelli spread his hands and shrugged.

"Yes, well," Dr. Klimov said after a moment. He unnecessarily rearranged some papers on his desk. He was clearly upset. Bertonelli wondered about it. His reaction seemed more than wounded professional pride. The man was reputed to be the very best on epilepsy in the Soviet Union, so Bertonelli had expected a prima donna. But there was more here.

"I will send a copy of her records over to you at the university, then, first thing in the morning."

"I would like to see her this afternoon, if I may."

"She is resting."

"I don't propose to examine her at this time. Not until I've had a chance to review her records, Doctor. But I would like to meet with her. I promised her husband I would look in on her."

"Impossible."

Bertonelli inclined his head. He had a flair for the dramatic. It was his upbringing. He took his time getting to his feet. "Thank you, in any event, for your time, Doctor. I'll make my excuses to the major. I'm leaving Moscow tomorrow, and it certainly will be at least two weeks before I'll return."

Dr. Klimov had gotten up as well. Contriteness showed in his face. He shook his head. "Please forgive me, Dr. Moore. But there is more here than you are aware of."

"With her condition?"

"A situation that in some ways exacerbates her epilepsy."

"Would you care to explain that to me?"

Dr. Klimov seemed to be having a great deal of trouble coming to a decision. It suddenly came to Bertonelli that the doctor was more than professionally interested in Tanya Kostikov. He had become personally involved.

"Have you ever met her?"

"No."

"But you know her husband?"

"I only know of him, actually."

"But you said he came to you . . ."

"Yes, he did. But before that I had never met him. I try to keep as far away from the KGB as I possibly can."

Dr. Klimov smiled sadly. He came around his desk. "So do we all, Doctor. Believe me, it is impossible. So I understand now your position. If you cooperate, your study grant will continue. If not . . ." He shrugged. "At least you are the lucky one. You will be allowed to leave."

"I understood you studied at the Menninger Clinic."

"Yes, I did. While I was there, however, my mother and my wife were required to remain in Gorky. It became a very long year's separation. One that resulted in the death of my mother, and ultimately my divorce."

"I'm sorry."

Dr. Klimov managed another slight smile. "Don't be." He took Bertonelli's arm and they went out into the corridor.

"You mentioned something about a situation that was affecting her condition?"

"Yes, yes," Dr. Klimov said. "When you meet her you will better understand. She is a frail woman—a child, actually. Physically as well as mentally. And yet she is quite bright, very artistic. A real talent."

"Her father was president of the Writer's Union."

Dr. Klimov looked sharply at Bertonelli. "Did her husband tell you that?"

"Yes."

"Did he also tell you that her father resigned in disgrace, and died a year later?"

"Did it have something to do with Major Kostikov?"

"Not directly. But when he and Tanya were married, Kostikov took her away to the United States. Washington, New York. His father, the general, was stationed overseas as well. They were one big happy family. Except that Tanya's father had never—could never—fit into their circle. So he felt he had truly lost a daughter. He began writing things."

"Things?"

"Poetry critical of a world in which his daughter had to be taken from his side because her husband was spying in a foreign land. Dreadful stuff, actually."

"He was asked to resign, and it killed him. Is that it?"

"Oh, yes," Dr. Klimov said. "As surely as if Valeri Kostikov had held a gun to his head and pulled the trigger. No less messy, either, I might add."

They had proceeded down the busy corridor to the elevators. Bertonelli felt like a giant next to the small man. His father had been short, and Bertonelli had a sense of déjà vu standing next to Dr. Klimov. It made him feel somewhat uncomfortable, gangly. He also found it extraordinary that the man spoke so openly about the KGB.

"I've moved her to a semiprivate room, but she is alone for the moment," Dr. Klimov said as they rode the elevator up to the sixth floor.

"Forgive me for asking such a delicate question, Doctor, but is there some trouble between Major Kostikov and his wife?"

"He loves her. There is no doubt about that," Dr. Klimov said curtly.

They stepped off the elevator and headed down the corridor past the busy nurses' station. The corridor smelled of disinfectant and cooked cabbage. The rooms were old-fashioned, with high ceilings, tall windows, and black and white tile on the floors. It reminded Bertonelli of hospitals in the States when he was a little boy.

"How long will she be here?" Bertonelli asked.

They had come to the end of the corridor and Dr. Klimov halted just before the last door. He looked up.

"She could go home now . . . if she wanted to."

"The situation you mentioned?"

Dr. Klimov's head bobbed. "Unfortunate. She no longer loves her husband. In fact she despises him . . . or, rather, she pities him."

Bertonelli's left eyebrow rose. "Has he done something to her?"

"No. It's not quite as simple as that, I'm afraid. As far as it goes, Major Kostikov is a good man. Bright, honest, dedicated."

"Then . . . ?"

"He is KGB and she is an artist. Honor is on top of his tongue, and a knife is under it."

"I'm sorry?"

Dr. Klimov smiled. "Forgive me. I forgot you might not understand some of our little proverbs. Major Kostikov is an honorable man. Yet he is KGB. Tanya cannot forget what the KGB has done . . . is doing."

"To her father."

"And to others. Her friends. She has no one left, actually, except for an elderly aunt in Leningrad."

"What does she want?"

Dr. Klimov looked at him. "To get better. To have a life of her own." He glanced toward the open door. "Wait just a moment and I'll tell her she has a visitor. But you mustn't be long."

"Of course," Bertonelli said.

Dr. Klimov went into the room. Bertonelli moved closer to the open door and leaned up against the wall as if he were merely waiting. But he could hear Klimov speaking and then a soft, woman's voice replying.

"How are you feeling, Tasha?"

"Like I'm going crazy, Dmitri."

Dr. Klimov chuckled. "Perhaps I will release you by Monday. But just now you have a visitor. An American neurologist who would like to speak with you for a minute or two."

"Did you call him?"

"Valeri did."

There was no reply from Tanya.

"He seems to be a sensitive man, for an American. But if you don't want to see him, I will send him away."

"Is he here now?"

"Just outside the door."

Bertonelli pushed away from the wall and went a few paces down the corridor. An old man, teetering on a walker, hobbled around the corner. He stopped, out of breath, and glared at Bertonelli. He murmured something, then shook his head and hobbled away.

Dr. Klimov came out of Tanya's room. "She will see you now, Dr. Moore. But please do not be long. She tires easily. It has been less than thirty-six hours since her last seizure."

"I understand," Bertonelli said. He was starting to feel like a heel. He had to keep reminding himself why he was there.

"I'll be in my office. If you would like to talk afterward, please come down."

"Yes, thank you."

Dr. Klimov turned and walked down the corridor where he stopped at the nurses' station. Bertonelli entered the room.

Tanya Kostikov, her skin like fine parchment, her long dark hair pinned up in the back, her dark eyes large and liquid, was sitting up in bed, a shawl around her tiny shoulders. She had been writing poetry. Her notebooks surrounded her on the bed. She smiled uncertainly.

"Hello, Tanya," Bertonelli said.

"Dr. Klimov said you are an American." She had a gentle, aristocratic voice. "My husband asked you to see me?"

"I know your husband. I thought I would stop by to see if I could help."

"Valeri is worried about me." She smiled. "But as you can see I am in very good hands here. Still, it cannot hurt to hear what it is you have to tell me."

It was a plain, three-bed room. Tanya was in the bed nearest the window. The other two were empty. It was the closest to a private room in Moscow. Bertonelli brought a chair over and sat down next to hear.

"I like your eau de cologne," she said, sniffing. "We epileptics depend upon our sense of smell. Just before a seizure we begin to smell the most dreadful odor, you know . . ." She laughed. "But, then, you are a doctor. You would know all of that."

"I understand you had a seizure very recently."

"Thursday morning," she said. She looked away. "It gets dark early now. I forgot to take my medicine. It was my own fault."

Bertonelli was brought back up against his own youth again. His mother had asthma. He remembered that he used to get mad at her because of her attacks, as if she had brought them on herself. His anger was genuine in those days. Later as an adult he had a lot of trouble accepting his guilt feelings. Seeing the edge of fear in Tanya's eyes made him realize again just what an egocentric bastard he had been.

"Dr. Klimov is a very competent man."

"Brilliant," she said, looking back. "I wish I'd known him in Kansas."

"Were you there . . . in Kansas?"

An odd expression came into her eyes. "How did you say you know my husband?"

"I didn't. But when I heard you were ill, I decided to come by to offer my help."

"Yes? What sort of help? You would work with Dmitri?"

"I was thinking of the Mayo Clinic in Minnesota."

Tanya's eyes brightened. "I have heard of it. A very good place." She sat up, the shawl slipping from her shoulders. "You have some influence? You could arrange for my admittance there?"

"Yes. But it would have to be with your husband's cooperation."

"There is no money. Not for that kind of thing." She laughed. "You know my husband. He will never leave Moscow. This is his city. His Uncle Gennadi is here."

"The money is no object. Arrangements could be made."

The flicker of hope that had lit up her eyes began to fade. "I do not think it can happen."

"Why?"

"Medically I am in good hands here."

"You could explain it to your husband. He would understand."

It was very warm in the room. A bead of perspiration had formed on Tanya's upper lip. She leaned forward, burying her face in her hands.

"I'm going crazy here," she said, her voice muffled.

Bertonelli wanted to reach out and touch her shoulder. But he did not. The back of her hospital gown was open. Her skin was creamy, her spine prominent because of her thinness.

"Your husband will know I was here, Tanya. It cannot hurt to talk to him. Perhaps something could be worked out."

"I will die here, in Moscow," she said.

Bertonelli wanted to hold her. Tell her it would work out. And he was astonished at himself for his feelings, and somewhat embarrassed. He got to his feet and put the chair back.

Tanya looked up, real anguish on her face.

"Talk to your husband about it," Bertonelli said gently. He took out a pen and wrote his embassy telephone number on the edge of one of her notebooks. "Have him telephone me."

She looked from the number back up to his face. "Thank you."

"I've not done a thing. Yet."

"I'll talk to my husband. I'll give him this number," she said. "But tell me something—you're not really a doctor, are you?"

Bertonelli was startled. "What makes you say that?"

She managed a slight smile. "Because all during this interview you didn't once ask anything specific about my physical condition. All you could speak of was my husband . . . who is KGB."

"I can help."

"I'm sure you could. But if your trade is his defection, forget about it."

"That isn't what I had in mind. Really."

"Oh?"

"I would simply like to talk with him."

"Leave me now. I don't think I can stand much more . . . hope, for this day."

Back at the embassy, before he went up to his office, Bertonelli arranged with the housing officer to get him a room for the next few nights at the Rossiya Hotel. Normally it was illegal, by Soviet law, for anyone who maintained an apartment within the city to check into a hotel. His excuse was that his apartment was being refurbished. By midnight, if not sooner, the KGB would know where he was staying, but it was exactly what he wanted.

Next, he stopped by the embassy telephone operator's booth next to the Consular Affairs office and told the night-shift girl that he was expecting a telephone call. He instructed her to take a message and then telephone him *en clair* at the Rossiya. He figured it was probably an unnecessary precaution because

Kostikov would probably not call here, but he wanted to cover all of his bases. He wanted to smoke out the KGB major. If the Soviet government wanted to repatriate the Americans they were holding, and if they had selected Colonel Okulov as the conduit or as the first contact, he wanted Kostikov to be dragged into the breech. It was only fitting, since the major had killed Okulov.

Grant showed up a few minutes later. They went up to Bertonelli's office. Grant unbuttoned his coat and perched on the edge of the desk.

"We missed you this morning."

"I had visitors last night, Wyatt. Sent directly from our friend Valeri Konstantinovich. A real pleasant trio."

"What? They came to your apartment?"

"Tore the place apart. But I beat the shit out of one of them."

Grant looked at Bertonelli with true amazement. "What are you trying to do? Get yourself killed?"

Bertonelli explained what had happened the previous night, and what he had done that afternoon at the Skifovsky Institute.

Grant shook his head. "You're sure going to get that boy's attention."

"He's the next best bet."

"And when it's all over, Mr. DeMille will take all the credit."

"Listen, he's a sharp bastard. You have to give him that. He's even maneuvered the ambassador. If this all falls apart, it will be Thomas Frederick Scott who'll take the blame . . . along with me. DeMille will be the next DDO no matter what happens here."

"But it's us who go out on a limb."

"Ah, but that's what we're getting paid for, isn't it?"

Grant had to grin despite himself. "It was getting a little boring around here."

"We'll all get a little famous if it does work out."

"Shit."

Grant had come out of the University of Texas at Austin. He had worked his way through school as an oil roustabout. His arms and upper chest were still very well developed. He and Bertonelli had sparred a few rounds in the gym, and come to a mutual understanding and respect for each other. Bertonelli had a lot more respect for a man of physical prowess than he did for what he (and Spiro Agnew) called the effete East Coast intellectual crowd—of which DeMille was a prominent member.

Bertonelli and Grant went upstairs to the empty cafeteria. It was closed because it was a Winter Festival Friday night and there weren't enough ranking embassy personnel on duty to justify its operation. Grant jimmied the liquor locker, but took only one bottle of bourbon. Bertonelli had gotten the glasses, and they sat by one of the windows looking down on Tchaikovsky Boulevard with its traffic as they drank.

"Have you been to the circus, Wyatt?"

"I don't like circuses," Grant said morosely.

"What? You don't like the clowns? The elephants?"

"I don't like looking at the freaks. They're selling themselves."

Bertonelli looked down into his glass. "That's part of human nature, my friend, to stare at the odd, the unusual."

"Shit."

"Come on, it's the optimist's dream. Capitalize on a shortcoming. Make your liabilities into your assets. Maximize your abilities . . ."

"Every silver cloud has a dark lining?" Grant offered, and they both laughed at the little joke.

Three army trucks, the red star bold on the canvas, rolled by below. Bertonelli and Grant watched until they had disappeared around the corner. The snow was falling much more heavily now, eddies of it swirling after the last truck.

"None of this probably makes any difference," Bertonelli said after a time.

Grant nodded. "I did find out about Novikov, though."

"I saw your note. But Hobbs is probably correct. This is a disinformation plot."

"Cold feet?"

Bertonelli sat back. "You should have seen her, Wyatt. She had me pegged almost from the start. She's sharp, but she's out of her element here. Lost." He shook his head. "But I honestly don't think she'd be better off in the States, though."

"You hate using her, I know."

"With a passion. I'm sorry I went over there. I felt like a sonofabitch the entire time I was talking with her, and I think she knew it."

"What's done is done," Grant muttered.

"True." Bertonelli poured them another drink. He raised his glass. "A toast."

"To what?"

"Truth. Justice. The American way."

"So, it's a shitty business. We all knew that when we started," Grant said. "Sometimes boring, but almost always shitty."

"Necessary, though."

Grant smiled wanly. "We keep telling ourselves that, don't we."

They drank for a while in silence as they watched the occasional car or truck pass on the street. The snow gave no sign of letting up. They'd probably have six inches on the ground by morning, with drifting because of the sharp wind. In Moscow they were used to the winter. The snow and cold never slowed them down.

"I think Novikov is probably a dead end," Bertonelli said.

Grant shrugged. "For what it's worth, I did find out his telephone number. We had it all along downstairs in some of the old telephone directories. The *dacha* actually belonged to the Novikov family. At any rate the number was there: one-seventy-five, seventy-three, thirty-six."

A common mistake visitors to the Soviet Union often made was interchanging the terms Soviet and Russian in describing her citizens. Actually, Russians only made up half the population. Officially there were one hundred and four different nationalities speaking one hundred and twenty different languages, living in fifty-three separate republics or regions. An Armenian, for example, would never refer to himself as a Russian. Britons understood this distinction quite well, for they referred to themselves as either Scottish, Welsh, or English. The differences were real, even beyond the languages. Estonians and Lithuanians were much like Scandinavians—tall, blond, good-looking; very Westernized in their habits and dress. Georgians were short, dark-haired, and Mediterranean. Uzbeks, Azerbaijanis, and Tadzhiks were Moslem. Each nationality had its own unique characteristic. Lithuanians were Catholic, Latvians were German, and the Siberians of Yakutia were akin to American Eskimos. Soviet internal passports included the bearer's nationality.

It was late afternoon and already dark. Valeri was parked around the corner from the gigantic Kazan Station off Komsomol Square. Streetlights were on, there was a lot of traffic, and people seemed in a hurry because of the snow and cold.

Valeri rolled down his window as Lipasov hurried across the street.

"Find anything?"

"There is a girl living up there. Number fourteen. Third floor. The *babushka* said she left about an hour ago."

"What's her name?"

"The old woman wasn't sure, but she thought it was Nadia

111

something or other. No one likes her. Said she was foreign. Probably Siberian.'' Lipasov glanced back the way he had come. The apartment building was just as Larissa Okulov had described it: a yellow brick building, three floors, rather plain but apparently well kept.

They'd found nothing at the other apartment; in fact it had not even been furnished, though the neighbor assured them that Colonel Okulov had been renting the place for nearly a year. Votrin had gone back to the office to check on the surveillance team following Bertonelli, and then he was going home to get some sleep.

Valeri got out of his car and followed Lipasov back across the street to the apartment building. Just inside, an old woman dressed in a long dark overcoat, a thick woolen scarf on her head, was seated behind a Dutch door, the top half of which was open. She was reading a newspaper and drinking tea. The corridor was very cold. Steam rose continuously from the hot drink.

Lipasov had found this place with no trouble, and had waited around, as Valeri had instructed him to, without directly approaching either the girl or the landlady.

After General Demin's warning, his father's call, and events of that afternoon, however, Valeri felt they might be running out of time, so he had decided a more direct approach was necessary. Lipasov offered no objections. He had a score to settle, although neither of them had any idea that this apartment had a connection with Bertonelli's contact.

''There are no rooms here,'' the old woman wheezed, looking up. Two of her front teeth were missing. The others were discolored from smoking. She was sweating despite the chill.

Valeri smiled. ''But there must be something, grandmother. Perhaps the basement. Maybe the attic?''

''But then there is no heat. Unless you keep the attic door open.''

''It wouldn't matter.''

The woman laughed. ''What are you two, then, queers?''

Lipasov stiffened.

''Simple men who would like a place to meet,'' Valeri said reasonably. ''To talk. To compare . . . literature.''

Again the old woman laughed; this time she broke out in a spasm of coughing. When her attack finally passed, she reached into a flat cabinet next to the door and brought out a key. "You will have to see it yourselves. I am too old to climb the stairs now. When my Stepan was alive—God rest his soul—he took care of things. Now my lazy good-for-nothing son is with the hooligans in Odessa, enjoying the sun. There is no peace."

Valeri took the key and he and Lipasov started up the narrow stairway. The woman got to her feet and leaned out the doorway.

"For you, fifty rubles," she called up. "But you mustn't report this. The room doesn't exist."

It was private enterprise on which there was a very stiff city tax. If a building contained five apartments, a certain tax was paid whether or not the units were rented, which, of course, in Moscow, they usually were. An extra room was like gravy on your potatoes. Found money. Perhaps fifteen percent of the rooms and apartments in Moscow were phantom properties not on the tax assessor's rolls.

They stopped on the third floor, and Lipasov had the cheap lock of number fourteen open in less than twenty seconds. Valeri motioned for him to stand watch in the stairwell, and he went inside.

The apartment was very small, only a sitting room and a tiny efficiency kitchen with an electric burner on a counter and a miniature refrigerator next to the chipped enamel sink. There were two chairs at a small table by the window. The couch had been made up as a bed, the covers in disarray. The only food in the place was a small tin of tea, half a loaf of dark bread, a piece of cooked fish on a plate in the refrigerator, and a quarter bottle of vodka on the table. The ashtray was filled with the butts of cheap cigarettes that were mostly cardboard filter. A heavy wool dress and a pair of cheap shoes were stored in a cabinet in one corner. A small chest of drawers contained a few panties, one bra, and a thin cotton sweater. The clothes were clean but well worn. There was nothing else in the apartment. No books or newspapers, no photographs or paintings, no radio or record player. Nothing that would indicate someone had lived there for any length of time. Most disturbing was the lack of a suitcase or carryall. Had the girl already moved out?

Valeri stood in the middle of the room trying to think about what he was seeing; trying to look beyond what was there, or wasn't there; trying to put himself into Okulov's position. If this was the apartment of his mistress, he certainly wasn't treating her well. There was no permanence here. In fact the apartment seemed even more temporary than a hotel.

"Comrade Major," Lipasov appeared at the open doorway. "Someone is coming."

Valeri took a last look around the room, then joined Lipasov in the corridor. They closed and relocked the door, and made their way to the back stairs. Halfway up, Valeri stopped and hunched down. From this angle he could just see the bottom half meter of the door to number fourteen. They could hear someone coming slowly up the stairs, the tread light. A woman's booted foot, the hem of her coat just visible from where Valeri crouched, appeared at the door, stopped a moment, and then the door opened and the woman disappeared inside.

If she was Okulov's mistress, Valeri wondered what would become of her now. Yet he had had the feeling in the apartment that the place was used as a safe house. If that were the case, who the hell was she?

He and Lipasov went the rest of the way upstairs to the tiny, unheated attic room. It was half the size of the girl's apartment just below, made even smaller by the sharply sloping ceiling. A narrow window looked down on the street. In the summer, this would not be unpleasant. Now, however, they could see their breath. On one side of the room was a small bedstead with two tattered throw pillows. A chest on the opposite wall, beside the window, was flanked by a decrepit old chair and a washstand with an old porcelain bowl and ewer. Except for the lack of a skylight, Valeri figured this could be a museum exhibit showing the studio of an impoverished nineteenth-century artist. Tanya would love the place if she saw it.

Lipasov tried the table lamp beside the bed. It worked, which meant the mains were hooked up.

Valeri was of two minds. On the one hand he wanted to pull the girl in, question her, and find out just what part she played, if any, in this business. On the other hand he felt that if he waited, sooner or later someone would show up to speak to her, or make some contact. Who it was, and what they might say perhaps would provide some clue.

"I'll stay awhile," Valeri told Lipasov. "Get back to the

office and pick up a recorder, telephone tap, and anything else you can think of.''

"The standard kit?"

"Right."

"And an electric heater?"

Valeri went to the window and looked down. "If you can find one. Some food. Vodka. And bring back the cognac from my desk."

"I'll be back in an hour."

Valeri turned around. Lipasov was hesitating at the doorway. "But?"

Lipasov shrugged. "I thought Bertonelli was important. What are we doing here?"

"Besides his wife and Bertonelli, this girl was Colonel Okulov's only other recent contact that does not fit anywhere. So we watch her."

"Yes, sir," Lipasov said. It was clear he wasn't particularly happy. He wanted the American.

After Lipasov left, Valeri lit a cigarette and stared out the window down at the street as he tried to make some sense of what he had learned so far. But he could not. Had Okulov been trying to defect, or not? What did Novikov's telephone number have to do with anything? Why had Okulov's brother, Uri Vladimir, come to pick up Larissa Okulov? And what part, if any, did the girl downstairs play in this business? A Siberian, the *babushka* had told Lipasov. It did not make any sense. He could not see what set of circumstances could force the facts into any logic.

Lipasov appeared on the street a moment or two later, after having paid the landlady for the apartment. He climbed into his tiny gray Zaporozhets and drove off.

Valeri put out his cigarette in the washbasin, then walked downstairs to the third floor where he knocked at the door to number fourteen.

The girl opened the door almost immediately, as if she had been expecting someone. She was nearly as tall as Valeri, with the round soft features of a Siberian but with something else, almost a Lithuanian or Estonian mix. She was definitely not a Muscovite. Her lips were thick and sensuous, her nose small and slightly turned up, accentuating her high, delicately formed cheekbones. Her shoulders were tiny as were her breasts beneath her thin print blouse. Her hair was dark. It fell around her shoulders. Valeri was reminded of the statue of the Little Mermaid in Copenhagen's harbor. Disappointment showed in her large, dark eyes.

"I'm your new neighbor," Valeri said.

"Yes?" She had a soft, round voice. Even in this one word, he could hear she was foreign.

"I just moved in. Upstairs."

She looked beyond him. "I didn't know there was an apartment up there."

Valeri smiled. "It isn't much, let me tell you."

She smiled too.

"I am Valeri Kostikov." He stuck out his hand. "The grandmother downstairs said they call you Nadia."

The girl looked at his hand, then shook it. Her grip was soft, her bones delicate. Valeri couldn't imagine Okulov with her. She was fragile, in some ways even more so than Tanya (though Valeri couldn't say exactly how), while Okulov had been almost gross.

"I am Nadia Burdine," she said.

Valeri couldn't tell from how she pronounced her name if there was an *E* at the end or not. In any event it was a curiously un-Russian name.

"My friends call me Valerik."

"I have no friends," she said.

"You live alone, then? The old lady thought you might have a husband. Maybe I could meet him . . . ?"

"I have no husband."

"There was a man . . ."

"This is my place. I live here alone."

"As a matter of fact the landlady told me that Colonel Okulov rented the apartment. Though, she said, he hadn't been around for the past day or so. I thought perhaps he lived here as well."

"I don't know the name," Nadia said with a straight face, although Valeri could tell she was lying.

He shook his head. "It is too bad, you know. But I heard that Okulov had been killed."

"Why do you tell me this?"

"The landlady mentioned his name. I thought I had heard it. I didn't know if you knew."

"She was mistaken. Obviously. Believe me, I live here all

alone, just as I prefer it. But was this Colonel Okulov a friend of yours?''

"Oh, no . . ."

"Then I fail to see what business it is of mine, or why you have come here with this story. If it is a line, then it is a poor one.''

"A line?'' Valeri asked, genuinely confused.

She smiled. "An excuse to meet a girl, you know.''

"No, I didn't. You're not from Moscow.''

"No, I am not. But I am pleased to meet you, Valeri Kostikov. If you will excuse me now, I am very tired.''

She started to close the door. Valeri blocked it.

"If there is anything I can do for you. Anything at all, just come upstairs and knock. Or, if I am gone, leave word with the grandmother downstairs.''

"Thank you.''

"I would like to be your friend.''

"Good night,'' Nadia said solemnly.

Valeri turned and went up the stairs, but not before he got to the top did he hear the door close. He sneaked back downstairs where he listened at her door. From inside he could hear her crying. Softly. In despair.

Votrin returned with Lipasov forty-five minutes later. Both of them seemed agitated.

"It's fantastic, but Bertonelli is on the move again,'' Votrin gushed. They set their cartons and packages down on the small table. "He's a dangerous man, Comrade Major, and something must be done about him. Next he'll be walking into the Center and taking it over.''

"Plug in the heater,'' Valeri said. "Now, what's he done this time?''

The two surveillance men looked at each other.

"He went to see your wife, Comrade Major,'' Votrin said.

For a moment Valeri wasn't sure he had heard correctly.

"At the Institute?''

"Sergei followed him from the embassy. At first he couldn't believe it himself.''

Lipasov had plugged in the portable heater, and already they could feel its warmth in the tiny room.

"Are you sure he actually spoke with my wife?''

Votrin nodded. "Sergei went inside right behind him.

Bertonelli apparently had an appointment with Dr. Klimov. They spoke for a few minutes and then Dr. Klimov brought him up to see your wife. The doctor left them there, alone, for several minutes.''

The thought of it made him sick. But Valeri hung on; he did not want to go off half-cocked.

''And then where? Where did he go afterward?''

''Back to the embassy.''

''Is he still there?''

''No, Comrade Major. He has checked into the Rossiya Hotel. As of a half hour ago he was having his supper there.''

''Is anyone with him?''

''No. He is alone.''

As incredible as it seemed, Valeri was beginning to believe that Bertonelli was out to get him, probably because of the incident at the zoo. But was it possible that the American could be so arrogant? So bold as to make an attack on a KGB officer and his family, right here, in Moscow? It was nearly beyond comprehension. The man had to have a death wish. He had to be a fanatic.

Votrin and Lipasov were staring at him with barely suppressed excitement. Ever since their encounter with Bertonelli at his apartment building, they had been straining at the leash to go after the man. They obviously were hoping that this would be it.

''Is Sergei still there, watching him?''

''Yes.''

''I want you to remain here,'' Valeri told Lipasov. ''Watch the girl. Her name is Nadia Burdine. I told her Okulov was dead. She might try to run, or someone may come here to see her. In either event I want you merely to observe, follow her if she moves or is moved.''

Lipasov was upset.

''Listen, Viktor, we all have a personal stake in Bertonelli now. He's attacked you and now he has come after me through my wife.''

''Let's take him,'' Lipasov said with real feeling.

''Not yet. We're going to continue to sidestep him, watch him. Sooner or later he's going to lead us to the information we need.''

''If Colonel Okulov was a traitor, what does it matter, Comrade Major? He is dead.''

"It matters to me! We could force Bertonelli's expulsion. But I want more than that. I want him stopped. Permanently."

Lipasvo's eyes were shining. He nodded.

"Get a room next to Bertonelli's," Valeri told Votrin. "Have Sergei and the others back off. I want you to take personal charge. I want him followed, but now I don't want him to know it."

"He'll know . . ."

"He'll *suspect*. He won't know for sure."

"Aren't you at least going to talk to him?"

"Not yet. We'll let him stew in his own juices for a little while longer. The future is his who knows how to wait."

Valeri left first. The old *babushka* had closed her door. With all the comings and goings she had probably suspected what was going on, and like a good citizen she had turned her back, not wanting to actually be a witness.

On the way across town he telephoned his office. Shevchenko had not returned that afternoon, and by now was probably home for the weekend. But General Demin had called with the message that Valeri *and* Tanya were to be at his apartment for drinks and dinner at seven o'clock tomorrow evening. There were to be other guests who wanted to meet them both.

As he drove he felt somewhat detached, almost light-headed. He had said nothing to Lipasov or Votrin, but he thought he understood why Bertonelli had gone to see Tanya. The notion went at least a part of the way toward explaining what was going on. Bertonelli had apparently tried and failed to turn Okulov. Now he was going to work on another target. There was little doubt that Bertonelli had offered Tanya some help. Medical help. A trade was being offered.

He turned onto Sadovaya Boulevard with its busy traffic, pulled up in front of the Institute, and went across the broad front entryway, between the columns, and took the marble stairs up to the fourth floor.

Dr. Klimov's office was dark, his secretary gone. Back in the corridor Valeri hurried across to the west wing, his shoe leather echoing hollowly. He raced up to the sixth floor, a sudden urgent premonition of doom washing over him.

Tanya was not in her room. Back at the nurses' station he was informed she had been moved to a private room, but that she was being examined at this moment, and the doctor was not to be interrupted.

Something in the nurse's eyes, some private, inner knowledge, struck Valeri as if he had just received a blow to his heart.

He turned and headed down the corridor.

"Major Kostikov," the nurse called after him.

Around the corner he headed resolutely to the end room, hesitated just a moment, then pushed the door open.

Tanya and Dr. Klimov, both nude, lay in each other's arms on the tall hospital bed. They had obviously just made love. Tanya's eyes were closed, a thin sheen of perspiration covered her thin body, her chest rising and falling, her nipples still erect. One long leg was thrown over Klimov's, who was stroking the side of her cheek with his fingertips.

Valeri had to think they looked natural together. The poetess and the Jewish intellectual. She would have no problem getting out of the country, and he could apply for another foreign study grant—which would be approved without question. They could be together in Kansas, or whatever place suited them. They would be that wonderful foreign couple. They would have a good life together. After all, who could dislike such an obviously sensitive, in-love couple?

Stepping back into the corridor, Valeri was about to pull the door closed, when Tanya suddenly sat up.

"Oh," she cried.

Dr. Klimov looked over his shoulder, his eyes growing large when he realized who it was.

Valeri turned and went to the window a few paces away at the end of the corridor. It was very dark in the courtyard below, though beyond the hospital he could see the lights of the Kremlin. He lit a cigarette and inhaled deeply. He had known for a long time that their marriage had gone sour, but never in his wildest imaginings had he ever dreamed he would become the cuckold. But then, what husband did? Behind him, back in the room he could hear their urgent whisperings, though he could not make out what they were saying. He tried to examine his feelings. His gut ached and his heart pounded a little harder than normal, but he found that he wasn't really very angry. Surprised. Perhaps hurt. But not the enraged husband seeking revenge. Another thought struck him: perhaps Bertonelli's visit had precipitated this.

Perhaps the American had offered Tanya and Dr. Klimov an easy way out of the Soviet Union. Perhaps Bertonelli had been sent here to Moscow to wreak havoc. He was the wrecker.

"Tanya would like to speak to you, Major Kostikov," Dr. Klimov said.

Valeri turned around. Klimov stood at the open door, fully clothed now, his head up defiantly. He looked frightened, though.

Smiling, Valeri stubbed out his cigarette on the window-sill. "You know, you can call me Valeri now that we have so much in common."

Dr. Klimov blinked rapidly. "I . . ." He started to turn away.

"Wait, please."

The doctor turned back.

"An American came here this afternoon. He spoke with you and then with Tanya."

Dr. Klimov's eyes narrowed, but he nodded. "Dr. Moore from the State University."

"What did he want?"

"I don't understand. He said you asked him to see Tanya."

"He was lying."

"I telephoned the university . . ."

"He is CIA."

Dr. Klimov stepped back. "God in heaven," he said heavily. He glanced inside at Tanya. "He wanted to help her."

Valeri smiled. "So, you see he was wrong. He wants me after all. But you have saved the day."

"Dmitri?" Tanya called softly.

Dr. Klimov jerked as if he had been shot. He looked again at Valeri, then spun on his heel and hurried down the corridor. Valeri noticed for the first time that three of the nurses had been watching from the nurses' station. He found he didn't give a damn.

Tanya was in bed, the covers pulled demurely up to her chin. She looked, at the moment, like a tiny, frightened child who knows she has done something wrong. Valeri had the almost overpowering urge to close the door, pull the covers back, and make love to her. But, he thought sadly, even though he was physically capable of such an act, such a thing was impossible for him.

"You could ruin his career. Have him thrown in jail," Tanya said.

Valeri stood at the end of the bed. "Yes, I could."

"Don't do it, Valerik. Dmitri . . . he is a good man."

Valeri wanted to ask her what exactly she meant by that, but he found he was beginning to lose his nerve.

She looked away. "I'm sorry you had to witness it."

"Sorry? So am I. Do you love him?"

She hesitated. "I don't know."

That hurt him. "But you don't love me."

She turned back. "No. We come from two different worlds."

"You knew that when you married me."

"We were young."

"Perhaps marrying a young KGB officer whose father was a general could enhance your father's career."

"How in God's name can you say something like that?" she flared.

Valeri shook his head. "It wasn't in God's name." He understood fully that there was no hope whatsoever for winning her back. And he felt almost relieved.

"Why don't you go away and leave us alone."

"Would you like a divorce?"

She nodded.

"I won't stand in your way, then. Nor will I take any actions against Klimov."

"Yes?"

"But first you must do me a small favor."

"What do you want?" Tanya asked suspiciously.

"We are expected at General Demin's apartment for dinner tomorrow night. I'll come here to pick you up. For a few hours you'll have to pretend we're still happily married, that everything is all right between us."

"He'll have to know sooner or later," she said. "What's the matter, are you afraid a divorce will affect your career?"

"It's not that at all. But you will be there with me. Afterward I'll bring you back here if you wish, and then I'll leave you alone."

Tanya studied his face for a long time as if she were trying to determine if he was telling her the truth. Satisfied, she nodded.

"All right."

"I'll come by a few minutes before six," Valeri said. He

turned to go but then came back. He had nearly forgotten the real reason he had come here. It was incredible.

Her eyes narrowed.

"An American came here to see you this afternoon. He claimed to be a doctor."

"CIA?"

"Yes."

"I thought so."

"What did he say to you?"

"He offered me a chance to go to the Mayo Clinic in the States." She reached over to her nightstand for one of her notebooks, then sat up and handed it to Valeri. "On the cover. The phone number. He wants you to call him."

Valeri recognized the number. It was for the American embassy. He started to lay the notebook on the bed, but she waved it away.

"Keep it," she said tiredly. "Now, just get out of here, please."

Valeri looked at her for a long time. "I'm sorry," he said. He pocketed the notebook, turned, and left.


He cleaned up and changed clothes at his apartment, but unable to face being alone, drove over to his office. It was possible that Shevchenko had left a message, or that Lipasov would have some word on Nadia Burdine. He kept thinking about her, and about Larissa Okulov. Two beautiful, intriguing women. Okulov had evidently been able to offer them some incentive to be with him. Perhaps the colonel had been a man of independent wealth. It would explain his very expensive apartment. Perhaps this entire affair had been nothing more than some capitalist adventure between Okulov and Bertonelli. If that were so, the joke would be on Valeri. Perhaps even General Demin had been in on the scheme. Generals had expensive tastes, and Americans did have a way with money. It was their national mania.

It was snowing very hard, the strong wind blowing the flakes almost horizontally. The roads were quite slippery, so it took him longer than usual to get downtown.

In his office he telephoned Shevchenko. In the background he could hear music playing, and the children singing and laughing. The place sounded like a madhouse.

"What did you find out, Mikhail?"

"Are you at the office?" Shevchenko shouted over the racket.

"Yes."

"Why don't you come over here? Sasha is fixing supper. There's plenty. And we have some vodka."

"Not tonight, thanks. What about Novikov's father? In the UPDK?"

"He died seven years ago in Mexico City. Heart attack. Worked at our embassy as assistant consul."

"So the *dacha* went to his son."

"Who was a rotter. Exactly. Listen, Valerik, I think this Novikov business is a dead end. From what I could tell, Bertonelli was never anywhere near Mexico City. I thought there could have been at least that connection. But no."

"I think you're right."

Shevchenko hesitated.

"What is it?"

"Do you want me to come in? Is everything all right?"

"Everything is fine, Mikhail. Give Sasha a hug for me. I'll see you on Monday."

"I'm taking the children to the circus on Sunday. Would you like to come along?"

"Tanya and I are having dinner with General Demin tomorrow night. It'll probably be a very late affair."

"How is she?"

"Just fine. Listen, have a good weekend."

"Valerik, are you all right?"

"Don't be an old woman."

"Fuck . . ."

"See you Monday." Valeri hung up the telephone. Tanya had not been able to have children. It had something to do with the narrowness of her uterus. Somehow they had never considered adoption, and now, he thought, it was just as well.

He had been alone before, but never this lonely. Before he left his office he extracted an address from the staff directory. He was being a fool, but then he couldn't help himself. Not tonight.

Fainna Skvorstov's apartment was across the Yauza River beyond the Androniev Monastery (which these days was a museum) on Moscow's far east side. Each day she rode the subway to and from work, and once she had confided in Valeri that for a single girl living so far outside the city it was constantly lonely. But she was not able to find a decent place closer in for the same amount of money.

She was dressed in blue jeans and a sweater, the sleeves pushed up above her elbows, no shoes on her feet, when she came to the door. Her hair was bundled up beneath a towel. She smelled of soap. Evidently she had just bathed. She didn't look as attractive now as she did in the office; her nose was a bit too large, her eyes too deep-set, her elbows and shoulders bony. He wondered what the hell he was doing here like this.

"Comrade Major," she said, surprised, but with pleasure.

Valeri had stopped along the way and bought a bottle of good French red wine. He held it up. "A present. I hope I'm not disturbing you."

"No, you're not," she said. She drew him into the apartment, closing and locking the door.

The place was small, but pleasantly furnished. Soft music played on the radio in the corner, and there was the odor of cooking. It smelled very good to Valeri.

She took the wine from him and brought it into the kitchen as he took off his overcoat and laid it on the couch.

"I was just fixing my supper," she called out to him. "Have you eaten yet?"

"No," Valeri said, looking around. He felt like a fool. Distant. Ineffectual.

Fainna came back in the living room, but stopped short. "What is it?" she asked in concern. "Are you all right?"

Valeri nodded. "Maybe I shouldn't have come."

She smiled. "It is lonely out there."

"I'm sorry . . ."

She came across the room to him, and suddenly she was in his arms, kissing him, her tongue darting against his, their bodies pressed tightly together. She pulled off his jacket, and he peeled her sweater over her head, then kissed her breasts, taking each nipple in his mouth as she arched her back and moaned.

More Winter Festival banners had been put up and they snapped sharply in the breeze that had driven the overnight snow into delicately sweeping sculptures. Moscow had been transformed into a gay wonderland of pretty scenery and happy people.

Yesterday afternoon at the Institute, Valeri had known, in an intellectual way, that his marriage was finished. Still, he could envision himself forgiving her. She would get better, and in the spring they would go to Yalta to heal their wounds in the sun. This morning, however, he knew in his soul that there was no going back.

Driving across town he thought about last night. Fainna had kept repeating how happy she was that he had come to her. But this morning she had cried when he left, knowing that it would never work for them.

Twice he almost turned around and went back to her, but he couldn't keep his mind off Nadia Burdine.

Valeri brought some groceries to the attic apartment. Lipasov had been ready to climb the walls with boredom until an hour ago.

Nadia Burdine had spent the evening alone in her apartment below. That morning at eight, however, she had gone out. Lipasov had heard her door opening, and he had hurried after her. She had seemed frightened. Often she looked over her shoulder to make sure she wasn't being followed. It gave Lipasov some difficulty, but he was a professional and she obviously an amateur. She had gone around the corner where she entered the busy Kazan Station with its heroic murals on the ceilings. At first Lipasov thought she might be trying to run, but all she carried was a scuffed leather shoulder bag.

"She tried to make a telephone call from one of the booths," Lipasov said. "But I don't think she got through. It was a local number."

"You got close enough to know that?" Valeri asked.

"I saw her dialing, then I took the next booth."

"Could you hear if she spoke?"

Lipasov shook his head. "But she wasn't in there very long, and if she did speak, she whispered."

"She didn't know you were behind her?"

"I don't think so, Comrade Major."

"She's in her apartment now?" Valeri asked, taking off his coat. "She came directly back?"

Lipasov nodded.

They had drilled a small hole in the floor through which a highly sensitive but directional microphone had been inserted so that it rested against the ceiling of the girl's apartment. The microphone was connected through an amplifier to a tape recorder that was sound-activated. Lipasov had adjusted the sensitivity control so that the slightest noise below triggered it.

Valeri donned the earphones, pressing them tightly to his ears. At first he could hear nothing other than a faint hum from the amplifier. Suddenly the tape recorder reels began turning at the same moment he heard a faint metallic click. A spoon against a cup?

The tape recorder stopped, but then started almost immediately with the sound of water running from a tap, then splashing into a pot, perhaps. She would be making her morning tea, Valeri suspected. He could see her at the sink and then at the electric hot plate.

Lipasov was staring at him. Valeri took off the earphones.

"She's making her tea."

"What are we doing here, Comrade Major?"

"Our jobs, Viktor Ivanovich."

"Let me switch places with Oleg at the Rossiya. I want Bertonelli."

Valeri shook his head absently. "Not yet." Her name was Nadia Burdine. She was foreign, possibly Siberian, and she had been the mistress of Okulov. It was all they knew about her. Perhaps that was all there was. Perhaps she had no connection with this business. Perhaps she was nothing more than an unfortunate little girl caught up with promises of a life in Moscow; of champagne and caviar, of nice clothing, of the ballet and restaurants. And now she was alone. Her protector, a traitor to more than his country, dead.

Whom had she tried to telephone this morning? Certainly not Okulov at his apartment. Valeri couldn't believe the colonel would have been so open with his mistress as to give her his home telephone. Had there been another number where messages could be left? A number no longer activated now that Okulov was dead?

"Colonel Okulov is dead," Lipasov was saying. "Let's arrest the girl and question her. We'll soon find out what she's all about, if that is your concern."

"Who do you suppose she tried to call, Viktor?"

Lipasov shrugged.

"She is Siberian."

"The old grandmother didn't know for sure."

Valeri listened for a moment in the earphones, but there were no sounds from below. The girl would be waiting for her water to boil. Patiently?

"I would very much like to look at her papers," Valeri said.

"Go downstairs and demand to see them."

Valeri looked up. He had a real respect for Lipasov, but the man had no imagination. It was, in many ways, a paradox in the Soviet Union. Music and poetry were her people's soul. Yet too much imagination—or imagination channeled in the wrong directions—was anathema to the system. Lipasov had chosen his route. Valeri wondered what his own might be.

"She is simply a little girl, Comrade Major," Lipasov said in frustration. "A colonel's whore."

"She would run."

"Then we would follow her."

"But I am her friend. I would like to keep it that way for now."

"I do not understand . . ."

Valeri got up and opened the door. The stairway and the corridor below were quiet. "Why do you suppose Colonel Okulov met with Bertonelli at the zoo?"

Lipasov was watching him. "Does it matter, Comrade Major, beyond the fact that he tried to kill you?"

Valeri turned back. "Colonel Okulov was attempting to defect, or was passing information. I would like to know which."

"Bertonelli has the answers, the sonofabitch!"

"First I would like to find out more about the girl downstairs. For that you will have to do some play acting, Viktor Ivanovich. Put on your coat."

Lipasov looked at him as if he were a madman.

"I'm going down to talk to her. You will be below on the stairs, listening. The moment I mention the name of Colonel Okulov, you will come up the stairs, show your identification, and demand to see hers."

"What excuse shall I give? Am I to arrest her?"

"No excuses, but I will protest, and you will treat me as if I were an ordinary citizen interfering in KGB affairs."

"And then what?" Lipasov was clearly uncomfortable.

"She will be the wrong girl after all. You will hand back her identification, with no apologies, and you will leave."

Lipasov was having trouble accepting it.

"What is wrong, Viktor?"

"Why are we going to this trouble over this girl? I do not understand, Comrade Major."

"It's probably nothing," Valeri said. "But I would like to know what her papers say, without her becoming suspicious of me. Now, get your coat."

When she came to the door, Nadia was wearing the wool dress Valeri had seen in the cabinet. It was too large and hung on her body. He got the impression she had recently lost weight. Her feet were bare. Her hair was pinned up, exposing her long neck and tiny ears. He thought she looked like a movie star in the role of a poor, starving revolutionary.

"Yes?" she said, with that same odd accent.

"I was going for something to eat. I thought you might like to join me."

Her eyes narrowed. She looked beyond him as if she expected someone else to be there. She shook her head slightly. "No, I am not hungry. Thank you." She started to swing the door shut.

"No, please wait," Valeri said.

Her right eyebrow arched. "Yes, what do you want with me?"

It struck Valeri that she was beautiful. She was obviously wary, frightened, and yet there was a certain quality of self-possession, some inner knowledge that separated her from anyone he had ever known. It wasn't Tanya's sad soul, it wasn't Larissa Okulov's haughtiness, nor was it Fainna's convictions. It was something else, something attractive.

"The grandmother downstairs is worried about you."

"The grandmother is a lecherous old bitch who is worried only about her rent."

"She thinks you have no food."

"Does she come up here and look through my cupboards? Tell her to mind her own business."

"She's worried about everything, I think. She keeps asking me about this Colonel Okulov."

Nadia started to say something, when they heard someone coming up the stairs. She stepped back as if she were a deer in the forest who had heard a branch snapping beneath a hunter's boot.

"I would like to be your friend," Valeri said, lowering his voice. "I would like to help you."

Lipasov appeared at the head of the stairs, hesitated, then came down the corridor. There was a stern expression on his face. He looked huge and very official. Valeri thought he was playing his role very well.

"Citizen Nadia Burdine?" Lipasov asked, taking out his KGB identification and holding it up.

Nadia's voice caught in her throat. She nodded.

"There has been a complaint. I want to see your papers. Now."

"What sort of a complaint?" she asked defiantly.

"Your papers," Lipasov insisted harshly.

Valeri stepped forward. "Pardon me, but you cannot barge in here like this. What does this woman stand accused of?"

"No, please," Nadia interrupted. "It's all right. I've done nothing wrong."

Leaving her door open she turned back into her apartment and a moment later came back with her purse from which she withdrew an internal passport.

Valeri had stepped back slightly so that he was looking over Lipasov's right elbow.

"When is the last time you visited Leningrad, Citizen Burdine?" Lipasov asked, taking her passport and opening it.

"I have never been to Leningrad," she said.

The photograph of her was recent. She was just twenty-one, had been born in the Siberian Autonomous Region of Yakut, and currently resided in the capital city of Yakutsk. Her travel visa had been stamped by Moscow Militia on December 20. She had been here less than ten days.

"What is the nature of your visit to Moscow?"

"It is a vacation."

"For the Winter Festival?"

She nodded, but Valeri got the impression she didn't know what Lipasov was talking about. Siberia was remote, but Winter Festival was the second or third most important holiday in Russia.

"You have never been to Leningrad? Not two weeks ago? And again the month before?" Lipasov asked harshly.

"Never," Nadia said. "What is this all about?"

Lipasov handed back her passport after a long moment. "Your visa expires in twenty-three days. See that you do not miss the deadline."

Lipasov gave Valeri a searching look, then turned on his heel and left.

"Bastard," Nadia said under his breath.

"Are you in some sort of trouble?" Valeri asked sympathetically.

"Who are you?" she demanded.

"A friend."

She smiled humorlessly. They heard the outside door slam below. "What do you know about this Colonel Okulov? Everyone keeps talking about him."

"Just what I read in the newspapers."

She was startled. "It is true then? He is dead?"

"An accident, I think. Then you did know him?"

She shook her head solemnly. "My tea is getting cold, you know." She turned and went back into her apartment, closing and locking the door, leaving Valeri standing there.

Lipasov came back up to the attic a couple of minutes later as Valeri was pulling on his coat.

"Now we know she is from Yakutsk, Comrade Major. So what?"

"You did a nice job, Viktor. I'll be back this afternoon

with your relief. In the meantime continue watching her. She just might try to run.''

"Run where?"

"I don't know," Valeri said at the door. "But it is very important that she doesn't get away from us."

"She is a very pretty girl, for a Siberian. But she is a liar," Lipasov said. He took off his coat and put on the earphones.

She had been lying, at least about Colonel Okulov. About what else?

On the way over to his office Valeri drove past the Skifovsky Institute with the intention of making sure Tanya would be ready for tonight. But he could not face her, so he didn't stop.

Yakutsk was six time zones to the east of Moscow. It was four in the afternoon there when Valeri reached Lieutenant Eduard Agadzhan who was in charge of the KGB Internal Residency. He was at home.

"How is the weather in Moscow?" the lieutenant shouted. The connection wasn't very good.

"It snowed last night. Today it is windy."

"It's always cold here, Comrade Major. These aren't the tropics."

Everyone but a Siberian talked about the weather during the winter. Valeri suspected the lieutenant was a transplant.

"I need some information about a girl. Nadia Burdine. Born in Yakut. Her internal passport gives her residence as Yakutsk."

"Is she there in Moscow?"

"Yes, she is."

"Send me her photograph, her fingerprints, and her passport number. I'll see what I can do on Monday. When did she leave here?"

"Last week," Valeri shouted. "But listen, Lieutenant, I need that information now, this afternoon."

"Do you realize how big Yakut is, Comrade Major?" the lieutenant shouted. His voice was very faint now.

"This is very important."

"Has she killed someone? Perhaps the party chairman?" In Siberia irreverence was a way of life. They spent too much time keeping warm to take anything else seriously. Besides, they already were in internal exile. What else could be done to them?

"Not yet," Valeri said. "Someone will be at my office to take the message."

"What do you want to know?"

"Everything. Who she is. Where she works. Who her friends are. Has she ever made other trips like this?"

The line was silent for several seconds. Valeri thought he had lost the connection. But then the lieutenant was back.

"I'll tell you how large our autonomous republic is, Comrade Major. Within our borders is thirteen percent of the entire landmass of the Soviet Union. That's how big . . ."

The line finally went dead. Valeri hung up. Thirteen percent, was it possible?


Valeri left word with the weekend duty officer downstairs that he was expecting a call later that afternoon, and then drove over to the Moscow City Soviet Building on Gorkovo Street, a few blocks from the Bolshoi Theater. The imposing structure housed most of the city's governmental functions including the Soviet itself, the city prosecutor's office, some courtrooms, and Militia Headquarters. It was a Saturday, so there wasn't much activity.

Inside, he turned left and walked down the broad corridor into the office that handled visa applications and residency permits. Two young girls and a short man wearing a thick wool sweater were on duty.

One of the girls came to the counter. Valeri showed her his identification.

"I would like some information about a girl who came here from Yakutsk on the twentieth."

"Has she a police record, Comrade Major?" the girl asked pleasantly. Her eyes were red. Valeri suspected she had partied last night, and was regretting it now. Still, she was good-natured.

"Not that I know of. I'd like to take a look at her visa application."

"The twentieth of this month?"

Valeri nodded.

"We should still have those files up here. The girl's name?"

Valeri gave it to her. She smiled tiredly. "It'll be just a moment, sir." She turned and went off across the large office to a bank of electrically driven horizontal filing machines along the back wall. The man and the other girl both looked up curiously at Valeri, but then went back to their work.

All of the thousands of people who showed up in Moscow each week from the outer republics with visa applications signed by their local Militia had to pass through this office. Their applications were checked and filed, and their passports stamped. During the week, Valeri suspected the place would be a madhouse. The counter was at least thirty meters long, and beyond it were two dozen desks, each with in-out baskets that bulged with files and paper work.

The girl came back a couple of minutes later. She seemed puzzled. "Are you certain the stamp was for the twentieth of this month, Comrade Major?"

"What's the trouble?"

"I'm sorry, but we have no record of a Nadia Burdine entering Moscow on that date from Yakutsk."

"Perhaps the file was misplaced?"

"I searched the records two days before as well as two days after. There is nothing."

"I saw it with my own eyes."

"I'm sorry, sir. Perhaps it was a forgery. It happens. Shall we report this to Special Investigations?"

"No," Valeri said absently. "This is a KGB matter."

Valeri drove across the river, in no great hurry, at least for the moment. It would be several hours before he got anything on the girl from Yakutsk. As far as Moscow Militia was concerned, she did not exist. Okulov had apparently arranged for her visa stamp. But why had he simply given her a thirty-day visa? Why not a permanent residence permit?

The day was turning out to be quite nice, though the temperature was dropping now that the cloud cover was mostly gone. Tonight a lot of drunks would freeze to death. It happened every Winter Festival. Even more banners had been put up. At many corners magicians or jugglers or mimes in whiteface were entertaining the people. At the fringes of each crowd were the obligatory pairs of Militia officers, their breath white in the cold. The holiday was building to a crescendo.

He turned into Gagarin Square and a block later pulled up at his apartment building. Upstairs he took off his coat, tossed it over the couch, and turned on the small black-and-white television. He wanted noise, any kind of noise. While the set was warming up he went into the kitchen and fixed a glass of tea that he brought back to the living room. He sat down in front of the TV set and put his feet up. The show was a live broadcast of one of the circuses at the Luzhniki Stadium. The cameras kept switching from the performer on the high wire to the faces of the audience, especially the little children whose eyes were wide.

Valeri had the notion that something was about to happen. First the telephone number for a burned-out *dacha*, and now a girl whose visa stamp was a forgery. She was a part of this business; there was little doubt of it any longer. But where did she fit?

Another thought struck him, and he sat up. Bertonelli had somehow known about the phone number. Did he also know about the girl? Had Okulov offered the phone number *and* the girl? Was she somehow part of the bargain?

He put down his tea and telephoned his office, getting the phone number of the room Votrin was occupying in the Rossiya Hotel. He dialed it and the clerk rang the room fifteen times, but there was no answer.

Votrin was gone, which meant Bertonelli was gone. Where? And why the hell had the American moved into the hotel in the first place? Granted his apartment had been ruined, but Valeri would have thought the man would have taken up temporary residence in the embassy. It would have been a lot safer for him.

Something was happening. And right now. Valeri could feel it in his bones. The high-wire artist had put on a blindfold and was standing on his head twenty meters above the netless ring. The crowd was holding its breath.

Bertonelli had the telephone number. He wanted the girl. He had moved to a hotel where his comings and goings wouldn't be nearly so restricted as they would from his apartment or from the embassy. There were so many ways in and out of a hotel such as the Rossiya.

His telephone rang. The caller was General Demin who asked about Tanya.

"She is much better, Uncle Gennadi," Valeri said. His heart was thumping.

"I am at my office, Valerik," General Demin said. "I understand she is still at the Institute. Will she be coming to dinner this evening?"

"I'm picking her up at six. But we may have to make an early night of it."

"I tried to telephone you last night." General Demin hesitated. "Is everything going well with you, nephew?"

"I was here," Valeri lied. "I just didn't hear the telephone."

Again General Demin hesitated. "Then we'll see you this evening?"

"Yes, sir."

"Oh, by the way, Valerik. You wanted to know about Colonel Okulov's gun. I received the report just this morning from downstairs."

"Yes, sir?"

"I don't think you will like this, but I don't want you to blame yourself for his death. You couldn't have possibly known."

"Sir?"

"Colonel Okulov's weapon. It was a museum piece. Only for show. The bullets had no powder, and the firing pin had been filed down. It was merely a harmless display. A toy."

"Why did he carry it to the zoo?"

"We will never know, Valerik. It was most unfortunate. A string of errors that led to his death. But listen, my nephew, when you live close to the graveyard you can't weep for everyone. You had no way of knowing the gun was harmless."

"Thank you, sir."

"We'll see you this evening?" General Demin asked again.

"Yes, sir," Valeri said and hung up.

The fabrication had been transparent. Okulov would not have drawn a harmless weapon. Valeri had seen his automatic reaction. He had drawn his gun and was turning around with every intention in the world of firing. There was no doubt of it in Valeri's mind. He closed his eyes and leaned his forehead against the cool wall. The girl fit somewhere. She had been brought illegally to Moscow. Why? Dammit! Why?

The telephone rang again. This time it was his office. Lieutenant Agadzhan had already called from Yakutsk with his message.

"He reported that no one by the name of Nadia Burdine left Yakutsk this month," the duty officer said. "In fact there is no one by that name anywhere in Yakut according to their records."

Excitement rose inside Valeri like a bright star on the

horizon. But he held himself in check. Okulov and Bertonelli.
Two thin threads connected them, first the telephone number
and now the girl.

"When did he call?"

"Just a few minutes ago, Comrade Major."

"He was quite certain about his information? He didn't say
he would continue checking?"

"No, sir. He was very sure that no such person existed
anywhere in Yakut."

"Thanks," Valeri said. He hung up.

Bertonelli had the telephone number, but he didn't have the
girl. Yet.

Valeri grabbed his coat, but before he left his apartment he
checked his gun. The Beretta's ejector slide was well oiled
and moved smoothly. A live round was in the firing chamber.


There were even more people out on the streets. In a few
places snowplows were still busy scraping away the last of
the snowdrifts. Shopkeepers had shoveled their sidewalks,
and along Kalinina Prospekt another circus parade had at-
tracted a crowd and temporarily diverted traffic.

Valeri took the ring on Kudrinskaya Street that circled the
center of the city, passing Kommunuy Park and turning off
finally at the Leningradskaya Hotel, a twenty-eight-story pile
of brick that looked a lot nicer than it was. Several big
Intourist buses were parked in front of the Kazan Station,
waiting for a group to come in on a train.

The KGB lieutenant at Yakutsk had called back too soon.
As he explained that morning on the phone, Yakut was very
large. With only a name and a date, the man's entire staff
could not possibly have searched their records that fast. It
meant that Okulov had brought the girl here to Moscow with
the cooperation of someone in the Yakutsk office. Someone
who would be expected to field inquiries about her.

Valeri did not allow himself to take that thought any further. It lead to an area that he was not ready to explore.

He drove slowly past the yellow brick apartment building,
but nothing out of the ordinary seemed to be going on. There
was a lot of traffic, a lot of pedestrians, but no cars with
official plates. No strange men hanging around the street
corner, no one across the street watching the apartment.

Around the corner half a block away he parked his car and went back on foot, crossing in the middle of the block and ducking into the building.

The *babushka's* door was closed, the lower corridor very cold, the building quiet. Valeri stood a moment listening, but he could hear nothing, absolutely nothing except for the sounds of traffic outside on the street.

Moving to the stairs he took out his gun, then started up silently, stopping to listen at each landing. There was nothing: no talking, no music playing, no laughing or arguing, no television or radio blaring.

The plaster walls were cracked and needed painting. The stair treads were dirty. Valeri supposed that the old grandmother's arthritis or other maladies prevented her from doing the cleaning, while her hooligan son was enjoying his friends in Odessa.

At the third-floor landing he stopped again. His heart was pounding. Nadia's door was closed. He had a sense that the building was deserted. He withstood a nearly overwhelming urge to call out, to shout for Lipasov upstairs in the attic.

Cautiously Valeri moved down the corridor. He put his ear to Nadia's door. There was no sound from within. He tried the doorknob, and it turned easily in his hand, the door opening inward.

The tiny apartment seemed unchanged, except that the bedcovers had been folded and neatly piled on one end of the tattered couch.

He stepped inside. A faint clean odor of perfume or perhaps soap hung in the air. A cup and saucer lay upside down on the drainboard beside the sink. The two chairs had been pushed up to the table by the window; the ashtray was clean. It came to him then that she had gone.

Across the room he opened the clothes cabinet. It was empty. So was the small chest of drawers.

Valeri turned on his heel, burst out into the corridor, and took the stairs up to the attic two at a time. He threw the door open. Viktor Ivanovich Lipasov, the hero of the Dynamo Stadium indoor pool, lay dead in a pool of his own blood. He had been shot at very close range, twice in the face and once in the neck. His teeth were mostly smashed, his nose was destroyed, and blood filled his eyes and had poured out of his ears. Most of the blood, however, had come from a severed carotid artery in his ravaged neck. The room stank of blood.

Pocketing his Beretta, Valeri carefully stepped around Lipasov's body, bent down, and touched his forehead. It was cool. This had happened at least an hour ago. Perhaps a little longer.

Valeri straightened up. No one had come to investigate, so there had been no noise. A silencer on the gun. Lipasov had not cried out. Had not suspected he was going to die. It had happened too fast for him.

The tape recorder was running, but the amplifier had been disconnected. The tape on the reel was nearly finished. Whoever had been there had had the presence of mind to pull the amplifier plug, rewind the tape, then put the machine on record, erasing what had already been recorded.

Valeri went to the narrow window and looked outside across the snow-covered roofs toward the bulk of the big railway station. One name kept running through his mind, threatening to dislodge his sanity. But he held himself together. It would be suicide for him to go off crazy, half-cocked.

He turned again to look down at Lipasov's devastated features. The family of the mother and child he had saved from drowning two years ago had had him to their apartment for dinner every Sunday a half-dozen weeks running. Finally he got tired of the gratitude—the hero business, as he called it—that he begged Valeri to assign him weekend duty. By then his swelled head from the *Pravda* article had already deflated, and he had reverted to his old self. Lipasov was not married, but someone was going to have to tell his brother and mother.

Valeri opened the window a crack, then turned off the electric heater. He took a blanket from the narrow bed and draped it over Lipasov's body and the big pool of blood. Within fifteen minutes the room would be as cool as an icebox. Within an hour it would be as cold as a deepfreeze.

He pocketed the key lying on the table, and at the door looked back at the shrouded figure. Lipasov had been a good man, but he had made a mistake that had cost him his life. It was a mistake Valeri was not going to make.

Bertonelli, he thought as he left the apartment, locking the door behind him. The American had made his mistake by thinking Moscow was his city. It wasn't. Moscow belonged to Valeri.

# 10

Russians are a suspicious people. Most foreigners lived in approved apartments guarded around the clock by Militia. Bill Hobbs was one of the rare exceptions.

Bertonelli parked his pool-issue Toyota on the narrow street that fronted the Yauza River on Moscow's east side near the Androniev Monastery Museum and knocked on the front door of one of the low, row houses. Hobbs, clad in a bathrobe, appeared.

"Good morning, Uncle Bill."

"DeMille is looking for you," Hobbs said wryly. "He missed you at the hotel."

Bertonelli had spent a bad night. This morning he awoke with a hangover, and had gotten out early to shake Kostikov's lapdog. He wasn't feeling any better now.

"Can I come in?"

Hobbs looked beyond him. "Were you followed?"

"I managed to lose him."

Hobbs was married. His wife had gone back to Washington six months ago for a visit, and decided not to return. Five years of Moscow had been more than enough for her. So far Hobbs had shown no inclination to transfer back to the States. Bertonelli couldn't understand it. He had thought their's was a good marriage.

"You'd better come in, then," Hobbs said.

The house was small and crammed, it seemed, with books, magazines, newspapers, maps, and papers. A wood fire burned in a heater in the corner of the messy living room. Bertonelli could feel a cold draft coming from the back of the house. He kept his coat on. He didn't want to stay long in any event. Sooner or later his car would be spotted.

"I heard your apartment was trashed," Hobbs said. "Kostikov?"

"His people," Bertonelli said. "But I didn't come here to talk about that."

"Coffee?" the West Pointer asked from a sideboard. "Or something a little stronger?"

Bertonelli held back a sharp remark. Hobbs did his thing at his own speed and in his own way. Pushing him wouldn't help. This was only a long shot, but it was worth taking.

"Brandy."

"DeMille is mad that you didn't report it." Hobbs poured some brandy in both of their coffees and handed Bertonelli his. "But he hasn't said anything to the ambassador yet."

"I'll bet," Bertonelli said. DeMille, true to form, was running scared just now. He was going to have to be avoided. Frightened little men were unpredictable.

They sat across from each other. Bertonelli had to move a pile of books from the couch. Hobbs smiled.

"This is just for show, you know. Impresses the hell out of Ivan when he sees the mess. Scholars are harmless so long as they're doing nothing but research. But that's not why you came to see me. Not simply for information."

"I came to ask for a favor . . ."

Hobbs went on as if he hadn't heard Bertonelli. "Ambassador Scott is on your side, you know. There has already been a lot of traffic between State as well as Langley over this business. I've even been asked to do an analysis. They think with my contacts I'd be the logical one to approach if the Russians are sincere about this business." Hobbs looked up. "But it's your ball game, Tony, if that's what you're worried about."

Bertonelli studied Hobbs's expression. He didn't know if the man was being honest, or was simply toying with him. "I didn't come here for a lecture . . ."

"I didn't think so. But maybe you're taking this too personally. Grant's day report said you went to see Major Kostikov's wife at the Skifovsky Institute. Ayers was worried about you. He came to me and asked for my opinion." Hobbs sipped his coffee. "Don't let this become a vendetta, Tony. He was doing his job in the zoo, nothing more. Had the tables been reversed, you would have shot him."

It came to Bertonelli that Hobbs was probably in agreement

with DeMille. After all, he had his position to protect here. A position so important to him that he let his wife leave him rather than give it up. But then, Bertonelli thought wryly, hadn't he done essentially the same thing to lose his wife? Still, he was going to need Hobbs's help.

"Okulov offered me two proofs."

"You mentioned that."

"The first was a seven-digit number. We thought it might have been a telephone number. But I don't think so."

"A telephone number for whom?"

"Vladimir I. Novikov. But the man is dead, his *dacha* destroyed. It's a dead end."

Hobbs thought a moment. "So you're left with a seven-digit number. How did you come by it?"

"That doesn't matter. There was a second proof, and I think Kostikov has got it."

"Then it is simple," Hobbs said, unimpressed. "Okulov was designated to make contact with you, but it failed. Perhaps it's Major Kostikov's turn now."

"I don't think he has the approval of his government."

"What's he doing, then?"

"Investigating what he thinks was an attempt on Okulov's part to defect, or, at the very least, to sell me state secrets."

"Then he's after you?"

"I think so."

"Which is why you went to his wife, to force his hand. To make him go off in a fit. Maybe make a mistake."

Bertonelli nodded. "But it hasn't worked. His people searched my apartment, and have been following me around Moscow. But he's made no effort to contact me."

"Why should he, Tony? When he feels he's ready, he'll simply arrest you, and there won't be a damned thing we can do about it. You have to give him credit. He's keeping his head. If you came here for my advice, I think you should get your ass back to the embassy and stay there until this all blows over."

A log fell in the stove. Hobbs put down his coffee, limped over to the stove, opened the door, and stirred the fire with a poker. The pleasant odor of burning birch filled the room.

"Wood is very expensive here," he said. "But I like the smell and the sound."

"If it's a disinformation plot, it won't go beyond me here in Moscow," Bertonelli said.

Hobbs put the poker aside and turned back. "You underestimate your worth. At least as concerns the Russians it would be a feather in Major Kostikov's cap to drive you out."

"But if it isn't a scam. . . . We can't simply walk away from it. I can't bury my head in the embassy." Bertonelli felt as if he were trying to wade through a pool of molasses. In some ways the entire business was like a nightmare from which he could not wake up. He kept making all the right sounds, only no one seemed to be hearing him. He had never run into anything like this before. But then, he told himself, this was Moscow.

"Who are these Americans? Have you given any thought to that? If they're not the people we know about, who then? Any ideas?"

Bertonelli lay his head back. He closed his eyes. Afghanistan was there. The high mountain road. He could feel the cold, thin air, even smell the fires. "No," he said softly.

"Then I can't fathom why you are so certain this isn't a disinformation plot of some sort . . ."

Bertonelli could hear Hobbs's voice as if it came from a long distance. He'd always been this way, hadn't he. Ever since he was a boy standing up to his father. Taking his beatings silently, stoically. Christ but he had been a little bastard. Maybe nothing had changed. Maybe things never changed.

" . . . It's so damned transparent. And not very original. Listen to me, Tony, things like this happen all the time. You were given your briefing when you first got here. Don't accept packages from strangers, all that. It's one of the oldest tricks in the book, and it works most of the time. Someone hands you an envelope, and a moment later you're under arrest for possession of state secrets. Major Kostikov simply jumped the gun, that's all. His timing was off."

Bertonelli opened his eyes and put his coffee down. "He shot his own man."

"His aim was off, too!" Hobbs snapped irritably. "Christ, you got out of there with your skin intact. Why push your luck?"

"I came here for some help, Uncle Bill."

"And I'm giving it to you, only you're too thick-headed to take it."

"I want to set up a meeting with Kostikov."

"You weren't listening to me. Back off, Tony. Return to the embassy, admit your mistake, and take your lumps. Believe me, the ambassador will support you. DeMille will gloat, of course, but that will be easier to endure than rotting in a Lubyanka cell."

"You have the connections. Throw a cocktail party. Invite some of your pals, along with Valeri Kostikov. It'll be safe for him as well as for me. We can talk."

"You can't be serious." Hobbs looked at him as if he were seeing a raving lunatic. "But then, I'm forgetting about your reputation. It's a wonder they sent you here in the first place."

"Kostikov is trying to find out what Okulov was up to, just as I am. We can help each other."

Hobbs laughed out loud. "That's rich, Tony. Amazing, actually, is what it is. The number two CIA officer in Moscow wants to compare notes with a KGB major. DeMille would shit in his pants, and then he'd happily set up the firing squad. You could be charged with treason."

"That's why I want you to set up the meeting."

"No, Tony. Absolutely, emphatically, no. You want to get your ass shot off, be my guest. But I'm not going to be a party to it."

Bertonelli thought back to his meeting with Colonel Okulov in the zoo. The man had been sincere. Perhaps even awed by the thing he was doing. Bertonelli remembered his own unease and skepticism. But he also remembered the Russian's eyes. Okulov had been doing something that he considered distasteful. Then there was the other thing.

"I can't help you."

"If Colonel Okulov was telling the truth, what then?"

"The ball is still in their court. This is a big country. If they wanted to hide a hundred thousand Americans, there'd be no way for us to find them without the Soviet government's cooperation. No way in hell."

Bertonelli considered that. He rose. "If I should prove it, what then?"

Hobbs looked up at him. "Bring me the two proofs, Tony, and we'll see."

"You're playing it safe here, aren't you . . . Bill."

"Get the hell out of here."

"It's this, a desk job at the Pentagon, or a forced retirement, isn't it. That's why you don't want to upset the apple cart."

"We live in a big indifferent world, my impetuous friend. The name of the game is making sure we don't get ourselves into an all-out nuclear war. No one gives a flying shit about the individual."

Hobbs was running scared. Bertonelli could see it, and the knowledge saddened him.

"Bullshit," he said, and he left. The books and papers in Hobbs's house perhaps were for show, but so was his entire existence. He reported on the status quo. Nothing more. His war wound and medals were from a long time past, from another very much different man.


Bertonelli had a two-kopeck coin in his pocket. He called the embassy from a pay phone near GUM, the huge government-run department store just off Red Square. DeMille was on the warpath and the embassy was about to be put on emergency footing. Grant sounded alarmed, nevertheless he agreed to meet with Bertonelli in front of the Intourist Hotel on Gorky Street. Immediately.


"DeMille wants me to bring you in," Grant said. It didn't seem as if he wanted to get too far away from his car.

"What about Kostikov? What the hell is going on? Talk to me, Wyatt."

Grant looked across the street at the heavy pedestrian traffic. The street scene could have been in New York City. It seemed very normal. "Everything is changed, Mr. Bertonelli. I don't know anymore."

"Where's Posman?"

"Back at the embassy."

"Who's on Kostikov?"

Grant looked back. "No one."

"Where is he?"

"Mr. DeMille has called off the operation."

"Where is he, goddamnit?"

"At the Rossiya Hotel," Grant blurted. "I think he's waiting for you."

It was finally starting, Bertonelli thought. Kostikov was finally making his move. But something else had happened. Something was wrong. "I think you'd better tell me what's going on."

"Are you coming back to the embassy with me?"

"No."

"I didn't think so," Grant hesitated, but then he seemed to come to a decision. "You'd better watch your ass, Mr. Bertonelli. The game has changed."

"Go on."

"Are you going to meet with Major Kostikov?"

"Yes."

Grant sighed. "Then you'd better take a look at something first. It might change everything for you, too."

Bertonelli followed Grant to a yellow brick apartment building around the corner from the Kazan Station. They made two passes before they settled directly across the street. Grant walked back and got in Bertonelli's car. There was a lot of traffic here too. The sun was shining, but it was very cold. Steam rose from a manhole cover in the middle of the street.

"Major Kostikov has been here three times in the past eighteen hours. His people set up a surveillance operation in the attic apartment."

"Surveillance of whom? Who are they watching, Wyatt?" Bertonelli looked up at the small window just beneath the roof. It was open. The room would have to be like a deepfreeze.

"I don't know. Whoever it was, they're gone."

"You went up?"

Grant nodded. He was clearly uncomfortable. "Major Kostikov showed up for the third time a couple of hours ago. He wasn't inside for more than ten or fifteen minutes when the attic window opened and he came out in a big hurry. I followed him directly over to the Rossiya. But I got to wondering why it was he had lit out in such a big hurry, so I left Ralph at the hotel and came back here."

Bertonelli waited.

"I shagged my ass back to the embassy afterward and told Mr. DeMille. You were gone, someone had to be informed.

Mr. DeMille pulled Ralph in and put out the word for you. The ambassador has been told as well."

Hobbs had lied at least about that. "Langley has been told?"

"I don't know. But I imagine they have," Grant said. "But listen to me, Mr. Bertonelli. I think you should come back to the embassy. Short of that, you'd better do your thing here and then get the hell away. I don't think the situation is going to remain stable for very long."

"That bad?"

"I just don't know anymore," Grant said. It seemed as if he had lost his nerve.

"Get the hell out of here," Bertonelli said gently. "Keep yourself available at the embassy on the duty phone in case I need some help."

Grant nodded. "Watch yourself, for God's sake." He got out, went back to his own car, and drove off.

Bertonelli waited a full minute before he got out and walked across the street. His nerves were jumpy. He'd known Grant only a few months, but in that time he had come to respect the man. Grant was level-headed, unflappable, a real professional. But he was frightened now. It was unsettling.

The corridor smelled of garbage and stale cigarette smoke. Bertonelli hesitated a moment, then started up slowly, quietly, listening as he went. The building was quiet. On the third floor the stairs ended. He moved down the corridor to the back where a much narrower staircase went up to the attic. *Watch yourself, for God's sake*, Grant had warned. Bertonelli pulled out his gun as he started up.

At the head of the stairs he put his ear to the door and listened. No sounds came from within. Kostikov had been there. And so had Grant. Both of them in the past two hours. Bertonelli tried the door. It was unlocked.

The tiny room was very cold, but it stank of blood. A body covered with a wool blanket lay in the middle of the floor. A tape recorder and another piece of electronic equipment had been set up on a small table. A wire led to a hole in the floor. Whoever they had been watching had occupied the apartment just below.

Bertonelli stepped inside, got down on his haunches, and pulled back the blanket. His stomach flopped. The first impression that came to mind was assassination, not murder. The

Russianness of the killing was unmistakable. The KGB killed its people this way. Destroyed their faces at point-blank range as a warning to others. Arabs slit their victims' throats, though Lebanese and Syrian death squads used bombs. Americans, especially Hispanic drug dealers, shot their victims a half-dozen times, then dumped the bodies in the nearest water. But Russians went for the face with large-caliber handguns.

He shivered, put the cover back, and straightened up. This was a Kostikov surveillance operation. So who had assassinated his man and why? Who had occupied the apartment below?

Run. The singular thought popped into Bertonelli's head. Get the hell out. Get back to the embassy. There was nothing here for him. Kostikov had set up a surveillance operation. He had returned three times to check on its progress. Two hours ago he had found his man shot to death. But he had not reported the crime. Instead he had covered the body and opened the window to preserve it.

Kostikov had run. To the Rossiya. To his prime suspect.

The amplifier connected to the microphones in Bertonelli's room was quiet. There was nothing but incidental noise on the tape recording Votrin had made overnight. Bertonelli had received no guests, had made no telephone calls—not even to room service—nor had he talked to himself.

Votrin was out there somewhere in the city. Dead like Lipasov?

Nadia Burdine was somewhere in Moscow too. Or at least Valeri hoped she was. He hadn't checked the train depots or the airports. She could be on her way back to Yakutsk. Valeri found he really cared.

*"I have no friends,"* she had said at her door.

She was a nonperson as far as concerned Militia records. And now Bertonelli probably had her. Valeri didn't know how long he could stand the waiting. Nor did he know what he would do when Bertonelli showed up.

He was afraid.

At two in the afternoon Valeri called Tanya at the Institute. "I'll be ready at six if you bring my clothes," she said.

"I may be a little late."

"You'd better not be. He called here about an hour ago to make sure I was well enough to come to dinner."

Valeri looked out the window. He was on the Rossiya's eighteenth floor. The onion domes of St. Basil's seemed near enough to touch. "Has anyone been by to see you today?"

"No. Just Dr. Klimov, of course. Valeri, are you all right?"

"The American didn't come back?"

"No. Listen to me, after tonight it is finished for us. I think you know it."

"Are you moving in with . . . your doctor?"

"I'm going to Leningrad. I telephoned my aunt. She said it would be all right. I think she's looking forward to my company." The woman was in her nineties and lived on yogurt.

"Do you still want a divorce?"

"No . . . I don't know. Not yet, anyway."

It was something, at least. "What does Dmitri say about it? About your leaving? What's his opinion? He seems decent enough."

"Don't do this, Valerik. Not now. I'm not up to it."

"Sorry," Valeri said, and he meant it. It hadn't come as a surprise, but it hurt nevertheless. It all hurt. "You don't have to be there tonight. I can make excuses."

"It's all right. Honestly. Pick me up at six."

"Thank you," Valeri said. He put the telephone down gently as if he were afraid it might break. Life would be better for her in Leningrad. Even with her ancient aunt. She could make friends in the Writers' Union once she was safely away from the corrosive influence of her husband's presence. Her poetry would probably be published after they were convinced someone wasn't looking over their shoulders. He thought about the vial of medicine he'd seen floating in the toilet. If she didn't pull another trick like that, she'd be fine.

Once again he turned his thoughts back to Nadia Burdine. If Bertonelli had taken her, he would not be bringing her here. The man was arrogant, but he wasn't stupid.

Where then?

The American embassy? Too many eyes watching. Unless she had the proper papers, the Militia would never let her pass. He had a hunch Votrin had gone there. Bertonelli would be stopped.

His apartment? There wasn't much left of it. And there would be the problem of the Militia guard, who had already been warned after the fiasco of the other evening. If Bertonelli showed up there, the Militia would report it.

Which left an unknown. Like Colonel Okulov, did Bertonelli maintain a safe house here in Moscow? A retreat? A snug little nest away from microphones, away from prying eyes? A love nest?

Valeri roused himself and left the room, taking the elevator down to the lobby on the ground floor. The Rossiya was one of the largest hotels in the world with more than three thousand rooms, two movie theaters, a vast concert hall, numerous shops and cafés, and a lovely twenty-first-floor restaurant. He used the public phone near the rest rooms. Shevchenko's number was busy. Sasha loved the telephone. It was Mikhail's only complaint about her.

He tried General Demin's office, but the duty officer said the general had gone home. General Demin's number was busy as well. Uncle Gennadi was going to be disappointed.

The Rossiya was always a beehive of activity during Winter Festival. Foreigners were in the city for the holidays; deluxe tours were fifteen percent off normal season rates. A certain element of Russian was here, too, like a scavenger fish following its shark, looking for black-market trade goods such as Western jeans, T-shirts, stereo albums, ballpoint pens, and Zippo lighters. The Militia was here watching the Russians, of course, and there were always a few KGB Surveillance Directorate legmen watching the foreign tourists. (But the KGB kept to themselves. Their mission was holy.)

It was depressing.

Valeri dialed the number Bertonelli had jotted on the corner of Tanya's notebook. His stomach knotted up. A man speaking English answered on the first ring. "Yes?"

"I would like to speak with Mr. Anthony Bertonelli," Valeri responded, also in English.

"Who is calling, please?"

"Is Mr. Bertonelli there?"

"I don't know, sir. If you could just give me your name . . ."

Valeri hung up. His hand was damp, and shaking. He thought about trying Uncle Gennadi again. He was going to need help, wasn't he? This time he'd tell everything. Bertonelli had murdered an officer of State Security. But what was Viktor Ivanovich doing at the apartment, Valerik? Tell me. Who is Nadia Burdine? Hadn't a specific warning been issued not to pursue the investigation of Colonel Okulov, a real hero of the state, dead only through a tragic series of mistakes and circumstances? Was this more of the deputy chief's destructive speculations?

A good-looking couple came in the front doors and sauntered across the lobby. They wore identical fur coats. They were obviously Americans, and very happy, confident, self-assured. Valeri found himself envying them, which astonished him. He had never envied anyone in his life. Especially not an American.

A huge concert banner hung from the tall ceiling. The East Berlin Symphony Orchestra was playing in the hotel's main hall tomorrow. It was a tradition.

Valeri went back upstairs. The amplifier was still quiet. He lit a cigarette and went to the window. He was running out of time. Where was the connection?

A pretty Siberian girl and an eight-digit number. It was maddening.

He felt as if he were looking at the world through the wrong end of a telescope. Objects were in focus and clear, but they were too distant to make out. Somehow, like in a dream, he could not seem to make his hands turn the instrument around. Yet he knew that once he did he would understand everything.

Bertonelli held the secret. Valeri wanted to kill him.

Valeri entered Bertonelli's room again.

The Rossiya was first class. Thick carpeting on the floor, nearly new drapes on the windows, patterned bedspreads on the twin beds and a gleaming chrome and porcelain private bath. A lovely photograph of the Kremlin lit in multicolored lights at night hung on one wall.

Bertonelli's suitcase lay open on a stand. It contained only a few items of underwear and a couple of pairs of socks. No files, no photographs, no maps. A dark sportcoat, two pairs of slacks, and a pair of shoes were neatly arranged in the closet. Toiletry items were laid out in the bathroom. Deodorant, hairbrush, toothbrush and toothpaste, electric razor and cologne. He was a fastidious man. Valeri remembered the cologne from the zoo.

Nothing to come back for in this room. Nothing to risk his life for. No holds. No ties.

Valeri was reaching for Bertonelli just as a man who has been ill for a very long time reaches for a memory of health. Impossible, but worth the try nevertheless.

\*   \*   \*

It would be dark by five. For now windows in the taller
buildings glowed blood-red. Shadows were lengthening with
the lowering sun by the time Votrin came in, his dark Siberian features livid with rage for having lost Bertonelli.

"I'm sorry, Comrade Major. One minute he was there, and
the next he was gone. He hasn't shown up at the embassy or
at his apartment."

Valeri wasn't surprised, just happy to see him. There were
dozens of ways in and out of a hotel the size of the Rossiya.

"This time we're going to stop the bastard once and for
all," Valeri told him. "Get back to the office and organize
two surveillance teams. I want one on the embassy and the
other on his apartment. Around the clock. The moment he
shows up, arrest him."

"What about Viktor?"

A sharp pain stabbed at Valeri's gut. "He's busy. You and
Sergei will have to do this on your own. I don't want him
harmed, Oleg. But you will have to be very careful. He's
armed."

"Here in Moscow?" Votrin said in amazement. "He's
done it this time, hasn't he."

"He surely has," Valeri said half to himself. "It's possible
he'll have a young woman with him. Pick her up as well."

"Okulov's whore?"

"I think he took her this morning."

"I don't understand," Votrin said. He was thinking about
Lipasov.

"Neither do I."

The telephone in Bertonelli's room rang at four o'clock.
Valeri was next door before it had a chance to ring three
times. He picked it up.

"I'm waiting for you, Kostikov," a voice said in Russian
but with an American accent. The same voice from the zoo.

Valeri said nothing.

"I saw your watchdog leave a few minutes ago, Deputy
Chief. I know you're there alone. And I know that you want a
piece of my ass."

"Where are you?" Valeri pulled out his Beretta and stuffed
it in his belt.

"Closer than you think," Bertonelli growled. "And we're going to meet face to face. But first we have to get something straight between us."

Valeri was having a little trouble following the idioms that the American was translating into Russian. He pulled out his gun again, and turned to face the door. He just remembered that there was a telephone in the floor lady's alcove not fifty feet down the corridor.

"Are you listening to me?"

"I'm here," Valeri said.

"We have to talk, you and I. Someplace private. Away from eavesdroppers."

"The zoo?"

Bertonelli hesitated. Valeri could hear traffic in the background.

"Come back to your room, Mr. Bertonelli. I'll wait for you."

"Is your tape recorder still running next door?"

"No," Valeri lied.

"For your sake, I hope you're telling the truth. You could end up dead like your man in the attic apartment near the Kazan Station."

Valeri's breath caught in his throat. Bertonelli had been there. He had admitted it. His arrogance was nearly beyond belief.

"You think I killed him and snatched whoever it was you were watching in the apartment below. But I didn't."

"Who then?"

"You know damned well it was a KGB assassination. We don't shoot our victims in the face like that."

Bertonelli had said it to throw him off. Valeri could not allow himself to believe such a possibility.

"Open your eyes, for chrissakes!" Bertonelli said. "What do you see, you stupid fuck?"

The profanities didn't translate well, but Valeri had spent enough time in the West to understand what was being said. Besides money, the major preoccupations of Americans seemed to involve either sex or other normal bodily functions, as well as a curious disregard for religion. Yet on their money were the words *In God We Trust*.

"I see the room of an American spy. A murderer."

"Had I killed your man, would I have called you? Think it out, Kostikov. What has your Uncle Demin told you about Colonel Okulov? Has he let you in on the big secret? Is that why you went back to the zoo and dug up the book of matches? Is that why you went to the telephone exchange and from there out to Novikov's *dacha*? Has he told you about the number—one-seven-five-seven-three-three-six? Is that why you went to see Larissa Okulov? We've watched you every step of the way."

Valeri closed his eyes. This was impossible. He could hardly believe what he was hearing. Bertonelli didn't have the manpower. Could not have the manpower. This was Moscow, not New York!

"Tell me about Colonel Okulov."

"Not yet," Bertonelli said. "First we meet. No microphones."

"I'll meet with you. Where?"

"Leave the hotel by the front door. Turn left and walk down to the river. When I think it's safe, I'll show myself."

"No," Valeri snapped. He was thinking ahead. There wouldn't be enough control.

"You don't have any choice. But let me give you one tidbit, Chief Deputy. Okulov was not a traitor. He had the support of his government. Do you?"

"What?" Valeri asked, but the line had gone dead. "Bertonelli?" he shouted without being aware that he had raised his voice. He was gripping the telephone so hard his knuckles were turning white.

If Okulov was not a traitor, then what did that make him? What was the number? Who was Nadia Burdine? But it was a lie. All of it had to be lies. General Demin would have told him. Uncle Gennadi would have said something . . . or had he?

Valeri crashed the telephone down and left the room on the run.

A big truck equipped with a plow lumbered across the frozen Moscow River, cutting a broad roadway through the recent snowfall. Valeri jumped down from the Rossiya's loading dock and hitched a ride in a bakery truck just leaving.

Red Square was busy with tourists, elderly women out with their grandchildren, and ordinary Russians getting a head start on the night's celebrations.

They passed in front of the hotel with no sign of Bertonelli, and headed north along the Kremlin wall toward Lenin's Mausoleum, closed at that hour, though there were four Zil limousines parked in front. Party officials paying their respects. They would be noticed, their devotion appreciated. Russians loved their dead leaders more than they did their live ones. Valeri thanked the nervous driver, got off at the Senate Tower, and headed back, anonymous now in the crowd. He moved past the Spassky Tower, the gate into the Kremlin. Closed. The broad avenue descended sharply there to the Moskvoretsky Bridge over the river. The hotel was just across Red Square. From that spot he had an unobstructed view of the route Bertonelli had instructed him to take. He slowed his pace as he scanned the crowd. Bertonelli was a large man. He would stand out. He would be watching the hotel and the bridge, expecting Valeri to emerge at any moment. His concentration would be diverted. Red Square was a sea of fur hats, though. It was very cold, but no one seemed to mind.

It was possible that Bertonelli had called from somewhere across the river. It made sense. He would be able to watch Valeri coming across on foot. If that were the case, it didn't matter how the approach was made.

A tour bus rumbled up Razina Street and pulled up to the Rossiya. Valeri watched as two dozen people clambered off and entered the hotel. They were all well dressed. Laughing, and gay. Porters came out and began grabbing suitcases from the luggage compartment. Another bus pulled up right behind the first, disgorging its passengers. Within two minutes, both buses pulled away.

A tall, husky man dressed in a light gray overcoat, a stylish felt hat on his head, got out of a taxi parked at the lower corner of the hotel. He bent down to say something to the driver, and when he straightened up he slammed the door and looked across the square toward the Kremlin wall. It was Bertonelli.

Valeri started to move, to merge with the crowd, but he was too late. Bertonelli stiffened slightly in recognition, then turned and headed briskly the rest of the way down the hill to the bridge, not bothering to look back to see if he were being followed. Again Valeri was struck by the raw arrogance of the man. This was Moscow! What was he expecting to accomplish here like this, unless he meant to shoot down a KGB major in broad daylight. It was incredible.

Valeri waited for a break in the traffic and then hurried across Red Square so that he would be on the same side of the roadway as Bertonelli, who had already reached the bridge.

Unless someone was waiting out ahead somewhere, Bertonelli was alone. But Valeri found he didn't care. He was either going to bring the American in, or kill him, at which point his investigation would be over. At which point he would be able to face General Demin tonight with a clear conscience. At which point he would be able to restore his life to some semblance of normalcy.

Bertonelli stopped midway across the bridge. Without looking back he lit a cigarette, then leaned on the broad concrete rail and stared out at the river.

Valeri had once again transferred his gun to his coat pocket. He pulled off his gloves as he approached, and reached into his pocket, his fingers curling around the Beretta's grip.

Bertonelli was a large man, much bigger than Valeri had remembered. His nose in profile was large, Roman, but it was to be expected from his name. Valeri was struck by the aura of self-confidence and power that seemed to surround the American.

Bertonelli looked up casually. "Did you know that KGB outnumbers CIA by three to one?"

Valeri stopped five feet away.

"Of course if you add our FBI and our Border Service, there isn't such a great disparity. But then we're talking about three separate chains of command." Bertonelli glanced at Valeri's hand in his pocket. "Do you mean to shoot me here and now?"

"I'm sincerely considering it."

"Then you would never know, Deputy Chief, if it actually was me who killed your man. Or what Colonel Okulov and I chatted about in the zoo."

"It wouldn't matter. The case would be solved and you would be eliminated."

Bertonelli smiled and looked away. Valeri stared at him.

He was just an ordinary man after all: his shoes and trouser legs were wet from the snow, his thick, dark hair curled out below his hat, his cheeks were red from the cold, his breath no less frosty than a Russian's.

"There's trouble in paradise, my friend."

"What?"

"Workers' paradise. You know, dissension among the troops." Bertonelli turned back. His eyes seemed lit by electricity. "You've been lied to. Up the state. Cornhole the proles."

"I'm taking you in."

"You're a scapegoat, Kostikov, and the hell of it is, you don't even know it."

Bertonelli could have been speaking Martian.

"Leviticus. Day of Atonement. Send your sins out into the desert on the head of a goat and all that."

"What are you saying to me?"

Bertonelli looked beyond Valeri. "You didn't come here to take me in. You'd have all your ducks lined up in a row. There'd be KGB by the truckload on either side of this bridge. I wouldn't even put it past you to send out an ice-breaker so the Navy could be standing by below in the river in case I jumped for it. You came here to talk to me."

Valeri took out his gun and pointed it at him. "I'm here, Mr. Bertonelli. You have my undivided attention. You've gone through a great deal of trouble to arrange this meeting. Talk to me."

Bertonelli took no notice of the gun. "First I have to ask you a couple of questions."

Valeri laughed contemptuously. "You're hardly in a position to ask questions."

"Assuming I didn't kill your man in the attic apartment, who did? And why? Ask yourself that."

"You killed him."

"I wouldn't be here talking with you if I had. Use your head. Who were you watching in the apartment below?"

"You're a spy, Mr. Bertonelli. You have impersonated an American doctor. You have impersonated a Militia officer. And you have had an unauthorized meeting with a Soviet citizen."

"And you're a lousy shot, which is neither here nor there."

"It's my duty to place you under arrest."

"Then you might as well shoot me right here."

"What?"

"How long do you think I'd last at Lubyanka? Not very long. Whoever killed your man would kill me. I would have to be silenced. A lid would have to be kept on this." Bertonelli shook his head. "It's my guess you've been told to back off with your investigation of Okulov."

Valeri was startled, and it must have shown on his face because Bertonelli nodded in satisfaction.

"I need your help, Kostikov. And I think you're going to need mine. Who were you watching in that apartment? Did it have anything to do with Colonel Okulov?"

"Help? What are you talking about? Do I appear insane to you? I'm going to take you in and question you. If you cooperate, all will be well . . . relatively speaking. If not, I'll turn the job over to the experts. And believe me, Mr. Bertonelli, when I tell you that we have the experts."

"General Demin told you that a mistake was made. But you're old family friends, so he has promised to protect you. I don't enjoy such an advantage. In fact at this moment my embassy rather desperately wants me to return."

"You should have done so. Now it is too late."

"They'll be showing up back at the hotel sooner or later. I'd like to get my things before that happens."

Valeri thought he was watching a television drama. He raised his gun. "I'm taking you in. Now."

"Fine. Let's go."

Valeri didn't move.

"What are you waiting for, Comrade Major?"

"I'm trying first to understand you. At the very least you will be on a plane for Washington, D.C., within twenty-four hours. At worst you will be sent to a gulag in Siberia for a very long time."

"I'll take my chances. How about you, Comrade Major? You'll never know who killed your friend, nor will you ever know what Colonel Okulov was up to."

"You will be finished."

"So will you. But the stakes are very important to me."

"How important?" Valeri asked.

"Important enough for me to defy my own chief of station. Important enough for me to risk my life by meeting you here like this."

Traffic rumbled past them at their backs. A biting wind had come up with the lowering sun. Bertonelli took a last drag on his cigarette and flipped it out over the frozen river. Valeri's gun hand was freezing.

"Tell me how the meeting between you and Colonel Okulov was set up, and why you took the precaution of the Militia uniform," Valeri said.

"I have to admit, I didn't trust him. I thought it might be a trap." Bertonelli lit another cigarette. "He approached me during an intermission at the Yermolova Theater earlier in the week."

"He was seeking to defect?"

"I thought it was a strong possibility, and so did some of the others at the embassy. At worst we thought it might be a disinformation plot aimed at my downfall. No matter what, we figured we'd learn something."

"Because of Ivanovich in New York?"

"Yes." Bertonelli almost smiled. "But he said something very curious that night at the theater. You have to understand we couldn't have been together for more than eight or ten seconds. Just before he walked off, though, he told me that our meeting would be very dangerous, but that it was of extreme importance and delicacy, and that he had the approval of a certain element of his government."

"Still, you certainly must have had second thoughts."

"Plenty of them. That's why I provided myself with an escape valve."

"You're a CIA spy. Didn't it strike you as fantastic that a KGB colonel wanted to arrange such a meeting?"

"To say the least." Bertonelli finally laughed. "But here we are, you and I, Major."

"What did he tell you?"

"Your life will be in danger as soon as you hear what I have to say."

Valeri pulled the Beretta's hammer back. "Your life is in danger at this moment."

Bertonelli hesitated.

"If I shoot you now I'll get a medal."

"Your government is holding prisoner, in some gulag somewhere, a number of American citizens. He didn't tell me where this gulag might be, or who the Americans were, or even how many of them were being held. Just that certain elements of his government wanted our people repatriated without prejudice."

"There are Americans in our prisons," Valeri said, momentarily confused. "Smugglers, black marketeers, dope dealers."

"We know about them. Colonel Okulov assured me that this was a different matter."

"Your government keeps records. You have your social security identification numbers. Who are these people? You tell me."

"There are no Americans missing in the Soviet Union other than the few Colonel Okulov excluded. No one else."

"I can't believe this . . ."

"Neither can I, Kostikov. But he offered me two proofs that night. The first was the number written in the matchbook you picked up. A telephone number for a dead man. He never had the chance to give me either."

Nadia Burdine's face swam into Valeri's mind. Was she the second proof? But she was Siberian, not American.

"Who were you watching in that apartment?"

Valeri was really beginning to feel the cold. *Make no mistake, Okulov was not breaking the law by meeting with Bertonelli. On the contrary, he died in the service of a grateful nation.* General Demin's words. To throw him off?

"Goddamnit it, you square-headed sonofabitch, these are my people we're talking about."

Square-headed? Valeri wondered. "One of my men is dead."

"I didn't kill him."

"How do I know that?"

"I wouldn't be here if I had killed him. I would have informed my government and let them take the appropriate steps from Washington."

"Why didn't you?" Valeri asked. "Why haven't you done just that? Why have you risked so much to meet me here like this? What is it you're not telling me, Mr. Bertonelli?"

Bertonelli turned away momentarily.

It suddenly came to Valeri that Bertonelli was telling the truth, so far as the American knew it. It also came to him that Bertonelli hadn't told his own people the entire story. It was extraordinary.

"What else did Colonel Okulov tell you in the zoo? You were together for an hour. Did he give you conditions?"

Bertonelli held his silence.

Valeri lowered his gun, carefully releasing the hammer. His heart was thumping. There'd be no going back now for either of them. Better to turn back than to lose your way, Uncle Gennadi would say. Larissa Okulov had reacted to Bertonelli's name. And Colonel Okulov himself had been ready to kill a fellow officer of State Security.

"What else haven't you told me, Mr. Bertonelli? What is it you haven't even told your own people?"

Bertonelli finally looked up. "He told me that the repercussions if he were caught and exposed would be enormous." Bertonelli paused. "He promised that if anything went wrong, anything at all, the Americans would be murdered, their bodies destroyed. No one would ever know."

Valeri recoiled in horror.

"My life here is in danger, Deputy Chief. And now so is yours."

"No."

"Why would I make up such a story? Why would I put myself out on a limb like this? Christ . . ."

Valeri's head was spinning. He felt almost physically ill. At first General Demin hadn't known a thing about the investigation. The next morning, however, all that had changed. It could only mean that Uncle Gennadi was on the side that wished to bury the Americans. But what if it were all lies . . . ? What if . . . ?

He could not take his thoughts away from the eight-digit number and the girl. Colonel Okulov had offered Bertonelli two proofs that Americans were being held. A number and a Siberian girl. Where did they fit? How did they fit?

Bertonelli was watching him. "We will have to move very fast now."

"I will go to my government," Valeri said. "I will find out who Colonel Okulov was representing. We can take up where he left off."

"Are you so sure, Kostikov, that you will be able to find out? Mention this to the wrong person and my people will be dead."

"I'm taking you in. You are going to be my proof. They won't dare kill you."

"Shit," Bertonelli swore. He hunched up his coat collar. "I'm not going to be taken to Lubyanka. You will have to shoot me here and now."

"My people are watching the embassy and your apartment with orders to arrest you."

"Call them off," Bertonelli said earnestly. "Help me, Kostikov! Who were you watching in that apartment?"

"Why did you go to see my wife at the Institute?"

Bertonelli sighed deeply. His expression softened. "I shouldn't have done that. I'm sorry. I meant no harm."

"Then why did you go there?"

"I wanted you to come after me."

Valeri nodded. He knew it was true, just as he understood now why Colonel Okulov had been chosen to approach Bertonelli. Okulov had the right family, the right connections. He was a loyal Russian. His friends and acquaintances were at the highest levels of the Soviet government. Bertonelli was approached because he was a high-ranking American spy here, whose track record was considered above reproach by Langley. He would be believed. Going to him like that would solve the problem of the Americans being held without revealing the KGB's knowledge that DeMille was in fact chief of station, not Scofield. It all fit. And yet the entire business was so sinister, Valeri was having a very difficult time reconciling such a notion with his trust and affection for Uncle Gennadi.

"Give me something, Kostikov," Bertonelli said softly.

"What will you give me in return?"

"I will leave Moscow when this is over. I'll return to Washington. You'll get your medal."

"The number had eight digits. The last was a zero. I don't think it was a telephone number."

Bertonelli's eyes were suddenly bright. "Novikov is a dead end?"

"I think so. Does such a number have any significance for you?"

"No. Who were you watching in that apartment?"

"I think that is all for now, Mr. Bertonelli."

"Goddamnit . . ."

"No. When you find out what the number might mean, we will talk again."

Bertonelli wanted to say more, but he held himself in check.

"Where will you go?"

"I don't know yet."

"How will I be able to reach you?"

"You won't. I'll contact you."

"Where?"

A bus rumbled by. "I'll think of something," Bertonelli said. He glanced at the gun in Valeri's hand, then turned and headed back across the bridge, the last rays of the sun gone, the red star atop the Spassky Tower glowing in the descending darkness.

# 12

Now that Tanya would not be coming back, the apartment seemed dark, cold, and very lonely. Valeri changed his clothes and got a few of her things from the closet. Before he drove to the Institute he telephoned his office with the message for both surveillance teams that Bertonelli was to be watched but not arrested.

"I'll wait out in the corridor while you change," Valeri said, laying Tanya's things on the bed. Tchaikovsky's *Swan Lake* was playing on a radio or television somewhere down the dark corridor.

"It's all right, Valerik," she said in a small voice. "I'll just be a moment." She had already put on some makeup and had brushed her hair. She took off her hospital robe. Beneath she wore only a bra and panties. Her body was very thin, her ribs prominent on her flanks, her knees knobby, the skin shiny where it was stretched taut at her shin bones.

As Valeri watched, she pulled on the blue dress he had brought, then stepped into her shoes. She turned her back and lifted her hair off her shoulders so that he could zip her up.

"It didn't have to turn out this way," he said. He wanted to kiss her.

She turned and looked up at him. "But it did, didn't it."

They were expected at 37 Kutuzovsky Prospekt by the obsequious security guard who had the elevator waiting. On the twenty-third floor General Demin himself stood at the open door to his apartment waiting for them. His face was slightly flushed. There was a smile on his thick, Georgian lips as he held out his arms for Tanya.

"Ah, my little Tanochka," he said.

She went to him and they embraced warmly, kissing each other on both cheeks.

He held her at arm's length while he inspected her with a critical but loving eye. He shook his head and clucked. "Forgive the indelicacies of an old man, little girl, but there is nothing to you. You need to put some meat on your bones."

She patted his ample belly playfully. "Like you, Uncle?"

General Demin threw his head back and roared. "The little one is too small; the big one is too big; the medium one is just right—but I can't get it." It was one of the many old Russian proverbs he was fond of.

"Hello, Uncle Gennadi," Valeri said. He felt strange here.

He and General Demin embraced, kissing on the lips.

"I'm glad you could come tonight, Valerik. There is someone here who would very much like to meet you." General Demin smiled, but there was something in the back of his eyes that seemed off. "You will have to be careful to live up to your reputation, though, or else they will think I exaggerated."

General Demin took his and Tanya's arms and led them into the apartment. Valeri had been here often. Nothing seemed changed to him. A narrow vestibule opened into a broader corridor that turned right into a long living room with tall, heavily draped windows overlooking the city. To the left was the dining room, beyond which was a large kitchen. In the back were two large bedrooms and General Demin's trophy room. During the war he had brought back a lot of captured German weapons, flags, medals, and other memorabilia that were displayed there with obvious pride.

Serafima, General Demin's short, roly-poly wife, came around the corner. She was beaming as she hugged Tanya first, then Valeri. She had never had children. Her disappointment was that Tanya had had no children either. Very un-Russian, she often chided.

"How are you feeling, dear? The truth," she asked as General Demin took their coats.

"I am getting better," Tanya said.

Madame Demin was fully as sharp as her husband; she herself was an astute political animal. Very little got past her.

Valeri could see from her eyes that she knew all was not well with the Kostikovs beyond Tanya's obvious illness.

"And it looks as if you are working too hard, as usual, Valerik."

"Father wants us to take the Yalta house in March."

"None too soon," Madame Demin said. "Now come meet our guests."

The living room was comfortably furnished with over-stuffed furniture (some of it older than Valeri), and massive tables of dark wood. A huge oriental rug, well worn, even faded in places, covered much of the parquet floor. In a far corner a baby grand piano was piled with sheet music. Both the general and his wife played very well. Valeri remembered as a youth coming to the Demin apartment and listening to music. They were fond, uncomplicated memories.

A man and woman sat together on the couch, sipping champagne. Valeri nearly stopped in his tracks with the shock of recognition.

"Comrade Chief Secretary of Western Research for the Politburo Uri Vladimir Okulov, and Madame Okulov, I would like you to meet Valeri Konstantinovich Kostikov, my First Department deputy chief, and his wife, Tanya Alexandrovna."

"Nice to see you again, Comrade Major," Larissa Okulov said languidly, her right eyebrow arched slightly in amusement.

Uri Vladimir Okulov rose, and he and Valeri shook hands over the low coffee table laden with a champagne bucket, bottles of vodka and cognac, and a large silver tray with caviar, chopped onions, lemon, and chopped hard-boiled egg. He was dressed in a severely cut dark suit, his tie knotted correctly, a small red star on his lapel, his dark hair slicked back. He was thin, almost ascetic, the very opposite of his brother. Though he had the pinched, faintly disapproving air of a bureaucrat and high-ranking party member, if he harbored any animosity toward Valeri, he hid it well.

"Your father commands our Northern Missile Defense," Okulov said. "A real hero."

"Yes, sir," Valeri said.

"Valerik is making his own mark," General Demin said. "Believe me, very little escapes his attention here in Moscow."

Okulov smiled, turning his attention to Tanya who had been staring openly at Larissa. "Madame Kostikov."

Tanya inclined her head slightly. Valeri could see that she

understood something was happening here other than a simple social engagement. It made her uncomfortable.

"Would you care for champagne, Tanya?" Larissa asked.

"Tanya is going to help me in the kitchen," Madame Demin said firmly. "We won't be long." She took Tanya's arm and together they left.

"We needn't ask Comrade Major if he would like a glass of wine," Larissa said. "I happen to know for a fact he doesn't like it."

Her dress was made of a shimmering silver material, and was very low cut. It made the rest of them seem drab. Her hair was pinned up, revealing a long, lovely neck and delicate silver earrings. Her makeup seemed too precise, however, too much like that of a mannequin.

"Vodka or cognac, Valerik?" General Demin asked.

"Cognac," Valeri said. He took a seat at the end of the table while General Demin poured him a stiff measure of fine French cognac in a large crystal snifter.

"I have long admired the necessary work of the Second Department, Comrade Major," Okulov said.

"Do you see our reports, then?" Valeri asked.

"Indeed we do. Since it is impossible for us to close our borders, you become, in essence, our first line of defense. I take a personal interest."

"Defense against what?"

"Encroachment."

General Demin handed Valeri his drink with a warning glance, then sat at the far side of the table.

"You believe we should not trade with the West?" Valeri asked. The atmosphere was dangerous.

Okulov laughed with a measured intensity. "On the contrary. Trade, properly controlled, is necessary . . . for the moment. Certainly, however, in your reading of history at the university you came across such anthropologists as Margaret Mead, who meddled in the affairs of New Guinea and Samoa in the thirties. Outside influences, even under the controlled guise of anthropological observation, forever changed the natives. The culture mix was devastating."

"They stopped eating each other," Valeri said.

Larissa laughed. She was enjoying this.

"Of course we can no longer live in such splendid isolation," Okulov continued. "But certainly we can learn from the mistakes of others. Certainly we *should* learn, don't you agree, Comrade Major?"

"Wasn't it in 1951 that Margaret Mead wrote a paper about us, Comrade Chief Secretary?"

General Demin stiffened.

" 'Soviet Attitudes Toward Authority,' wasn't it?"

Larissa laughed again. "Didn't I tell you, Volodya? Rich. Very rich."

"Perhaps you have made my point for me. Who better to understand the real dangers of the rabid dog than the veterinarian?"

Valeri could hardly believe his ears. He had thought such rhetoric had gone out with Khrushchev in the late fifties or early sixties.

"You have spent time in the West, Major. Here in Moscow you keep track of foreigners. In your estimation, are there in fact true differences between us . . . other than the superficialities, of course?"

"I'm sorry, I don't think I understand what you mean to say," Valeri said.

Okulov leaned forward. "Would you believe it possible for a Westerner, let's say an American, to find a life for himself here in the Soviet Union? In that I mean to say, become a part of our fabric?"

"It's been done."

"Or a Russian, let's say. Could he successfully become an American? A Chicago cowboy?"

"Baryshnikov."

Okulov's eyes narrowed. "But then he wasn't a true Russian, was he."

Valeri didn't know what to say.

"He could not have been Russian. Not and become so utterly Western in such a terribly short time."

There it was, then, Valeri thought. The circular argument in which once a view was stated, any party purist worth his salt could prove it to his own satisfaction. If the politician had enough power, his personal satisfaction would become universal truth, *ipso facto*. The shortages would be divided among the peasants, the Stalinist Russian was fond of saying. Therefore there are no shortages, because the peasants are poor anyway.

"You, for instance, Major Kostikov. Could you successfully emigrate to the United States? Could you become an American?''

Valeri thought of Bertonelli. He shook his head. ''No.''

''And why not?''

''I'm Russian.''

Okulov actually smiled. ''But what do you mean by that, Comrade Major? Beyond the happenstance geographical location of your birth?''

Valeri sipped his cognac. Larissa was watching him, a faint smirk on her lips. General Demin was looking at him, an expression of paternal pride in his eyes. But was something else there too? He was beginning to understand why he *and* Tanya had been invited to dinner like this. He would not be surprised if they brought out the flag and played the national anthem before dinner. Valeri was here with Tanya to remind him of the Soviet pride. A man and a woman going forward together, working hand in hand to build communism. Uncle Gennadi and Serafima were here to reinforce the ideal of the extended family: one generation handing the job to the next; the younger generation revering the older. Chief Secretary Okulov was here to present Valeri with a needed lesson in party unity. We all needed reminders from time to time, reminders of who we were, of what was expected of us, and what were the rewards of our labors. Finally Larissa Okulov was here to remind him of the virtue of humility and the terrible abyss of individualism, egoism, and the cult of personality. But there was only one reason this evening had been so carefully orchestrated on his behalf, and it made him sick to think of it.

''The Soviet Union is the *rodina*—my mother, our mother. I could no more leave her than I could leave my own biological mother.'' The response was textbook perfect. The Komsomol line. Every schoolchild could recite it.

General Demin was clearly relieved. He looked at Okulov, then Valeri. He smiled. ''Nor betray her,'' he suggested gently.

''Nor that,'' Valeri said—and before anyone else could respond—''But it is a universal principle isn't it?''

''Of course,'' Okulov replied.

''One that must apply to everyone.''

''Naturally . . .''

''At all levels, Comrade Chief Secretary?''

Larissa's eyes widened. No one said a word. The silence grew until General Demin got up.

"More cognac, Valerik?"

"Yes, thank you," Valeri said. He finished his drink and held out his glass.

General Demin poured him a generous measure. Then he refilled the Okulovs' champagne glasses. "I'll see how dinner is coming," he said, and left.

Okulov got up and went over to the piano where he looked through the sheet music, leaving Larissa and Valeri alone for the moment.

"Curious to be meeting like this again," she said. "I suppose Gennadi even calls your wife 'Tanochka'?"

Valeri was no longer intimidated by her. In fact he found that he felt sorry for her. She seemed shallow. Her brother-in-law had her well under control for her to be here. He nodded.

"Quaint. As was your little speech."

"Have I done something to make you angry?"

She shook her head in amazement, but not in sadness. "Only murder my husband."

So she knew. He could stop pretending.

"In self-defense. He tried to kill me. He was trying to defect."

Her cheeks reddened. For just a moment she looked haggard, worn out, used up. "He was a very good man."

"A defector."

"Be careful that you don't dig yourself a premature grave. It can happen."

"The true power of our people has always been in her art, her poetry, and her music," Okulov said from across the room.

"And chess?" Valeri offered, looking up.

Okulov turned. "Yes, and chess. Human endeavor. Games and gentle persuasions that emulate life, wouldn't you agree?"

"Celebrate life, I'd think."

Okulov hit some piano keys, the sound discordant. "Do you treat everything with such seriousness, Deputy Chief?"

"That which moves me."

"And what is it that moves you?"

Valeri no longer felt he was on the defensive as he did when he and Tanya had first walked in the room. With a sudden clarity he saw that Larissa and her brother-in-law were frightened of him. So was Bertonelli. Somehow he had become the pivot point, the fulcrum around which so many lives seemed to hang in the balance. He'd never thought of himself as a threat. Until now he had been cautious, even apologetic. But this was a nation of laws, after all, wasn't it?

"Justice," Valeri said.

"The greatest good for the greatest number, Plato wrote."

"Truth. The great Soviet experiment."

"Not an experiment, I think, Comrade Major. Reality now, tempered by a clear understanding of the exigencies of the international nuclear status quo."

"Are you afraid of nuclear war?"

"What sane man isn't?" Okulov answered too quickly.

Valeri got the impression he was lying. It was disturbing. The Russian term for it was adventurism. A nearly equal number of Russians had been awarded medals for such radical thinking as had been destroyed by firing squads. Stalin and Khrushchev were now in disgrace for precisely the same reasons they had come to power. Who set the policy these days? The Okulovs of the Soviet system?

Tanya appeared at the archway. She wore an apron over her blue dress, which somehow made her seem even more diminutive than she was.

"Dinner is served."

"At last," Larissa said, getting up. She was a little unsteady on her feet. Okulov took her arm and they went into the dining room.

Tanya stopped Valeri at the archway. "What is going on here, Valerik?" she whispered. "Who are these people?"

"They're trying to get me to stop an investigation, I think. Or at least divert it. We're going to get out of here early."

Tanya looked at him. "Are you in some kind of trouble?"

"They are," Valeri said tersely.

The table was covered with a crisp white linen tablecloth and filled with a variety of dishes, all of which Madame Demin had personally prepared. It was another of the things Valeri remembered from his boyhood. Dinners at the Demins were always wonderful affairs of endless dishes and endless toasts. Tonight was different, though. They all felt it. General Demin sat Tanya and Okulov to one side, and Valeri with Larissa on the other. He poured their first spiced vodka.

"The Deputy Chief and I were just getting into an interesting conversation," Okulov said. "We were trying to decide what made a Russian different from an American. Practically every day I read about one of our people attempting to emigrate. On the surface it would seem we've bred a generation of malcontents. But only on the surface. Upon closer examination, I've found that the ones who go over are defective. Unhappy childhood. Failure with their career. Perhaps they've run afoul of another man's wife, or perhaps even the party. In any event, they become exiles."

Madame Demin dished up their borshch and a platter of *pirozhki*, little pastries filled with ground meat.

"Fantastic," Okulov said to her. "The point I am trying to make, Major, is that the particular Russian I'm talking about is a misfit. I spent a couple of years in New York. I saw these people at close range. I watched them. They were a sad lot. For all their initial bravado about becoming American—free, they say, as if that were some magical ideal—they tend to stick together. They subscribe to Soviet newspapers and magazines, they go to Russian specialty restaurants, see Russian plays, read Russian novels, drink Russian vodka. They gather in each other's apartments to talk not about the supposedly great opportunities they are enjoying, but about Moscow, or Leningrad, or Odessa. About places they remember, about people they've left behind. In short, they bring with them their Russianness. They can't escape it."

"Then we should allow them to return home without slapping them into prison the moment they get off the airplane," Valeri said.

"That's the saddest aspect of all. Their experiences have tainted them. You don't put the rotten apple back into the barrel with the others. Isolate it, for certain. Perhaps cut out the spoiled bit if you can. But that is not always possible, or even desirable."

"So these people should be destroyed?"

"Sometimes the most difficult course is the best."

"But then someone has to make those decisions. It must be a terrible burden."

"The price of civilization, Major. You're an educated, well-traveled man, and a student of human nature by virtue of your occupation. You watch Americans. In fact one might even say that you have an intimate knowledge of their habits. At least of a certain class of American. Your job is to isolate them. Not out of fear, but out of necessity, wouldn't you agree?''

''A task which Valerik does very well,'' General Demin said from the end of the table.

''I agree one hundred percent, Gennadi,'' Okulov said. ''Which is why the terrible episode of Thursday night must be put in its proper perspective.''

Madame Demin had gone into the kitchen. She came back with a large bowl of *pelmeni*, small, meat-filled dumplings served with sour cream. The general poured more vodka. Larissa had averted her eyes, refusing to look at Valeri. She was the bereaved widow here with her brother-in-law to convince Valeri . . . of what? That Colonel Okulov was a hero who had tried to cause Bertonelli's downfall? That signals had been crossed, and the word had somehow not been given to Valeri's department? That Colonel Okulov's death was a tragic mistake? Nothing more?

Then it came to him what they were really trying to say. Bertonelli had told the truth on the bridge. Now Chief Secretary Okulov and whoever he worked for were running scared. Colonel Okulov had been privy to the terrible secret, but he was already dead. The secret was safe with him. Which left Bertonelli. He would have to be eliminated, but it would have to be by someone neutral. Someone not connected with the plot. Someone who could logically be expected to go after Bertonelli. By the same man who had inadvertently broken up the meeting at the zoo. They wanted him to kill Bertonelli for them.

''Tell me, Comrade Chief Secretary, why wasn't I informed?'' Valeri said.

''Informed about what?'' Okulov asked. He glanced at General Demin.

''What your brother was doing at the zoo with an American spy.''

''I don't want it to weigh on your conscience, Valerik,'' General Demin broke in.

The dining room was deathly still. Valeri didn't really know why he was pushing so hard, but he couldn't help himself. He looked directly at Larissa. ''Should it?''

She looked up. Their eyes locked. ''You bastard,'' she hissed. She jumped up, knocking over her glass of vodka.

Madame Demin's eyes sparked. "I will not have such talk at my table!"

"Sit down, Larissa," Okulov said evenly.

General Demin got up and held her chair for her. For a long time she stood there glaring at Valeri. Then she lowered her eyes. "Please forgive me, Madame Demin," she said contritely. She sat down.

"You have been under a terrible strain these days, my dear," Madame Demin said coolly. "We do understand."

Tanya was confused, but she knew enough to hold her silence, for which Valeri was grateful.

General Demin cleaned up Larissa's spilled vodka and poured her more. She drank it down and held out her glass for another. General Demin poured it.

"We've all been under a strain," Okulov said, looking down at his hands. "He was my brother, after all."

"I'm sorry, comrade Chief Secretary, but there is a lot here that I do not understand," Valeri said.

"It is something on my conscience, Major. A terrible burden that I must live with. Believe me, it is the very reason I asked Gennadi to arrange for us to meet like this. To clear the air. He was working for me. I sent him to the zoo."

"Which is why, Valerik, I knew nothing about it when we spoke in your office that morning," General Demin explained.

"But why, Comrade Chief Secretary? What was he doing there for you?"

Okulov looked to General Demin, who nodded. Madame Demin's lips were compressed.

"I sent him to kill Anthony Bertonelli."

Madame Demin sighed. Larissa lowered her head, tears coming to her eyes. Valeri thought he might be watching a poor stage drama.

"I'm sorry I had to lie to you on the telephone about the colonel's gun," General Demin said.

"My fault entirely," Okulov said. "I asked him to tell you that white lie so that I could explain the entire situation to you in person. And I wanted to do it here, like this, tonight, while you were among . . . family. So that you could better understand why I did what I did."

"Understand what?"

"Why I wanted Bertonelli dead. Why I was willing to risk

my brother's life in the deed. Why it must not go any further than this table tonight. I am baring my soul to you."

General Demin leaned forward. "He wanted to offer you a promotion. I told him with you that would not work."

"I was desperate. I *am* desperate."

Very large lies are much easier to believe than small lies. Valeri had read that somewhere. It struck home now.

"Just tell it to him, Volodya," Larissa cried. "Get it over with."

"Larissa and I . . . are in love," Okulov said. "We've been in love for years. We've been having an affair. Bertonelli found out about it somehow, and threatened me with exposure. It happened while I was in New York. It is why no objections were raised on his diplomatic visa application."

Valeri wanted to laugh out loud. It was so transparent. Or was it? Who to believe—Uncle Gennadi and a chief secretary of the Politburo, or an American intelligence officer? Which story was the most fantastic?

"Why didn't you deal with him yourself, then?" Valeri demanded.

"At first I thought I would do just that. Lure him here to Moscow and simply kill him. But it is more complicated than that."

You can't drive straight on a twisting lane, Valeri thought.

"My brother found out about us on his own. When he came to me, I told him about Bertonelli's blackmail. At first my brother thought I deserved whatever would come of it. He refused to help. For that I can't blame him. I would have been dismissed from the party, at the very least. Likely internal exile. Certainly separation from Larissa."

"But you had a better plan."

"Yes, and my brother went along with it. He approached Bertonelli at the Yermolova Theater last week and told him that he knew everything, and that he wanted to ruin me. He was planning on giving Bertonelli the Novikov files."

"What?"

"Novikov, the elder, was instrumental in developing an agent network on the North American continent under his cover as a UPDK diplomat. Our deep-cover people are still in place. Mexico City, Washington, New York, Ottawa, Toronto."

"How would that information hurt you?"

"My job is the recruitment and placement of our people. If the network were to be destroyed, my downfall would be assured."

"So Bertonelli took the bait?"

"Yes, he did," Okulov said. "There was no other way to get the man to such a meeting. We had to tell him something important enough to get him there alone. At that point my brother was going to kill him."

Valeri felt a premonition of doom. The fatal flaw in Okulov's story was that it failed to explain Nadia Burdine's existence, or poor Lipasov's murder. But what about Bertonelli's two proofs? The number was a code, but what about the girl? She wasn't an American. She was a Siberian. No matter from which angle he looked, Nadia Burdine simply did not fit.

"You now have my life in your hands, Comrade Major. Quite literally," Okulov said softly.

It was an extraordinary thing for one Russian to say to another. Valeri shrugged absently. "Even if I wanted to ruin you, Comrade Chief Secretary, who would I turn to? Who would believe me? Pardon me, Uncle Gennadi, but without your help there would be little I could accomplish."

General Demin nodded.

"Why have I been told all this?"

"Bertonelli has to be stopped."

"You and your brother tried to kill him, but he is very good. Do you know how he escaped from the zoo?"

Okulov nodded. "Gennadi told me."

"Did you also know that he has had surveillance people on me ever since that night?"

Okulov sat forward. "What? Now? He followed you here?"

"No," Valeri said, satisfied with the reaction. "I managed to slip away from them."

Okulov and General Demin exchanged glances.

"You are his next victim, then, Valerik," the general said heavily. "He's stalking you, and when he feels it is time, he will pounce."

"And I will kill him."

Madame Demin looked sadly at Valeri, then got up and went into the kitchen. Tanya was staring at him, her eyes wide. The dining room was suddenly airless, and very strange, an alien land from which Valeri had the urge to flee.

"He will tell you fantastic stories," Okulov said. He had

become animated. "He will twist the truth, and promise you anything. He has the power."

Tanya started to speak up, but Valeri cut her off.

"What happens afterward?"

"We will protect you, naturally."

"I meant with you, Comrade Chief Secretary."

Okulov was startled. "I don't intend to throw away my career, if that is what you mean, Major. I will continue to make a meaningful contribution to my government. I've made my sacrifices."

"Still you have taken a risk by being so open with me."

"You could cause trouble, with or without Gennadi's help."

"But you could cause more."

Okulov nodded. "We have a common goal, you and I."

"Bertonelli."

"Protecting the state."

From whom? Valeri wondered. And what about poor Lipasov? Or the girl? Where was she? Where did it all fit? Lies within lies. Half truths spun into a delicately complex web of deception and dangerous associations. Above and beyond everything else, Valeri realized with a deep feeling of loss that his relationship with Uncle Gennadi could never be the same again. All of them would forever be changed for the worse by this thing. It was a cancer. And who was supposed to protect the state from itself?

"You will do this?" General Demin asked softly.

Valeri put his napkin down. The food was very good, but none of them had eaten very much. He wanted to go into the kitchen and apologize to Madame Demin, but he couldn't. Not now. Perhaps never. He got to his feet.

"I'll do what's right, Uncle Gennadi."

"That's all we can ask of you, Valerik."

"If you need anything, anything at all, Major, you can contact me through Gennadi," Okulov said. "But you will have to be very careful. Bertonelli is a powerful force."

"Yes, he is," Valeri said.

Tanya got up and came around the table. General Demin started to get up, but Valeri waved him back.

"We can find our own way out."

"Take care, nephew," General Demin said. "I don't want to lose you and Tanochka."

\*     \*     \*

On the way back to the Institute, Tanya sat hunched down in her seat against the passenger side door as far away from Valeri as she could get. She had shuddered and pulled away when he had taken her arm in the elevator. She wanted to maintain her distance now.

Their marriage was over before this night began. But now even the last thin threads of contact they had had were severed too. Valeri thought they could have been two animals of completely different species. She was the dove and he was the shark. The sea creature might dream of flying, but the bird could not conceive of an existence beneath the surface of the waves over which she flew.

"I don't even hate you," she said at one point.

Valeri looked over at her. "I'm glad."

"I'm amazed that we were ever married."

"Was it terrible?"

She shook her head. "I don't know. I look back and honestly try to remember what I felt—even two hours ago— but I cannot. It's blank."

"We lived our lives together . . ."

"No. It was not life, Valerik. Not for you, not for me. Wasted existence, nothing more."

She looked at him, and for a terrible moment he had no idea who either of them were. When it passed he felt a frightening weakness, as if he were a mindless chip of wood being swept over a waterfall.

# 13

The frigid night air hung still like the breath of a corpse along Tchaikovsky Boulevard. Standing in the shadows across the road from the American embassy, Bertonelli had watched the late weekend shift coming off duty, and the night operators coming in. He had also watched the gray Zaporozhets sedan parked halfway up the block.

At some lower level of his consciousness, Bertonelli felt that he should know what the eight-digit number meant. Not a phone number or a code, something else. He had repeated it to himself over and over again in varying combinations: one digit at a time, then two at a time, four, the entire eight. But he was a field operative, not an analyst. There were others much better at the game than he.

Two minutes into his meeting with Kostikov on the bridge, Bertonelli had convinced himself that the Russian was either a very good actor, or was innocent of any complicity in the Okulov business. If the latter were the case, Kostikov would be in serious danger now. No matter what happened, it was likely the man would be assassinated. The trick was going to be keeping him alive long enough to find out the rest of the story. Bertonelli wasn't quite sure how he was going to manage that.

A few minutes after eight, a dark blue Zhiguli came around the corner from Kalinina Prospekt and pulled up alongside the Zaporozhets. The plates were official. The driver jumped out, said something to the man in the smaller car, then got back into his own car and left. A moment or two later, the Zaporozhets's headlights came on, and the tiny car pulled away.

That was Kostikov's doing. To this point he was playing it straight. They had had an exchange of information, and the major had called off his watchdogs. Bertonelli waited for a break in the traffic and then hurried across the street.

The embassy was well lit in the front. Militia guards watched the outside, while U.S. Marines in dress uniform watched from within. By mutual agreement no one was supposed to be armed. The Moscow Militia wore their sidearms in plain view. The Marines hid theirs beneath their tunics.

Bertonelli took out his identification and held it up before the young Militia officer, dressed in greatcoat, tall boots, and fur hat, could ask. The man looked from the plastic ID card to Bertonelli's face and then stepped respectfully aside. He was there not to stop or harass Americans, only to screen Soviet citizens who had no business there.

Bertonelli crossed the inner courtyard and entered the embassy.

The Marine guard behind the reception window looked up and then got to his feet. "Mr. Bertonelli," he said.

"Is Ambassador Scott in residence this evening?"

"No, sir. But Mr. DeMille has been asking for you. He's still here."

"Thanks," Bertonelli said. He walked down the dark corridor and took the back stairs up to the third floor where he hesitated a moment on the landing. Scofield was just getting on the elevator. The doors closed and the car started up. The corridor was empty for the moment. Bertonelli slipped out of the stairwell and hurried to his office. He closed and locked the door before he flipped on the lights.

His office had been searched. The seal on his safe had been broken, his file cabinets unlocked and emptied, books taken off the shelves and piled on the floor in the corner. Bertonelli stepped around his desk. This was DeMille's doing. It made his blood boil. The only thing they had not touched was the photograph of his ex-wife and daughter. He took it down from atop the file cabinet and looked at the only two women other than his mother who had ever meant anything to him. They seemed too far away now, too impossibly remote. There had come the day when JoAnn had found out what he really did for a living, and it did not fit with her notions of success and of fair play. She had simply divorced him. No fuss, no arguments, no strain at first.

His daughter was wearing braces now; he knew because he got the bills. She would be in junior high school next year. For a long time, staring at the photograph, he thought seriously about giving up, about resigning here and now, and returning to the States.

"When your principles get in the way of good common sense," JoAnn had told him, "it's time to reexamine your principles."

He had. If anything, he'd been strengthened in his resolve. Even that seemed remote now, though. But nothing came easy, did it? His old man had been bitter at twenty-five, old at thirty-five, and dead at forty-five. The war had done it, prejudice had done it, or . . . what? Who to blame? A recalcitrant, difficult child, a chronically ill wife, too little income as a laborer in a town where industry had been dying since 1950. The great American dream had been alive and well at the turn of the century in places like Pittsburgh, Erie, Gary. But it had died after the Second World War, about the same time the CIA had been formed and the cold war spawned a generation of Kim Philbys and Israel Beers.

Bertonelli replaced the photograph, took off his overcoat and hat, laying them aside, and looked at his watch. It was just a few minutes after noon in Washington. Though it was a Saturday, Langley would be fully staffed from the Operations level down. The DCI and his division chiefs would be gone of course, so decisions would have to be made by junior staffers.

He pulled out his snub-nosed .38 with the squat silencer cylinder screwed onto the end of the barrel and checked it. DeMille would know that he was armed. For that alone his tenure in Moscow was at an end. Perhaps, he thought, he had no decision to make. The game was over. DeMille would be coming down at any moment.

For a second or two he was back in Afghanistan. His muscles bunched up, his jaw tightened. They were young boys who had done the massacre. Uzbeks, Armenians, Georgians. A lot of them farmers, some of them sons of factory workers. An ignorant, savage lot. The bloodlust among the people of the steppes was more than a thousand years old. Even before the Vikings were bloodying England's shores, the Tartars were bashing in each other's heads with great enthusiasm. Today the typical Russian office building was

constructed to look more like a tomb than a place of business.
It was a national mania: poetry, music, and chess in the
evening after a hard day on the killing fields.

Bertonelli stuffed his gun back in his jacket pocket, unlocked his door, and stepped out.

Hobbs and Grant were just coming down the corridor.
They were deep in discussion. Hobbs looked up.

"Ah, the prodigal son returns."

The elevator was on the fifth floor; the indicator started
down.

"Do you know where Ambassador Scott is this evening?"
Bertonelli growled.

Grant turned and looked at the elevator indicator.

"At the Bolshoi," Hobbs said genially.

"Get him here," Bertonelli demanded. He turned on his
heel and started for the stairs.

"Roland would very much like to speak with you, my
boy," Hobbs said.

"Mr. Bertonelli . . . ?" Grant called.

Bertonelli hurried down the stairs. He figured he was going
to have one shot at this, and only one. It was a big gamble,
his career on the line. But then he was finished here in any
event.

On the first floor there was a commotion in the main entry
hall. Bertonelli peered out the small window in the stairwell
door. Posman was giving instructions to a half-dozen Marines. Above, a stairwell door banged open.

"Bertonelli!" DeMille shouted, his voice echoing.

Posman and the Marines looked around.

Bertonelli yanked out his gun and raced down the last flight
of stairs to the basement. At the bottom he threw open a
wooden door in a bulkhead and hurried down the narrow,
low-ceilinged corridor, holding the .38 behind him. A steel
door with no exterior lock or knob was set into the thick stone
wall. Bertonelli hit the buzzer, his heart racing. Technical
Control for communications was on the top floor, just below
the antennae on the roof. But the actual on-line cryptographic
equipment was here. There would only be a maintenance man
and an operator on duty tonight, both of them borrowed from
the Air force, who maintained the equipment.

He was about to ring the buzzer again, when the narrow
slot in the door slid open.

"Let me in," Bertonelli demanded.

"Yes, sir," the young man said. The lock slid back and the door started to swing aside just as the bulkhead door at the far end of the corridor banged open.

"Bertonelli!" DeMille shouted.

Bertonelli shoved his way into the crypto center, pushing the young sergeant out of his way, slamming and locking the steel door behind him.

"Sir?" the young man said in alarm. His name tag said Anderson.

The room was long and narrow. It smelled strongly of electronic equipment and cigarette smoke. Tall equipment racks lined one wall and a half-dozen teletype machines lined the opposite wall. At one end of the room was a workbench and parts bins. In the center of the room the other Air Force sergeant was seated at a steel table. He jumped up.

The door buzzer rang, the sound shrill. Bertonelli brought out his gun.

"Christ," Anderson swore.

"Nobody's going to get hurt tonight if you do exactly as I say."

The door buzzer rang again. Very soon DeMille was going to figure out what was going on down there, and he'd order the circuits pulled from upstairs.

Bertonelli motioned toward the teletype equipment with his gun. "I want to send a query to Langley."

Anderson hesitated, his eyes flicking from Bertonelli to the door and back. The buzzer rang again, insistently. Someone began pounding on the door. The other sergeant, whose name tag read Walsh, was edging away from the table toward the equipment racks on which hung a military .45 automatic in an open holster.

"If you get any closer to that gun, I will shoot you, Walsh," Bertonelli said.

The young man stopped in his tracks.

"I want that circuit to Langley. *Now.*"

"Yes, sir," Anderson said, swallowing his words. "What designation?"

The buzzer was silent. They were running out of time.

"Top Secret, Flash."

"Who is the addressee?"

"Assistant Director of Intelligence, or whoever is ranking on duty there."

The telephone on one of the equipment bays rang. Walsh started for it.

"Sit down," Bertonelli ordered.

Walsh complied. He was beginning to sweat. Anderson went over to one of the teletype machines without being told again. He sat down, flipped a switch, and hit the letter key. The carriage jumped and returned flush left. The young man looked up.

"Top Secret, Flash. Message as follows,' Bertonelli said, and Anderson tapped it out.

```
TOP SECRET
282334Z***********001A
FLASH
TO: LANGLEY ADI-OD
FM: MOSCOW OPS****02
1. REF. PREVIOUS OKULOV QUE-
RIES XX
2. REF. PREVIOUS QUERY ANALY-
SIS SEVEN-DIGIT NUMBER XX
3. QUERY ANALYSIS MODIFIED XX
NUMBER AS FOLLOWS XX 1-7-5-7-
3-3-6-0 XX
4. QUERY XX REQUEST IMMEDIATE
ANALYSIS XX BELIEVE INFORMA-
TION CONNECTED IN SOME WAY WITH
AMERICANS HELD U.S.S.R. XX

END FLASH
MOSCOW OPS ****02
282 . . . . . . .
```

The carriages of all six teletype machines began to jump at the same time, indicating an open circuit. DeMille had pulled the plug, but he was too late.

"Any way to wire around them upstairs?"

Anderson looked up.

"No, sir," Walsh said from where he sat at the table. He nodded toward the crypto machines. "We've been cut off at the source. All our circuits are down. Out of sync."

"But my message got through?"

Anderson nodded. "Yes, sir."

The telephone on the equipment bay rang again.

"That'll be Tech Control," Walsh said.

Bertonelli crossed to the telephone, pocketing his gun. He pulled the .45 out of its holster, removed the clip, and checked to make sure the breech was empty. He reholstered the gun and picked up the phone.

"Is everyone all right down there, Tony?" DeMille asked.

"We're fine. My message did get through."

"I saw it. Where did you come up with the last digit?"

"Major Kostikov."

"You met with him?"

"Three hours ago."

DeMille sighed deeply. "Wyatt tells us that one of Kostikov's people was shot to death sometime today."

"I had nothing to do with it."

"I want to believe you . . ."

"You'd better believe me. A lot of lives are on the line here. American lives."

"We've gone through all of that."

"No, listen to me. I wasn't completely honest with you or Ambassador Scott. There's more."

There was a long silence. Bertonelli glanced over at Walsh and Anderson. They were staring at him, open-mouthed.

"I'm listening."

"Has Ambassador Scott been contacted?"

"I think you and I can work this out."

"Has he been called from the ballet? I want him here. I want to talk to him."

DeMille laughed. "You know our position on hostages, Tony."

"Try to raise above yourself for once, you stupid asshole. I don't want him down here, I simply want to talk to him. And I want our circuit with Langley reopened."

"Or else? Come on, give me your ultimatum. Are you going to kill those two young boys down there with you? Are you going to destroy the equipment? Are you going to take

the maintenance manuals with you and try to get them out to
your KGB pal? Is that your game?''

"There were two proofs, Roland. The first is the number.
The second is a person. Major Kostikov knows who it is.''

"One of your missing Americans?'' DeMille asked sarcas-
tically.

"Colonel Okulov told me that if anything went wrong, all
of them would be killed, their bodies destroyed.''

A few seconds passed.

"When you think about it, Tony, they're sharp bastards.
Your little stunt in New York caused them a lot of embarrassment. From the day you arrived here, we've all been expecting something like this to happen. I personally thought it
would have come a lot sooner. But now that it's here, you
have to admire their planning. They wanted your ass, and
they've got it. Really, it's fantastic how they got you to
cooperate with them. Think about it, Tony. Look around you.
No Russians. Just you, your gun, and two United States Air
Force noncoms being held hostage.''

Was it simply a disinformation plot after all? Bertonelli
found himself looking back at his meeting with Colonel Okulov.
Had it been a sham? But he had seen the dead man in the attic
apartment. Russians might be gleeful killers, but there had to
be a reason.

"What if there really are Americans being held in some
gulag?''

"Colonel Okulov approached you. Someone else will make
the approach if they are serious.''

"He said they would be destroyed.''

"No government in the world would do such a thing,
Tony.''

Bertonelli thought about the bodies still being found in
Argentina, buried all over the countryside; he thought about
the downtown stadium in Santiago, Chile, that had been used
as an execution arena; about the Marine barracks in Beirut;
about the *Achille Lauro*; about passengers killed on a dozen
airplanes and trains hijacked around the world; about the
Olympics in Munich. He thought about Afghanistan. He thought
about My Lai.

"The right people, backed into a corner, would,'' Bertonelli
replied.

"What people?''

Bertonelli cut the connection. He waited a moment, then dialed Hobbs's office. Grant answered on the first ring.

"Has Ambassador Scott been called?"

"He's on his way, Mr. Bertonelli. But DeMille is determined to get you out of there before the ambassador arrives."

"Listen, Wyatt, no matter what happens, the ambassador has to be told what's going on here. Can you help me . . . ?"

The line clicked.

"We're giving you ninety seconds, Tony, and then we're blowing the door," DeMille said.

Bertonelli looked at Walsh and Anderson. He shook his head. "That won't be necessary, Roland. I'm giving myself up."

"Fine. Leave your weapon on the table, and come out into the corridor with your hands in plain sight."

"I think not. I wouldn't want a nervous Marine pulling the trigger. Better you come down here."

"Ninety seconds."

"I'll hand over my gun to Anderson. The door will be unlocked."

"No."

"Bring Hobbs and Grant down with you. Once the situation has been stabilized, I'll walk out of here. You don't want a bloodbath on your hands. It wouldn't look good on your record."

DeMille said nothing.

"Come on, Roland. You owe me that much at least. Consider the possibility that I'm not a traitor, that I'm simply a stupid sonofabitch. Within twenty-four hours you can have me on a plane for Washington."

"Let me speak to Anderson."

Bertonelli took out his gun, pulled the hammer back, and pointed it at Anderson. "Mr. DeMille would like to speak to you, Sergeant. He wants to know that I've handed over my gun, and that it's all right down here."

Anderson slowly got to his feet. He looked at the .38 in Bertonelli's hand. The silencer cylinder made the weapon seem even more deadly than it was.

"Here," Bertonelli said, holding out the telephone.

Anderson approached slowly and took the phone. Bertonelli laid the .38's barrel on the side of the man's head just behind his ear.

"This is Sergeant Anderson, sir." The young man looked at Bertonelli out of the corner of his eye. He nodded very carefully. "Yes, sir, I . . . have his gun."

Walsh stared at Bertonelli with open hostility in his eyes.

"Yes, sir, we'll unlock the door," Anderson said. He slowly hung up.

Bertonelli stepped back. "I'd like to stop and explain what's going on, but there isn't time." He motioned with the gun. "Unlock the door."

Anderson went across the room and turned the lock. Bertonelli took the .45 from the holster on the equipment rack and handed it to Walsh. When Anderson returned they all sat down. Bertonelli laid his gun on the table and instructed Walsh to cover him with the empty .45.

"They won't let you get out of here, Mr. Bertonelli," Walsh said after a long silence.

"I don't want to get out," Bertonelli said. He took out a cigarette and lit it with one hand.

"Can you tell us what's going on, then?"

"No."

"Has it something to do with the Flash you sent out the other day?"

"Stay out of it, Sergeant," Bertonelli said softly. He was weary. "Believe me, you don't want to get involved."

Five minutes later they heard someone in the corridor. Bertonelli put out his cigarette.

"Sergeant Anderson?" DeMille called from outside.

"Yes, sir," Anderson said.

"Is everything correct in there?"

Bertonelli nodded.

"Yes, sir," Anderson called out.

The steel door swung slowly inward. DeMille peered cautiously around the corner, then stepped into full view. He held a small automatic in his right hand. Grant and Hobbs were right behind him. He spotted the .45 in Walsh's hand.

"You went too far this time, Tony. But you have to admit I gave you fair warning. I don't think you can find fault with me in that respect. I told you that we could not afford to have cowboys here in Moscow. The balances are simply too delicate."

"The ambassador will be here soon."

"Won't do you any good, Tony. I'm placing you under arrest. You're going to stand trial."

"What am I charged with?"

DeMille looked surprised. "Why, murder, of course. Of a Soviet citizen. Naturally we won't turn you over to the Soviet authorities because of your CIA involvement. But you will be tried in Washington, and the Soviets will be satisfied. Believe me. When it's over we'll be able to get back to work here." DeMille looked over his shoulder. "Get Lieutenant Lewis in here."

Bertonelli picked up his gun and pulled the hammer back.

DeMille turned back. His eyes widened. He started to raise his gun.

"Don't do it, Roland. I don't want to shoot you."

"But you would."

"If need be."

DeMille considered it. "Then Sergeant Walsh would kill you. He has a gun aimed at your chest."

Walsh laid the .45 down. "It's unloaded, sir."

"I should have known better," DeMille said bitterly. "I was warned about you. Do you want to get out of here? Is that it?"

"No."

"What then, Tony? This can't last indefinitely."

"I want the Langley circuit restored, and then I want to speak with Ambassador Scott."

"This is my station . . ."

"When it's over with, you're welcome to it."

Again DeMille seemed to consider Bertonelli's words. He shook his head. "I can't let you do this."

"Then I'll kill you."

"Why? For your Russian friend?"

"For the possibility that there are some Americans being held in a Gulag. I want to know who they are, where they are, and then I want to get them out. I want to take them home."

"Six shots in your little gun. There are twice as many Marines in the corridor."

"I understand."

DeMille opened his mouth to call out. Bertonelli started to squeeze the trigger. Hobbs's eyes went wide, and he stepped aside. DeMille stiffened.

"Please don't call out, Mr. DeMille," Grant said. He had a gun at DeMille's back.

The breath caught in DeMille's throat. "Why?" he croaked.

"Let's just say that if we do it your way, sir, someone is bound to get hurt. I'd like you to pass your gun back here to me."

"The man is a traitor, and a murderer."

"No, sir. I don't believe he is. I discovered the body."

"Tony," Hobbs said. "What if we do restore the circuit, and Langley tells you that the number has no significance?"

"Then I'll back off."

"You'll put your gun down and give yourself up?"

"You have my word on it."

"You won't pursue this any longer? You'll have no further contact with Major Kostikov?"

Everything seemed to come down to a simple choice. Even the most disjointed operation Bertonelli could remember teetered on some pivotal point, some break-even juncture at which everything hung on one simple act. He nodded.

"Roland?" Hobbs said.

DeMille's eyes bored into Bertonelli's. Slowly he handed his gun back to Grant. "No matter what happens, Tony—no matter what—you're finished."

Bertonelli lowered his gun.

"I'll have the circuits restored," Hobbs said. "And as soon as Ambassador Scott arrives, I'll have him call down here."

"Do that, Uncle Bill," Bertonelli said.

"You're dead, mister," DeMille whispered.

# 14

A thin blue glow rose from the U.S. Situation Room at the Warehouse, its light diffused through the tall windows in Valeri's office. A harsh circle of yellow light illuminated his desk and typewriter, throwing the rest of the room in shadow.

Someone had cleaned up the glass from the floor and the tea mess from the large wall map. His father looked sternly at him from one of the photos. Each time Valeri glanced up, his father's eyes seemed to be telling him something: "Take care, Valerik, all the brave men are in prison."

His report was as complete as he could make it at this point in his investigation. He had not spared his speculations, nor had he hesitated to name names and set down conversations, including those with Larissa Okulov and her brother-in-law, as well as with General Demin and Bertonelli. An exercise in futility, he wondered, for who would see the report? Not Uncle Gennadi. Perhaps Chairman Chernetsov. Perhaps no one. Perhaps it would be cremated with him.

Someone was on the iron stairs. Valeri looked up as Votrin came in. The little surveillance man looked angry and confused. Steam rose from his coat. He reeked of vodka.

"Can you tell me what the fuck is going on, Comrade Major?" He took off his hat and tossed it aside, then unbuttoned his coat with thick fingers. "First we're sent to watch Bertonelli, then we're called off. Next we're sent to search his apartment, but again we're called off. Finally we're sent to arrest him. At long last, I say to myself, we'll have a go at the bastard in Lubyanka. But no, once again we're called off. Frankly, I'm a confused fucker."

Valeri locked his report in a desk drawer, and pulled out a

bottle of cognac and two glasses. He poured them both a drink and handed Votrin his. He raised his glass.

"What shall we drink to, Oleg Dimitrivich? It looks as if you've already had a very good start."

Votrin tossed his drink back and held out his glass for more. Valeri poured it.

"Don't be antisocial. You have something on your chest. Spit it out. Between us we will be able to work out your problem. Never let it be said that the efficiency of our office suffered because of a basic lack of understanding."

"Are we going to arrest that bastard or not?"

"Not yet."

"Pardon me, sir, but Mikhail is just as confused as I am."

"Mikhail?" Valeri asked in wonderment.

"Captain Shevchenko. I was just with him. It was he who called me off. Said they were your orders. He bought me supper across the street."

Valeri closed his eyes. Mikhail was supposed to be home with his family, celebrating Winter Festival. He had offered to come in. His telephone had been busy the same time as General Demin's. Coincidence?

"He thinks Colonel Okulov was trying to get something on Bertonelli so that we could arrest him, you know. It was Bertonelli's fault. All of it. But we have to take him before he runs off. Mikhail said it was very important. We can't let a man like that simply walk off."

Valeri opened his eyes. Votrin was staring at him. A sheen of sweat covered Votrin's big forehead. His eyes were bright from drink. Valeri knew the man as a steady and efficient if somewhat unimaginative worker, but he had never known Votrin to be disrespectful of his superiors. It was the alcohol, Valeri thought. That and outrage that a criminal against the state was being allowed to walk free. But Mikhail had put him up to this, and it made Valeri sad to think what that might imply.

"Where is Captain Shevchenko at this moment? Still across the street?"

"I don't know. Home, I think. He said his wife was giving him hell."

Valeri switched off his desk lamp and got up. He was stiff from hunching over his typewriter for the past hour and a half. He was also bone weary. He had not slept decently in what seemed like weeks.

"Let me take him. Please." Votrin said it with great feeling.

"Where is Sergei? Has he gone home as well?"

Votrin nodded.

"Then you go home too, Oleg. Get some sleep. Have a relaxing Sunday. On Monday we will begin again. I promise you."

"It could be too late by then. Fuck."

Too late for what, Valeri wondered. "I'll speak with Captain Shevchenko. Together we will deal with the Americans."

"Now!" Votrin said, straightening up.

Valeri let his gaze grow cold. He held Votrin's eyes for a moment, then stepped from around behind his desk, and pulled on his hat and coat. "You would be wise, Oleg Dimitrivich, to give some thought to what you are saying, and just how you are saying it."

Votrin opened his mouth, but no sound came out.

"We are all cut from the same mold in the eyes of the law. Our constitution guarantees it. Nevertheless, unanimity of purpose demands organization. There is a top and a bottom. For everyone."

Valeri picked up Votrin's hat and handed it to him.

"I'm sorry, Comrade Major. I didn't mean anything . . ."

Valeri patted him on the shoulder. "Believe me, I understand fully the pressure you must feel. But you too must comprehend that there is a larger picture here in which Mr. Bertonelli is simply one element. Naturally I don't expect, or want, you to know everything. Suffice your knowledge to include your specific duties, leaving the broader scope of this investigation to your lawful superiors."

Votrin was impressed by the speech. He hung his head. "I'm sorry."

Valeri forced a smile. "Not to worry. Justice will be done. Believe me."

Votrin put down his glass and left. Valeri checked his Beretta, waited a few minutes, and went out.

The streets were filled with partygoers. This was the biggest night during Winter Festival. Last year he and Tanya had celebrated with the Shevchenkos and some other people at

General Demin's *dacha* on the Istra River outside the city. This year there would be no celebration, nor would there be next year, or the year after.

He took the Kudrinskaya Ring around the city center, his driving reflexes automatic, as his thoughts wandered back and forth from Uncle Gennadi to Mikhail. Betrayal seemed to be the order of the day. He felt as if he were a starving man looking through a window into a room of diners enjoying a banquet. He wanted to join them, desperately wanted to partake in their feast, but he knew that he did not have the price of admission; he would never have the price.

He slowed and stopped for a traffic light across from Kommuny Park. Lights had been strung up in the trees. It was ten below zero, but Gypsies were playing on the corner to a small crowd of men who passed around the vodka.

Valeri rolled down his window and listened to the gay, in some ways almost carefree music. Still there was an edge of sadness to the tune. A Russian could not escape it. Live and scratch, his grandmother used to tell him; when you're dead, the itching will stop. She had been very proud of her son, Valeri's father, but she used to delight the children with tales of his misbehavior as a boy. Lara was the one, though, who was forever trying to imitate their father's misdeeds, while Valeri stayed home and followed the straight and narrow path.

He had never known his grandfather, who had been killed while helping to put down the revolt of the sailors at the Kronstadt garrison in 1921. But the stories handed down about his role in the great Revolution, along with his son's exploits during the Second World War, served as an unbroken chain of proud history for the Kostikov family. "With history comes responsibility," Uncle Gennadi used to say. Valeri had never really understood what was meant by such a statement, until just now.

The light changed and he accelerated away from the music, rolling up his window as he turned off at the Leningradskaya Hotel, and parked a block away behind the Kazan Station. He turned off the headlights and the engine, and as the interior of the car turned into a deepfreeze he smoked a cigarette and watched the front of the yellow brick apartment building.

Komsomol Square behind him was busy, but finally this narrow side street had quieted for the night. In this neighborhood all the parties were inside. Elsewhere across the big city, however, it seemed as if half the population had turned restless and were driven to be outside. It was the same on May Day, which was an even larger holiday. But that was spring, when the parks and boulevards were naturally filled with people. This was winter, when it took more to get even the hardy Muscovites outside.

After a few minutes he flipped out his cigarette, got out of the car, and went the rest of the way on foot. A cat lay frozen at the side of the road, which was very rare because there were not many domestic animals in the city. In the old days such a waste of protein wouldn't have been allowed. The thought came unbidden to Valeri, and he shuddered.

He went across the street and entered the building. As before, the corridor was very cold and quiet. The stairs were in darkness. He had to slowly grope his way up to the third floor. This time the building smelled neutral. It was as if everyone had moved out. Only the dead man in the attic apartment remained in residence, and there was no need for him to boil his cabbage or light his stove.

Valeri stepped to the end of the corridor and went upstairs. He took the key out of his pocket and at the top tried the lock, but it was open. For a second or two he tried to imagine the significance of it. Bertonelli had admitted he was here. Which meant he had picked the lock and had not bothered to relock it.

No one was there. No one but Lipasov. Valeri took the gun out of his pocket and slowly pushed the door inward with his toe.

The room was intensely cold. Lipasov's body still lay beneath the blanket. Nothing had been disturbed.

Inside, Valeri pocketed his gun and closed the door. He closed the window and drew the curtains, then turned on the lamp. He could see his breath, and already his fingers were turning numb.

Promising himself that this would be the worst of it, he pulled the cover off Lipasov's body. The blood had all coagulated to a black mass, and then had frozen solid. Pieces of brown fuzz from the wool blanket stuck to the horrible wounds on Lipasov's face. Valeri's knees went weak for a moment. He had to avert his eyes and tell himself that the thing lying on the floor was not Viktor Ivanovich any more than the frozen creature outside on the street was a domestic cat. The quality that had made them what they had been was gone; it had been robbed from them by some terrible force.

Valeri tossed the blanket aside, then went to the bedstead, which he pulled apart—pillows, cushions, blanket, sheets—scattering the bedding all over the room as if there had been a great struggle. He yanked the wire out of the microphone they'd used to monitor the girl's movements, then tipped over the tape machine and amplifier, ripping off the reels, and with the butt of his gun he smashed the dials and knobs on the front panels. He tipped over a chair and knocked the table lamp onto the floor. The bulb, overheated in the frigid room, went out with a soft *pop*, plunging the attic into complete darkness.

Controlling an almost atavistic urge to flee the death chamber, Valeri stepped wide of where he knew Lipasov's body lay, yanked open the door, and stepped out, his stomach heaving, his bowels like water, and sweat beginning to pop out on his forehead. He left the door ajar and descended to the third-floor corridor.

A door opened and closed somewhere below. Valeri stiffened. Someone was on the stairs. But then he could hear they were going downstairs, not coming up. A minute later he heard the front door open and close, and once again the building was quiet.

As his heart began to return to normal, Valeri entered the apartment Nadia Burdine had occupied. He turned on the light, but remained with his back to the closed door as he let his eyes search the room.

He was missing something, had missed something the last time he'd been there. It was like the game of hide the thimble; the most successful hiding places were those out in the open. The obvious almost always seemed to be overlooked.

A cup and saucer lay upside down on the drainboard beside the sink. Two blankets were neatly folded on the end of the couch. The table was clean, the ashtray empty, the chairs pushed in. . . .

It came to him.

She had not been taken. There had been no struggle here. She had packed up her few things, had straightened up the apartment, and had left. Of her own volition.

Valeri looked up at the ceiling. Lipasov had to have heard

her preparations. Had to have heard her packing up and then leaving. Unless he was already dead. But then, who had killed him? And why hadn't they come for the girl? What else was he missing?

It was no longer possible, he told himself, to think that the girl had nothing to do with this business. Colonel Okulov had brought her here in secret and now she had vanished. Moscow was a big city, all of Russia so large, its vast empty regions were hard to envision in ordinary terms. But now she was cut off from her protector, and Valeri found that he genuinely cared. She had been set adrift. Where would she run? Where could she run?

Three days ago Larissa Okulov had told him about this apartment. Evidently, however, she had known nothing about Nadia, only that her husband was seeing another woman. Poetic justice, in a way, he thought. But that didn't seem to fit either; yet if she had known about Nadia, why hadn't someone come for the girl?

Valeri turned off the light and went back out into the corridor. Downstairs he stopped to listen at the old grandmother's door. From inside he thought he heard a radio or television playing. It sounded like American rock and roll. Perhaps the woman's hooligan son had returned from Odessa.

Outside, he hunched up his coat and hurried back to where he had parked his car. Bells sounded in the crisp night air down toward the Kremlin. It was eleven o'clock. A night to be out partying. Short of that, a night to be home, snug in bed. Yalta in the spring seemed like it belonged to another universe.

He crossed the parking lot on foot and entered the Kazan Station through a side door. The Volgograd train left at midnight every night except Sunday. Already the station was beginning to fill with passengers. At a public telephone he dialed 02, which was the emergency number for the police. After fifteen rings it was answered by a man who sounded angry that his evening was being disturbed.

"I want to report a murder in the Central East District, near the Kazan Station," Valeri said.

"What?"

"It's a man. He's been shot in the face. I think he's been dead for hours." Valeri gave the address. "He's in the attic apartment."

"Listen here, who is this? Where are you calling from?"

"Someone has been murdered. Aren't you going to do something about it?"

"Don't you know that it's a criminal offense to play a joke on the Militia?"

The Militia cooperated with the KGB in monitoring and running traces on telephone calls throughout the city. Their equipment was very good. They'd be tracing this call now.

"Maybe I'll call the KGB. I think he was one of theirs."

"You'd better give me your name."

Valeri hung up, and went back outside to his car. He started the engine and turned on the heater but left the lights off. From where he sat he was out of the way of traffic, but he had an unobstructed view of the apartment building three quarters of a block away. The Militia would be coming soon, followed by the coroner's unit. Once Lipasov's identity was established, Valeri's own department would be notified, and General Demin would be informed. He had no idea what might happen after that, but besides the eight-digit number, the missing girl was his only real lead.

He lit a cigarette as he waited, and then turned on his communications radio. Nothing came over the frequency, however, other than routine transmissions in code with grid references. They were surveillance operations in progress, some of which he recognized, others he did not.

Fully ten minutes after he had made his call, he heard the first sirens. A minute or so later a Militia car, its blue lights flashing, raced up from Komsomol Square, screamed past Valeri, and screeched to a halt in front of the apartment building. Two uniformed Militiamen got out and hurried inside. Moments later a second and third Militia car raced past Valeri.

It would take some time, Valeri had to keep telling himself. The Militia would have to go through its routines first. Telephone calls would be made, more units brought out, everyone in the apartment building questioned, especially the *babushka* on the ground floor, before General Demin would have the chance to understand the significance of the report.

The attic window was lit with a wavering yellow glow. Flashlights, Valeri figured, since the lamp had burned out. They would know now that the telephone call had not been a hoax. He could not get the vision of Lipasov's horribly mutilated face out of his mind's eye.

A dozen people had come out of the railroad station and stood at the edge of the parking area watching the commotion in front of the apartment building. Four uniformed Militiamen were busy pulling portable roadblock signs from the trunks of their cars and setting them up on the street on either side of the building. Four drunks stumbled up from Komsomol Square and joined the growing crowd from the station. No one noticed Valeri sitting in his car.

Other lights began coming on in the apartment building, including those in Nadia Burdine's apartment.

A four-door Zhiguli came around the corner, pulled up by the roadblocks, and two men in civilian clothes got out. The uniformed Militiamen on duty saluted, and the investigators entered the building.

By now they knew that Lipasov was KGB, and had been involved in a surveillance operation of someone in the apartment directly below the attic. They also knew that whoever had occupied the apartment was gone. If they were sharp, and the old grandmother was cooperating, they had also learned that Lipasov had not been alone. There had been others in and out of the apartment during the past thirty-six hours. By now there would be a lot of nervous people up there wondering just what they had stumbled into.

Very soon the calls would be starting.


More roadblocks were set up. Other Militia units arrived. The ambulance came around midnight, and was allowed through to the front door. Two attendants took a stretcher into the building, but by twelve-thirty they still had not emerged with Lipasov's body.


There were the self-assured Russians who ran the Soviet Union. And there were the Ukrainians, known as Little Russians, who were always trying to prove themselves for recognition.

Lipasov told Valeri a story about his father, a Ukrainian intellectual of great appetite for recognition in Moscow. The

old man had come to visit his son a few months after the
life-saving incident in the Dynamo Stadium pool.

At the university he presented a paper on prime integrals to
the Soviet Academy of Sciences. "Yes, Comrade Doctor,"
he was asked afterward, "but what about your son, a real
hero?"

At the plush restaurant in the National Hotel, where the old
man was hosted to a dinner by his peers, talk turned from
mathematics to the ideal of the Soviet man—one ready to risk
his life to save others.

Shopping at GUM, his son was recognized from the
newspaper photo.

The old man was clearly frustrated. He had come to Moscow for recognition for a lifetime of work, and was being
ignored.

"I should never have allowed you to learn how to swim,"
the old man had told his son at the train depot before he left.

Lipasov had smiled, knowing his father was only half
making a joke and needed something in return. "But then you
would only have your mathematics to be proud of. Now you
also have a son who is a hero."

It was enough. The elder Lipasov had returned home, a
man who had proved himself in Moscow!

A little after one in the morning one of the investigators in
civilian clothes hurried out of the building, jumped into his
car, and drove off.

"I have no friends," Nadia had told him the first time he
had laid eyes on her. He remembered her touch, soft and
delicate, when they had shaken hands.

The heater in Valeri's car wasn't very good. By three
o'clock he figured it had to be nearly twenty below zero
outside and not much warmer inside. He was numb with the
cold, his nose and ears ached, his fingers tingled. A small
dark blue Zhiguli came from the opposite direction and pulled
up politely before the roadblocks. Valeri sat forward and
scraped some frost off his windshield as he watched Shevchenko's tall, lank figure unfold from the little car. He was
carrying a package that he handed to one of the Militiamen,
then he stepped over one of the roadblocks and crossed the

street to the apartment building. Before he went inside he looked toward where Valeri was parked, but if he saw anything he gave no outward sign. The Militiaman took something out of the package, tipped it up to his mouth, then passed it to one of the others. Vodka.

It was logical that Mikhail was here, Valeri told himself. Lipasov had been identified, and undoubtedly they had tried to reach the deputy chief to no avail, so they had called his chief of staff. "Let it be so simple," Valeri sighed. He lit another cigarette. He had gone through nearly the whole pack and his throat was raw.

Another few minutes went by.

The front door of the apartment building opened and the two ambulance attendants came out carrying Lipasov's shrouded body on the stretcher. One of the Militiamen thoughtfully opened the rear door of the ambulance, and the stretcher was put inside.

Hope began to rise in Valeri's breast. Perhaps it was going to be simple. Lipasov's body found, Valeri's chief of staff claims it, and the investigation is over as far as concerns Militia.

It bothered Valeri that no one was closing the ambulance door.

Shevchenko emerged from the apartment building a minute or so later. He checked his watch, then went over to the ambulance where he spoke with the attendants and a couple of the Militiamen standing around.

It was obvious they were waiting for someone. Who? The coroner? But the body had already been moved.

A gray Mercedes came around the corner, its big square headlights flashing past Valeri as it moved sedately up the street. Its license plates were official; Valeri recognized that much. But they were not KGB. The Militiamen hurriedly removed the roadblocks, and the car came to a halt a couple of meters behind the ambulance. Two men in sheepskin coats and fur hats got out of the car.

Valeri closed his eyes for a moment, willing the scene to change. Willing Shevchenko away. "Go home, Mikhail," he said. When he opened his eyes Shevchenko was speaking earnestly with the two newcomers. One of the ambulance attendants pulled the stretcher halfway out and the other drew back the sheet. Shevchenko looked away, but the other two didn't. One of them took out a flashlight and shined it on Lipasov's face.

Who were they? Valeri memorized the license plate number, though he didn't think it would do him much good. These two probably worked for Okulov. No one else could possibly be interested in the case. If they were smart, the car would be reported stolen. If they weren't so sharp, it would be a pool-issue car, the records for tonight lost. If they were arrogant, it wouldn't matter, because Valeri had already been warned.

Lipasov's body was shoved back into the ambulance, and the rear doors finally closed. One of the men took Shevchenko's arm and led him a few steps away. They seemed to be arguing about something. A moment later the other one joined them, made a gesture, and Shevchenko stepped back. The first one jabbed his gloved finger into Shevchenko's chest, then abruptly turned on his heel and went back to the Mercedes. The other one said something else to Shevchenko, then joined his companion.

The Mercedes took off around the ambulance and passed through the far set of roadblocks. Unable to follow that way, Valeri turned around and raced a block and a half to the Yaroslavsky Station. He pulled up and doused his lights. Thirty seconds later the Mercedes came down Rusakovskaya at a high rate of speed, ignoring the red light at Pereyaslavskaya Boulevard.

Two big trucks lumbered across the intersection before Valeri was able to follow. He kept a respectful distance behind. It would be no trouble recognizing the German car's taillights. He did not want them to know that they were being followed.

They turned west on the ring at the Leningradskaya Hotel, the same way Valeri had come from his office. For an insane moment he almost suspected they were going to the Warehouse where they would meet with General Demin. But they turned north finally on Leningradsky Prospekt, passing the Byelorussia Station, and farther out, the Hippodrome. For a bit he began to think they were heading out to the burned remains of the Novikov *dacha*. Perhaps it wasn't a dead end after all.

In the end, however, he finally realized where they were headed, and he cursed himself for his stupidity. He just hoped they were wrong, because he didn't know what he might have to do if they found Nadia.

The apartment building was white, and very tall, just as Larissa Okulov had described it, rising at least twenty stories from a low, birch-covered hill. Only a few lights were on, making a loose mosaic pattern in the apartment windows. There weren't very many cars in front. It was a new building. Earth-moving equipment, shrouded by snow, some of it covered with canvas tarpaulins, was parked in the back. When Lipasov had checked out this place, he had reported that the apartment in Colonel Okulov's name was empty of furniture and appliances. Valeri had never suspected Nadia would run there.

Traffic had thinned out. For the moment nothing moved on the highway. To the west an Ilyushin jet roared in for a landing at Frunze Central Airfield. The Mercedes pulled into the apartment building's driveway and swung around to the back. Both men got out and went inside.

Valeri flipped off his headlights and drifted to a stop behind a large front-end loader, its rear wheels towering above his car. He got out, hurried the rest of the way across the deeply rutted, unpaved parking lot, and entered the building by the front door.

A half-dozen steel fire doors were stacked against the stairs, chained to the railing. A large jagged hole had been chiseled into the concrete wall exposing a jumble of electrical wiring. No one had bothered to sweep up the debris that included several pieces of rusted metal pipe, some waxed paper, and three empty vodka bottles as well as hunks of concrete and dust from the hole.

The elevator was stopped on the eighteenth floor. Colonel Okulov's apartment was on the sixth. The two men had apparently taken the back stairs up. Inside, Valeri stopped a moment to listen, but the building was quiet. He started up. The first- and second-floor landings were choked with bags and boxes of garbage, some of it spilling down the stairs. The third-floor landing was clean. None of the fire doors were in place. He heard music playing and someone laughing from one of the apartments down the broad, well-lit corridor. The walls and ceiling had been freshly painted. The paint-splattered drop cloths were still lying on the floor that had already been carpeted.

By the time Valeri reached the sixth-floor landing, he was winded. This corridor was darker than the others, the floor bare concrete, the walls unpainted plaster. For a moment or two he hung back within the stairwell until his eyes grew accustomed to the dim light.

Just as he started out, the two men from the Mercedes emerged from the stairwell at the opposite end of the corridor, and Valeri stepped back. They were talking, their voices soft and indistinct. He could not make out their words. At an apartment halfway up the corridor they stopped. One of them put his ear to the door, listened a moment, then straightened up and shook his head. They both were very large men, bulky in their sheepskin coats. One of them took something out of his pocket and bent down to the lock. The other one stepped back and pulled a gun out of his coat pocket.

The first man was very good at his job; he had the lock picked in under ten seconds. He straightened up, pocketed his tool, and pulled out his gun. Then he stepped to one side, glanced at his partner, and carefully eased the door open.

Nothing happened for several seconds. Valeri could see that the apartment was dark. These two obviously had a great deal of respect for whoever they thought was inside. It came to him that they suspected whoever was here had murdered Lipasov. He tried to think that out. Nadia had not been taken. Was it possible she had a gun in her purse? Colonel Okulov could have given it to her for protection. Lipasov would not have expected any danger from her. He would have had no reason to cry out. He would have heard her coming up the stairs, opened the door for her, and she could have shot him at point-blank range. Afterward she erased the tape, then packed her things and left. Siberians were a harsh people, but she had seemed so delicate, so lost. So desperate that her colonel had not come back for her?

The first man stepped into the apartment. A second or two later the other man went inside.

Turn around and leave, a voice in Valeri's head told him. Stay out of it. If she had killed Lipasov so brutally, she deserved no one's help. But the answer was not that simple for him. He could not get Bertonelli's warning out of his mind, that the Americans, whoever they were, would soon be eliminated. That knowledge could have driven her to kill. Yet

Valeri could not fathom what she had to do with Americans. She was Siberian.

A soft popping noise came from the apartment, a man grunted in pain, and two shots were fired from an unsilenced gun, the noise shockingly loud in the corridor.

Valeri pulled out his Beretta and thumbed the safety off as he raced down the corridor.

One of the men stumbled out of the apartment, blood soaking through a black hole in his coat just below his right collarbone. He looked up, spotted Valeri, and started to bring his gun around.

"No!" Valeri shouted. He fired once, his shot catching the man in the chest, driving him backward, his body bouncing heavily off the wall.

"Leonid?" the man inside the apartment called out sharply in alarm.

Valeri was in the doorway. The man was looking over his shoulder, his dark pig eyes narrowed. Nadia lay in a bundle at his feet, her dress hiked halfway up her thighs, one shoe half off, a big silenced Makarov just beyond her outstretched hand. Blood oozed from a long streak at the side of her head.

"Get out of here, Major," the man said. "Before it is too late."

Valeri's gun hand shook. This one knew him. "Put your gun down and step away from the girl."

The man seemed to consider it. "She killed your surveillance man in the attic apartment."

"Put down your gun . . ." Valeri started to demand again, when the man spun around, bringing his gun up. Valeri fired twice, the first shot catching the man in the shoulder, shoving him off-balance, and the second catching him at the base of his skull just behind his left ear, blood pouring out of the wound as if his head had exploded as he went down.

Valeri dropped down beside the girl, who was starting to come around. He was surprised that his mind was so clear, yet it seemed as if he were in a dream. In less than seventy-two hours he had killed three men, had met with an American spy, had one of his own people shot out from under him, had defied his superior officer and a high-ranking party official, and had lost his wife. Valeri examined Nadia's head wound. The bullet had merely grazed her scalp. She had been lucky. Her eyes fluttered open, finally focused on his face, and she pushed herself up with surprising strength. Valeri grabbed her gun and pocketed it along with his own.

"Can you stand?" he asked. "We have to get out of here before the Militia arrives."

"What are you doing here . . ." she started to ask, but then she spotted the dead man, and she shuddered. "Stupid," she said.

Valeri helped her to her feet, where she swayed a moment, but then she stood on her own.

"Where are your things?"

"Where are you taking me?"

"Someplace safe. Your things. We haven't got much time."

"There," she said, pointing to the corner.

Her few belongings were heaped in a pile. She put on her shoe and he helped her on with her threadbare cloth coat and wool scarf, then picked up her purse and a net bag that held her other clothes and a few toiletry items.

"Is there anything else?"

"What are you expecting, a fur coat, maybe some furniture?"

She was weak. She stumbled at the door. Valeri took her arm and led her out of the apartment. She looked down at the other dead man.

"Why did you do this?" she asked. She looked up at Valeri.

"I know about the American prisoners."

"What prisoners?" she asked.

Valeri led her to the end of the corridor and they started down the stairs. The blood had coagulated on the side of her head, plastering her dark hair against her neck. Twice more on the way down she stumbled and nearly fell. By the time they reached the bottom, Valeri was half carrying her, his arm around her tiny waist. He felt as though he could crush her bones with only a slight pressure.

They crossed the narrow entry vestibule, and outside she was seized with a bout of shivering, her teeth chattering. He literally dragged her the last twenty meters to his car.

Fainna was half asleep when she answered the telephone, but she woke up as soon as she realized who was calling.

"I need your help. But it will be very dangerous," Valeri said. Nadia was hunched up in the car; her color was bad and she could not stop shaking.

"What's wrong? What can I do?"

He hesitated. He could not take her to his apartment. After tonight it would almost certainly be under surveillance. Nor could he take her back to the attic apartment, and the room at the Rossiya was definitely out. There was nowhere else.

"I can't explain on the phone, but I have to bring someone to stay at your apartment for tonight at least."

"Of course," Fainna said instantly. "Who is it?"

"Are you alone?"

"Yes," Fainna said in a small voice. "What's wrong? Are you in trouble?"

"Yes."

"Oh, God," she said. "Are you hurt?"

"No, but she is," Valeri said, and he felt terrible.

Valeri carried the girl into Fainna's apartment and laid her down on the bed.

"What happened to her?" Fainna brushed Valeri aside and looked at the wound on the side of Nadia's head.

"She was shot."

Fainna looked up, her lips compressed. "Who shot her?"

"I don't know. But there were two of them, and they worked for someone very important in the party."

"Are they still after her? Will they come here?"

"They're dead. I killed them. But there will be others."

Fainna was dressed in a heavy robe, her hair was pinned up, she wore nothing on her feet. A very stolid look came into her eyes. "I don't ever want to know how this came to happen. Just tell me that this is worthwhile, Valeri. That you are right and they are wrong."

"I don't know. But I'm not a traitor. This is very important."

"Get out of here, then," she said. "There's still some cognac left."

In the kitchen Valeri took down the cognac and a glass, poured himself some, then sat down at the small table. He hadn't bothered to take off his coat. The events of the past days began to catch up with him and he hung his head in weariness, cradling the drink in his hands, warming the liquor.

Nadia cried out in the bedroom. Valeri looked up. He heard Fainna's voice, soft, soothing; reassuring the girl that everything would be all right. Then he heard water running in the tub.

The number and the girl. The girl and the number. They intertwined like dancers in an improbable ballet. Who was the choreographer? Where was the score? The two men from the Mercedes had known him, perhaps had expected him. His mind was spinning.

After a while Fainna came back into the kitchen. She helped him off with his coat.

"Have you eaten? Are you hungry?"

Valeri looked up. "How is she?"

"She's sleeping," Fainna said, her hands on her hips. "What next?"

"Have you someplace to go?"

"You want me to leave?"

"I had nowhere else to take her. But it is very dangerous. It would be better if you weren't here."

"They're going to come after her?"

"And me."

Fainna thought it out. "If I left now, it would create suspicion. I'll leave in the morning. There is plenty of food in the cupboards. I'll leave the key for the heater oil. The tank is in the basement. But you'll have to get her some clothes. Nothing I have would fit her."

Valeri nodded. He was beginning to come apart.

"Now, are you hungry?"

"I don't think so. Just tired." Valeri dragged himself to his feet.

"She's in the bed. You and I are going to have to share the couch."

Valeri had no idea what time it was. Fainna did not awaken when he got up. He pushed open the bedroom door and looked in. Nadia was awake. Tears rolled down her cheeks.

"I'm sorry," Valeri said softly, but he had no idea what he meant.

## 15

At eight in the morning Valeri went into the kitchen. Fainna had made tea and had laid out a plate of bread with butter and jam.

"She's still asleep?" he asked.

"Yes. What is her name? Do you know?"

"Nadia Burdine." Valeri sat down at the table. "She's Siberian, I think."

Fainna poured him a cup of tea. "I knew she was a foreigner. But she is very pretty for a Siberian."

"There's nothing to her. It looks as if she's been starving."

Fainna stared at him for a moment. She was dressed to go out, wool slacks and a bulky sweater. Her boots were waiting with her coat and a small overnight bag by the door. "She's very young, Valeri. Maybe twenty-one."

"How do you know that?" He thought she had looked at the girl's internal passport.

Fainna shrugged. "Only a man could ask such a question." She put the teapot down. "At any rate, you'll have her all to yourself. I'm staying with a friend today and tonight. Tomorrow at work you can let me know how long this is to go on."

She was jealous. But Valeri had no idea what to say to her.

"There is broth in the refrigerator. And eggs and more butter. If she has been starving, she'll have to go slow at first. Perhaps she should be in a hospital."

"They would arrest her."

"It might be for the best."

Valeri shook his head.

"Then be very careful, Valerik."

In the small living room, Fainna pulled on her boots, and

210

put on her coat and rabbit fur hat. She didn't look back as she went out. For a long time Valeri remained in the kitchen doorway, listening to the sounds of the apartment building, and the traffic outside on busy Entuziastov Road. Anyone else would be reporting him to General Demin. But not Fainna. Sad for her, she was in love with him, and she knew it could never work.

He went to the bedroom. Nadia was still sleeping, her slight figure bundled up beneath the covers, her dark hair spilling over the pillow. Valeri had expected a bandage, but there wasn't one. A little blood had leaked down across her ear and cheek from her hairline. Her skin was very pale by contrast to the blood.

What next, he asked himself. He had Okulov's second clue, but it wouldn't do him any good unless she cooperated with him. Despite her frailty, Valeri suspected she was a tough little girl. If she had actually killed Lipasov, she was heartless, too. Because of her he had killed two men. Last night didn't seem real to him.

Nadia stirred in the bed. Valeri went back into the kitchen where he heated up the broth Fainna had left, and then scrambled an egg and buttered a piece of bread. When he brought it in to her, she was sitting up, Fainna's flannel nightshirt hanging off her shoulder like a sack.

"I dreamed someone undressed me, bathed me, and then put me to bed," she said, hungrily attacking the food. "Was it you?" She looked up, her mouth full.

Valeri brought a chair over to the bed and sat down. "It was Fainna."

"Your wife?"

"A friend."

Nadia looked serious. "Do you have a wife?"

"Tell me about the man in the attic apartment."

"Your apartment?"

"Why did you kill him?"

Her eyes opened round, the picture of innocence. "I don't know what you're talking about, Valeri Kostikov. What man?"

Valeri was inexplicably pleased that she remembered his name.

"Tell me about yourself, then."

She had already finished the egg, and she started on the cup of broth and the bread. "What about me? I am just a simple Siberian from Yakutsk."

"Here in Moscow for the Winter Festival."

She smiled. "Even we Siberians like to have a little fun once in a while, you know."

"There is no record of you in Yakutsk."

"It is a big place."

"Nor does the Militia here in Moscow have any record of your arrival."

"I have their stamp in my passport—"

"Of which they have no record."

She had the piece of buttered bread in her hand. She gestured at Valeri with it. "Then I am to be indicted for the inefficiency of your Moscow police?" She laughed disdainfully. "Let me tell you about inefficiency. Have you heard the story about the greedy monkey who tried to get the bananas out of the narrow-necked jar? He could get his hand inside, but with the bananas, his fist was too big to get out. And he didn't know what to do. He was too stupid to think of another way."

"I've heard it."

She seemed surprised. "Then you know about inefficiency: it's the same as stupidity," she said as if she'd made a salient point. She looked at him over the rim of her cup. "But I don't know who you are. Militia because of my passport?"

"KGB. Second Chief Directorate."

"Of course," she said. "Then why haven't you arrested me?"

"I want to know why you killed my friend in the attic apartment. I want to know about Colonel Okulov. I want to know about the Americans. And I want to know about a number: one-seven-five-seven-three-three-six-zero."

"I don't know what you're talking about."

"Who were the two men last night, and why were they trying to kill you?"

"They were drunk. They were trying to rape me."

"What were you doing in that apartment?"

"It was empty. No one lived there. I didn't think anyone would mind."

"Why did you move out of your apartment by the Kazan Station?"

"I was tired of the old grandmother. She was getting on my nerves."

"Where is your family?"

"I have no family."

"Where are the rest of your things?"

"Things?" she cried, throwing up her hands. "Does everyone have to have some enormous pile of things? You ought to see my dog sled."

Valeri just looked at her. He didn't know if he wanted to laugh or cry. He thought about taking her shoulders and giving her a big shake until she came out with the truth.

"I would very much like to see that," he said.

She laughed again.

"So what happens now, Nadia?"

Her left eyebrow rose.

"I meant now that Colonel Okulov is dead, and no one was at the number you tried to call from the telephone in the Kazan Station—and especially now that they're trying to silence you. What now? Will you return to Yakutsk?"

"What do you want from me?"

"The truth."

"You wouldn't know the truth if it came up and bit you on the nose."

"Try me."

She looked away. "Where are my clothes?"

"They're not fit to wear. I'll get you some more."

"It's not necessary."

"*What have you to do with those American prisoners?*" Valeri said in English.

"What?" she asked.

"I wondered if you spoke English."

She shook her head. She put the cup down. "Do you have a cigarette?"

Valeri lit one and handed it to her. She sat back, her head against the wall, took a deep drag, and blew the smoke out of her nose. Valeri had never seen anyone but a Frenchman do that. It was somehow sensual. Disturbing to him.

"How do you feel now?" he asked.

"Better."

Valeri got up and put the chair back against the wall beside the bureau. Nadia watched him but said nothing. He thought he could get to her, but he hadn't. Perhaps it was impossible with her. Perhaps she would be gone when he got back. he couldn't understand who she was, or what she was doing here.

"Colonel Okulov had some very powerful enemies who want you dead. They also want to kill all the Americans and destroy their bodies. I'm going to try to stop that, with or without your help."

"I don't know what you're talking about."

"No one knows you're here. If you stay put you might be safe. I'll be back in a few hours."

In the living room Valeri picked up the telephone, unscrewed the mouthpiece, and took out the microphone, which he dropped in his pocket. Then he screwed the mouthpiece back on and hung up the telephone. She would not be able to make any calls.

The streets were nearly deserted when Valeri drove across town. He had had a lot of trouble starting his car, and it did not warm up until well past Red Square as he turned onto the broad Bolshaya Pirogovskaya Street. A few people were lined up in front of the Tolstoy Museum, their breath hanging like white fog in the very still air. To the west a few clouds were beginning to build. By night they would have snow again, but it meant the temperatures would moderate. The huge Luzhniki Sports Center was busy. Circus wagons were parked in long rows outside the Great Stadium in which a hundred thousand spectators could watch a soccer game. The circus didn't start until one o'clock, but already there were a lot of people wandering around.

His thoughts were on the girl, who had not cooperated at all. He half doubted that she would still be at Fainna's apartment when he returned. They'd find her if she tried to run. He could only hope that she understood that.

There was a little traffic on the river as he crossed the Komsomolsky Bridge and continued the last few blocks toward his apartment. Chief Secretary Okulov was going to have two choices to consider with the death of his two men. He would have to suspect that either Bertonelli or Valeri had killed them. Bertonelli would be his easiest choice. Once it was established who really did it, however, and ballistics would take care of that, Okulov would understand that Valeri knew more of what really was going on than he had admitted last night at the Demins'.

Valeri parked his car a block and a half from his apartment and went the rest of the way on foot. This was an area of fairly new and well-tended buildings. General Demin's influence had put him and Tanya at the head of the list for their apartment a couple of years ago.

A yellow Moskva station wagon was parked in front of Valeri's building, the engine running. Two men sat in the car, obviously waiting. The plates were the same series as the Mercedes's.

Valeri backed away and returned to his car. Okulov had already made his decision. The question was, had they been ordered to kill him, or simply arrest him?

Sasha Shevchenko, dressed in a dirty quilted robe, felt boots on her feet, the baby Tonia, their only girl, on her hip, came to the door.

The apartment looked like a disaster area, as it almost always did. The only time there seemed to be any order was when they had guests for dinner. And then only the living room was reasonably neat.

"Valerik," she said tiredly. "Mischa isn't here."

"May I come in?"

"Sure," she said, sighing. "Do you want some tea?" She turned back into the apartment, and Valeri followed her inside. Nika, their three-year-old boy, screamed something from one of the back rooms, and Sasha shouted for him to keep quiet.

"I'll get the pot," Valeri said.

She smiled gratefully at him. "Be right back," she said, and she disappeared toward a bedroom.

The kitchen was a pigsty, dirty dishes stacked everywhere, butter spread on the back of one of the chairs, a bowl of baby cereal upside down on the floor beneath the highchair, and a half bottle of milk getting warm on top of the refrigerator.

Valeri put on the teapot, put the milk away, and rinsed out a couple of cups. He could hear Sasha and the boy yelling at each other. The Shevchenko children weren't particularly bad; in school they did very well, according to Mikhail. It was just that they were a boisterous family. At home they did everything at the top of their lungs, and they were always spilling or breaking something.

Valeri took off his hat and coat, laying them on a reasonably clean chair. When the water was ready he brewed the tea, put three spoons of sugar in Sasha's cup, and brought it back into the living room.

She was curled up on the couch, her hairy legs folded beneath her. She didn't have the baby. "Tonia didn't sleep well all night. Maybe she'll do us a favor and drop off now."

"Where's Mikhail, and the rest of the kids?" Valeri asked, handing her her tea.

"Thanks," she said. "They went early to the circus. The boys wanted to meet some of the clowns. Mischa knows everyone down there. He's been promising for weeks, and thank God they took him up on it."

Valeri sat down across from her with his tea. Big sheets of plastic had been taped up over the windows to conserve heat. Water had condensed on the inner surfaces, and had frozen in pretty patterns. Light came in, but you couldn't see out very clearly.

"I'd like to talk to him, Sasha. This morning. Do you know exactly where he'll be?"

"I don't know," she said tiredly.

"Did he mention a name? Anything? Perhaps he was going to drop by the office?"

She shook her head. "Who knows?" But then she brightened. "Ovakimyan."

"Who?"

"His first name is Gaik, or something like that. He was here two days ago. He is a clown. Mischa probably took the children to see him. But I don't know where." She smiled faintly. "The children liked him. That's why I remembered."

The baby cried out, but Sasha didn't seem to hear. She was obviously very tired, but Valeri thought she was worried about something as well. She was having a hard time looking him in the eye.

"What is it, Sasha? What's the trouble?"

"I need a vacation, and here it is with winter just getting started."

"Mikhail went out last night. Very late. Did he tell you what happened?"

"No," she said softly.

"He didn't tell you about Viktor Ivanovich?"

She shook her head again, then raised the tea mug to her lips. "It's good," she said. "Mischa loves you like a brother."

"Someone killed Viktor."

"They think you are involved, Valerik. But Mischa doesn't believe it."

"He's right," Valeri said. "Has he spoken with General Demin?"

"Three times. It's driving him crazy. He doesn't know what to do." She looked up. "Go find him. Talk to him. He really looks up to you."

"Has anyone been here to see him?"

"No one but Ovakimyan the clown." Her mood darkened. "He's a good man. But the children weigh him down sometimes. You know we have to deal with the black market almost every day just to feed the babies. It's awful. He worries about his career. Without the KGB nothing would be possible." She looked up around the apartment. "Not even this. But we don't have any real friends."

"He'll be all right, Sasha."

Tears began to leak out of her big brown eyes.

"Where did it go wrong, Valerik?" she lamented. "Last year it wasn't like this. Remember the summer on the river? Remember Winter Festival at General Demin's? I was never so proud. The children played on the ice. The general bought them skates. Six pairs, and a sleigh for me to use."

Valeri remembered. "Mischa got drunk."

"Me being pregnant didn't stop me from making a pass at you."

"I was flattered."

"Tanya wasn't."

They laughed sadly. "Are you going to be all right here?"

"What can happen to me, Valerik? I'm a mother."

Heartbreak, Valeri thought. He put down his cup and got up. In the kitchen he put on his coat and hat. Nika started to scream and the baby began to cry. By the time Valeri got back into the living room, Sasha had gone to check on the children. He let himself out.


The circus, to the Russian way of thinking, was Disney World, cable TV, and Hollywood all wrapped up into one. It represented the great fantasy escape from a humdrum world in which personal choice and individualism were legislated out of public existence. The *kollektiv* might put up the high wire or the trapeze, but it still was the individual who faced the dangerous heights or the uncertain great cats; and it was still the individual who put on the clown face and made the children laugh. The Russian spirit, not yet jaded with entertainment overkill, took this ideal to its heart. The circus knew no season; outdoors in the summer, inside during the winter, the bears and the clowns and the acrobats entertained an appreciative audience. The circus had its superstars.

Valeri showed his identification at the Luzhniki service gate to an old Gypsy woman playing records in a small wooden hut. She looked to be a hundred years old.

"Where can I find Gaik Ovakimyan the clown?"

She leaned out the window, grinned toothlessly, and pointed across the vast parking lot toward a large display of the intertwined Olympic circles, beyond which were dozens of gaudily painted aluminum trailers.

"He'll have an audience, you can be sure of that, comrade," she cackled.

She reminded Valeri of the witch in *Hansel und Gretel*. He drove across the parking lot, under the gate, and parked beside a huge truck filled with steaming manure and hay. Two swarthy Gypsies in hipboots were standing atop the pile, shoveling the muck into the corners. They were in shirtsleeves despite the fact that it was still well below zero. One of them called down something to Valeri. He waved up at them, and headed back toward the trailers.

There were a lot of people milling about. A half-dozen old men stood around a steel barrel in which trash was being burned. A young girl in nothing more than leotards and an open sheepskin vest was performing magic tricks with large complicated twists of stainless steel rod. Her nipples were hard because of the cold. None of the old men even pretended to pay attention to her magic, but when she passed the hat they were generous.

Two young girls were selling spiced vodka in gaily painted porcelain cups from an open window of one of the trailers.

At another, an old woman held a young man's hand and, much to the boy's chagrin, was earnestly reading his palm at the top of her voice to the delight of the dozens or so onlookers.

At still another trailer, a brisk business was taking place with meat pies and *kvas*.

A corrugated plastic roof had been thrown between a dozen trailers along one lane. Valeri wandered down this arcade at which Gypsies were selling everything from American cigarettes to *genuine* diamonds and sable-lined boots, mittens, and hats.

Shevchenko stood drinking a vodka at the last trailer as he watched his two oldest sons trying to shoot tin ducks with .22 rifles in a shooting gallery. Each shot pinged like the clink of milk bottles on a cold winter's morning. The other children were eating big oranges, the juice running down their coat sleeves. There was no sign of a clown.

Valeri hung back and watched his old friend in profile. His trousers were unpressed and the cuffs were wet from the snow. He was a slob, but he was a man with a very large heart.

Shevchenko turned, finally, and spotted Valeri. For just an instant he looked frightened, but then he smiled. It was enough, however, for Valeri to realize that his suspicions were correct.

"It's a little early to be drinking, isn't it?" Valeri said good-naturedly. The boys gathered around him, jumping up and down and shouting his name. He gave them some money and they all raced down the arcade to where cotton candy was being sold at a small stand.

"You spoil them, Valerik," Shevchenko said.

"That's what uncles are for."

"Where were you? I tried to telephone."

"I spoke with Sasha. She said you were called out last night. Anything I should know about?"

Shevchenko looked worn out, frightened now, and very guilty. Like Sasha he was having a hard time looking Valeri in the eye.

"She told me General Demin has called you several times."

"He was trying to find you."

"Tanya and I were at his apartment last night for dinner."

"I know—" Shevchenko started to say, but he cut himself off.

"What's happening, Mikhail? What did General Demin want?"

"Like I said, he wanted to find you. He wants to know how our investigation of Bertonelli is coming along. He's very worried about you."

"And what did you tell him?"

"The truth," Shevchenko said defensively.

"What truth?"

"Call him, Valerik. Go see him. Talk to him. He is a good man. He can help you."

"But?" Valeri asked.

Shevchenko looked away. "Fuck," he said, and he shook his head. "He can't help you, none of us can unless you want it. General Demin thinks you should go out to see your father. Take a vacation. Both you and Tanya."

"What happens in the meantime?"

"We'll take care of Bertonelli. Listen, the man is the devil. He turned Colonel Okulov, and now he's got a new target."

"Me?"

"Everyone can see it but you."

"Do you believe that?"

"I don't know what to believe anymore. But he killed Viktor Ivanovich. You knew, but you didn't do a thing about it. Why, Valerik? He was a good man. Our friend."

"What if I tell you that Bertonelli didn't kill him."

"Who, then?"

"Would you go to General Demin with it, Mikhail? Would you report our conversation?"

"He's our general," Shevchenko said softly, appealing to Valeri. He turned abruptly, stepped across to the trailer at which vodka was being sold, and bought himself another. Valeri lit a cigarette. The Shevchenko children had disappeared around the end of the arcade toward where the animals were in cages.

"Call him," Shevchenko said, returning.

"Did he offer you a promotion? My job?"

Shevchenko stepped back, stung by the accusation. But Valeri could see that it was the truth. Shevchenko wore his emotions on his sleeve.

"Someone is watching my apartment, you know."

"It's no one from our department."

"They work for Chief Secretary Okulov—the colonel's brother. The same as the two from the Mercedes last night."

Again Shevchenko was shocked. "You were there?"

"I saw you. But Bertonelli didn't kill poor Viktor."

"Who was he watching in the apartment below?"

Valeri thought about Votrin, who at this moment was the weak link, even if the old grandmother hadn't told them. Votrin knew that Lipasov was watching the girl. Evidently no one had gotten to him yet. That wouldn't last, however.

Tomorrow at the office it would come out, if not sooner. He was definitely running out of time. Now it all depended upon the girl, and Bertonelli's discovery of what the number meant.

"I'm going to need your help, Mikhail."

"Anything."

"I'm not Bertonelli's target. Something else is going on here."

Shevchenko started to protest, but Valeri held him off.

"I need twenty-four hours."

"I don't know."

"Enjoy the circus this afternoon, and then go home to Sasha. Forget I was here."

"What if he asks me? Directly?"

"Lie."

"I don't know if I can do that, Valerik," Shevchenko said softly.

The children were coming back.

"Twenty-four hours, Mikhail. It's all I ask," Valeri said. "Tomorrow at the office I'll explain everything. I promise you."

Shevchenko nodded.

"It'll turn out all right." Valeri turned and left, waving good-bye to the children as he hurried around the corner.

He wasn't able to return to his apartment and no stores were open on Sunday, so he was unable to get the girl any clothes. When he got back to Fainna's, Nadia was up. She had put on her wool dress, and had washed out her other things, hanging them in the bathroom.

"You took the telephone apart," she said. "What are you afraid of?"

"Who did you try to call from the Kazan Station? Colonel Okulov?"

"I don't know who you're talking about."

Valeri had tossed his coat over the couch. He took the telephone transmitter from his pocket and put it back in the telephone handset.

"There. The telephone is fixed. If you want to call someone, go ahead."

"I don't know anyone in Moscow."

Valeri shrugged. "Then call your friends in Yakutsk."

"They don't have telephones."

"We can send them a telegram. They're probably worried about you."

She shrugged, imitating his gesture.

"The thing I don't understand is your connection with the American prisoners. If I knew that, I might be able to understand why you don't care."

"You don't know anything," she said with the first spark of emotion he had seen.

Valeri went into the kitchen where he made them some tea. He poured a little cognac in his cup. Cigarettes and alcohol seemed to be all that were keeping him going.

Nadia stood in the doorway, resting her weight on one leg, her hip and shoulder against the wall. The pose seemed to be a calculated insolence.

"I'm sure when ballistics makes its report we'll discover that my friend was killed with a silenced Makarov."

"Those men who tried to rape me planted the gun."

"Then they must have killed my friend," Valeri said. "Now we're getting somewhere."

She sipped her tea.

"Of course, that still leaves us with a big question. Why did they come after you in a deserted apartment?"

"They must have followed me."

"*I* followed *them*, remember? If you are going to lie to me, at least keep your lies straight. Don't contradict yourself."

"I don't care if you believe me or not."

"I don't," Valeri said, smiling. "But let's talk about Colonel Okulov for a moment."

"Who?"

"Actually, you know, you should really hate me. My department is in charge of watching American spies here in Moscow. Wednesday night we followed an American CIA agent to a meeting at the Moscow zoo with the colonel. No one had told me a thing about it. When I went inside to arrest them, Colonel Okulov actually pulled out a gun and tried to shoot me. But, unfortunately, I had the element of surprise and I killed him instead."

Her eyes were bright.

"And the American got away."

"Why tell me this?"

"Ah, the point is, Nadia, that I felt very bad about shooting one of my own people. so I went to his wife to apologize.

But you know, she didn't seem to care. It was then that she told me about his two apartments. You know, the one behind the Kazan Station where you and I first met, and then the other one, where I saved your life. Quite a coincidence, wouldn't you say?''

''Why did you bother?'' she asked, her voice very soft.

''Actually, I don't know. Now my very best friend and chief of staff thinks I'm crazy. My own general thinks I am a traitor, and Colonel Okulov's brother—who is very big in the party—wants me dead.''

''Why should I believe you anyway?'' she flared.

''Why would I lie to you?''

Nadia fried them some potatoes and onions which they ate with sour cream, bread and butter, and coffee. If they were going to have supper tonight, Valeri figured he would have to go out and shop for more food. Fainna's larder was getting bare.

''Colonel Okulov went through a lot of trouble to get you here. The KGB has no record of you in Yakutsk, and when I checked with Moscow Militia they had no record of your entry. They wanted to turn your name and description over to Special Investigations.''

''And they're looking for me now?''

''No. I stopped them. But it won't last long, of course. Colonel Okulov's brother knows you're in Moscow and he knows that I killed his men.''

She looked up from her food. Valeri was struck again how like a startled doe she seemed. She would fit naturally in the broad, empty expanses of Siberia, he decided.

''I don't know how long either of us can hold out, here. My people want me dead, and Bertonelli's people don't believe him.''

''Who is Bertonelli?'' she asked.

''An American.''

She wanted to ask him more. He could see it in her eyes, in the set of her shoulders, in the way she held herself erect. For the first time Valeri thought he was getting to her.

''Bertonelli was Colonel Okulov's contact. The one at the zoo.''

Nadia held her silence.

''Colonel Okulov brought two proofs of the existence of

the American prisoners. One was the number, and the other was you. Unfortunately he never had the chance to give them to the American. I got there too soon.''

Nadia sagged. Her eyes closed, and tears began to leak from beneath the lids.

"Can you at least tell me what the number means?''

She pushed away her plate and got up.

"How many Americans are being held prisoner?''

She left the kitchen. Valeri got up and followed her into the bedroom where she lay down on the bed, her back to him.

"They're in Siberia, somewhere in Yakut,'' he said. "What is your relationship to them? Are you the gulag secretary? Perhaps your father is a camp supplier and you know about it? How did you make contact with Colonel Okulov in the first place? What was he to you?''

Nadia curled up in a fetal ball and cried silently.

"What did he tell you? What did he promise you?'' Valeri was looking for the bridge to cross the gap between them. He sensed that she was very close to breaking down and telling him everything.

He sat on the edge of the bed and touched her shoulder. She didn't respond.

"I spoke with Bertonelli. I gave him the number, but I didn't tell him about you. I don't know about you.''

"Why should I believe you?'' she asked, her voice muffled.

"Colonel Okulov told him that if anything went wrong, anything at all, the Americans would be killed, their bodies destroyed.''

"Go away,'' she cried.

"I don't want that to happen.''

She was silent.

"Nadia?'' He wanted to hold her.

## 16

The Militia guards watching the front of the U.S. embassy stamped their feet and clapped their gloved hands together against the cold as they walked back and forth. What little traffic there was mostly went in. Very few people came out.

Valeri's problem was one of conception and understanding. Away from the girl he was able to put a blank face on her body. In that way he could conceive of her climbing the stairs to the attic apartment. He could see Lipasov opening the door; poor, unsuspecting Lipasov who had shaken with the anticipation of arresting Bertonelli certainly had been surprised by her visit, but he could not have been alarmed. Curious but not frightened. He could see an arm raised; he could hear the silenced Makarov bucking in that slender grip; he could see Lipasov falling backward, his face destroyed, blood spurting from three massive, fatal wounds.

As soon as he thought too hard about it, though, Nadia's face came into focus, and he was unable to imagine her the brutal murderess. Nor could he understand why she had been driven to do it.

Wyatt Grant emerged from the embassy.

Valeri started his car, waited for a cab to pass, and then pulled out, hanging far enough back so that he would not be obvious, but keeping close enough so that he wouldn't lose the Toyota Celica. Grant worked in the Consular section, but some months ago he had been pegged as CIA. Probably a surveillance specialist. If that were the case, he would be good.

The Toyota crossed the river, turned right by the Kiev

225

Station, and headed up toward the Lenin Hills on Berezh-kovskaya. Grant was going to be a difficult man to approach. But he was a professional, and would be less likely to go off half-cocked than a legitimate embassy employee. There was no guarantee, of course, that Grant would cooperate, or if he did, and passed the message along, that Bertonelli would come out.

The embassy car cut east again in front of Moscow University, and at Gagarin Square Valeri realized where the American was heading. He sped up past the Sputnik Hotel, and hurried the last couple of blocks north, pulling up just around the corner from his own apartment. The yellow station wagon was still parked in front. Less than a minute later, Grant came around the corner, cruised past Valeri's building, spotted the Moskva, and continued past where Valeri was parked.

Bertonelli's apartment was less than a kilometer away. Grant drove directly over to it, swung through the parking lot, stopped a moment at the driveway, and then headed back into the city at exactly sixty kilometers per hour, the speed limit. He was taking no chances. But it was fairly obvious that Grant was looking for Valeri.

Twenty minutes later they came off the Kudrinskaya Ring at the Kazan Station, and the Toyota turned down the street in front of the yellow brick apartment building. Grant slowed down, and for a moment or two Valeri thought the American was going to park and go in, but then he sped up. Valeri glanced up at the attic window in time to see a movement. Someone was up there, waiting. He sped up, continuing to tail the Toyota as it circled the block and again headed back into the city center.

Grant circled the Rossiya Hotel once, and then parked along the river quay just below the Moskvoretsky Bridge where Valeri and Bertonelli had had their meeting. Valeri parked right behind him and got out of his car. Grant got out and they met halfway. He was a rather plain-looking man of medium build. His eyes were a pale blue. Shrewd, Valeri thought.

"I wanted to make sure you knew what I was doing," Grant said in English.

"Looking for me," Valeri replied, also in English.

Grand nodded thoughtfully. He seemed to be studying Valeri, measuring him. He glanced across the boulevard toward the hotel, and beyond it, Red Square. "Looks like you're not a very popular guy just now."

Valeri couldn't quite catch the idiom, but he understood what Grant was trying to say. He smiled. "I'm being watched."

"Everyone is in this country."

Valeri thought about the FBI in New York, but it wasn't worth mentioning. "You have gone through a lot of trouble to attract my attention."

"You followed me, remember?"

"I would like to speak with Mr. Bertonelli."

Something sparked in Grant's eyes. He nodded. "And he would like to speak with you, Major."

"He has news?"

"He would like to meet with you as soon as possible. And yes, he does have news. Disturbing news. So disturbing, in fact, that it would give me a great big charge to pull out my gun and shoot your ass dead right here and now."

Valeri was startled with the measure of the man's intensity, though once again he wasn't completely sure of the idiomatic expressions the American seemed to need for communication. Also, Grant's accent was strange.

"It will be difficult since I'm being watched . . ."

"They're on you like stink on shit, Major. But first we want to know Mr. Bertonelli's status."

That Valeri understood. "I've been ordered to kill him."

Grant's eyes widened. "Well, that's plain enough. Anyone else besides you gunning for him?"

"As you say, Mr. Grant, in this country everyone is being watched. And at the moment everyone is gunning for Mr. Bertonelli."

"Why?"

Valeri was suddenly tired of the game. He looked at his watch. "It is nearly two o'clock. I will meet with Mr. Bertonelli at the same place we met before, at exactly three. He will come alone."

"Now, just hold up a minute."

"There are many lives at stake here, not the least of which is my own. Three o'clock. Alone." Valeri turned and walked back to his car.

"Goddamnit," Grant swore.

Valeri looked over his shoulder and grinned. "By the way, Grant, say hello to Mr. DeMille for me."

* * *

Valeri drove around the city for an hour. Twice he almost went to Fainna's apartment to check on the girl, but each time he decided against it. If Bertonelli had news—disturbing news, according to Grant—he wanted to hear it before he tried again with her. On the far north side of the city, Valeri stopped across from the USSR Economic Achievement Exhibition, where a big truck was parked along the side of the road, the driver sitting on the open tailgate. The man flipped his cigarette away and came across to Valeri who rolled down his window.

"A happy good afternoon to you, comrade," the driver said through black, broken teeth. It was impossible to guess his age.

"I think I have car trouble," Valeri said. It was a code.

The driver grinned. "Maybe you're low on gas. Have you checked your gauge?"

"That's it, I'm sure. Maybe twenty liters?"

"For you, my friend, I can help. Sixteen rubles."

It was twice as much as at a service station. But there weren't many of them in all of Moscow, and none open on Sunday. Valeri nodded, and the driver hurried across the road to his truck. He came back with a jerry can, but he did not pour the gasoline until Valeri handed over the money.

"I'm usually here every Sunday," the driver said conversationally when he was finished. "But I don't do windshields." He laughed uproariously at his own little joke, and he was still laughing when Valeri drove off.

At five minutes before three Valeri parked his car behind the Rossiya Hotel, and headed on foot up to the street level, then across the bridge. There was a little more traffic now than before, including a few pedestrians crossing. But there was no sign of Bertonelli. This time, he suspected, the American would approach with a lot more caution because of Grant's report.

Halfway across the bridge, at about the same spot as their last meeting, Valeri stopped, lit a cigarette, and leaned on the broad concrete balustrade. The sun had gone beneath the building clouds, and although it was much warmer than this morning, Valeri shivered. There were no shadows. The city downriver had taken on a curiously flat, two-dimensional appearance, making it seem unreal, as if it were a painted backdrop. Already some streetlights were coming on.

His thoughts kept drifting back to not only what Grant had said, but how he had said it. Bertonelli had news, presumably about the eight-digit number. But it was news so disturbing that Grant wanted to kill a KGB major in broad daylight not one block from Red Square. It was extraordinary. Yet Valeri was no closer now to understanding what was going on than he had been that night at the zoo. Nothing seemed to fit. Nothing.

He became aware that someone was approaching and he looked up. Bertonelli, wearing the same light gray overcoat and felt hat as before, had come from the opposite side of the river. Again Valeri was struck by the power that seemed to emanate from the man. Only this time Bertonelli was not smiling; his mood wasn't as easy as it had been the last time, and he looked tired and strung out, almost haunted. Valeri could not remember ever seeing a man who looked so dangerous.

Bertonelli stopped a couple of meters away. He looked first at Valeri, then beyond to the far side of the bridge, then back again as if he were sure a trap had been laid. His stood solidly, his feet apart, his knees slightly bent, as if he were ready to fight or run. His lips were compressed, his nostrils flared.

Valeri was suddenly very wary. It looked as if Bertonelli had come here to kill him. He started to reach in his pocket.

"The moment you touch your gun, I'll pick you up and throw you over the side," Bertonelli said, his voice low, nearly inflectionless.

Valeri's hand stopped.

"I won't fuck with you any longer, Major. Who were you watching in the third-floor apartment behind the Kazan Station?"

"First the number."

"Tell me now, you bastard, or I swear to Christ I'll kill you."

Valeri shook his head in amazement. "You may try to kill me, Mr. Bertonelli. But do not be so certain that you would succeed."

Again Bertonelli looked beyond Valeri.

"I came alone, and not to fight you. Mr. Grant told me that you have some news. Disturbing news. Tell me."

"What did you come here for, Kostikov?"

"To talk to you. For an exchange of information."

"Why?"

The question startled Valeri. He knew that whatever answer he gave, the American would not believe him. "We don't have a lot of time, you and I."

"You've been ordered to kill me?"

"Yes."

"Why did you tell that to Grant? Are you a traitor too?"

Valeri lowered his eyes. "It would appear so, wouldn't it." He looked up. "I wanted your attention."

"Who gave those orders?"

"My superior officer."

"General Demin," Bertonelli said. It wasn't a question. "Why? What have I done?"

Valeri considered the question for a moment. "I was told that you were attempting to blackmail Colonel Okulov."

"Jesus Christ!" Bertonelli exploded. "You fucking people are all alike. Every goddamned one of you. What about the two proofs?"

"The number was a code for Novikov, who was said to have created a North American continent spy network."

Bertonelli took a step forward. Valeri held his ground.

"And you believed that?"

"I'm here. I sought you out. Talk to me."

"Do you really want to know what the number means, Kostikov? Are you sure? Because I'm telling you, if you lie to me afterward, if you hold back, I swear to God I will kill you with my bare hands."

Valeri was taken aback by such hatred.

"The number you gave me wasn't complete, Kostikov."

"I gave you everything that was written on the match cover."

"I sent it to Langley. They figured it out."

"Yes?"

"There was more, Major. Two letters. *A* and *F*."

Valeri said nothing.

"AF stands for Air Force. The number is an American military serial number."

Valeri thought he understood. "For a U-2 pilot? But there is no one like that in any of our prisons."

"He's a pilot, all right. An Air Force captain, but he wasn't shot down over the Soviet Union."

"I don't know what you're talking about."

"He was shot down over North Vietnam at the beginning of 1963."

"That's impossible," Valeri blurted.

"Colonel Okulov had the man's serial number. It was one of his proofs. The Air Force captain is listed on our records as missing in action in Vietnam. Missing in action, Kostikov, along with hundreds, thousands, of others. Now he's here in the Soviet Union."

"It's been nearly twenty-five years."

"The second proof, Major. The one you were watching. Was it . . . is it one of our people? Are they right here in Moscow?"

Valeri shook his head. This was not what he expected at all. It simply made no sense. "No," he said.

"Goddamnit . . ."

"It is a girl. A Siberian."

"What?"

"I don't understand either. But I think it was she who killed my surveillance man. Okulov brought her here from Yakutsk, but there is no record of her there, nor here in Moscow."

"What else has she told you?"

"Nothing," Valeri said. His mind was racing ahead, trying to make some sense of what Bertonelli had just told him. The Soviet Union had supplied arms and equipment to the government of North Vietnam early in the sixties, and later. But why bring American POWs here to the Soviet Union now? What earthly reason could there be?

"Where is she?"

Valeri looked up. He thought about Fainna. "I can't tell you that."

Bertonelli came closer. "He wanted me to have both proofs. The serial number and the girl. Who is she? Where is she? Have you taken her to Lubyanka?"

"No. Not there. I have her someplace where no one will get to her for the moment."

"Take me to her, then, Kostikov. At least do that much for me."

"And then what?"

"We'll make her talk."

Valeri shook his head. "We're going to do this my way . . ."

"Listen to me. Do you understand what it means to us, our MIAs? Do you understand about the families who haven't known all these years?"

"Twenty million of my countrymen were killed in the Second World War. I think I understand."

"Then help me, Major. In God's name, help me."

Valeri turned away and looked downriver. For a few moments he was only vaguely aware of Bertonelli, or of the traffic passing on the bridge. Incongruously he was thinking again about his youth, about the stories he had been told by his grandmother and his uncles and his father. He had been raised on stories . . . on heroic tales that, as often as not, made his mother cry. She had been a kind, gentle soul who had taught Valeri morality while his father taught him principles. The state was greater than the sum of its parts because of men and women who were willing to make sacrifices. It was the secret of the great Soviet experiment.

Bertonelli leaned on the railing next to Valeri. He too looked downriver. His anger seemed to be gone, leaving behind a great weariness.

Valeri looked at him.

"You're a good man, Kostikov. Not a typical Russian, I think. But then neither was Captain Burdine a typical American. He was one of the best."

The air disappeared, leaving all of Moscow in a vacuum. It seemed to Valeri as if his heart had stopped and his body had turned to stone. Bertonelli didn't notice.

"He was an Acadamy graduate. But he came up the hard way from some country school in Iowa, according to his records. Never married. No children. Never had the chance. He was only twenty-five when he was shot down."

"Burdine?" Valeri asked softly.

Bertonelli slowly straightened up. "Robert Burdine," he said.

A bus rumbled by. Nadia's face swam into view. He could hear her voice. Her accent was at once Siberian and yet . . . somehow it was subtly different. She was twenty-one. She had been born in 1965. Two years *after* Captain Robert Burdine had been shot down over North Vietnam.

"You'd better talk to me," Bertonelli said softly. There was no menace left in his voice.

"Her name is Nadia Burdine."

Bertonelli was rocked as if from a physical blow.

"She's Captain Burdine's . . . daughter, I think," Valeri said. His mind was racing ahead. What did this mean? What could it mean?

Bertonelli closed his eyes. "How old is she?"

"Twenty-one."

"He's been here all this time, then," Bertonelli said, opening his eyes. "Colonel Okulov's two proofs were his serial number and his daughter. What has happened, Kostikov? What in God's name have your people done?"

His presence at the Warehouse would be reported, but it no longer mattered to Valeri as he parked in the back and took the stairs up to the U.S. Situation Room. The computer operators on duty were surprised to see him, but no one said a thing. Bertonelli had given him a secure telephone number at the embassy. Reluctantly he had agreed to let Valeri work this out in his own way. They were going to have to find out who, other than Captain Burdine, was being held, and exactly where they were being held. There wasn't much time; they both agreed on that. Colonel Okulov had made the initial approach, but he was dead. And now, apparently, the prevailing mood was to destroy all the evidence of the POWs. That meant killing the girl, Bertonelli, and Valeri. Before that happened, Valeri wanted some insurance. If he could get his report to his father, he thought there might be a chance for them all.

Valeri hurried up the iron stairs to his office. General Demin was seated behind his desk, the drawers open, Valeri's report in front of him.

"What are you doing here on a Sunday, nephew?" he said.

Valeri stopped just within the doorway. "I came for something."

"This?" General Demin asked, holding up the report. He shook his massive, Georgian head. "Nothing more than dangerous speculation."

"It's the truth."

"Do you think you know the truth, Valerik?"

"Now I do, Uncle Gennadi. Now that I've spoken again with Bertonelli."

General Demin slapped the file down on the desk, and got to his feet. His tie was loose, his uniform tunic unbuttoned. His face was lined, his eyes red and puffy. He hadn't gotten much sleep lately.

"What do you think you know, nephew?"

"I know who the Americans are, though I don't know how many of them we're holding, or where we're holding them."

"Then you don't know very much."

"I know that Colonel Okulov was probably a good man. He wanted to repatriate them. He wanted to send them home. To their families."

"Them?" General Demin sneered.

"At least one of them is an American POW shot down over Vietnam."

"The great colonialist misadventure. Just why is it, do you think, that we have these men here?"

"I don't know. At least I don't know yet. But we have had them since 1964."

"All that time." General Demin went to the window and looked outside, his back to Valeri who thought he looked haggard.

"The number I thought was Novikov's telephone number was in reality the American's military serial number," Valeri said. He glanced at his desk. General Demin had read his report, but he hadn't ordered his arrest. At least not yet.

"That would mean Chief Secretary Okulov was lying. That's quite an accusation. I love you like family, Valerik, but that does not mean I can continue to protect you if you keep on with this craziness."

Valeri stepped the rest of the way into his office and took the report off his desk. He stuffed it into his coat pocket. General Demin heard him, but he didn't move.

"When you were a little boy your father used to despair that you would never learn to walk. You were forever bumping into things. Falling over. In fact you never did learn. You ran before you walked."

"He was a pilot in the U.S. Air Force, Uncle Gennadi." Valeri didn't know why he was telling everything. But it felt right. If anyone besides his father could make things turn out, it would be Uncle Gennadi. "A captain. His name is Robert Burdine."

"You have the proof? You have this man?"

"I have his daughter. Colonel Okulov brought her here from Yakutsk. It was she who killed Lipasov."

"And how do you feel about this, Valeri? Harboring a criminal. I saw nothing about her in your report. Are you taking her word about this American captain? What is it you really know? You want to bring down a respected officer of the Politburo, no less, and yet you bring me no hard evidence."

"I think you know what I am saying is true, Uncle."

General Demin turned around. He had a gun in his thick fist. "I can't let you leave this office, Valerik. And it's a sad state of affairs. Once a word is out of your mouth, you can't swallow it. That applies to the state as well as the individual."

"Don't do it, Uncle. Bertonelli is safe in his embassy, and Washington already knows about Captain Burdine."

General Demin smiled sadly. "They knew about Hungary; they know about Afghanistan. But there is nothing they can do about it."

"There's the girl."

"She can't last long. Not in Moscow, without papers."

"And Tanya? And Aunty Serafima? And my father and sister? Are they to be part of this too? Or have you irrevocably allied yourself with Chief Secretary Okulov?"

A gust of wind rattled the window, and the first snowflakes began to fall. Already it was nearly night outside. The lights of Moscow were coming on, but Valeri's office was dark.

"He wants me and Bertonelli and the girl dead. And then he wants to kill all the Americans and destroy their bodies. Is that what we have become, Uncle Gennadi? Is that what you have become?"

"Even a general has his limits."

"What if I get the proof?"

"What if you do, Valerik? There is nothing I can do about it."

"I was going to send it to my father."

General Demin smiled. "Afterward what do you think would happen?"

"We can take it to Mr. Gorbachev. He is a moderate."

"No one can get to him. He is surrounded by the old guard."

"Chief Secretary Okulov."

General Demin nodded. "Do you suppose your Mr. Bertonelli has such easy access to his President Reagan?"

"I have to try, Uncle. Not everything they say about us in the West is true."

General Demin looked at him in genuine amazement. "All this for idealism, Valerik? Or is it this girl of yours? Serafima said all was not well between you and Tanya. Even I could see it. Is that it?"

Valeri said nothing.

"Then go," General Demin said, lowering his gun. "Take the girl and run. Leave the country. Time is all I can give you, nephew. It's not within my power to grant you anything else."

Valeri turned and left his office.

Nadia was sitting in the dark, looking out the window when Valeri returned to Fainna's apartment. He had stopped off to buy a few potatoes, a sausage, some milk, more bread, and cigarettes with the last of his money. He put the things in the kitchen and came back out to her.

"Why are you sitting in the dark?" he asked.

"Dark, light, what does it matter?"

Valeri took off his hat and coat. "Has anyone come here, or called?"

She shook her head. It was snowing in earnest now. She reached out with a fingertip and traced a pattern on the window.

"Why did Colonel Okulov single you out to bring you to Moscow, Nadia?"

She looked up. "I don't know what you're talking about," she replied tiredly.

Valeri sat on the arm of the couch across from her. She looked very pale. There wasn't much color in her cheeks, but her eyes were bright.

"I met with the American. he found out what the number means."

"You're lying to me."

"No. They know in Washington now about your father. Captain Robert Burdine. He was shot down over North Vietnam in 1963. But I don't understand why he was brought to the Soviet Union."

"These are lies!" she shrieked. "You don't know anything!"

"Why, Nadia? Why would I lie to you?"

She clapped her hands over her ears to block out his voice. He went to her and pulled her hands away. She was surprisingly strong.

"I'm trying to help you. Believe me. But there isn't much time."

"No!"

"Yes, Nadia. The Americans want to help, I want to help, but we need more information. We must know about the others. Who they are, and where they are."

"No. Get away from me. It's all lies. He lied to me . . ."

"Who lied to you?"

She shook her head.

"Who lied to you, Nadia? Was it Colonel Okulov?"

She looked away. "No one can help us now."

"Why did he bring you to Moscow? Why you?"

"I'm a Siberian," she said proudly. "But he made promises."

"What promises?"

"I didn't want to come with him. He was in love with me. But they made me do it."

"Who made you do it?"

"My father," she said in a very small voice. "Some of the others. But not all of them."

"Who is there besides your father? What other Americans?"

"A lot of them."

"Who? How many?"

"More than a hundred."

Valeri was stunned. He could not believe it was possible. "Pilots?"

"Some of them."

"All from Vietnam?"

"Yes."

"Why were they brought here?" Valeri asked.

"I don't know," Nadia said, and she began to cry silently, big tears rolling down her sallow cheeks. It came to Valeri that she did not want to go to the United States. He suspected that given the chance she would rather return to wherever it was she had come from.

"What promises did he make to you, Nadia?" Valeri asked

gently. He wanted to hold her. "That whoever wanted to remain behind could stay?"

"Go away. Leave me alone."

"But you can't go back without help. And Colonel Okulov is dead."

Nadia was shivering now. Valeri wondered about her mother. He felt a great pity for the girl whose father was an American POW and whose mother was a Siberian. Where were her loyalties? Where was her future?

"Colonel Okulov's brother wants to kill all of you and destroy the evidence."

"Good," she snapped savagely.

"No, Nadia! You don't have the right to make that decision! No one does!"

"What then?"

"I want to stop that from happening. But I need your help. We need each other. Tell me where they are being held, and tell me who is there. As many names as you can remember."

"What then, Valeri Kostikov? What do you think you can do?"

"I will give that information to the Americans. Once the knowledge is out, my government would not dare kill your father and the others."

"You would be a traitor to your own country?"

"Not to my country, only to some very evil men who would cover up a terrible mistake with an even bigger crime."

"You are so naïve," she said. "And I hate you. If I could kill you I would, just like I did your friend."

Valeri hardened his heart. "Where are the Americans?"

"They will kill you first."

"They've already tried."

"They'll try again."

"Where are they?"

"Karaginskiy."

"Karaginskiy what? Is that a region? A city?"

"An island in the Bering Sea."

"What else is on that island?" Valeri asked.

"Nothing," she said. "Only the prison camp, the forests, and the charcoal kilns."

Valeri got up. "I'll get some paper and a pencil. You can write out all the names you can remember."

She looked up at him. "That won't be necessary."

"I need the names, Nadia."

"I brought a list with me. Of the Americans."

"Where is it? Here, with you?" Valeri asked. He was excited.

She shook her head. "On the first day I hid it in the Kazan Station," she said. She told him exactly where. "The families are not on the list."

"What families?"

She looked at him. "I hate you, Valeri Kostikov. I shall always hate you."

# 17

Of the nine railway stations in Moscow through which more than 400 million passengers passed each year, the Kazan Station was one of the largest. From there trains began their journeys across the far-flung reaches of the Central Asian republics and Siberia. At busy times the mezzanine was a beehive of activity, dozens of different national tongues rising in a constant, droning babble. This night the vast depot was relatively quiet, almost hollow; no one started for Siberia on a Winter Festival Sunday.

Valeri stopped just within the main entrance and pretended to study the schedule as he looked toward the broad stairs that led down to the boarding gates.

A half-dozen old *babushkas* pushing cleaning carts were mopping the floor and polishing the lower meter and a half of the marble pillars that rose up to the ornately vaulted ceiling far overhead.

Nadia said she had arrived early in the morning of the twentieth. Colonel Okulov had left her for a few moments at trackside while he went to check on something. During that brief time she had hidden the small paperbound notebook wrapped in plastic. Her father had pressed it on her before she left. None of them trusted the colonel, she said, despite his promises.

A pair of soldiers came up the stairs, crossed the main hall, and sat down with their duffel bags on one of the long benches. They didn't look happy. Evidently their leaves were over, and they were waiting for a train that would take them back to their base. One of them took out a bottle of vodka, took a deep drink, and handed it to his companion.

Valeri walked across the mezzanine and took the stairs

down. At the bottom a sleepy Militiaman was leaning against the steel fence. He straightened up. Valeri showed him his ID.

"There isn't a train scheduled until ten o'clock, Comrade Major," the young man said politely.

"I know. But has anyone come this way in the past half hour or so?"

"No, sir."

"No one?"

The Militiaman straightened up a little taller. "Merely the maintenance people, sir."

"There, you see? Just who I might be looking for," Valeri said. "Don't let anyone else through until I come back."

"Yes, sir," the Militiaman said, only too happy to cooperate with the KGB.

Valeri went through the gate and headed down the long boarding platform. For a couple of hundred meters the tracks were covered by an iron roof. Beyond that the snow seemed to fall in a thick gray sheet.

Nadia's train had been parked here. She stood next to a stanchion, she said, marked " Д ". The platform had been busy. No one paid her the slightest attention. The moment Colonel Okulov was out of sight she dropped her purse. Bending down to gather her things, she reached over the edge of the platform, her fingers searching for and finding a hole in the bricks into which she hurriedly stuffed the small notebook. It only took a few seconds, and then she waited for the colonel to return for her.

An empty passenger train had been shunted to a far set of tracks. Above, in a glass booth, Valeri could see two men talking, their backs to the tracks.

He stopped at the " Д " stanchion. No one was watching. He bent down and reached over the edge, finding the hole. His fingers curled around a small package wrapped in plastic and he withdrew it, standing up and stuffing it into his coat pocket.

It had only taken a second or two, and no one had noticed him. He turned and went back to the Militiaman who was waiting for him.

"I was mistaken," Valeri said. "He is not here."

"Perhaps I could be of help, sir?"

"Yes, by keeping alert for anyone else coming here, just as I have, and asking about strangers."

The Militiaman would worry about it for the rest of the night. But it would be something to keep him awake between trains.

Back in his car across Komsomol Square, Valeri turned on the dome light and unwrapped the plastic covering from the small, cheap notebook. There wasn't much traffic at this hour. What little there was moved slowly because of the heavy snow. Valeri felt as if he were in a cocoon.

The notebook was filled with names, written in pencil in a tight, neat hand. Beside each name was a serial number or a social security number, and a brief comment or two: *Shot down Nam Dinh 4/17/64. Captured Khe Sanh 1/1/64. Photo mission Hue, others killed. Song Bo 3/11/65.* A few of the names had been placed in parentheses with a second, more recent date following. Valeri realized that these were people who had died in the Soviet Union.

After a few minutes he rewrapped the notebook in the plastic and stuffed it back into his pocket. A trolley bus rattled by, its few passengers looking straight ahead.

There were more than a hundred names, perhaps as many as two hundred, in the little notebook. But there was no explanation why the North Vietnamese had turned them over, or what purpose they were to serve in the Soviet Union. The dates of their original capture, however, all fell in the years 1963 through 1965. It held a clue, Valeri supposed. But there was no real significance in it for him. Someone had created an operation in which American POWs were needed. They were brought to the Soviet Union, set up in a gulag on Karaginskiy Island, and then . . . what? Had they simply been forgotten in Siberia, the fact of their existence hidden perhaps under the guise of a dissident gulag, or perhaps a prison for ordinary criminals? Siberia was the land of the forgotten exile. But all these years supplies were flown out to the island. There were the camp administrators and the guards. Dissident exiles themselves with absolutely no hope of escape? Siberia was said to be one of the last unfenced regions of human habitation on earth. No need for prison walls and electrified fences, not when the gulag itself was a man's only hope for survival. To wander off, even in the summer, would mean certain death. And an island in the inhospitable Bering Sea was even more secure. The timing of Colonel Okulov's move had bothered Valeri at first. But now he could appreciate it. The government of Vietnam was finally beginning to cooperate with the Americans in finding all of the MIAs. Sooner or later it would come out that the Soviet government had taken more than a hundred American prisoners and still had them. It was the ultimate debacle of an overzealous KGB in a not-so-cold cold war between the superpowers. The repercussions of discovery would be awesome. For years the Soviet Union had told the world that it deplored the excesses of Joseph Stalin. This now gave proof to the opposite. The entire government would fall; it would make the shooting down of the Korean airliner seem like a tempest in a teacup by comparison. Kill them or repatriate them—either way the risks were enormous. How safe was any national border, after all? Kill them and deny everything, thus protecting the state. Or, the more difficult choice, arrange to have them returned home. With the correct approach the Americans might have gone along with it, happy to have their people returned. But who could be sure how any government would react? Wars had been fought for much less. Certainly the propaganda value to the American position was inestimable. At the very least the Soviet Union would be censured within the U.N.; the worst was impossible to predict, but certainly Mother Russia would lose enormous respect worldwide. And there were those in the government who simply couldn't conceive of taking such a risk. The terrible choice, in the end, had pitted brother against brother. Colonel Okulov the moderate and his brother Uri Vladimir the old guard.

Valeri realized he had done them a favor by mistakenly killing the colonel. If he hadn't done it, someone else would have had to do it. Perhaps his own brother, perhaps his wife. But the situation had gotten out of hand. Now Chief Secretary Okulov would do everything within his power to make sure that Valeri and Bertonelli did not survive.

He touched his pocket where the notebook lay heavy against his hip. There was no way to predict what the American government would do once Washington knew about the MIAs. Valeri shuddered to think of the possibilities. Bertonelli could be discredited, still, the story denied, and eventually the storm would die down.

Again Valeri thought about Tanya's poetry. *Snow fell across my world/It raged even in my soul./A hearth held a flame./Oh that the hearth were snow!*

He started his car and headed back out to Fainna's apartment. He would turn the girl and the list over to Bertonelli. From that point on not even Okulov would be able to contain the secret any longer. When the sheath is broken, he thought of the old Russian proverb, you cannot hide the sword.

Valeri parked his car in front of Fainna's building, crossed the street, and went upstairs. A grandmother and two children came down. The old woman smiled and nodded as they passed. He opened the door and went in. The kitchen light was on, casting a soft glow into the living room.

"I wondered when you would return," Shevchenko said. He was sitting in shadow across the room.

Valeri's heart fell. "What are you doing here, Mikhail? You promised me twenty-four hours."

"The question is, what are *you* doing here? Is this where you hold your meetings with Bertonelli?"

Valeri closed the door. There was no sign of Nadia. Had she run, or had they taken her? "How did you find me?"

"You weren't home. You weren't at the Institute. So I went down the list. When I came to Comrade Skvorstov's name, I didn't have to look any farther."

Mikhail was drunk. A thin sheen of sweat covered his face. His eyes were bright when he leaned into the light. He held his TK automatic pistol loosely in his lap. Valeri thought with sadness that this was the second time that day that someone close had held a gun on him.

"General Demin asked you to find me?"

"You have to be stopped. Who better than a friend for the task. And together we are going to bring in Bertonelli."

"I just spoke with General Demin this afternoon."

"I know. Afterward I'm going to take you out to his *dacha.* You'll be safe there."

"Safe from what, Mikhail?"

"You'd be surprised, but they want you dead. They're going to try to kill you, and then say you were a traitor."

"Who are they?"

Shevchenko shrugged. "Somebody. But General Demin says it will all turn out for the best. Tanya is already on her way. She is very worried about you as well, you know. You have made some very powerful enemies. Even Sasha said you didn't look well, and I have to agree with her."

"And then what?"

"It'll take a while for the dust to settle, I suppose. Then you and Tanya will go off on a state-sponsored vacation. Afterward you will receive a promotion, get a new job, and your life will start all over again."

"With a bullet in the back of my head?"

Shevchenko was aghast. "No."

"At the very least, I'll be sent away from Moscow."

"Your father does well by himself in far-off Khabarovsk. We're all related, Valerik; the same sun dries our rags."

Valeri took off his hat and unbuttoned his coat. Ignoring Shevchenko, he went into the kitchen where he poured himself a cognac. There was no sign that Nadia had ever been here. Their breakfast dishes had been washed, dried, and put away. He was sure that Mikhail would have said something about her if she had been there when he arrived. He lit a cigarette. General Demin was being pressured by Chief Secretary Okulov. He remembered an old American military expression: Shit runs downhill. Uncle Gennadi had set Mikhail to the task of finding the deputy chief. It was likely, then, that Okulov's strong-arm squad would be lurking somewhere nearby.

"Valerik?" Shevchenko called nervously from the living room.

Valeri went back in.

Shevchenko had gotten to his feet. "You're going to have to help me."

"With what?"

"We need you to get Bertonelli here."

"I can't do that."

"You must. For me."

Valeri nodded toward the window. "Who is waiting out there, Mikhail?"

"No one."

"Then it won't matter, will it, if Bertonelli doesn't come.

We will have done our best, but the American simply wouldn't cooperate. Who's to know differently?"

"They'll know."

Valeri went to the window and looked down at the street and the park across. A Mercedes had pulled up behind his car. The angle was wrong for him to see inside, and the blowing snow obscured the car's exhaust so that he could not tell if the engine was still running. He had no doubt, though, that Chief Secretary Okulov's people were down there. He turned. Mikhail was watching him.

"I don't know how to get in contact with him."

"I think you do."

"No. But has anyone explained to you exactly what is going on here? I mean have you been told about the American prisoners we're holding? They're POWs from North Vietnam. A lot of them pilots. We've had them for more than twenty years in a gulag on Karaginskiy Island in the Bering Sea."

"What are you talking about?"

"Chief Secretary Okulov thinks they should be killed, their bodies destroyed."

Shevchenko said nothing.

"I just want you to know what's happening, Mikhail."

"No."

"Bertonelli and I are the only ones who know. If he comes here, they will kill him. And me. And now you."

Shevchenko was shaking his head.

"They're waiting outside."

"Call him."

"Mikhail." Valeri sighed. He put out his cigarette. "I think maybe you and I can get out of here through the basement, and then out the back. Where is your car? I didn't see it when I came in."

Shevchenko held his silence, but he looked guilty.

"You were driven here." Valeri understood now the setup. "Tanya's not really on her way out to Istra, is she? You were lying to me about that part. What else? Did General Demin order you to kill me once I called Bertonelli?"

"I swear to you, Valerik, nothing will happen to you. But Bertonelli has to be stopped. He murdered Viktor Ivanovich. General Demin has the proof."

"You said someone wanted to kill me. Who?"

"I don't know."

"I do, Mikhail. And they're right outside at this moment."

Shevchenko glanced toward the window. He was unsteady on his feet. Valeri thought if he could disarm his old friend, they could get out. It would give him the freedom to arrange a meeting with Bertonelli and hand over the notebook. The only problem was Nadia. Had she wandered off, or had she been taken?

"It's your own fault," Shevchenko blurted. "General Demin warned you to stay away. He said it was none of your business. And it wasn't."

"It's too late for that now . . ."

"Fuck. There's nothing I can do, Valerik."

"Put down your gun and let me leave."

"No." Shevchenko was in real anguish.

Someone was out in the corridor. They both heard it. Valeri stepped back and put his hand in his coat pocket, his fingers curling around his Beretta. Shevchenko turned to face the door as it came open.

Nadia came into the apartment, her cheeks flushed from the cold. Her eyes opened wide when she saw Shevchenko with the gun. "Oh," she said, stepping back.

Shevchenko was concentrating on the girl. She was clearly a surprise to him. For a moment he did not know what to do.

Valeri pulled out his gun and thumbed off the safety.

"Who are you . . . ? Shevchenko started to ask.

"Mikhail," Valeri said softly.

Shevchenko glanced over his shoulder. He saw the gun in Valeri's hand. "What?"

"Put your gun down, Mikhail. I honestly do not want to shoot you."

"Shit. You can't do this, Valerik."

"Put your gun down. Now."

Shevchenko was befuddled. He didn't know what to do. He hadn't counted on this.

"Mikhail . . ." Valeri said.

Nadia was suddenly pulled aside, and Valeri looked up in time to see a very large man, a thick arm around her neck, the barrel of a big gun at the side of her head, fill the doorway.

"Put your gun down, Major, or the girl dies right now."

It was over. He had tried and lost. Valeri carefully laid his

Beretta down on the floor. Nadia was looking at him. But she didn't seem frightened. He admired her strength at that moment.

"He refused to call Bertonelli," Shevchenko said.

"Put your gun down as well, Captain," the man said.

Shevchenko was surprised. "Where is General Demin?" he demanded.

The man took his gun away from Nadia's head, pointed it at Shevchenko, and fired, the noise incredibly loud in the confines of the tiny apartment. Shevchenko's body, flung backward, crashed over a coffee table, breaking it in half. A huge dark stain spread across his chest. His right hand twitched, the knuckles rapping a death code on the floor. Then he was still.

Valeri had reached into his left pocket for Nadia's silenced Makarov, but the man turned to him. Valeri stiffened for the shot.

It did not come.

"You will please call Bertonelli now, Comrade Major," the man said.

Valeri shook his head. "It's too late. He knows everything."

The man seemed to consider it. He smiled, and turned his gun back to Nadia's head. "How important is her life to you, Major? Important enough for you to make one telephone call?"

Valeri's breath caught in his throat. His eyes were locked with hers. She started to shake her head, but the man tightened his grip. Valeri thought her neck would break.

"Wait," Valeri said.

"All this rough stuff certainly isn't necessary, Nikolai," a familiar voice said from the corridor.

The man stepped aside, dragging Nadia with him, and Chief Secretary Okulov came in. He was wearing a smartly tailored black overcoat and a fur hat. He had a Graz Burya in his gloved hand. He glanced at Shevchenko's body and shook his head. Then he looked at Valeri, his eyes dark, piercing, inhuman in their animal intensity.

"So, my brother was full of surprises. We never suspected he'd brought the girl here."

"Bertonelli knows everything, and he's transmitted it to Langley," Valeri said.

Okulov smiled. "I think not, Valeri Konstantinovich. But we'll soon see."

"I've sent a complete report to my father. He'll get it to Mr. Gorbachev."

"You once told me, Major, that you were a true Russian. That you could no more betray your country than you could your mother."

"We're not talking about the *Rodina* now, Comrade Chief Secretary, we're talking about your insanity."

"Not mine, I think. Yours. Here we are with so much death and destruction of good, hard-working men because of your aberration."

"Too many people know about the American POWs. Give it up, Comrade Chief Secretary. Become a true hero."

Okulov smiled again, but there was a dangerous glint in his eyes. "Take the girl out of here," he said to his man. "Kill her in one hour unless I call you. Have the others at the rendezvous."

"No!" Valeri shouted.

"Believe me, I'm touched, Comrade Major," Okulov said.

His man dragged Nadia out into the corridor and they were gone. Okulov reached back and closed the door.

"Now, Comrade Major, you are going to call Mr. Bertonelli and arrange another meeting with him on the Moskvoretsky Bridge."

"No."

"It will have to be done within the hour, or else the girl dies. I wonder just how strong your resolve might be?"

Valeri took his hand out of his coat pocket and went over to the window. Okulov's men were bundling an unresisting Nadia into the back seat of the Mercedes. A minute later the car left. But there would be others out there somewhere, he figured. Okulov would not stay here alone with a raving lunatic.

"Time passes, Major."

Valeri turned back. "If you kill me and the girl, it will still leave Bertonelli. And no matter what you think, he knows enough that his government will have to act."

"I think not."

"Do you know who that girl is?"

"A whore."

"The daughter of U.S. Air Force Captain Robert Burdine, serial number AF17573360, shot down over North Vietnam in 1963, and held prisoner on Karaginskiy Island since at least 1964. There are between a hundred and two hundred other Americans there—pilots, journalists, advisers, CIA agents. And their families. Siberian women, children. They cut trees and make charcoal. None of them trusted your brother.''

"A nice speech, Kostikov. Call Bertonelli.''

Valeri nodded. He turned and went to the phone. Okulov followed him with the gun.

"This is necessary, believe me, Major.''

Valeri picked up the telephone, hesitated a moment, and then yanked the cord out of the wall. He let the telephone clatter to the floor.

Okulov was livid with rage. "Traitor,'' he hissed. "The girl will die.''

"She will die in any event.''

The apartment door crashed open. Okulov started to turn as Bertonelli and Grant barged in. Valeri pulled out the Makarov and fired at the same moment Bertonelli and Grant also fired, all three shots catching the Chief Secretary in the torso, his body lifting up on its tiptoes before it flopped over on the couch.

Grant had dropped into a crouch. He held his gun at arm's length on Valeri.

"They took the girl,'' Valeri said.

"We saw,'' Bertonelli replied. "There are more of his people outside. They'll be coming up at any moment. We have to get the hell out of here.''

Valeri stepped back. He shook his head. "I'm not going with you.''

"Goddamnit, we don't have time to fuck around.''

Valeri took the plastic-wrapped notebook out of his pocket and tossed it to the American. "All their names are in there. Serial numbers. Everything. They're being held on Karaginskiy Island in the Bering Sea. Nadia isn't the only civilian. There are other children and Siberian wives.''

Grant's eyes were glazed. He got to his feet. "If you stay here, Major, they'll kill you.''

Valeri shrugged.

"We could force you to come with us,'' Bertonelli said.

"No.''

"Why?'' Grant demanded.

"This is my country. I'm a Russian, not a traitor.''

Grant wanted to protest, but Bertonelli grabbed his arm and

pulled him toward the door. "We won't forget you, Kostikov," he said. Then they were gone.

Valeri let the Makarov drop to the floor. He lit himself a cigarette, and then went over to Shevchenko's body. He sat down, and looked into his old friend's face. He had no idea how he was going to tell Sasha or the children, or even if he would survive to tell them. But he had accomplished what he set out to accomplish. Only it didn't make him feel very good. In fact he felt dirty, and very used.

Nadia's face swam up into his mind's eye. Then so did Tanya's and Fainna's, all of them melding into one sad visage of betrayal that he could not face.

Valeri lowered his head and wept.

# II

# THE INTERROGATION

## 18

Valeri was in exile in his own country. His KGB identification and internal passport had been taken from him. It was understood that his mail would be censored, and under no circumstances was he to use the telephone or telegraph services. His driver's license had been taken from him as well.

He was honestly surprised that he had not been shot, or at the very least sent to prison. He had been held in isolation at Lubyanka for twenty-four hours, then had been flown by military transport here to Khabarovsk. Days ago? Weeks? His sense of time seemed warped. Of course his sister moved around him as if she were treading on eggshells, but his father was a surprise. He said nothing about what happened. In fact his staff officers had come to the house last night for dinner to meet the general's son from Moscow. It seemed to Valeri as if they were studying him, politely perhaps, but with the respect that a prison guard might have for a mass murderer condemned to death. He was a dangerous curiosity. An oddity. When they left they had been full of subdued bonhomie, a certain cheer, but none had shaken his hand. Valeri didn't really care. Had the tables been reversed he wouldn't have bothered shaking the hand of a traitor himself.

At night, alone in his own room, he began to think about his mother. The thoughts always began innocently for him—he thought about when he was very young, in the United States, and later in Paris. He thought about Leningrad and even Yalta. Always, though, his mind turned elsewhere, to the other woman in his life: to poor sick Tanya; to haughty Larissa Okulov; to Mikhail's wife Sasha (he didn't want to think about how she had taken the news of Mikhail's death); and finally, like a magnet, his thoughts were pulled inexorably back to Nadia. Poor little innocent, doelike Nadia, daughter of an American POW from the Vietnam conflict, and . . . who? Obviously a Siberian woman. Had many women been brought to the gulag at Karaginskiy Island for the pleasure of the American prisoners?

In the morning his father went off to the base on the plains east of the city, and Lara had tried to get Valeri to come shopping with her. Afterward they would have lunch, she said, and then drive out to the civil war statue and museum at Volochayevka. But he did not care about the Amur partisans, and the civil war was a very long time ago.

"You will have to make a life for yourself here, Valerik," his sister told him gently. She had inherited their mother's eyes and cheeks, but her body was boyish, almost athletic. She rode in the summer, did cross-country skiing in the long winter, and competed with the men under her father's command in shooting.

"Why?" Valeri asked.

Lara had been ready to leave. She came back into the breakfast room. "You don't know what you've done, do you?"

Valeri shrugged.

"If we knew beforehand where we were going to fall, we could lay down a carpet. But . . . here is where you will stay, my brother."

"Until they put a bullet into the back of my head."

She reared back. "Not while father is alive!" Her nostrils flared.

Valeri looked away. Even his sister was beginning to remind him of Nadia. It was crazy, but for him Nadia was the only reality. Yet she was the most elusive creature he had ever known in his life. He knew that his sister still stood there, but he could not turn and face her.

What had become of Nadia? Chief Secretary Okulov had promised she would be shot.

"They're still trying to figure out what to do with you," Lara said.

Valeri listened to her words; they flowed around him with little effect. After a time she left and he sat alone in the breakfast room trying to make some sense of what had happened to him.

\*　　\*　　\*

General Demin had arrived a half hour after Bertonelli and Grant left. He was in uniform, and he had his gun drawn as he stood in the doorway looking at the bodies of the chief secretary and Valeri's chief of staff.

"You have gone too far this time, my nephew," he said, his voice echoing in Valeri's head. "I can't protect you. Not from this. Too many questions are bound to be asked. They simply will not believe anything you tell them, unless it is the truth they want to hear. That will be your only salvation."

Valeri looked up. "It's too late for them, Uncle Gennadi."

General Demin shook his massive head, saddened by Valeri's answer. "Don't ever think that. It is never too late for them. Believe me."

Someone was coming up the stairs.

"Do not blame yourself, Uncle," Valeri said. "You warned me, but I would not listen. It will be our story. But save Nadia. Please!"

General Konstantin Illyich Kostikov was a tall, stern-looking man. He was dressed expensively in a civilian fur coat and hat as he walked with his son across Komsomol Square at the end of Karl Marx Street. It was an exceedingly cold, dark afternoon. Their footfalls crunched crisply in the snow.

"They tell me that it was some sort of a vendetta," the general said. "First the colonel, and then his brother, a chief secretary of the Politburo, of all people. No one can understand what you have done. Why, for instance, did you lure the chief secretary to that apartment? And why is it you attempted to blackmail the colonel's wife with some story about a love tryst between her and her brother-in-law?"

With an almost preternatural clarity Valeri was beginning to understand what it was they were trying to do to him. He'd been sent here to his father to be straightened out. He was to be reeducated. By carefully examining each facet of a truth from wholly different and unexpected angles, they would wear him down, confuse him, make him finally see the error of his ways. If one fact in a body of knowledge can be shown to be wrong, all else in the encyclopedia must, at the very least, be suspect. Display a fact in a new light; prove that such-and-such is not in actuality as it first appeared, then one must suspect his vision and outlook. Show where a single act of judgment is faulty, and a solid case can be constructed for the dismissal of the entire brain.

"Clever," Valeri muttered. He meant it.

Everyone else seemed to be hurrying. But for Valeri and his father time didn't seem to have any significance. At the far end of the square they passed an old, very large, ornately designed red brick building. It reminded Valeri of something, but for the life of him he could not think what it was. He stopped. A sign announced the building to be the headquarters of the Amur Steamship Company, which seemed out of place, an anachronism in this age of nuclear missiles, Soyuz, and televised Tchaikovsky. It was a Tanya building, he decided; a thing he just knew without thinking about it, just as he knew they once were in love, but that it had faded.

"What about the girl, Father?" Valeri asked, turning.

"What girl?"

"Nadia Burdine. Her father was . . ."

The general sighed, his breath white like steam in front of his face. "I have heard this story, Valeri. You have even called out her name in your sleep. Lara tells me you talk of nothing else. Uncle Gennadi is deeply concerned about your mental health. They say you are suffering delusions."

"Her father is an American, her mother a Siberian."

"No, Valerik," the general said. He took his son's arm and they went the rest of the way across the square.

Somehow it was even colder by the river. Across the ice was the treeless Siberian steppe. China was barely eighteen miles away. In the days of Mao Tse-tung this region was fortress Khabarovsk; every second citizen, it seemed, was a tank commander. It was different now. These days they were specialists, scientists, and technicians—prima donnas.

"It has been documented that you met with an American intelligence officer on several occasions. In front of the Rossiya Hotel, and then on a bridge over the Moscow River. In broad daylight."

"Colonel Okulov was trying to pass him information that night in the zoo," Valeri said tiredly. He couldn't drag his eyes away from the nearly flat, white landscape. It was hypnotic.

"Disinformation, Valeri. Your own staff recommended the

American's arrest. There were sufficient grounds. But you hesitated. Until in the end it was simply too late."

"We're holding American POWs."

"That was Bertonelli's fabrication in order to sway you. In order to turn you away from your lawful job. He is a master of deceit. You have said as much yourself. Uncle Gennadi tells me you hated Bertonelli. You called him the devil. Perhaps he bewitched you."

"Then who is the girl?"

"If there was a girl, she was Colonel Okulov's whore."

"The serial number?"

"A telephone number, Valeri. For a man by the name of Novikov. You uncovered that fact yourself, don't you remember it? Novikov's father apparently created a spy network in Mexico, or perhaps even in the United States. I don't have all the facts, you know. You must help me!"

They started along the river walk. Valeri didn't think he could remember what it was like to be warm. His father, however, seemed mindless of the cold. Streetlights were beginning to come on. A steam haze had settled over the town.

His father looked at him. "Are you cold, Valeri? I suppose you're not used to it."

Valeri had spent his life trying to live up to his father. He was finding it difficult now to turn away from that ideal. In that direction, though, lay a trap for him.

He could admire the technique, only it made him sad the extent they were willing to go to get at him. He himself had never been a great interrogator because he was not willing to pull out all the stops, use anything and everything against the subject. But in a detached sort of way he could understand what was happening around him. The method was fairly simple: show the subject he was at your mercy, prove to the subject that you loved him, and finally, allow the subject the room to tell you everything.

They'd dumped him unceremoniously here in Khabarovsk. They'd set his father and sister up as his interrogators. And he ached now to tell them everything, absolutely everything.

He realized that he was beginning to live his life in the past. In many ways he was regressing, going back to a simpler age when he was a young boy and his parents made the decisions for him.

After dinner Lara joined him in the great room, a fire crackling in the massive stone fireplace. She was dressed in a gray wool knit dress. It was almost a carbon copy of the dress Nadia had worn.

"I received a call from Tanya this afternoon," Lara said. "She's a lot better now. She's back in the apartment."

"She was going to move to Leningrad. Move in with her aunt."

"Her aunt has died."

For some reason Valeri was not surprised. "Is she going to stay in Moscow, then?" Tanya and his sister had never gotten along, which was strange because they had so much in common. Tanya was a poet, and Lara had been married to a dissident poet.

"I don't know. She didn't say. But she is worried about you." Lara crossed the room and poured them both a cognac in snifters. She brought them back to the fireplace.

The cognac was good, as usual. His father and sister had always surrounded themselves with the best, no matter where they were. Valeri sipped his drink, wondering what Lara's next move would be.

"She wants you back," Lara said soberly. "She sounded very . . . sad."

"I'm sorry."

"We never did get along. But she is a good woman, Valerik."

"Yes, she is."

Lara's eyes were wide. "I don't have to try to fool you, do I?"

Valeri shook his head.

"You're an intelligent man, sometimes. But I think you should have listened to Uncle Gennadi. He tried to set you straight. But, Christ, you wouldn't listen. At times you're a stupid sonofabitch, you know."

Valeri turned from the fireplace to look at his sister. Her face was a little red. She wore no makeup, and her hair was pulled back. When she was a little girl she had won the science prize in the third, fourth, and fifth forms. But afterward science didn't mean a thing to her. Valeri had always wondered if she had been distracted by a boy, or if she had simply lost interest.

"Do you know anything about Nadia Burdine?"

"Who?"

"Nadia Burdine."

"Father said something about her."

Valeri felt out of balance. His father had denied her existence; now his sister acknowledged it. The house was quiet except for the crackle of the fire, and the Siberian wind outside around the eaves.

"Was she your lover, Valeri "

"No . . ."

"Tanya can help you."

Valeri felt distant. The cognac was settling in his stomach like a pool of molten steel.

"We can all help you."

"Only . . . ?" Valeri prompted.

"Only what?"

"You want me to tell you something," Valeri said. He put his cognac snifter down on the fireplace mantel and looked around the big room. "Is it in the telephone, Lara? Or the lamps? The couches? Chairs? Maybe they put them in the walls?"

Lara had stepped back. "What are you talking about?"

"The microphones. The surveillance devices." He stepped away from the fireplace. "How about the paintings? Are the cameras there, Lara? Where should I look? Where do you want me to speak?"

"What are you talking about?"

"Don't lie to me. It's not necessary. I can understand."

"You're crazy."

Valeri looked back at her and laughed. "You're right, Lara. I'm crazy." He advanced toward her and she backed up in real fear. "There's no telling what I might do. I could go completely insane. I could run amok, you know." He reached dramatically into a pocket. "I could pull out a gun and shoot everyone dead!"

Lara stopped and looked at him. She shook her head. "You know we're trying to help you, Valerik."

"Don't call me that," he said tiredly.

"What?"

Valeri went back to his cognac on the mantel. The fire was warm. He was beginning to sweat.

"I don't understand you anymore," Lara said.

"Just don't call me Valerik."

"Why?"

"You never did before. Why begin now?" Valeri turned. "Who got to you, Lara? Was it Father? Or was it someone else?"

"I don't know what you're talking about."

"Tell me, Lara, that I need a friend. That I need a confidant. That my wife needs me. That my father trusts me. That my uncle loves me. That you respect me."

Lara puffed up. "It's all true, you know. But you don't want any help. You don't want to be loved."

Valeri forced a smile. "You were never very sincere."

"What are you talking about? You can't even keep a wife. She is having an affair. With a Jew."

"And you are more concerned about appearances than you are about family."

"Don't talk to me about family!" Lara shouted. "You gave up your family long ago. You made your choice, now you can live with it!"

"Or die with it."

"I truly think, sometimes, that is what you want."

"It wouldn't be so bad."

Lara shook her head in irritation. She finished her cognac and put her snifter down. "Listen to me. Life may be unbearable, my brother, but death isn't so pleasant either."

Valeri began to laugh. A little at first, and then almost uncontrollably, though he really wanted to cry. His sister had lived with his father for so long that she had picked up a lot of his mannerisms, including the frequent use of old Russian proverbs. He had come in here to be alone with his thoughts. But they could not allow that. His interrogation was taking much too long. There was no telling what damage his aberration had already done. Steps would have to be taken to rectify his errors. But first they had to know everything. Every last detail. Because they did not want to believe his reports, nor did they want to believe what they had seen with their own eyes. He had been sent here not only for the isolation, but because his father and sister were loyal Russians who meant a lot to him. A firing squad was final. Drugs were dangerous. But family . . . now *that* was a splendid idea.

"If you can't trust your own father . . . if you can't trust your sister, who can you trust?" Lara asked.

In many ways his sister was a lot like Larissa Okulov. Even their names were nearly the same. They both were disdainful, but Valeri suspected they both had inferiority complexes a kilometer deep: Larissa Okulov because of her youth, and because she did not fit in Moscow; and Lara because she had never fit anywhere. She was her father's girl, doomed to remain under his control and by his side for the remainder of his life.

"What's wrong with you?" Lara asked. "Have you totally lost control?"

Valeri turned away from her and looked at the fire. It was too warm on this side of the room and too cold on the other. It was the story of his life, he thought. He knew no middle ground. He tried to think what it would be like if he jumped into the fire and lay there. He didn't know if he would have the stamina to endure the pain. He had read somewhere that in burning to death it took fifteen seconds for the human body's sensory mechanisms to finally overload to the point that pain became meaningless. But fifteen seconds was an immensely long time, an eternity; fifteen seconds of the most unendurable pain imaginable to a human being was horrifying even to contemplate.

Lara watched her brother for a long moment, then turned and left the room.

By the end of the week Valeri was beginning to come back to reality. He was beginning to take an interest in his surroundings. For instance, he began to notice that he was being guarded, in a manner of speaking, day and night. Always there seemed to be at least one of his father's men around somewhere. Doing work on the house, repairing the oil furnace, fixing the car (a big Zil limousine, one of the only ones in all of Khabarovsk), painting one of the spare rooms, serving dinner, doing the marketing, even courting his sister.

One of them, Fedyanin, who came to fix a fuse in the electrical panel in the kitchen, was a young lieutenant in communications. Valeri sat drinking his morning tea watching him work. They struck up a conversation and soon Valeri was answering innocent questions about Moscow and the girls at the university.

The next afternoon Fedyanin was back to fix something else, though this time he had not bothered to bring his tools.

"How did they get you to come out here for this kind of work?" Valeri asked.

"I was born here," Fedyanin said naïvely. "Easier than bringing in an outsider."

"No, I meant to watch me."

Fedyanin was embarrassed. He jumped up and went to the fuse panel where he began pulling out glass fuses.

"Be careful that you don't electrocute yourself," Valeri said.

Fedyanin hid his head in shame. He was very young.

"It's not your fault," Valeri said kindly. "I'll talk to my father. He'll assign someone else. There won't be any trouble."

"No," the young lieutenant said, turning around.

"You'd rather stay?"

"Yes."

Valeri had to smile. The lieutenant was being very obvious. "My sister?"

"She is beautiful," Fedyanin said, glowing.

"I won't say anything if you don't."

When Fedyanin was gone, Valeri put on his coat and left the house. No one stopped him; in fact no one even talked to him. But when he looked back two men were walking fifty meters behind him. Beyond them was a car. When he stopped, they stopped. When he started, they did. There was no way for him to escape, of course. But he wondered if they would try to prevent him from committing suicide. It was an intriguing thought.

For the remainder of that afternoon Valeri amused himself by devising several suicide schemes. The best part was that none of them knew what he was thinking. If they did, he suspected they'd have him put in restraints.

It was a Monday, Valeri thought, when Lieutenant Fedyanin came for him in a Zhiguli with military markings. Fedyanin would not talk on the long ride out to the Northern Missile

Defense Command's base headquarters, nor would he come inside. Valeri was directed to the second-floor conference room where he was greeted by an older, kindly-looking man with gray hair and thin wire-rimmed glasses who sat on the far side of the long table.

"Come in, Valerik, please do come in," the man said. He wore civilian clothes, and looked rather shabby. Valeri almost felt sorry for him.

A wire mesh covered the three windows that looked out over the parade grounds, beyond which was an ice-skating rink. The boys here under his father's command had it easy compared to those in other Siberian commands.

The civilian had a thick stack of file folders in front of him on the highly polished table. "Please, sit down, Valerik."

Valeri closed the door and sat down across from the civilian who reached across the table. They shook hands.

"Please, I am called Romanov."

Valeri smiled.

"Ah," Romanov shrugged. "A romantic name, you are thinking. But I am no relation to the dynasty, though in all honesty the name did help in the United States."

With what, Valeri wondered, but he didn't ask.

Romanov busied himself with his files. He laid out a large tablet and several sharpened pencils, then took off his wrist-watch and propped it up in front of him as a reminder of just how precious his time really was.

He looked up.

"So, Valerik. We have spoken with all the principals back in Moscow . . . as far as that has been possible . . . and we think we have a fairly complete handle on the story. Madame Okulov, General Demin"—here the interrogator glanced down at an open file folder—"Oleg Votrin, Fainna Skvorstov."

"Nadia Burdine?"

Romanov looked up again. "Who?" he asked innocently. He flipped through several other file folders. "Who?" he asked again.

"You know," Valeri said.

The interrogator took off his glasses and rubbed his watery eyes. Somehow the act made him seem vulnerable. Valeri was beginning to see that it was all put on to throw him off.

"This is the girl you have mentioned before?"

"She is the daughter of an American POW we are holding on Karaginskiy Island."

"Have you ever been to Karaginskiy Island?" Romanov asked.

Valeri shook his head.

"A desolate place, let me tell you. There isn't much there. A few seals. A lot of birds."

"Bertonelli knows everything."

"Anthony Bertonelli?" Romanov asked. He held his glasses to his eyes and examined a photograph in one of his files. He lifted it out and handed it across. "This one?"

Valeri looked at the photo. It showed the body of a man who had been shot in the face with a high-caliber weapon at least three times. It was impossible to say who the man was. But it definitely could have been Bertonelli. The build was the same, the shape of the face and neck the same. The clothing the same.

"There was another man with him, I believe. Grant . . . ? Something like that."

"They still know."

"Know, Valerik? Know what? And who are *they*?"

"The Americans. Langley. They know about the POWs."

"And how do they know about these people?"

"I told them."

"Maybe we are getting somewhere. How did you communicate with Langley?"

"I told Bertonelli and Grant."

"They are dead," Romanov said irritably. "Don't you believe your own eyes?"

"That's not Bertonelli's body."

"But it is," Romanov insisted. He took the photo from Valeri and turned it over. "See?" he said, holding it up. Bertonelli's name was printed on the back along with a KGB file number.

"They still know enough."

"Even though you now admit that Bertonelli . . . could be dead?"

"I gave him a number . . . what I thought was a telephone number. He transmitted this to Langley, and they replied that the number was a serial number for a United States Air Force pilot . . . Captain Robert Burdine."

"American military serial numbers are the same as their

national social security system identification codes. Nine digits, I believe.''

''In the sixties when Captain Burdine was shot down and taken prisoner in Vietnam, American serial numbers were different.''

Romanov seemed to think about that for a moment or two. He nodded at length, as if he were willing to accept at least that much for the time being. ''And this number, it came from where?''

''A matchbook.''

''Ah, yes,'' Romanov said, suddenly remembering. ''The matchbook that you claim Colonel Okulov may have dropped when you shot him.''

''When I confronted the girl with what I knew, she finally admitted that Captain Burdine was her father. She said she was brought to Moscow by Colonel Okulov to prove to the Americans that we are holding American POWs.''

''Extraordinary. And you believed this?''

Valeri said nothing.

''You say, then, that this meeting was arranged between Colonel Okulov and Bertonelli to effect the exchange of the girl. She was defecting?''

''I don't know. But she had the knowledge of the POWs.'' Valeri hesitated. If the KGB had killed Bertonelli and Grant, then the KGB had Nadia's notebook. It would not matter, then, whether or not Valeri told Romanov about it. But if Bertonelli was not dead, if he had made it back to his embassy, then there was a very real possibility that the KGB had no knowledge of the POW list.

''Yes, go on,'' Romanov prompted.

''What have you done with her?''

''Can you give me the names or serial numbers of some of the other Americans allegedly being held?''

Valeri said nothing.

''Just one name?'' Romanov asked. He shook his head. ''Ah, Valerik. Just when things were beginning to go along so nicely between us. Now you balk at a simple question.''

''What have you done with Nadia?''

''We sent her home.''

''To Karaginskiy Island?''

Romanov laughed. ''Of course not. Her home is in Yakutsk. With her parents.''

"I called the KGB in Yakutsk. They have no record of her."

"A stupid error. Of course they have a record of her, as they do of all their citizens. Much of what you have done cannot strictly be blamed on you because you were given false information at various stages of your investigation. If you would like to see Nadia Burdinsky's birth certificate, her work and travel permits, I can produce them all."

Valeri was sure he could. Nor had he missed the interrogator's change of Nadia's last name to one that sounded more Russian than Siberian.

"But now that I have answered your questions, Valerik, please answer one of mine. Can you give me the name or serial number of just one more American you claim we are holding?"

"No," Valeri said. "I only know the one name."

Romanov stared at him for a moment or two, a hard look coming into his eyes. "You were heard to mention a number. You apparently hold the belief that as many as two hundred Americans are being held. How did you come by this figure?"

Valeri felt a sudden flush of triumph. Suddenly he knew that he had won at least this round with his interrogator. They were afraid of him, just as Chief Secretary Okulov had been. As long as he held back at least one fact, or made them *think* he was holding something back, they would have to keep him alive.

"I don't recall having mentioned anything like that."

"I came here to help, Valerik. To get everything straightened out."

"I can return to work when this is over? Are you saying that to me, Romanov?"

Romanov slapped a file folder shut. "A little cooperation was all I asked," he said, hurt.

"Wash a pig as much as you like, it goes right back to the mud, eh?" Valeri said. "What are you afraid of, Romanov? What really frightens you?"


Two days later he walked alone downtown from his father's house. It was early, well before noon when he crossed Komsomol Square and went down to the river. China was just across the steppe. He found that fact intriguing, almost overwhelmingly so. He climbed over the iron fence at the end of the quay, picked his way across the rocks, and started across the ice.

Lieutenant Fedyanin and a bull-necked sergeant came after him. "Major Kostikov. Please," Fedyanin called to him.

Valeri stopped reluctantly and turned back. He was finally starting to feel the confinement of Siberia. It was the Soviet Union's greatest paradox and most monstrous joke.

For several days Valeri allowed himself the luxury of remembering his past (recent as well as far) in daydream snatches. He played a game with himself, trying to remember only the good scenes for as long as possible, only giving in to the bad when his head throbbed, his stomach ached, and his heart pounded.

As before, his thoughts seemed to be drawn each time back to Nadia. Nadia of the dark hair and doe eyes. Nadia—Valeri's daughter of the Nile, his mystery. He couldn't help himself.

Uncle Gennadi arrived on the eighteenth, barely three hours before the blizzard. War, even from the great Northern Missile Defense Command, was impossible for the duration of the storm. A cyclical peace had come to Khabarovsk. A lot of people looked forward to these interims.

"Aunty Serafima sends her greetings," General Demin said. He looked winded and a bit bemused, as any city creature does upon first reaching the deep country.

"I meant to apologize for my behavior at dinner that night."

"That is not necessary, nephew."

"I don't get any news out here."

They were in a corner of the great kitchen, by a big window that looked down over a pond across from which was a pleasant copse of woods. This afternoon they could see nothing but the white driving snow. It gave Valeri a particularly claustrophobic feeling.

"I came out to see what I could do to help."

"What about Nadia?" Valeri asked, lowering his voice.

"Who?"

Valeri's breath left him. "Uncle Gennadi?"

"It was always the same with you, Valerik. You were forever trying to run before you could walk."

"You know the whole story."

"We're trying to save your life," General Demin said with much feeling. "But you are going to have to cooperate."

"I counted on you, Uncle."

"There are microphones in this house," General Demin whispered, leaning forward over the great table.

"I know. They hear you as well as me."

"But there can be friends editing the tape."

"You want me to cheat?"

"I want you to live, Valerik!"

"Then tell me the truth," Valeri urged. "Short of that, sign the order for me to return to Moscow."

General Demin sat back. "I am truly sorry."

"So am I, Uncle Gennadi," Valeri said tiredly. He hadn't been getting much sleep lately. And just now the blizzard blowing past the big window was hypnotic. "They say Bertonelli was killed and that Nadia was returned to Yakutsk. I don't believe either story."

"Why do you fight . . . ?"

"When I tell the entire story, Uncle . . . when they know everything that I know, then they will kill me."

"Your father will not allow it."

"My father is only a general."

"A hero of the state—"

"Who is ashamed of his son."

"No, Valerik. You are wrong. Terribly wrong."

Valeri got to his feet, looked down at his Uncle Gennadi for a long time, then turned and left the big kitchen. It was infinitely easier to deal with an interrogator such as Romanov than it was to deal with a father or a sister or an uncle. A family member could inflict more pain than the most adept torturer.

## 19

After the departure of General Demin and the interrogator Romanov, they left him alone. Not even the guards bothered to come around any longer. Valeri supposed that Lieutenant Fedyanin was sad that he could no longer visit with Lara. But it was just as well, because Lara, once disappointed in love, would never again place her heart on the line.

By the beginning of February the winter storms had fallen into a pattern; two or three days of calm, relatively warm weather would be followed by increasing cloudiness, a big wind, a lot of snow, and a sudden clearing that would leave behind crystal skies and temperatures twenty and thirty degrees below zero Fahrenheit. A week later it would begin to warm up again and the pattern would repeat itself.

His father and sister no longer mentioned Moscow, though from time to time he would catch them looking at him oddly.

He began to wonder why the KGB still had not killed him. He supposed it was possible that Bertonelli had somehow made it out of the country and now they were holding their breath to see what might happen next. Then again, he realized that it was possible he could have been all wrong. Bertonelli could have been the deceiver after all.

But, then, who was Nadia? Where was Nadia? At times during the night he would pace his room, barely able to control himself, barely able to keep from screaming out into the night.

One morning after Valeri's father had gone off to the base and Lara had already gone into town, Lieutenant Fedyanin showed up. He was flushed from the cold.

"My sister is not here," Valeri said. "Didn't you see her leave?"

271

"I saw her," Fedyanin said. He was young, probably not more than twenty-five or twenty-six, Valeri figured. His face was baby smooth, his eyes wide and blue and guileless. "As a matter of fact I got to speak with her. For just a moment."

"You came to see me?"

"Your father asked me to speak with you."

"About what?"

"A job."

Valeri had to laugh, though he didn't want to be unkind. "In case you haven't noticed, I no longer have a staff, so I could not offer you a job if I wanted to."

"No," Fedyanin said eagerly, "I've come to ask if *you* would like a job."

"That is very good. Now I am to be a lieutenant's assistant."

Fedyanin was embarrassed. "No, Comrade Major. You would be working as an intelligence evaluator at base head-quarters. GRU. Directly under your father."

Valeri just looked at him. He didn't know why he was making it so hard for the younger man. "I would have to work in the vault, I suppose."

Fedyanin nodded.

"Behind lock and key. Hunched over a desk. Seeing reports and data, never knowing what was happening outside unless a weather report crossed my desk."

Fedyanin's face darkened.

"No, Comrade Lieutenant, I do not want such a job. I would rather sweep snow with the other prisoners, or the *babushkas*."

This latest development was disturbing to Valeri. He simply did not know what to make of it. Unless it was a ploy to throw him off his guard, bring him back into the fold—show him by example that the state had his best interests at heart. By offering him a job they could also be sending him the message that he was going to be out here for a long time to come; he might just as well earn his keep. Fedyanin was crestfallen. He left without another word.


Valeri got into the habit of walking into town at noon for lunch at the Amur Hotel on Lenin Street, unless the weather was impossible. The building was primitive, nothing like the ten-story Intourist Hotel for foreign tourists, but to him it was old Russia. It made him remember his grandmother. He sat by the window looking out at the passersby on the street.

"You may be here for a long time, Comrade Major,' Fedyanin said.

Valeri looked up. He hadn't noticed the younger man come in. "Have you had lunch yet?"

"I would like to be your friend."

"Sit down and have some vodka, then. Let me tell you something."

Fedyanin hesitated.

"Please. I don't even know your first name."

"Anatoli," the young lieutenant said, sitting down. "Anatoli Vasilevich, after my father who was an officer. It is why I was sent to the university."

Valeri emptied a tea glass and poured Fedyanin a stiff measure of vodka.

"If you want to be my friend, Anatoli Vasilevich, you will have to drink with me."

"I am on duty."

"So am I."

Fedyanin was startled. It showed.

"Have you been told why I am here?"

"You're the general's son. It is enough for me . . ."

Valeri wagged his finger. "If we are to be friends, Vasha, then you must be truthful with me. Always truthful."

"I want to be your friend. And not just because of your . . . father, or your sister. I've watched you. You are a good man. Your father has a lot of respect for you, but your sister is afraid of you."

It was a big speech for Fedyanin. "In Moscow, you know, I killed a chief secretary of the Politburo. And I stand accused of being a traitor."

Fedyanin hung his head. "I know," he muttered.

"I am a general's son and they can't kill me, is that it?"

Fedyanin said nothing.

"Or, Vasha, could it be something else?"

He wondered what blot Fedyanin had on his record to get him this assignment. "Have you been sent today to offer me another job?"

"Border surveillance. They need a communications man in the air."

"The Chinese border?"

"Yes, Comrade Major."

"Odd job for a traitor, wouldn't you think?"

"I was sent to offer you the job," Fedyanin said. He pushed his tea glass away and got to his feet.

"I'll take it," Valeri said. "But I would like to ask you a question before you go off."

Fedyanin stood there looking at Valeri, not knowing if he should stay or go, at once fascinated and frightened.

"Do you believe in your country, Vasha? Really believe in it?"

Fedyanin turned and fled.

His patrols began the first week in March. For ten days he attended briefings about the threat of the Chinese government against the peaceful peoples of the Soviet Union. The yellow horde bred like mindless animals, he was told. A mathematician even spent an afternoon showing him the exponential curve the Chinese population was taking, so that by the midpoint of the next century the combined weight of all Chinese citizens would equal that of the entire planet. When Valeri suggested nuclear weapons be dropped on the mainland to control such a threat, the mathematician left.

They figured they could teach him what he had to know in the air. The big, slow-flying Tupolevs had a range of two thousand kilometers with a healthy reserve. He was given a powerful set of binoculars, a headset with a microphone, a heavy flying suit, and he was told to carefully watch the passing landscape forward of the wing. On one side of the Amur River was China. On the other, of course, was the Soviet Union. If anything moved between the two, anything at all, he was to report at once. Fedyanin came along, and he got very adept in the first few days at spotting the big Siberian elk. It became their joke, much to his chagrin. Every day he was asked just how it was he could spot a good Soviet elk, versus an elk about to defect. They were the Red Seven crew—the pilot, the copilot, the political officer, and Valeri and Fedyanin, spotters who were listed as radio operators.

On Mondays they were given one hour of crash drill, in addition to their eight-hour flight. On Tuesdays they had motivational briefings. On Wednesdays, in-air maintenance exercises on an old wreck that was called the simulator. On

Thursdays they attended commander's call, and on Fridays, political briefings. Saturdays were designated nontraining days. And for Red Seven, for the month of March, Sundays were off days.

The border was an amazing thing, to Valeri. At first he was unable to distinguish between the two sides of the river. To him there simply was no difference. The border was nothing more than an arbitrary political division. But in time he began to see how the land to the south could be Chinese, and how the land to the north could be the *Rodina*, the mother, Russia. After a while he was amazed that he hadn't always seen what was so evident. There was a wholly different look and texture to each side of the river. Each was clearly distinguishable from the other at the five hundred meters at which they flew their patterns.

On the second week of patrols their hydraulics failed a hundred kilometers out of Khabarovsk, and they crashed. Their pilot, Viktor Rogachev, a young kid from Omsk who could and had flown nearly everything that could fly and a few things that could not, told them calmly that they were going in.

"Sorry, boys, but you're going to have to hang on to your testicles or you'll have them roasted for lunch," he said with a laugh. But they could hear the strain in his voice.

Valeri could see that they were in trouble. They always remained at least half a kilometer within the Soviet side of the river, but now they were angling directly toward the river, across the midpoint of which was China.

Apanaenko, the political officer, was screaming incoherently into his microphone. Valeri yanked off his headset and shouted at the man to be silent. No one could hear him.

They were going in much faster than Valeri expected they should. He got the impression that the riverbanks were much higher there than they were around Khabarovsk, and then he yanked his seat harness tightly around his middle and chest, braced his legs against the forward bulkhead, and lowered his head into his arms.

"Valerik!" Fedyanin screamed as they hit the ice with a tremendous squeal of twisting, torn metal and a two-hundred-kilometer-per-hour toboggan-hiss of snow beneath the fuselage. They were airborne again for a second or two and this time when they hit, something crumpled and broke at the rear of the airplane.

Valeri looked up as they bounced into the air again, and the aft third of the aircraft fell away, a tremendous blast of subzero air and snow whipping into the open cabin. They hit a third time, bounced, hit a fourth, and then began to twist to the left, toward China, Valeri thought, snow flying everywhere.

He couldn't seem to control his arms and legs. Each time the airplane spun around they seemed to fly away from his body as if they were iron nails being drawn out by a powerful magnet.

But then the plane tipped forward up on its nose with a huge bang and fell over on its side.

Then it was still. Valeri hung from his seat harness listening to his own heart, listening to the wind, and smelling the rich, heady odor of aviation fuel over the warm, ticking-oil smell of a cooling engine that was less than a meter away from his left shoulder.

He looked up after a while. The fuselage all around him had been peeled open like a sardine tin. His position had been directly over the portside wingroot. The wing itself had been crumpled upward, bending over the top of him, offering him some protection. Mostly he had survived by pure, blind luck. But the fuel tank in that wing had ruptured and was leaking now, down on the hot engine manifold.

The notion of fire suddenly galvanized his mind, and he started to move, slowly at first, then as the urgency of his situation penetrated his dazed mind, faster and more frantically.

His harness released all of a sudden, and he fell nearly three meters down onto Fedyanin's crushed, decapitated body.

"Vasha?" he croaked.

Valeri undid the lieutenant's harness, pulled his soft body out of the twisted chair, and then backed out of the open rear of the wreckage, leaving behind a long red streak in the snow.

A hundred meters from the aircraft Valeri let go of Fedyanin's broken arms and struggled back through the snow and scattered wreckage into the body of the plane.

Apanaenko's crushed body was easy to find, as was the copilot's. It took him a very long time to drag them out of the plane and across the bloodied snow to lay beside Fedyanin's remains. He had to rest then for a minute or so, and the cold wind was like a razor-sharp knife even through his thick, nylon arctic gear.

Smoke poured from the wreckage as Valeri dragged himself back for the last time. Inside, he worked his way forward, but Rogachev's body was nowhere to be found. Had he survived the crash and crawled away from the wreckage?

Valeri stood panting in the forward section of the fuselage trying to think it out, trying to make some sense of the cockpit that was crumpled and turned on its side. The window was gone, and the aircraft's nose was completely buried in the snow. The pilot's chair was gone. It should have been hanging from what now was the ceiling, but it simply was not there. Valeri reached up and tried to hoist himself to the edge of the opening, but he no longer seemed to have very much strength.

Someone or something thumped against the side of the fuselage. Valeri turned in time to see the interior of the airplane fill with bright yellow flames. It would be a clean, honorable way to die, he thought. But he was afraid.

Valeri jumped up on the broken armrest of the copilot's chair, which gave him just enough height to reach the jagged edge of the broken window. He heaved himself up as a very hot blast of air rushed into the cockpit, searing and half melting his nylon flight suit.

A ragged edge of metal cut through his sleeve and bit deeply into his arm as he tumbled out onto the aircraft's nose and slid down into the snow. The very air around him seemed to dance and waver, and the odor of aviation fuel was everywhere, causing him to gag and vomit down the front of his singed parka.

He moved on instinct alone, directly away from the airplane, across the river to the south. He fell down, cracking his head on a patch of bare ice, but he got up almost immediately and stumbled ten meters farther, blood streaming down into his eyes. The Tupolev exploded in a tremendous ball of fire, the shock wave lifting Valeri off his feet and propelling him fifteen meters farther across the river into a deep snowdrift.

He was conscious the entire time. Now he was temporarily relieved. Although he would probably freeze to death, at least he had escaped from the searing flames. He felt very sorry about Lieutenant Fedyanin, though. Maybe Lara would cry for him.

\* \* \*

Valeri's burns and injuries were mostly superficial. Though he had spent more than two hours buried in the snowdrift before the rescue helicopters arrived, he suffered only a minor case of frostbite. After a night in the military hospital for observation, he was allowed to return home.

"They say you have requested to join another crew," his father said. "It isn't necessary, of course. You have proved your point against them: that you are not some coward or someone who hates his fellow countrymen. They can never question you about those values again. Even the doorstep of the rich finds itself embarrassed by the poor. What I can't understand is why you haven't agreed to cooperate with the KGB. They are merely trying to help. What are you trying to prove, Valeri? It simply does not make sense."

"Yes, it does, Father. If you just think about it long enough."

"They want to give you a medal for what you did out there."

"Pull dead bodies out of an airplane?"

"You didn't know they were dead. You risked your life. Lara is very proud of you."

"Lara is afraid of me. Lieutenant Fedyanin, who was in love with her, by the way, told me."

"I want you to call Tanya. Tell her that you are all right."

Valeri shook his head. "No, Father, I will not. There is nothing between us in any event. But I will accept their medal."

His father got to his feet. "Valeri, you must understand that even I cannot get you back to Moscow. They will never let you return."

"I suppose not."

"You must see it from their position."

"I can be happy here."

His father looked away.

"Could we still go to Yalta in the spring?" Valeri asked.

"Why are you doing this?"

"Doing what, Father?"

"Defying the system. Denying your Russianness."

"I'm only doing one of those, not the other."

"Maybe they won't give you a medal after all."

"No need for it."

"But it would be nice."

"Yes, Father. It would be nice."

His father left, his eyes glistening. Valeri realized that it was the very first time he had ever seen his father cry.

Valeri no longer had a Fedyanin to watch over him, and he came to miss the young man. Lara avoided him, and he let himself imagine that she was mourning her timid suitor. It made him think more of her, somehow; it made him believe she was human, that she had a softness that he'd never seen.

In four days he was assigned to another crew. This time he had no feeling for them. They were faces without personalities.

This time, instead of flying along the Father Amur, they flew south along the Ussuri River, China to the west. Their aircraft was newer and could fly faster and remain in the air longer. Special view ports had been built into the belly of the airplane so that the observers could lie in pods with a 360-degree view below, foothills and mountains rising on either side of the river. Bordachev was the second observer, Artemyev the political officer, Lyalin the copilot, and Trusov the pilot.

Valeri never really watched below. Instead his mind kept coming back to an image of Nadia as she had looked at the doorway of the apartment the first time he had ever seen her, then later as she lay wounded in the other apartment, and finally as he had seen her last, frightened, sad, and yet defiant.

At times he thought he was going insane. He was falling in love with the image of a twenty-one-year-old girl who by all rights had to hate him and everything he stood for.

*I have no friends.* He could hear her voice over and over again in his head.

*I hate you, Valeri Kostikov. I shall always hate you.*

He could feel her skin. He could smell her odor. He could see her clearly in his mind's eye. He knew her clothes, he knew her walk, and the way she lay on her side when she slept. He knew her, he realized, more intimately than he knew Tanya, which didn't make any sense at all. Yet it felt so very real to him. So very natural.

"There is no reason that you should remain on my crew,"

the pilot told him. "I don't give a damn if your father is the commander. I have a job to do and deadheads do not help me. If you want to come along as a passenger, there isn't much I can do about it. But I will have someone else in the starboard pod. I don't know who the hell you think you are, but you don't impress me very much."

It was the end of March. All of Siberia was still gripped in the icy clutches of winter. Valeri stole a Nazi Luger and ammunition from his father's war collection. As far as he could determine, the weapon was still in working order. The next morning he hitched a ride early out to the base with his father. They did not say much to each other during the long drive, which was just as well because Valeri felt certain he would betray himself if he had to answer questions. (It made him smile inwardly to think that if the interrogator Romanov were here now, he could have anything he wanted.)

"Come to my office when you get back, Valeri," his father said in front of base operations. "We can have supper at the club."

"Sure," Valeri said. He turned and angled directly across to where Trusov was checking their aircraft. The others had not shown up yet. It was far too early for them.

"Ah, Kostikov," Trusov said, looking over his shoulder. "I have not changed my mind, you know."

Valeri took out the Luger, cycled a live round into the firing chamber, and making sure that none of the maintenance personnel were near enough to see what was happening, pointed the gun at the pilot, whose mouth dropped open.

"We're going flying, Captain. Now."

"Are you crazy, or what?"

"Either do as I say, or I shall kill you. I have nothing to lose. I think you know that."

Trusov looked back toward the maintenance supervisor's office.

"Now," Valeri said, and he began to squeeze the trigger. He had no idea how much pressure it took to fire. It would be just as much a surprise to him as it would be to Trusov.

"Wait," the pilot said.

Valeri relaxed the pressure.

"Where do you want to go? We can't make Moscow without refueling, and our own jets would shoot us down before we reached Japan. Why don't you just give me the gun and we'll forget about it.''

"I don't want to shoot you.''

"They would kill you.''

"Yes.''

"Then where do you want to go, you crazy bastard? What is more important to you than your own life?''

"Karaginskiy Island.''

Trusov looked stupidly at him. He did not understand. He could not understand.

"You will either climb up into the aircraft within the next five seconds, or I will kill you.''

"We won't get very far,'' Trusov said, but he turned and climbed up into the airplane.

Valeri came in behind him, closed and dogged the hatch, and together they went forward to the cockpit where Valeri took the copilot's seat.

"Tell the tower that we have our crew aboard. We're leaving a little early, that's all,'' Valeri said, holding the Luger on the pilot.

Trusov looked from the gun to Valeri's eyes and then nodded and began flipping switches. "Radar will see which direction we are heading.''

"We will go in the direction we are supposed to go for the first few kilometers, then we will drop below radar and turn northeast.''

"You have this all worked out.''

"I wish I had.''

"What is there on Karaginskiy Island for you?''

"You will see when we get there.''

"It is more than a thousand kilometers, with no place to refuel or land.''

"There is a landing strip on the island.''

"I don't think so.''

"Then we will die out there, won't we,'' Valeri said, raising the Luger.

Trusov looked away and shook his head. "I said: 'If Major Kostikov is pushed, he will push back. And there is no telling in which direction he will push.' 'Trust us, Stanislav,' they said. 'The Major is crazy, not violent.' ''

Valeri's heart was sinking. "I killed a man in Moscow.''

"I know,'' Trusov said. "I told them this. But they said

that it was a grudge killing. With me there could be no grudge."

"Are you going to take off?"

"I couldn't if I wanted to, Comrade Major," the thick-necked pilot said almost sadly. He reached forward and tapped a pair of gauges on the panel. The legend over one read Fuel Pressure, over the other, Fuel Weight. Both read near zero.

Valeri stared at the gauges for a long time. He'd been outmaneuvered again, which, considering everything, was not particularly surprising. He became aware of the oil and electronic smells of the aircraft.

"I'm sorry, comrade."

"There is no reason for you to apologize to me, Captain. You simply are doing your job."

Trusov nodded. "But what really is on Karaginskiy Island?"

"You haven't been told?"

"No, sir."

"Then you do not want to know, believe me," Valeri said. He looked out the cockpit window. A dozen armed Border Guard troops had gathered around the airplane, their weapons pointed at the cockpit. He handed the Luger over to Trusov. "You win," he said.

"Bastard," Trusov swore, and he smashed the butt of the Luger into the side of Valeri's head.

**20**

Valeri was taken to the stockade where he was isolated from the other prisoners. During the first thirty-six hours his only visitors were a pinch-faced little captain with acne scars who was the base courts-martial officer, the pilot Trusov who testified in front of him into a tape machine, and finally, in the early evening of the second day, the interrogator Romanov back from Moscow. Valeri was almost glad to see a familiar face.

"So, Valerik, I could have almost predicted this." Romanov clucked his tongue. "Yet I read how you risked your life to pull your comrades out of a burning airplane while under fire from Chinese border guards. All of Moscow is talking about your exploits."

"They were already dead, and there were no Chinese," Valeri said

"Do you deny going back to the airplane? In risking your life?"

Valeri shook his head.

"Then what does it matter, the details of your heroism? Hardly anyone is surprised, you know. Your father is a hero of the Soviet people, as was your grandfather. You are merely following your heritage. And a glorious heritage it is." Romanov led him down the corridor into the orderly room where he was given a parka, and then they went outside and started across the parade ground past base administration.

"Where are we going?" Valeri asked.

Romanov grinned. "You'll see. You really will see this time, and perhaps we can get this entire silly business over with. Spring will be here soon. A beginning. New life, new ideas. But first the old have to be laid to rest, so to speak."

Romanov took Valeri's arm. "Actually I have an apology to make to you, Valerik. This could have been done months ago, or at least weeks ago, saving us all trouble. If only I had seen the light. If only I had understood what it was you truly wanted. You know you could have told me this and saved us all the trouble."

"I don't understand."

"It is the girl. She is the key. She's been the key all along. Silly me, I didn't see it. The fact of the matter is, I am here finally, and so is she."

Valeri stopped short, his heart in his throat. "Nadia Burdine is here? From Karaginskiy Island?"

"Nadia Burdinskly from Yakutsk is here," Romanov said impatiently. "Come. She is waiting for you."

Valeri shook his head. He understood what they were trying to do now. They were using Nadia against him. He would be expected to confess about the notebook, about the fact he knew how many Americans were being held prisoner. "What if I don't want to see her?"

"You have no choice."

"No?"

Romanov shook his head. "No."

They stopped outside the bachelor officers' quarters, which were housed in a modern three-story concrete-block building. The walls had been badly stuccoed and were peeling, showing in spots the imperfectly fitted blocks and crumbling mortar.

"She is on the third floor, at the end. We have isolated the entire section for you two."

There were no lights on up there. Valeri didn't know what to do.

"We will meet again in the morning. Eight o'clock. Someone will come for both of you." Romanov turned and walked off.

Valeri went inside and took the stairs up. Somewhere else in the building he could hear music playing, and the sounds of conversation and laughter. He could smell the delicious odors of dinner being served in the mess on the first floor.

The third-floor corridor was dimly lit. He walked to the end room, pushed open the door, and went in.

Nadia stood by the window looking down across the way he and Romanov had come. She wore the same knit dress as before. This time her hair was down around her shoulders.

"I didn't know why they had brought me here until I saw you coming across the base with that other one," she said without turning around. "They told me that I was to say I was from Yakutsk. No matter what happened, I wasn't supposed to change my story."

Valeri just looked at her. Obviously they were listening. It was also possible that they had hidden a video camera somewhere in the room. But he found he did not care.

Nadia turned around. She had put on a little weight since Moscow. Her cheeks had filled out, her breasts were larger, and her hips more rounded. She looked good.

Valeri closed the door. He took off his parka and tossed it over a chair. She was watching him, her eyes wide, her nostrils flared, a little color in her cheeks.

"What happened?" she asked, her voice soft.

"It got out."

"Are you sure, Valeri Kostikov?"

Valeri nodded. "We wouldn't be here together if it hadn't. But I thought you were dead."

She shivered. "I've been in Moscow all this time. Waiting. They would not allow me to return. I have been going mad not knowing what is happening."

"They're afraid of us."

"Why?"

"Because of what we know. Because we are right."

She smiled, then turned and looked out the window. "You are a fool, Valeri Kostikov. An even bigger fool than I am."

Valeri crossed the room to her. She had a musky, alive odor. He was shaking with the desire to touch her. She turned back again, looked up into his eyes, and then seemed to glide forward into his arms.

# III

# GULAG

# 21

It was a warm Washington spring. The sidewalks through the park behind the Central Intelligence Agency complex were filled with employees this noon.

Admiral F. Stewart Taylor (Ret.) was a large, barrel-chested man with thick white hair and dark gray, serious eyes. He wore a blue pin-striped suit and black wing-tipped shoes. His bodyguards walked ten paces behind him and Bertonelli. He created quite a stir. It wasn't often the director of the Central Intelligence Agency was seen in person. He was like a television or movie star; bigger than life, surprising in the flesh.

The park wasn't so pleasant now because of the construction still going on for the new wing. But it was nice to be outside, especially for Bertonelli who at long last was getting his hearing.

"Have you overlooked the obvious, Anthony?" Admiral Taylor asked.

"I've heard the argument, sir. It has been three months since Moscow. I've spoken with a lot of people."

"The names and serial numbers of our MIAs are not classified information. Anyone could pick a couple of hundred names and numbers, jot them down in a notebook, and pass them along."

"Yes, sir."

A jumbo jet roared overhead, coming down for a landing at Dulles Airport fifteen miles to the west. The sky was pale blue, but a haze hung on the horizon toward the city across the river.

"But you do not believe that happens to be the case."

"No, sir. They would not have killed their own people to simply encourage a disinformation plot."

289

"Are you so certain "

"Yes, sir," Bertonelli said without hesitation.

Admiral Taylor smiled tolerantly. "I'm not. Neither is Chuck Canfield. Neither, from what I gather, were DeMille or Ambassador Scott."

"They did not meet with Colonel Okulov or with Major Kostikov."

"KGB."

"Yes, sir. But what does the President say?" Bertonelli knew that he was going way out on a limb.

The admiral stopped and turned to face Bertonelli, a stern expression on his face. "Needless to say, the President has not been bothered with this."

Bertonelli felt a flush come to his face. He started to protest, but the DCI held him off adroitly.

"I think you had best listen to me now, Anthony. And listen with a closed mouth and an open mind. Can you do that for me?"

Bertonelli nodded.

"In the Soviet Union anything is possible. That is not rabid anticommunist doctrine. You must have an understanding of nondemocratic national purpose. It has to do with accountability . . . not to a people, but to a quite simple, and certainly publicly invisible, chain of command."

Bertonelli's first reaction was one of disdain. He could see DeMille as a power within the Agency's administration, and it was a frustrating vision. It was as if he were in a nightmare; he was trying to run, but he couldn't seem to make his legs work properly. But then he began to hear what the DCI was telling him.

"As an agency we can do nothing. You must understand that, Anthony. At least that much. Else we would be subject to knee-jerk reactions to every single vagary that came our way. We would literally shake ourselves to death. The Brits did it over the Philby business, and that was of little consequence in comparison to what you are bringing to us. We must maintain a certain inertia of conservative analysis and reaction. You can see that. We as an agency must be slow to act."

"We as an agency?"

"Exactly," Admiral Taylor said. They started to walk

again. "I'm glad you are beginning to understand what we are facing here."

"But it has been three months, sir. They could be dead."

"Yes, they could be. What are you going to do about it?"

The DCI was trying to tell him something. It was the reason they were not in his office. But Bertonelli felt stupid. "I don't understand what you are trying to tell me, sir."

"What proof are you searching for at this moment, Anthony? What data are you gathering? What witnesses are you interviewing? In short, what are you doing other than trying to convince as many high-ranking officials as you can that you are sincere and the rest of the world is wrong, merely on your say-so?"

"There's been no authorization . . ."

Admiral Taylor laughed. "From what I gather, such a consideration has never stopped you before. Have you, for instance, interviewed any of the North Vietnamese military officers now living in this country?"

"Sir?"

The director took a slip of paper from his pocket and handed it to Bertonelli. "Kim Phauong Tri. He was a colonel in the North Vietnamese army."

A New York address was written below Tri's name. It was in Greenwich Village.

"Colonel Tri defected to the south in May of 1972, shortly after the VC captured Quangtri. I was with Naval Intelligence at the time. In fact I interviewed the colonel."

"He has information?"

"It's possible. He teaches at New York University. Well respected, from what I hear."

"Excuse me, sir, but I don't understand what you're saying to me, at all. Who is Colonel Tri, and what exactly did he tell you when he defected?"

"You haven't heard a word I've said, have you, Anthony. It's quite extraordinary that you've come so far. Colonel Tri is just a name from the past. Nothing more. He was a high-ranking North Vietnamese officer. If anyone might have information for you, his kind would."

"Why him, Mr. Director?"

"Why not him?"

"There had to be dozens, perhaps hundreds of defectors. Many of them must be living here now. Why not them? What is so special about this one? What did he tell you in your interviews with him? Did he tell you about our POWs being taken to the Soviet Union?''

''I'm trying very hard to keep my patience with you,'' Admiral Taylor said sternly. ''You have been running around Washington irritating people to the point that even the Soviet embassy is stirred up.''

Bertonelli suddenly found it difficult to speak. They walked past some stone benches. A lot of secretaries and mid-level Agency employees looked up startled that they were seeing the director out here in the open. They started then down a long, looping walkway that led to a rear entrance to the building.

''I won't mention any names, of course, but I've been advised by some top people that this is still part of a sophisticated disinformation plot to bring not only you down, but anyone else who will believe you.''

''I'll go see Colonel Tri.''

''On your own Anthony. The Bureau would take unkindly to us snooping around on their home turf.''

They had come all the way around to the rear entrance of the main building. Admiral Taylor's bodyguard held the door open. Just down a short corridor was the director's private elevator up to his seventh-floor suite.

''Tell me something, Mr. Director,'' Bertonelli asked. ''Are the KGB watching Colonel Tri?''

''Not that I know of.''

''Am I being watched, sir?'' Bertonelli asked impulsively.

Admiral Taylor walked to the elevator. As he stepped inside the car he looked back. ''When you return from New York I will show you some satellite photos of a village. On Karaginskiy Island.''

The elevator door closed before Bertonelli could move a muscle. He realized that he was standing in the corridor with his mouth open. He had been handed the key on a silver platter. Why? And why had it taken them three months to do it? He was getting a very bad feeling about this, a very bad feeling indeed.

*        *        *

From the Agency, Bertonelli drove down to his apartment in North Arlington's Waverly Hills, where he packed an overnight bag. Since he had been back from the Soviet Union he had not seen his ex or his daughter. They were in California. He missed his daughter very much just now.

He caught the three o'clock flight out of National Airport to New York's JFK. The passengers were all businessmen, diplomats, or lobbyists, and were drinking heavily already.

Somehow the past three months never seemed to have happened for Bertonelli. On his return from Moscow he had figured on immediate action. He had confirmed the names and serial numbers of the MIAs in the notebook Kostikov had given him. All that remained was to come up with the satellite surveillance photographs of Karaginskiy Island, and then get the information to the President who would have to make the final delicate decision. But the photos were unavailable. The satellites were busy. Nor had he been able to see anyone of importance within the Agency. He had almost come to the conclusion that he would have to go to the *New York Times* with his story and blow the lid off what he was coming to think of as a cover-up.

All that was changed now. But he could not understand why he was being sent to interview a North Vietnamese colonel. If North Vietnamese defectors had had information as early as 1972 about Russians taking American POWs, why hadn't something been done about it? If, on the other hand, Colonel Tri had no information, why had the director offered him up? Bertonelli was getting the terrible feeling that he was being set up. But for what? A fall? He found himself watching everything around him. Being careful of his own moves. Always leaving himself an escape route.

In the meantime, Valeri Kostikov and the girl, Nadia Burdine, were probably dead by now. Bertonelli would never forget the look on the major's face in that apartment. He was a dispossessed man. He had lost his friend, he had lost the girl, and he had lost his country. But he was hanging on even though he would probably lose his life. Bertonelli realized that despite himself, despite his prejudices, he had come to admire and respect Kostikov.

And on Karaginskiy Island were two hundred American MIAs, and presumably their Siberian wives and offspring.

The plane landed at New York's JFK Airport a few minutes after four of a busy afternoon.

Bertonelli had checked his overnight bag through so that he could take his handgun. He retrieved the black leather bag from the carousel, then called New York University from a pay phone by the front doors. The operator connected him with Tri's department.

"Foreign Studies," a woman with a strong Asian accent answered.

"Is Mr. Tri in this afternoon?"

"Dr. Tri is in. Who may I say is calling?"

"A friend," Bertonelli said. "From Quangtri, 1972."

The woman hesitated. "Sir?"

"He'll know."

"One moment, sir," the woman said.

While he waited, Bertonelli glanced across the crowded terminal. Two men in dark suits were watching him. He was absolutely certain of it. One of them lowered what looked like a camera, said something to the other one, and they turned and walked out.

"Yes? Who is this?" A man's singsong voice came on the line.

Bertonelli watched as the two men crossed the sidewalk and climbed into a waiting Ford LTD that took off immediately. It was no coincidence. They had been watching him. It was possible they had the telephone number he had just dialed.

"Hello?" the man was saying on the line.

Bertonelli turned back. "Dr. Tri?"

"Yes, who is this, please?"

"I am a friend of Admiral Taylor. I've come here to speak to you on a matter of great importance. But you may be in danger at this moment."

"What are you talking about?"

"American POWs taken during the war."

"Who is this speaking?"

"Admiral Taylor sent me. We know about the American MIAs being held in the Soviet Union."

Someone said something in the background, and it sounded

as if Tri had covered the mouthpiece of the telephone. Bertonelli could hear voices, but the words were muffled.

"Colonel Tri?"

"I don't know who you are, or what you want, but I can assure you I have never heard the name Admiral Taylor, nor do I have any idea what you are talking about."

The voices continued in the background, but then the line went dead, and Bertonelli was left listening to a dial tone. He hung up.

For a long moment Bertonelli did not move from the phone. He had been set up. He thought about trying to reach the director, but he had a feeling the admiral would be out. No one had played straight with him in Moscow. The game apparently was the same in Washington. But why? What were they afraid of? The truth?


It was rush hour. Bertonelli's digital watch beeped twice for six o'clock by the time the cab left him off at Washington Square South and Broadway in Greenwich Village. The afternoon was warm. There were a lot of people in the park, playing chess, eating hot dogs from the carts, or playing Frisbee. The area had the feeling of a small-town neighborhood. All year the park was populated. A banner was draped across the arch on the opposite side of the park. Bertonelli could not read it from where he stood.

He walked across the street onto the university campus. A lot of students seemed to be in a big hurry. In the distance Bertonelli could hear sirens. Always in New York you expected to hear sirens, but this was different somehow. There seemed to be a lot of them, and they seemed to be heading this way.

A crowd had gathered in front of a building on the far side of a narrow mall. Bertonelli hurried across but then held up at the fringes. A plaque on the brown brick building read FOR-EIGN STUDIES. Two police cars, their red lights flashing, were parked at either end of the short street. Three other police cars, then an ambulance, arrived.


From a telephone booth three blocks away Bertonelli stopped long enough to telephone Dr. Tri's office. He wanted to make sure. A man answered.

"Sergeant Owens. Who is this?"

"Dr. Tri, please."

"Right. Who's calling?"

Bertonelli hung up, but not before he heard the commotion in the background, and the tension in Sergeant Owens's voice.

# 22

For the first time in more than two weeks the sun came up on the clear eastern horizon. A high pressure system had come through during the night and cleared the air, though the temperatures had dropped to record lows.

Valeri was hungry. He got dressed and went downstairs to the officers' mess at six, just as it opened. He was the first in line. No one said a thing about the fact that he filled his tray with two of everything: tea, toast, sturgeon, *aládyi* with jam, and two *ponchiki*, hot sugared doughnuts.

On the way out he stopped at the door and looked back. The cooks had come out of the kitchen and, along with the line servers, were watching him as if he were a fox who had just come into the coop and filched a chicken.

When Valeri returned, Nadia was sitting up in the bed, the sheet and blanket drawn up around her neck. Her eyes glistened in the early-morning light. She might have been crying.

"Are you all right?" he asked.

"Did you bring food?"

"Yes. Are you hungry?"

"Of course. I didn't have anything yesterday. I think they were afraid to feed me on the airplane."

Valeri set the tray on the bed, and she sat forward. The blanket·fell away exposing her small breasts and her flat stomach down to her navel. She didn't care. She was too hungry. She wolfed down her breakfast, and a part of Valeri's.

"Should I get more?" he asked when she was done.

She shook her head and smiled. "I'm eating like a Porky Pig."

"Where did they keep you in Moscow?"

"I don't know," she shrugged. "Lubyanka, I think. Do you have a cigarette?"

Valeri gave her one, and held a light for her. "What did you tell them?"

"Nothing," she said, looking up. She twisted the long cardboard filter between her thumb and forefinger. "But it is just a game, you know. They have drugs that will loosen our tongues."

"Sometimes there is brain damage."

She shook her head. "There, you see? You are one of them. I knew it all along."

"Who are *them*?"

"You know."

"No, I don't," Valeri said. He was thinking about Mikhail and Lipasov and Votrin. They were good men. But to Nadia they were the menacing *them*.

"Well, then, what are you doing here? Why didn't they already kill you?"

"I don't know. But they will not let me return to Moscow."

"To your wife?"

"I have no wife. Not now."

"Nor will they send me home," she said. She pulled the covers up and hunched her knees up to her chest. Her eyes were wide and clear, but very sad. "I don't understand what they want of us, Valerik. Most of the time I am afraid that they mean to kill my father and all the others. But then why have they arranged this meeting between us?"

Valeri had no answer for her.

"There is a reason. And when it comes it will not be pleasant."

It came to Valeri that he had fallen in love with her. He was sorry about it, because it made them both more vulnerable to Romanov and the others, yet he knew that he was glad.


It was just about eight o'clock. Romanov would be sending someone for them soon. Nadia had gotten dressed. She sat on the edge of the bed like a novitiate waiting for her exams.

Valeri stood looking out the window. The base had gradually come alive with the morning. There was no wind, and the plumes of smoke rose vertically from the chimneys. Everyone was in a hurry; no one lingered outside. Even the reveille ceremony on the parade ground went with dispatch.

In the beginning he had thought they were afraid of him: the Romanovs and whatever faction the interrogator represented from Moscow. Valeri Kostikov, son of a Soviet hero. A lot of power there not so easily dismissed. But then he had begun to wonder.

There had to be a good reason for keeping him alive, and for bringing Nadia here like this. But he could not see it.


"What did Colonel Okulov tell you? Did he actually come to Karaginskiy? Did he speak to your father and the others?" Valeri asked.

"Colonel Okulov never existed."

"I killed him in the Moscow Zoo. I thought he was defecting to the American . . . or at the very least passing state secrets."

"No secrets, Valerik. Just lies. There was no Colonel Okulov, just as there is no Karaginskiy Island. I am a runaway from Yakutsk. KGB has my records. You'll see."

She was playing devil's advocate, but she couldn't keep the bitterness out of her voice. It was well past eight now, and she was very nervous.

"He told you that your father and the others would be repatriated. But he also told you that whoever wanted to remain behind could do so. But didn't you realize that once the Americans found out about their people, they would insist on all of them coming home?"

"Yes," she said, "I thought of it."

"But it was easier to believe him, wasn't it?"

She nodded.

"Because the truth was too difficult to accept."

"What truth?" she asked.

"You know, Nadia."

"No."

"The Americans would take their own people back. They would insist on all of them returning. They would never allow even one to remain behind."

"No," she whispered.

"But their wives and children would not be allowed to come with them, would they?"

"Valerik . . ."

"My government wouldn't allow it. The Americans would not accept them. And there would be no place for them in any event, would there?"

"Why are you doing this?"

"Some of these men have wives and children in the United States. That's it, isn't it? No matter what happens, your mother could never return with your father."

"My mother is dead!" Nadia cried.

"No one could return but the Americans."

"Not true."

"All of you would have to be left behind."

"No."

"And what would become of you? Have you thought of that?"

She said nothing.

"Nadia?"

"Yes . . . Yes!" she screeched, holding her head.

"Yet you came to Moscow with Colonel Okulov. You believed him. You were ready to speak to the American."

"Yes."

"Why, Nadia?"

"Because . . ."

"Because why?"

"I was elected."

Valeri was standing over her. At first he was not quite sure he heard what he knew he had heard. She looked up into his eyes.

"There were two messages," she said. "One for Colonel Okulov's benefit, and the other only for the CIA representative. Only I never got to give it to him."

"You, along with your father's serial number, were the two proofs. Colonel Okulov brought you to Moscow as a proof. What else?"

Nadia said nothing.

"Nadia, what else?"

She jumped up and tried to push her way past him. He grabbed her arm and pulled her back.

"Nadia! Tell me!" he shouted. Romanov would be getting all this. Valeri did not care.

"You're hurting me."

He let her go and shoved her onto the bed. "You're a liar!"

She jumped up before he could turn to go and she clung to him. "Valerik!" she breathed into his ear. "Please believe me! They won't leave without us. That is the second message. They won't leave Karaginskiy without us. Oh God, it's their death warrant and everyone knows it."

The microphones could not have picked up her words. She had whispered too low and too close into his ear for it. He could feel her body beneath her dress against him; he could feel her heart mingling with his, the rise and fall of her chest with his, the sensuousness of her breasts and her long legs against his body.

Her face was turned up to his. Tears streamed down her cheeks. She was incredibly beautiful. But he had known that from the very first time he had laid eyes on her. Since that first time all of his thoughts had been dominated by a vision of her—by her smell, by her touch, by the snatches of brief impressions he had gotten on their first meeting.

He kissed her salty lips. At first she did not respond, but then she held him very close and he lifted her off her feet as he turned slowly around and around, drinking her very essence as if he were a man at an oasis after crossing a long, terrible desert.

He undressed her and gently lowered her to the bed, then took off his clothes and lay beside her. She shivered when he touched her flanks, but she arched her back and moaned when he took her breasts in his mouth, working his tongue around her nipples. She was crying and laughing at the same time as he entered her, her pelvis rising to meet his, her legs wrapped tightly around his waist, her fingers buried in his hair.

"Valerik," she cried out once from deep within her chest.

"I love you, Nadia," he heard himself say.

A young, nervous lieutenant came for them around ten. They wore parkas and thick felt boots against the cold that was so intense it took Valeri's breath away. The officer led them back across the parade ground to the base headquarters building, and up to the same second-floor conference room where Valeri had first met Romanov. They left their coats in the corridor. When they went in, the interrogator got heavily to his feet, his face long. This time in addition to his notes and files he had brought along a tape recorder and a stack of tapes. A samovar steamed on the sideboard.

"From what I've listened to so far, I believe you have told us almost everything we need to know."

Nadia stopped short. Her eyes were wide. "It was he at Lubyanka who questioned me," she said.

"You look none the worse for wear, my dear," Romanov said.

"Then you do know the mysterious Nadia Burdine from Karaginskiy Island," Valeri snapped.

"Yes? You have proof of this girl's identity? Of her birthplace? Her residence?" Romanov was impatient. "You yourself called her a liar just this morning. Do you deny that?"

"You listened," Valeri said foolishly.

"Did you think we would not, Comrade Kostikov? Do you think I am playing games with you here? Do you think all of this has been engineered for your amusement? So that you could get a piece of ass from a little Siberian whore?"

Valeri's muscles bunched up. He wanted to leap across the table and take the interrogator's throat in his hands, squeeze until the man's myopic eyes bulged out of their sockets, until his face turned purple. . . .

"We have nearly run out of time. Most of it you have used up these past months with your foolishness. Now it is time for us to get down to business."

Nadia touched Valeri's sleeve, and he could feel himself calming down.

"I don't know what you are talking about, Comrade Romanov."

"Don't turn against the very people who are trying to help you."

"Let us return to Moscow."

"That is not possible."

"Let us go to Karaginskiy Island, then."

Romanov sighed deeply. He took off his glasses and wiped them with a handkerchief. It was a habit of his. "There is an old saying. Be careful what you wish for; you just might get it." He put his glasses on. "Now, please, sit down. Will you have a glass of tea with me?"

"We've just had our breakfast," Valeri said. "But you would know that."

They sat together at the far end of the table. Nadia perched on the edge of her chair as if she were about to leap up and run away. She was shivering though the room was quite warm.

Romanov poured himself a glass of tea, added lemon, then came back to his things at the head of the table where he settled into his chair as if he were getting ready for a very long and probably arduous task.

He opened one of the files and extracted several sheets of paper. "What, for instance, did you mean when you said 'It got out.' That was you speaking, Valerik. Last night."

"I don't recall saying anything of the sort."

Romanov glanced back at his file. "Or you, Nadia. 'Are you sure, Valeri Kostikov?' " He looked up. "Sure of what? What is this mysterious *it* you two spoke of? The first words between you."

"What do you plan on doing with us, Romanov?" Valeri asked.

"That depends upon you."

"Are you going to kill us?"

"The thought has crossed my mind."

"And the Americans on Karaginskiy Island, will they be killed as well?"

"What Americans?"

"And their families? Their wives and children? They too?"

Romanov looked again at his file. " 'There were two messages.' Those are Nadia's words this morning. 'One for Colonel Okulov's benefit, and the other only for the CIA representative.' What were those messages?"

"Bertonelli is back in the United States with enough information to make you sweat," Valeri said.

"What information?"

"You can't risk killing them now, you know. If the United States government should happen to ask about them, it will be very difficult to deny their existence."

Romanov shrugged deprecatingly. "It is an unlikely story, Valerik. Even you must have had your doubts at the beginning, before you lost your heart. For instance, why would we have taken prisoners from Southeast Asia in the first place?"

"To work for the Soviet Union," Nadia said.

Valeri turned to look at her.

"You will tell me they were brainwashed," Romanov said.

"At first. But it stopped in the beginning."

"And afterward?"

"Nothing. We were left alone."

"Why?"

"I don't know. No one does."

"Why didn't you escape?"

"There are guards. And besides, there is nowhere to go. The sea is too wide and too cold; Siberia is too vast and too empty."

Nadia was lying, of course. It was obvious to Valeri. He wondered if Romanov had seen it. In the first years there would have been a lot of guards, fences perhaps, torture, deprivation of food and adequate shelter, the whole litany. But after the first wife had been taken, after the first baby had been born, the fences would have begun to come down. The prisoners themselves, as always was the case in a Soviet gulag, built their own psychological fences.

"Does the name Colonel Kim Phauong Tri mean anything to you?" Romanov asked. Valeri noticed that the interrogator had paid very close attention to Nadia's eyes in the asking.

"No," she said.

"I see," Romanov replied, disappointed. He got to his feet and went to the screened window where he lit a cigarette.

Nadia reached out and covered Valeri's hand with her own.

He looked into her eyes. "Why don't we just let them go, Comrade Romanov?" he said.

"Let who go?"

"The American MIAs from Southeast Asia whom we are holding on Karaginskiy Island. What have we been talking about?"

Romanov turned. "What prisoners? Goddamn you! Tell me! Convince me! Prove to me that we are holding prisoners . . . any prisoners . . . anywhere!"

"Nadia is the living proof."

"Of what? She is a little Siberian girl with an underfed body and an overripe imagination."

"Her father's serial number."

"Serial numbers of American soldiers have never been a state secret," Romanov said. "Is this all your Bertonelli has? This number and this girl's story?"

"Bertonelli is dead. You showed me his photograph."

Romanov came back to the table and looked into Valeri's

eyes. "Tell me, Major, why did you kill Colonel Okulov, and then engineer his brother's death as well? What did you hope to gain by such heinous crimes? Or were they murders of passion because you believed they both were sleeping with this little girl?"

Valeri had to work to keep his temper in check. Romanov was very good.

"I thought the colonel was defecting. It is in my report. When I tried to arrest him and his CIA contact, he pulled a gun on me."

"So you shot the colonel in self-defense. Are you a cowboy?" Romanov shook his head. His eyes were watery. "What of his brother, Chief Secretary Okulov? Why did you lure him to the apartment of your other lover, and then gun him down?"

"It did not happen that way, and I think you know it."

Romanov said nothing.

"I didn't lure him there. He followed my chief of staff—"

"Captain Shevchenko?"

"Yes," Valeri said. "His people killed Captain Shevchenko, and then took Nadia."

"Why, Comrade Major? Why did they kill your chief of staff? Had he made a threatening gesture?"

"No. He was just standing there, and they killed him for no reason."

Romanov straightened up. "Ah, Valerik, you must understand that nothing, absolutely nothing happens without reason." He flipped through some of his files. "Lipasov. One of your employees was found shot to death in a downtown apartment."

"Yes."

"Who killed him?"

"I did," Nadia said.

Romanov loooked over the edge of the file folder at her. "A liar and now a self-admitted murderess. Why did you kill this man? Did he offer you harm?"

Valeri was staring straight ahead. He was afraid to turn and look at her.

"I thought he worked for . . ."

"Yes?"

"The ones who want to kill everyone at the gulag."

"You know these others?"

"Only of them."

"From the colonel?"

"Yes," she said softly.

Romanov put down his file folder. "I appreciate your honesty with me, in at least this. Did you sleep with Colonel Okulov?"

"Now you have it all," Valeri interjected. "By our own admissions we are murderers. We can stand trial, and we can be banished to Siberia."

"That is true."

"But it still leaves you with the problem of the Americans on Karaginskiy Island. Bertonelli is not dead. He had enough information."

"It has been three months. Why do you suppose nothing has happened yet? Maybe his government doesn't believe him any more than I believe you."

"But it is true."

"You are willing to bet your life on it."

"Yes."

"What proof do you have? What else did you give Bertonelli?"

It had been three months, and nothing had happened. That much was true. Perhaps Bertonelli had not gotten out after all. Or, if he had, perhaps no one in his government believed him. Romanov had plugged all the leaks now, except for one: he did not know about the list. Apparently, however, it made no difference. There was truly nothing left now for them except a bullet in the back of the head.

"I'm trying to help you," Romanov said earnestly.

Valeri got to his feet and helped Nadia up. At the door something else occurred to him and he stopped and looked back.

"Who is Colonel Kim Tri? You mentioned his name."

Romanov looked at them both for a long time. Then he turned his back to them. "You are not ready for that. Not yet. You have a secret, so do I."

Valeri's sister was waiting for them in her Zhiguli. She jumped out of the car when they emerged from the building. Her cheeks and nose were red from the cold. But she looked very stylish in her fur coat and matching hat. Their lieutenant escort saluted and went back inside.

"Father said I should come out to get you," Lara offered. "He said we could all have lunch together at the house."

"Who else will be there?"

She opened the passenger side doors. She was hiding something, Valeri could tell.

"Father, of course," she said. "And Uncle Gennadi has come out from Moscow."

"Yes?"

"They wanted to meet Nadia."

"Who else, Lara?"

She looked cornered. "I don't understand this, Valeri. Not at all. But we are told it is important. So we do what we must."

"We don't have a choice?"

"I don't have a gun, if that's what you mean. Why are you fighting us like this?"

"Why are you helping them, Lara?" Valeri asked. "Who else will be there?"

"Larissa Okulov."

Nadia sucked in her breath, and took a half step backward.

"I thought that might get to you," Lara snapped. "Your lover's widow, you bitch! It has been you who has caused all this trouble for us." She turned on Valeri. "Father's promotion has been turned down, and we don't know if it will ever come up for review. Our house in Yalta is not available, and we've been told there will be special exercises all next month. And all for what? I don't know!"

"You haven't been told?" Valeri asked. He felt sorry for her. She had absolutely nothing. He used to wonder what would happen to her when their father died. Now he knew. She would die too.

"We've been told you are a traitor. At first I did not believe it. But now, seeing you with her, I'm not so sure."

"Then you don't want to know," Valeri said. "You want to stay out of it. Both you and Father." Valeri took Nadia's arm and started away from the car.

"You can't do this to me, Valeri!" Lara screeched in real terror. "They are waiting for me to bring you to them."

Valeri stopped.

Nadia looked up at him. "She is your sister?"

He nodded.

"Valeri, I am sorry. Truly. I did not mean to call her a

name. I don't know what got into me. It's the tension, that's all. I didn't mean a thing by it. I promise.''

"Names mean nothing, Valerik," Nadia said softly. "They want to see us. There is some reason here."

"For Father's sake, then," Lara pleaded.

"All right," Valeri said. He and Nadia turned back. "All right."

"You will come back with me?"

"Yes."

He and Nadia walked back to the car and got in the rear seat together. It wasn't quite what Lara had expected. But after an indecisive moment she accepted it. There wasn't much else she could do.

They drove into town in silence. The knowledge that his government was using his own family against him had a depressing effect. In the United States, justice was for the wealthy. He had seen it with his own eyes. Here, justice was for the innocent. His family was certainly innocent of his aberrations. They weren't peasants to be treated this way. At the same time he could be fatalistic about his own future; he could worry about his father and sister. That too was disturbing to him, as was the probability that Romanov understood his filial feelings and was using them against him.

On the other side of the coin there was Nadia. He turned to look at her profile as she stared straight ahead down the road they were taking. Her cheekbones were high, her eyebrows dark and naturally formed, her lips full, red, and moist. He could admire her strength even though he understood her vulnerability. Her very existence depended upon so much that Valeri did not yet comprehend that he was frightened for her.

General Demin was waiting in the great room, a fire blazing on the hearth. He had a drink in his hand. There were a lot of things in this room from Valeri's childhood. He realized that he knew nothing about Nadia's upbringing on Karaginskiy Island, nor did she know a thing about his youth. Here was a very good place for him to begin his history for her. If they could be given the time and the privacy.

"You," Nadia said from just within the doorway.

General Demin smiled wanly. "There, you see, Valerik?

She is here, unharmed. I brought her to you all the way from Moscow. But it was not easy, let me tell you."

"You know this man?" Valeri asked her.

She nodded. "That day at the apartment. The men who took me were stopped. Some others took me to this one's office. He and Romanov were my interrogators."

Valeri turned back to General Demin. "Uncle Gennadi, why didn't you tell me? All these months . . ."

"You were not ready, nephew."

"Did Father know?"

"Some of it. Not everything. None of us knew that, of course. In fact the last pieces of the puzzle were not put together until yesterday evening, and then this morning."

"The Americans we are holding on Karaginskiy?"

"Yes?"

"You know about them, and now you admit it?"

"As much as it pains me to say so, Valerik, yes."

General Demin finished his vodka and went to the table where he poured himself another. Like Romanov his mood seemed heavy, darker than normal. He was frightened; Valeri could see it. They all were frightened. But not of him and Nadia.

"You're a traitor too," Valeri said. "Why would you do such a thing?"

"Because I am a simple man, Valerik. Not a monster. Neither was Colonel Okulov."

"I killed the wrong man," Valeri said dully.

General Demin nodded. "The most tragic act of all. But it was not your fault. You had no way of knowing that he was trying to save lives, in his own way. And he had no way of knowing that you were not working for his brother, the chief secretary. It was brother against brother from the beginning. Ironically you killed them both. In Moscow they do not know whether to stand you in front of a firing squad, or give you a medal. Those who know anything at all, that is."

The front door opened. Valeri turned and looked out into the stairhall as his father entered, took off his overcoat and hat, and joined them.

"So this is Nadia," he said.

Nadia's eyes were wide. She was staring at General Kostikov's stars and the ribbons on his uniform.

"Hello, Father," Valeri said.

His father searched his eyes. "Hello, Valerik." He turned to General Demin. "Have they been told yet?"

"We were getting to it, Kosta."

"Where is Madame Okulov?"

"I believe Lara went to fetch her. She was not feeling well. Did Sergei come with you?"

"He'll be along in a minute." General Kostikov was frightened too. "Let's sit down and get started. We should have done this months ago. As it is we may be too late."

"Too late for what, Father?"

"To save their lives. Our lives. To avoid a disaster that could take us to the brink of nuclear war, to prevent the greatest catastrophe that our government could be expected to endure, namely, the censure of every single nation on earth."

They sat down in front of the fireplace, Valeri and Nadia together on the long couch. His father and General Demin sat in chairs opposite them.

"Did Sergei Romanov ask you about a North Vietnamese colonel?" General Kostikov asked his son.

"Kim Tri. This morning. I'd never heard of him."

"Nadia?"

"No, sir. I was not familiar with the name."

"Who is he?"

"We don't know, Valerik," General Demin said. "We got word that your Mr. Bertonelli went to New York City to see him. Before they could meet, however, Colonel Tri was assassinated. It was a *mokrie dela*."

"One of our people killed him?"

"Yes. But we still don't know who, or exactly why. They were working out of the United Nations. Apparently Bertonelli is under very close surveillance. Even I cannot find out who is directing it."

"Then he did get out?"

"Yes, but nothing has happened, Valerik. Nothing." General Demin sighed. "It was to be expected with what little he had to go on. A serial number and this little girl's name."

Was it all an elaborate ruse simply to get him to talk? Valeri wondered. Who ever was pulling the strings would have to be very clever to so adroitly manipulate his father and his uncle—men he had known all of his life. They were genuinely frightened. That much was certainly clear. But were they lying too?

"There is more," he heard himself saying as if from a long distance. Nadia squeezed his hand. He didn't know if it was a gesture of reassurance or one of warning. But it was too late to stop now. It was, as his father suggested, dangerously too late.

"What?" Romanov said from the doorway. None of them had heard him arrive.

They all looked up.

"Come in, Sergei," General Demin said.

"What else did Bertonelli take out with him, Valerik? Now you will finally tell us," the interrogator said, coming the rest of the way into the room. He hadn't bothered taking off his heavy overcoat. His glasses were steamed up.

"A notebook," Valeri said. "Nadia brought it with her from Karaginskiy."

"Clever child," Romanov said.

Nadia had closed her eyes.

"In it were the names and serial numbers or social security numbers of all the Americans, including the ones who have already died."

The air seemed to go out of Valeri's father. General Demin's face turned white. Romanov took off his glasses and began wiping them with his handkerchief.

"We discussed this possibility," Romanov said.

"Their bodies will have to be exhumed," General Demin said tiredly.

"Yes, but there will be no time for autopsies. You can see that, Comrade General." Romanov turned to Nadia who had opened her eyes. Her hand on Valeri's was cold and sweaty.

"How many are dead already?"

"I don't know. A dozen, maybe," she said softly. She was shivering again.

"Do you know the circumstances of their deaths? Of any of them? What I mean to say is, were they murdered or were their deaths natural?"

"Unnatural," she intoned. "Too much cold, you see. Too much work, too little food, too little clothing. You should go there, interrogator, and see how long your fat belly would last."

"There were two messages," Romanov prompted. "One for Colonel Okulov's benefit, the other—"

"They won't leave Karaginskiy—no matter what—unless

they are allowed to bring their wives and children.'' Tears streamed down Nadia's cheeks. "They would rather stay there for the remainder of their lives than lose their families. Do you know what that means? Any of you old men? Do you understand what you have done to us? God in heaven, I speak four languages. I have been taught mathematics and history and science. But for what? I have no hopes. You have robbed me of my future!''

"Not us,'' Romanov said.

"Yes, you!'' Nadia cried.

"No. But together we are going to try to rectify the terrible mistake. but you must understand that only the Americans will be allowed to leave.''

"Then they will die. We will all die.''

"In any event, if nothing is done, you *will* all die. There is a group in Moscow, in the Politburo—we can't pinpoint them—who are stopping up all the leaks. When they are certain that Bertonelli has been discredited, that his story is finally not believed, then everyone on Karaginskiy Island will be put to death, their bodies destroyed, all record of their existence obliterated.''

"No,'' Nadia sobbed.

"Nature at her worst is not half so cruel as men with a holy purpose.''

"Why?'' Valeri asked. "Why did we take these people? How did we do it? What were we trying to accomplish? I don't understand.''

"It was a KGB operation, that much we do know,'' General Demin said. He was looking into his empty vodka glass. "We were passing arms to the North Vietnamese people. In trade we took some American prisoners of war. From what I can gather it was an old Line F operation.''

"Department Viktor.''

"Yes,'' General Demin said. "They would have been brainwashed, then returned home through a POW repatriation program with the North Vietnamese. Once back in the United States they would have been used as tools to further disrupt the American people's trust in their government. If you remember, a lot of us believed the United States government was coming apart at the seams in those days.''

There had been other harebrained KGB operations, of course. Plenty of them. Valeri remembered reading about one in

particular. In 101 School outside Moscow they talked about
the disaster as an example of how *not* to do things. In the
early sixties a barrel of strontium 90-laced seawater was
dumped into the harbor of a Far Eastern nation at which
American nuclear submarines called. It was supposed to em-
barrass the Americans, who would be charged with polluting
the waters of a friendly nation. Enrage world opinion. Nothing happened, except the four Soviet contract agents—for-
tunately all Arabs—died horrible deaths of radiation poisoning.

"They were difficult times for the Americans," General
Demin said. "Drugs, flag burnings, demonstrations in Washington, D.C., riots in the Negro ghettos, panic, distrust.
Many young men even fled to Canada to avoid military
service."

"It would never happen here," General Kostikov said.

"What are they still doing on Karaginskiy, Uncle Gennadi?"

"Inertia. Who knows?" General Demin said, throwing up
his hands. "The camp is operated by the Chief Border Guard
Directorate. They were the ones who served as advisers in
Hanoi during the war of independence. They are simply still
doing the job they were told to do."

"Why weren't they sent back to Vietnam before the end of
the war?"

"I don't know, Valerik. There was an airplane crash in
1969 near there, in which General Yermilichev and some of
his staff were killed. He headed Department Viktor. With them
possibly went the true identities of the Karaginskiy prisoners.
This is a vast country."

"And that's it?" Valeri asked, hardly believing his ears.
"It is as simple as that? We took American prisoners of war,
placed them in a gulag, and then simply forgot about them?"
He shook his head. "Comrade Romanov . . . Uncle Gennadi
. . . Father . . . what are you telling me? Let's admit our
mistake. Let us give these people back. Let us return them
home."

"I wish we could, Valerik. Honestly, I wish we could. But
it is not so simple."

"Talk to Mr. Gorbachev. He is a moderate."

"We don't know who to trust to get to him. No one except
us in this room, and Madame Okulov, knows the entire
story."

"She worked for you, Uncle?" Valeri asked, still another piece of the puzzle falling into place.

General Demin sighed deeply and nodded. "Yes. She was spying on her brother-in-law to find out when the Americans were to be executed."

Valeri lowered his head. "I killed them both." There was no going back for him. Not to Moscow, not to his old life, certainly not to his job or his friends. All of that was a vast empty landscape, as was his future.

"Will you help us?" Romanov asked gently.

"With what?"

"You and Nadia must go to the United States. You must convince the American government, through Bertonelli, that a terrible mistake is now to be rectified. We want these people repatriated. But silently. Quietly. They will understand."

"No retributions," General Demin said.

"What about the families?"

"If the Americans will not take them, we will find a place for them. I promise you that," Romanov said. But he could not look at Nadia. "We will not be traitors to our country."

What choice was there? Valeri wondered. He thought, incongruously, about Tanya and Larissa Okulov, two women for whom he had been a source of great pain. But that seemed to be his specialty just lately. There were poor Mikhail and the dead hero Lipasov, whose passing had been at least indirectly engineered because of him. Wherever he looked, whichever way he turned, he saw pain. He was surrounded by a sea of suffering. Perhaps it was time to begin mending.

He looked up. "Bertonelli has the list of all the prisoners. Yet he apparently has accomplished nothing in his three months home."

General Demin nodded.

"Then we will have to bring him something else. Something more compelling."

"Nadia," Romanov suggested.

"Even more than that, Comrade Interrogator. I will bring them messages from the prisoners themselves. Something only they could know."

Romanov glanced at General Demin, then at Valeri's father. He shook his head. "We might be able to get you out there, Valerik. But there is no guarantee that we could get you back. Already there has been too much activity concerning the gulag. If they become spooked, they might kill every-one immediately and worry about picking up the pieces later.''

"Nadia will come with me to the gulag.''

"No,'' Romanov said. "Too risky for them as well as us. I forbid it.''

"Madame Okulov can go to the United States with you,'' General Demin suggested. "Hers will be a third voice. She knows about—''

"That is not possible, Uncle Gennadi,'' Lara said from the doorway. She was pale and shaking.

General Kostikov jumped up in alarm. "Lara?''

"She is dead, Father. Suicide in her room.''

# 23

Roy Sanders and Jordan Good, field men on rotation back to the Foreign Desk in Operations at Langley, showed up at National Airport. Bertonelli vaguely recognized them, but they showed him their IDs so that no one would get nervous.

"You didn't have to kill the poor bastard," Good said. He was a large, Semitic-looking man with a barrel chest and a huge nose.

"I didn't," Bertonelli said.

"Yeah. But you did telephone his office from JFK, didn't you?" Good asked. "You might just as well have killed him."

"We weren't expecting that, you see," Sanders put in. He was a much shorter, slighter, scholarly-looking man with a pockmarked face.

They hurried across the busy terminal. It wasn't quite ten in the morning. Bertonelli had spent the night in a small hotel in New York trying, without success, to get through to Admiral Taylor.

"What about my bag?" he asked.

"It'll catch up to you," Good said. "Unless you were planning on shooting someone here in Washington this morning."

Bertonelli stopped. "Look, I don't have to take this shit from you guys."

Good started to say something else, but Sanders held him off. "Sorry, Mr. Bertonelli, we meant nothing by it."

"What is going on here? Who sent you out to pick me up?"

"General Canfield. There are some people who want to talk to you this morning."

316

"What people?"

"Piss on it," Good muttered.

"Please, Mr. Bertonelli, we're just doing our jobs. We have a car just out front. It's been one bitch of a night."

"Sorry," Bertonelli said. "I didn't have much fun either."

They went out to the cab ranks and passenger pick-up area, where they got into a big Oldsmobile, the two agents in the front, Bertonelli in back. Good drove. He hauled the big car around as if it were a truck, while Sanders stared into his sideview mirror.

"You spotted him yet?" Good asked when they turned onto the George Washington Memorial Parkway.

"He's back there," Sanders said matter-of-factly. "Don't turn around, Mr. Bertonelli. Light blue Chevy."

Good glanced in his rearview mirror. "Got him. Bastards."

"KGB?" Bertonelli asked. The hairs were prickling on the nape of his neck. He felt as if he were getting very close to something . . . and he wasn't quite sure it was what he wanted after all.

"They've been on you ever since you got back," Good snapped.

"And you've been on me *and* them."

"For the past nine weeks," Sanders said.

Bertonelli sat back in the thickly upholstered seat. They were pretty good, he had to admit. He had gotten the over-the-shoulder feeling a few times during the past weeks, but he had never spotted anyone until JFK yesterday afternoon. But then he had been busy trying to present his case to anyone who would listen; he hadn't really been doing his job. Someone else had been, though.

"Who was Colonel Tri? Can you tell me that much?" he asked.

"North Vietnamese regular army when he came to us, from what I understand," Sanders said. "Before that he was a college professor in Hanoi. Just picked up where he left off over here after Saigon fell."

"KGB kill him?"

"Standard Moscow Center assassination device," Sanders said. "Not very pretty."

"The NYPD is pissed off. The Bureau is pissed off. And the shit's about to hit the fan," Good added.

"So, who was he?" Bertonelli asked again. "What did he

have that they wanted? He denied everything when I talked to him on the phone."

"You *are* dense," Good said, looking into the rearview mirror. "I expected a lot more from your reputation. But this is shit."

Bertonelli was about ready to go over the seat, but again Sanders became the moderator.

"Colonel Tri was nothing," he explained. "Just a former North Vietnamese living and working here. Of course, the Russians didn't know that. Soon as you went after him, they figured he had something, so they got to him first. It was our mistake, actually. We should have protected him better."

"He was a decoy?"

"Something like that."

"Who cares?" Good mumbled. "The sonofabitch probably couldn't speak English worth a damn anyway."

Sanders turned around. "Jordan's brother was killed in 'Nam," he explained. "He's a little gunshy when it comes to the VC or anything close."

"You two don't know what's going on here, do you?" Bertonelli said.

Sanders shrugged. "You came back from Moscow with something the Russians want. It's up to us to see they don't get it or you."

"Who set up Colonel Tri?"

"I don't know. It came down through channels. But we were told it was damned important."

"Our asses are on the line here," Good said.

The Rayburn House Office Building was just across Independence Avenue from the House wing of the Capitol. Sanders and Good made no effort to conceal the fact they had brought Bertonelli there. The light blue Chevrolet with two men in it drove slowly past and turned down South Capitol past the Longworth Building.

Inside, they hurried down a long marble corridor, their footfalls echoing like pistol shots. They entered a busy office complex through tall, highly polished wooden doors marked Suite 2120. Beside the doors was a plaque: UNITED STATES HOUSE OF REPRESENTATIVES: ARMED SERVICES COMMITTEE. They passed through the outer office, no one paying them the slightest attention, walked down a short corridor, and turned into a long, narrow, high-ceilinged waiting room, a door at the far end, wooden benches on either side, paintings of famous military scenes on both walls. General Canfield, deputy director of the Central Intelligence Agency, was talking with another man at the far end of the room. They looked up, General Canfield said something, and the other man went through the door.

"Any troubles on the way in?" the DCI asked sharply, joining them. He wore a blue serge suit, the cut of which was military. His hair was short, his mustache trimmed neatly, his shoes highly polished.

"No, sir," Sanders replied. "We did pick up a tail, though."

"Good," the general said. He stared at Bertonelli, his eyes dark gray, almost charcoal. He looked up. "Thanks, gentlemen. We'll handle it from here."

"Yes, sir," Good said. He and Sanders glanced one last time at Bertonelli, then turned and left.

"Well," the general said. He seemed to be having trouble forming his words. "From that first twixt, I have prayed to God you were wrong, Bertonelli, for all the obvious reasons. But I've also prayed that you were right, for all the obvious reasons."

"General . . ."

Canfield shook his head. "But, goddamn, no matter which way it turns out, it won't be neat or clean. It'll be the Iran hostage thing all over again, only ten times more difficult and a hundred times more critical. You know that. You know what is at stake here."

"Yes, sir. I didn't want to believe it either. But I am sorry about Colonel Tri."

"Don't be. He was doing consulting work for us on student activity groups all the while he was selling information to the Cubans."

"Sir?"

"If a man is a traitor to his own country, do you honestly think he can remain loyal to his newly adopted country for very long?" General Canfield laughed disdainfully. "Once a traitor, always a traitor. Wait here."

The general turned and went into the other room.

\*    \*    \*

By himself for the moment, Bertonelli lit a cigarette as he turned and looked up at a large painting of the Marines raising the flag on Iwo Jima. Working in the field he had come to expect lies and deceit. He supposed that here at home among friends he would not have to be on his guard. Nothing, however, seemed much different here than it had been in Moscow.

Colonel Tri had been set up as a decoy. Never mind he was selling only petty little secrets to the Cubans. He had been set up for the kill. Bertonelli had never considered himself to be a naïve man. Now he was beginning to doubt his judgment.

General Canfield returned a few minutes later. He and Bertonelli sat together on one of the benches.

"We're going inside in just a bit," the general said. "You'll be the star. Admiral Taylor and I want you to answer each and every question they'll put to you to the very best of your abilities. Do you understand that, Anthony?"

"What am I doing here, General? What's going on? Really."

General Canfield looked at him incredulously. "This is the House Armed Services Committee, for chrissakes. What the hell do you think you're doing here?"

"I don't know."

"They want to know about our MIAs. They want to know the entire story."

"What have they been told so far?"

This time the general's look was less incredulous, more appraising.

"Don't be a smartass. I've been in this business too long to have to put up with the crap from some prima donna. The committee has had its briefing. They've seen the satellite shots of the village on Karaginskiy . . . this meeting, by the way, is classified top secret. Keep it in mind."

"Do they know what happened to me in Moscow? Do they know about the KGB major, Kostikov, and the girl . . . Captain Burdine's daughter?"

General Canfield stiffened. "Just hold on here, mister. That particular bit is hearsay and nothing more. We've gone through that with you more than once. Nothing about any Russian families, or anything of the sort, has been proven."

"Then you *don't* want me to tell the committee everything," Bertonelli said. "How about Colonel Tri? Will questions arise as to exactly how he was set up for the kill? Or will you be handling that one, sir?''

"I'll be sitting next to you. On your right," General Canfield said, getting to his feet. "Mr. Thiesen will be on your left.''

"Who is he?''

"The Agency's chief counsel. If you have any doubt about what your answer should be, you *will* hold a hand over your microphone and consult with either or both of us. Is that clear, mister?''

"I hear you, General," Bertonelli said after a hesitation.

Bertonelli had never been particularly overawed by power or rank. It didn't bother him now that a dozen powerful Congressmen sat at the front of the room, or that the small audience consisted mostly of very high-ranking, highly decorated Army officers. The door from the waiting room was a side entrance to the large committee chamber. General Canfield led him across to the witness table that faced the Congressmen. The man the general had been speaking with when Bertonelli had first shown up was seated at the table. He jumped up and stuck out his hand.

"Nice to see you, Anthony. Paul Thiesen.''

Bertonelli shook hands with him, and took the empty place by the microphone. Not until that moment did he realize that a lot of the men in the room had loosened their ties and unbuttoned their jackets or tunics. Empty coffee cups and overflowing ashtrays littered the chamber. They'd been there for hours. Possibly overnight. It was extraordinary.

Several of the Congressmen had been arguing about something. They broke it off and the committee chairman, Thomas O'Day, a Republican from New Jersey, turned around. An aide scurried around the long table, a Bible in his hand. Bertonelli got to his feet, raised his right hand, and placed his left on the Bible.

"Do you swear that the testimony you are about to give to this committee is the truth, the whole truth, and nothing but the truth, so help you God?''

"I do," Bertonelli said.

"Please be seated, sir.''

"Mr. Bertonelli, have you been briefed that this hearing is classified top secret?'' O'Day asked.

Bertonelli leaned forward to the microphone. "Yes, sir, I have."

"What else were you told?"

"To tell the truth to the best of my knowledge."

O'Day sat back and said something to one of the other Congressmen, and when he turned back he nodded. "I appreciate that, Mr. Bertonelli. Believe me." He was a thick-jowled man with a mane of white hair. He'd been on the Armed Services Committee since the Korean War. He was an institution in Washington.

"Have you also been told the nature of this hearing?"

"Not exactly, sir. Except that it concerns our MIAs being held by the Soviet Union on Karaginskiy Island."

"You've been told nothing more?"

"No, sir."

"You have not previously met with Colonel Jared Kraus concerning this business?"

"No, sir," Bertonelli said. He turned to General Canfield, who was beginning to look worried.

"Kraus runs the Army's First Special Forces Operational Detachment," the general whispered.

"Delta Force?" Bertonelli asked, holding the microphone, barely trusting his own voice.

Canfield looked over his shoulder and nodded toward a bull-necked Army colonel with a chestful of ribbons. "That's him." Bertonelli followed his gaze.

"Mr. Bertonelli," O'Day was saying.

Bertonelli turned back. His heart was racing, his stomach was fluttering, his muscles jumping. It was the same way he felt that night in the Moscow Zoo when Kostikov had shown up with a drawn gun.

"In your estimation, you were not involved in a Soviet disinformation plot?" the New Jersey Republican asked. "That is to say, you believe that the Soviet Union has, and is presently, holding American Vietnam-era prisoners of war on Karaginskiy Island?"

"Yes, sir, I do."

"On what do you base that belief, Mr. Bertonelli, other than the testimony of a KGB Colonel Rotislav Okulov, your cooperative agreement with a KGB Major Valeri Kostikov, and the notebook that Colonel Okulov smuggled out of the prison?"

General Canfield reached out and covered Bertonelli's microphone. "Careful, Anthony. No rumors." He withdrew his hand.

"There is a certain amount of what we call tradecraft, Congressman, involved with my answer. But first may I ask a question of the committee?"

O'Day looked at the others. He nodded. "Yes."

"You mentioned, sir, a possible contact between Colonel Kraus and myself. We have never met. It is my understanding, however, that he is in command of the Army's Delta Force."

"That is correct, Mr. Bertonelli. This is significant to you?"

"Yes, it is, Congressman. Can you tell me if this committee is authorizing a Delta Force strike on Karaginskiy Island, with the intent of freeing our people?"

Again General Canfield's hand clamped over Bertonelli's microphone. "What the hell do you think you're trying to do, mister?" he hissed.

"General Canfield?" O'Day called.

Canfield looked up.

"Remove your hand from Mr. Bertonelli's microphone, please."

For a long moment Bertonelli thought Canfield was actually going to defy the Congressman. But then he pulled his hand away and sat back with a dark scowl.

"Would you object to such a rescue mission, Mr. Bertonelli? Do you have further information for us?"

Bertonelli glanced back at Colonel Kraus and the other Army officers. One of them he was sure was General Stanley Robbins, the Army's chief of staff. There were a lot of heavyweights here.

"I can't directly address the tactical problem of making such a strike into Soviet territory, Congressman, but there is another issue that must be addressed here. One that will affect not only the logistical aspects of such a mission, but the moral issues as well."

Canfield's hand shot out and covered Bertonelli's microphone again. O'Day banged his gavel.

"Go on with this, you sonofabitch, and I'll have your ass."

"What would you do with them, General?" Bertonelli

snapped, not bothering to lower his voice. "Leave them? Kill them? You tell me."

"Goddamn you . . ."

Bertonelli shoved Canfield's hand aside. "Colonel Okulov did not smuggle that notebook out of Karaginskiy Island, Congressman. A young woman by the name of Nadia Burdine brought it out. She is the daughter of a Siberian woman living on Karaginskiy Island and U.S. Air Force Captain Robert Burdine. There are other such unions at the gulag from what I was told, and numerous offspring who deserve our consideration."

The color drained from O'Day's face. Other Congressmen were shouting to be heard. General Canfield had gotten up and he stalked out of the room. The CSA, General Robbins, looked thunderstruck, his officers all worried.

Bertonelli turned again and looked at Colonel Kraus. The man had not moved a muscle.

Sanders and Good showed up and drove Bertonelli back to his apartment in Waverly Hills. This time there was no talk between them until they turned down his street and pulled up in front of his six-unit redwood building. His car was in the driveway. They had brought his overnight bag from the airport.

"Stay home, Mr. Bertonelli," Sanders said politely. "Your phone is tapped, so I wouldn't use it for anything personal."

"Am I under arrest?"

"Did you do something wrong?" Good snapped.

"Screw yourself," Bertonelli said. He grabbed his bag, got out of the car, and went up the driveway.

"We'll be around," Sanders called. "So don't worry about anything."

Bertonelli was frightened. They had planned on making a Delta Force strike on Karaginskiy and they had no idea that women and children would be involved. Nor, in the end, would they tell him anything else.

There was no political solution, of course. Not now. Colonel Okulov had tried in his own way, and with the support, apparently, of others within the Politburo, to effect such a thing, but he had been killed for his efforts and the others had gone to ground. If Kostikov had not pulled the trigger by mistake, someone else would have. Colonel Okulov's own brother, for instance. It was the Russian ego all over again. Russians simply could not stand to lose face. Backed into a corner they would rather tell the most outrageous, damaging lies than have to tell a simple but embarrassing truth. They'd rather die than expose themselves to ridicule. It was one of the reasons the Russian propaganda machine had always been so effective: they understood, as a nation, what face was all about—losing it, maintaining it. That national mania, combined with a nearly mystical patriotism, would make it impossible for them to strike any kind of a bargain. In the beginning, perhaps, a deal could have been made. But now, so many years after the fact, so long after a time when their actions could be justified, there would be nothing for them but massive political embarrassment, an embarrassment that every man, woman, and child in the country would have to share. It was not possible.

Sanders and Good were parked half a block away. There wasn't much traffic at this time of the afternoon. He hoped they were bored.

His gun had been taken out of his overnight bag, and his apartment had been searched, but not very efficiently. From beneath the insulation in the crawl space over the second bedroom closet he brought down a small plastic package in which was wrapped a Smith & Wesson snub-nosed .38. He sat at the kitchen table drinking coffee while he cleaned and oiled the revolver, then loaded it.

He had expected more from the Agency, though he could understand the logic of using him as a decoy. They had the notebook, they had his testimony, they even had the KH-12 Satellite Eye-in-the-Sky photographs showing an installation on Karaginskiy Island. The minute the KGB came after him here in Washington, it would prove they were worried.

The Agency had not done a very good job protecting Colonel Tri from assassination. He wondered how much of an effort they would put forth on his behalf.

The DeMilles of the world would inherit the earth, he was afraid.

He heated some soup, made a cheese sandwich, and opened a beer. He ate his lunch in front of the television set, though he didn't pay much attention to either.

What did they want of him? He had done his job. He had

brought them the ultimate prize. Yet his hadn't been the hero's welcome. JoAnn used to tell him that he expected too much from people. It was one of their automatic arguments. Expect nothing and you'll never be disappointed, was her line. I've never been disappointed with you, was his. It would set them both off. He found that he was missing her now. Being alone was convenient most of the time, but it was never very comforting.

The KGB had followed him to New York and had killed Colonel Tri. They would have to be very desperate to come after him here.

There had been no tradecraft involved getting him from the airport to the House Armed Services Committee meeting. Or had there? he wondered.

He put the chain on the front door, checked to make sure Sanders and Good were still outside, then took a shower and changed into some clean clothes. Afterward he felt a lot better, though he was still bothered, and worried about what would happen next. He was a man out of control on a roller coaster. He was plunging down into a tunnel with no way of knowing what was inside.

He mixed himself a stiff bourbon and water and brought it back into the living room.

Moscow seemed like another century. There, it was winter. Here, it was spring. Valeri Kostikov had been driven: a man with a cause that ultimately led him to betray his country. He was dead or in prison by now. For what?

Bertonelli also wondered about Nadia Burdine, the girl for whom Major Kostikov had sacrificed everything. What had become of her?

Everyone in the Soviet Union and everyone here in the United States was afraid of the Karaginskiy women and children.

Bertonelli was afraid *for* them.

Night intensified all of his feelings. He had the television on for background noise, but he wasn't really watching it. From time to time he looked out the window, down at the sodium vapor-lit street. Sanders and Good were his watch-dogs. There was no way of knowing, though, what they were thinking, or what they had been told.

\* \* \*

They came for him a few minutes before ten.

He was in the kitchen, fixing himself a hamburger. In Moscow you expected to be watched. Here in Washington it was unnatural. It made him feel as if he were a stranger in his own home. But something was about to happen. He could feel it. He hadn't felt this jumpy since Afghanistan.

Something made him look over his shoulder. A large man with thick, dark eyebrows and a bushy mustache stood in the doorway from the living room. He was young, and he was dressed in dark slacks and a dark pullover. He was apparently unarmed.

"Shit," Bertonelli swore. He had left his gun in the living room on the table beside the couch. He lunged for the paring knife he'd left lying on the counter.

"We're friends, Mr. Bertonelli," the man whispered urgently.

Bertonelli stopped. The man suddenly had some sort of a small, deadly-looking silenced gun in his hands. Bertonelli hadn't seen him draw it.

"Steve?" someone called softly from the living room.

"Here."

"Who the hell are you?" Bertonelli asked. His right hand was on the paring knife.

"Sergeant Steve Monahan. Delta."

Another similarly dressed man came from the living room. His hair was startlingly blond. He looked as if he were fifteen or sixteen at the most, except for his eyes, which seemed to be those of a very old man.

"Sorry to break in on you like this, sir," he said. "Do you know your telephone was tapped?"

Monahan turned and silently went back into the living room.

There wasn't the slightest hint of a Russian accent in either of their voices. Bertonelli relaxed. "What are you doing here? How the hell did you get in?"

"I'm Lieutenant Geoff Hill, sir. Delta. Jerry Kraus sent us to fetch you." He pulled Bertonelli's .38 out of his pocket and tossed it over to him. "Shouldn't leave things like this lying around, sir."

Bertonelli checked the cylinder. It was still loaded. He stuffed the gun in his belt. "How'd you get in, Lieutenant? What's going on?"

"Back way. You've got your friendlies watching you from up the block. Tan Olds. BYF one-two-four. Two men. I believe at least one of them is from your organization."

"KGB anywhere?"

"Two teams. One in the building just across the street. Apartment three-oh-seven. Second team at the end of the block."

"No one in back?"

"No, sir," Hill said. "Is there anyone else in the apartment with you?"

"No."

"Please pack a small bag with your things, sir." Hill backed away from the door. "But hurry. I don't believe the situation is going to remain stable for very long."

Bertonelli hurried out of the kitchen and into his bedroom where Sergeant Monahan stood to one side of the open window.

"No lights, sir," Monahan said.

Quickly Bertonelli tossed a few things into the same leather overnight bag he had brought up to New York with him, then pulled on a light jacket.

Lieutenant Hill came in. "Were you expecting anyone tonight?"

"No," Bertonelli said.

"Someone is out in the corridor working on your door, right now. My instructions were to get you out."

He nodded and Monahan disappeared over the windowsill with absolutely no noise.

"We must leave now, Mr. Bertonelli," Hill said softly. He closed the bedroom door.

Bertonelli went to the window. Monahan was already on the ground. A rope led down from a grappling hook on the roof.

"Where are we going?"

"Karaginskiy Island, sir," Hill said. "I thought you knew."

# 24

Karaginskiy Island rose up out of the sea like a malevolent monster some seventy kilometers off the coast of the Kamchatka Peninsula.

Nadia was in the back of the airplane with Bordachev, and the political officer, Artemyev. Something had happened to the heater. They were bundled up against the cold.

There were more trees than Valeri had imagined there would be. The island was much larger, the landmass rose much higher than he had expected. But Nadia had not told them very much. Not really.

"You will have to see for yourself, Valerik," she had said.

From the air it was an island of contrasts. Startlingly white snow punctuated by the green-black forests. Solid angular rock cliffs battered by an angry, ice-studded sea. Harsh summers wrapped by grim winters. Summer night sun and winter afternoon darkness. An island prison in the middle of a vast, free expanse of wilderness.

She told them the gulag was on the northern tip of the island, where sometimes there wasn't much protection from the fierce arctic winds.

"There isn't much chance that we will succeed," General Demin had said before they left.

Valeri agreed. He thought about it now. Seriously. But he was sorry that Uncle Gennadi had voiced the doubt. That never did anyone any good.

They angled north at about eight hundred meters, along the bay side of the long island. The land was wild and primitive, rising in the center to a range of stubby, snow-covered peaks. There was wildlife here: salmon and seals in the sea; deer, moose, otter, and even sable on land. They felled trees,

Nadia told them. All day long. Winter, summer, no matter, from which they made charcoal. Simple, easy, basic. Charcoal was their lifeline, providing heat, and providing steam to run a small generator for their electricity.

"You asked for this crew just to get back at me for what I did to you, didn't you?" Trusov the pilot said.

Valeri held no grudge against the man. In fact he felt nothing one way or the other about the pilot. He had simply not wanted to involve anyone else. It was fitting this way. Valeri was sick of death and misery. Sick of complications, of lies, of fear.

"We wouldn't have a chance in hell if we had to ditch in that water," Trusov said to his copilot, Lyalin, who was just a kid.

"We won't have to ditch," Valeri said.

"How can you be so sure?"

"I am."

"There is no airstrip shown on my charts. Not on this island, not anywhere within four hundred kilometers. Just mountains, and trees, and sea, and ice."

"We'll land on the island."

Trusov was getting excited. There was nothing to see except rugged wilderness. To the northwest, back toward the peninsula, and beyond to the mainland, weather was beginning to build up. By evening it would snow.

"What if I turn around and head down to Ust'-Kamchatsk? They have an airstrip there."

"I would take out my gun and shoot you and we would crash anyway," Valeri said.

"Bastard," Trusov spat. Lyalin was afraid to turn around.

No one knew what kind of reception they would get. Nadia did not know the chain of command, of course. And she said little except that most of their guards—and there were not many of them—were brutish, some of them nearly subhuman. But they had shown a great deal of respect for Colonel Okulov. It was something.

Romanov and Uncle Gennadi had left for Moscow to see if they could hold things off, though an investigation into poor Larissa Okulov's suicide would have to be carried out soon. She had been a traitor to too many people, to too many ideals for her to go on. The first time Valeri had met her he had seen a certain brittle quality to her.

Nadia was afraid that something had already happened on the island, while Valeri had become almost inured to disaster, which seemed to surround him like a devil's halo.

He thought, for some reason, again about Shevchenko. Valeri had not had the freedom of movement to face Sasha with the news of her husband's death. He worried not only about what she had been told, but how she had been told, and who had brought her the news. Probably some insensitive Armenian, or Uzbeki. How he hated the clodhopping farmers, yet they undoubtedly understood the realities of life and death better than the average Russian.

It was very cold in the cockpit of the airplane, but he was sweating. He pulled out a bottle of cognac from his pocket and took a deep drink. The young kid Lyalin was sitting forward in the right seat, looking out the window. Valeri still couldn't quite understand why they had killed poor dumb Mikhail who was incapable of hurting a fly. Unless they were dumber and more frightened than he'd been. If ever there had been a model communist, Mikhail was it. Even Sasha's admission that they dealt with the black market (out of necessity, but a state crime nevertheless) didn't diminish his qualities. If the men of the Politburo were the best, then Shevchenko and his kind were ultimate Reds.

"Bloody hell," Trusov said softly, in real awe. "It's there."

Valeri leaned forward in the jump seat as they banked toward the island. A long, narrow strip had been hacked out of the forest. There was nothing around it. No vehicles, no buildings, not even a windsock. But it was obvious the slash was an airstrip. A substantial airstrip.

"Valerik?" Nadia called from the back.

"Strap down back there," Valeri shouted. "We're coming in." He tightened his own seat belt.

Trusov glanced over his shoulder. "What is down there, Comrade Major? What has caused so much trouble? What are we going to find?"

"I don't know," Valeri told him. "I honestly don't know."

The air was supernaturally transparent. The airstrip was on top of a long, flat hill. Below, in the valley, they could hear a gust of wind coming through the treetops like water running down a slope. Somewhere in the distance they could hear the distinct, hollow raps of axes hitting trees. And in the very far distance they thought they could hear the Pacific Ocean crashing against the rocks, but that was forty kilometers away, on the other side of the island.

Valeri and Nadia stood with Trusov by the side of the big Tupolev. They had taxied to the far end of the runway where a road disappeared down the hill through the thick woods. Nadia was very nervous. She was shivering almost uncontrollably. It made Valeri jumpy.

"Where are they?" he asked her.

"Down there," she said, pointing down the road. "Maybe four or five kilometers."

"Will we walk?"

She shook her head. "They have seen the airplane. Someone will come for us with the bus."

"What is this place, Comrade Major?" Trusov asked. The foreboding dark forest that surrounded them made them all whisper.

"A gulag, Comrade Pilot."

The color drained from Trusov's face. He stepped back, looking from Valeri to Nadia and back again. "What?" he squeaked.

"Just down the hill."

"Let's get out of here. We can still make Ust'-Kamchatsk before the storm hits."

"When I am finished with my business."

"I will take off . . ."

"When you return to base, my father will have you shot. Think about it."

"I don't care," Trusov stammered.

"So far"—Valeri stepped a little closer—"you haven't broken any regulations. If you should, however, it is very possible you could be sent to a place such as this. Five years, perhaps. Ten? Twenty?"

Now they could hear the roar of an unmuffled engine. The bus was coming.

Trusov looked back at the plane. "I'll fix the heater. Bordachev is pretty good. He can help me. We'll just stay here. We have rations, sleeping bags. We'll be all right."

"Good idea," Valeri said.

Trusov scrambled up into the airplane and closed the hatch. He would not take off without them. He might be frightened here, but he was more frightened of the consequences of abandoning the commander's son . . . even if the son was accused of being a traitor.

Valeri stepped away from the wing. He let his eyes roam around the runway and the woods on either side of it. Something was wrong. He could feel it. The hairs on the nape of his neck bristled. The trees were laden with snow. Only the upper branches were bare. It was the wind. The runway had been recently plowed, all the snow piled in continuous long banks on either side.

The sound of the bus was much louder now.

Valeri turned back to Nadia. "How often is the runway plowed?"

She shook her head in confusion. "I don't know . . ." She hesitated. Then her eyes got wide. "Valerik," she breathed.

The bus was very loud. Valeri looked down the road as it came into view. It was a large half-track with what looked like a canvas enclosure on back. It was barely a hundred meters down the hill now.

"The runway is never plowed," Nadia whispered. "Before a plane comes in, the prisoners . . . all of us . . . shovel it by hand."

"Maybe this time is different."

"We have no plow here!" Nadia's eyes were beginning to get wild. "Valerik?"

Valeri's heart was hammering. There was no place to run, finally. Even if they could get off before the half-track blocked the runway, where would they go? Ust'-Kamchatsk to the south? Where? He had worked toward this end, though. He had dragged his friends and coworkers into it, into his own sphere of insanity, of antisocial behavior; he had done his very best to drag his wife and his father into it, with success. He wished he could face this alone. Their crime was abbreviated ChS, which stood for Members of a Family convicted under an antisocial code.

The half-track bumped up from the road, through the opening in the snowbank, and angled across the runway. Valeri watched the snow coming off the tracks, the front skis throwing sparks on the occasional stone. Nadia took his arm. He could feel her shaking. The half-track slowed and came to a halt a few meters away. Valeri could see only one man in addition to the driver in the cab.

Four soldiers in the uniform of the KGB's Border Guard Directorate jumped out of the rear of the half-track and crisply arrayed themselves, two on either side of where Nadia and Valeri stood, their Kalashnikov assault rifles at the ready.

"These are not our camp guards," Nadia whispered.

"No."

A very large man got out of the passenger side of the half-track. He wore a fur hat, highly polished leather boots, and a Border Guard's greatcoat, full colonel's pips on his shoulder boards. His face was red and glistening, his nose broad, almost Tartar, his eyebrows dark, thick, meeting over the bridge of his nose. Valeri got the impression that the man was bald.

The colonel came forward. "I suspected we would meet sooner or later, Major Kostikov." He smiled. "Permit me to introduce myself. I am Colonel Yezhov. Petr Yakovlevich."

"Why have you taken over this gulag?"

"I have my orders. Surely even a man such as yourself can understand this."

"You work for the same people Chief Secretary Okulov worked for?"

The colonel nodded. He looked at Nadia, his eyes lingering on her for a moment, and then he gazed up at the airplane. He turned back to Valeri at length.

"I will send someone back for your crew. They will have to be interrogated first, and then they will be processed and billeted. Not exactly like home here, but then this is Siberia, after all. Miss Burdine will be returned to her father who anxiously awaits her, which will leave you and me. We will have some dinner and a little chat tonight. There are a number of things I would like to know."

"We radioed our landing instructions back to Khabarovsk," Valeri said.

"It is of no consequence. Your father is a good man, but there is little more he can do than sacrifice an obseervation crew and his own son."

"There are others on their way to Moscow . . ."

"I have bad news for you," Yezhov said seriously. "Sergei Romanov and General Gennadi Demin have been killed in an airplane crash. We only just got word of this tragedy."

Nadia's grip on Valeri's arm stiffened. He felt sick to his stomach. The four Border Guard troopers stood impassively

at the ready. They could have been marble statues in a graveyard. They looked capable, though. Hard. Valeri thought they
looked like Nazis.

"All your friends are dead. Think of it. All dead. Some by
us, some by your own hand. Even this little slut's hands are
not free of blood."

"You are no better than the Germans," Valeri said. It was
quite an insult for a Russian.

"There are greater issues here, Comrade Major," Yezhov
said menacingly.

"Saving face?" Valeri spat. "Is that what this is all about,
Comrade Colonel?"

"No matter the reason, it was and is a decision of the state.
Of your government—a government you have betrayed. Your
father and grandfather were heroes. Your friends, heroes.
General Demin, a hero. All of them dead now. And you, a
traitor, still alive. It makes no sense, does it? In fact it makes
an honest, hard-working communist sick to his stomach."

Yezhov glanced up at the airplane. Trusov and the others
had not made a move, though they certainly could see the
armed men on the runway.

"Are you armed?" Yezhov asked. "Please drop it on the
ground."

Valeri hesitated.

"Are you going to try to shoot me?"

"No," Valeri said. Very carefully he lifted the Beretta his
father had given him out of his coat pocket. The troops
stiffened, bringing their rifles a little higher. He dropped the
automatic on the ground.

"Pick it up and get the crew out of the aircraft," Yezhov
told his men.

One of the troopers came forward, snatched up Valeri's
gun, and then the others hurried around the wing and started
banging on the side of the airplane.

"Shall we go?" Yezhov said to Valeri. "The girl can
come with you for now. We'll drop her off on the way in."

Valeri glanced over his shoulder. The Tupolev's hatch
swung open.

"I'll send the bus back for them. Don't worry, Major."

The troopers bodily yanked poor fat Bordachev out of the
airplane, his head banging on the frozen ground. Two of them
scrambled up into the airplane.

Valeri stepped around Nadia. One of the troops spun around, brought his rifle up, and levered a round into the firing chamber with a loud snap.

"Valerik!" Nadia cried.

"You bastard," Valeri said, turning back to Yezhov. "They don't know a thing. They merely flew me here. In fact the pilot wanted—"

A gunshot came from within the airplane. Valeri started forward, toward the colonel, Nadia raised her hand as if to ward off a blow, but Yezhov simply stood his ground, a faint smile curling his lip.

Something terribly hard smashed into the back of Valeri's head. His vision seemed to shatter into a billion scintillating shards but not before he watched the ground coming up to meet his face.

"I have always wanted to go to America, you know. Just to see it. New York. Chicago. San Francisco. Perhaps for a vacation. One week. Ten days. I would like to see with my own eyes all these cars and superhighways one hears so much about. I would like to see if the crime rate can possibly be as horrible as we are told."

Valeri sat in a chair, his parka off, his uniform tunic unbuttoned. His face was battered, and he was hot. He could hear the wind shrieking outside, and smell the dead odor of charcoal burning in an imperfectly drawing flue. His stomach was giving him trouble, which he found odd since he had been hit on the back of the head. He wanted to vomit.

"I understand that as a young man you spent some time in the United States. In Washington, D.C. You speak the language, you even understand many of their customs. Do you think like them as well, Comrade Major? Is that your trouble?"

Valeri managed to raise his head off his chest. Colonel Yezhov sat across a rough wooden table from him. He was bald after all. His jacket was off. He wore only a sleeveless undershirt. His shoulders were massive and hairy, his wrists as big around as Valeri's biceps. Sweat poured down his face. He was drinking vodka.

They were in a large room of rough-hewn beams and dirt chinking between the boards. The windows were covered with thick pieces of felt. The floor was made of wooden pallets from which arose a terrible stench.

"Where is Nadia?" Valeri asked. His front teeth were loose. He tasted blood.

The colonel poured himself another vodka. "Is that it, then, Major? Did you betray your country for lust?"

"Where is she?"

Yezhov poured a second glass of vodka and he leaned forward far enough to place it in front of Valeri. He sat back.

"She is with her father. I think you know that."

"I would like to see her."

"Not now," Yezhov said. He drank his vodka and poured himself another. There were plates of food on the table. Eggs, salmon, sausage, potatoes and vinegar, some kind of meat with sour cream and dark bread. It was a banquet.

"What about my pilot and crew?" Valeri asked. It took all his effort to keep his head up, and keep balanced on the chair. He raised his hands and rested them on the table, the glass of vodka between them.

"They are next door. You will see them in a little bit. I promise you that much."

A particularly strong gust of wind caused the roof beams to creak, and a puff of smoke rose out of the fireplace toward the attic.

"Have something to drink, to eat, Major. You will need your strength," Yezhov said. He had a secret.

"You are here to kill them, aren't you."

"Yes, I am."

"A very foolish decision, Comrade Colonel," Valeri said. Carefully he lifted the glass of vodka to his lips and drank. The warm liquor hit his stomach and rebounded. Bile rose bitter at the back of his throat. He fought down his nausea.

Yezhov reached forward and poured him another. "An interesting view, comrade."

"You yourself will be executed for your actions here. You will be vilified in the history books."

Yezhov guffawed, then laughed out loud. "Stupid Siberians do not write history books. Nor do the seals or the moose. They do not even read them!"

"The Americans do." Valeri tossed back the second vodka.

Again Yezhov reached forward and poured him another. "What Americans? The only Americans here will die tomorrow. Do you want to know how we are going to do it?"

"Bertonelli will write the history."

"Your Bertonelli is a fool and a has-been. His own government does not believe him. His only link, besides yourself, was eliminated."

This one was well informed. Valeri took a long shot. He smiled. "Your people think Colonel Kim Tri was the only witness. There are others."

Yezhov's eyes narrowed, but he said nothing.

"In addition, comrade, Bertonelli has a list. It was made here in this gulag, Nadia brought it with her, she gave it to me, and I gave it to the American."

"Yes?"

The room was still; even the wind seemed to be temporarily at a lull.

"It is a list of every American here. Names, military serial numbers, civilian social security identification codes. Even the names of those already dead and buried."

"You are a traitor. Yes, we know that. But I spit on your list. What has it done? Nothing. There will be no help here for you, Comrade Major." Spittle flew from Yezhov's mouth. He was getting agitated. His face was beet-red now. "Tomorrow you will die along with the others. Even your little piece will burn."

Valeri knocked his glass over, spilling his vodka. He watched as it ran across the table and dripped over the edge. "Fuck your mother," he said softly.

Yezhov got unsteadily to his feet. "It will be a sight to behold. We will poison you all." He laughed. "Then your bodies will be taken to the charcoal kilns. Destructive distillation, they call it."

Valeri looked up. The colonel came around the table, grabbed a handful of Valeri's tunic, and dragged him to his feet. The man was huge, powerful, not even human. His eyes were those of an animal's, a feral creature of the night.

"Very scientific. What little is left over will be dumped far out to sea." Yezhov shook Valeri like a rag doll. "You will be with them, Major. You and your little whore."

"Leave Karaginskiy, Colonel, before it is too late for you," Valeri said. "For you there will be no hero's welcome in Moscow if you continue with this insanity."

Yezhov shook him again. 'Do you want to see your crew?' he bellowed.

It was suddenly cold. Yezhov dragged Valeri across the

room, threw open the door, and shoved him outside into the
raging wind and snow and incredible arctic cold.

"Your crew," the colonel screamed like a demented monster from hell.

A Border Guard trooper, bundled up in a parka, his eyebrows and nostril hairs loaded with hoarfrost, appeared out of
the darkness. Halos of light seemed to rise in the night all
around them. To the left, a dull red glow lit the maelstrom of
wind and snow, the odor of charring wood surrounding them.

"Here!" Colonel Yezhov wailed satanically. He shoved
Valeri forward onto his knees.

The pilot, Trusov, the back of his head smashed in, lay in
the snow, his eyes open, his tongue protruding from his
mouth. Beside him the copilot, Lyalin, lay on his side, his
left arm crooked at the elbow, his fingers pointing up to the
sky. Beyond him, Bordachev, his face bloody, and Artemyev,
the political officer, the side of his face shot away, also lay
frozen in the snow.

Valeri crawled backward, away from the terrible apparitions.

"Put him in the isolator!" Colonel Yezhov shrieked.

Another trooper appeared out of the blizzard and together
with the first, they dragged Valeri to his feet.

"Have a pleasant night, Comrade Major," Yezhov shouted
over the wind.

The building was barely twenty feet on a side. It was
divided into cells so small that a man could not lie down; at
best he could only crouch in the five or six centimeters of
water that covered the mud floor. It was called the isolator,
every gulag had one, and they all stank of death and decay, of
unwashed bodies, of urine and human feces.

Valeri got a brief impression of a central corridor off which
thick, windowless doors opened, and then he was shoved into
his cell, his door was closed and barred, and he could hear
the guards leaving.

His cell was pitch-black. For a long time he listened to the
wind outside, to his own breathing, hoping to gain his night
vision, waiting for even the dimmest of outlines. But he could
have been blind. There was absolutely no light in his cell.

Valeri slowly squatted down on his haunches, his back
against one wall, his knees against the opposite side. It wasn't
very cold in his cell. In fact he could smell burning charcoal,

and for a moment or two he nearly panicked thinking he
would suffocate. He forced himself to calm down. They
would not have gone through the effort of constructing something like this to use it as an execution chamber. This was the
softener. A few days in here and a man's brains would
become scrambled. Gone would be his defiance, his plans
and plots of revolt or escape. From the isolator emerged
docile, tractable men. At least that was the theory.

The water on the floor was cold, though. Already it was
beginning to seep through the seams of his boots. He reached
in his tunic pocket for a cigarette, but the pack wasn't there.
He soon discovered they had left him nothing, not his identification, no matches, not even the few kopecks he had been
carrying.

Truly Moscow was never farther. He felt a curiously detached sensation, as if his life had never occurred. Friends,
uncles, interrogators were all gone. His wife had left him. His
father had been rendered helpless. And Nadia had been taken
away from him. Now, so too had his freedom, and even his
sense of sight.

Only Bertonelli remained. Strange and ironic, he thought,
to pin so many hopes on a man against whose kind he had
fought so diligently. Up close, however, the American had
not been a monster. Just an ordinary man doing his job.

"Is that you, Michael?" a tired voice called, in English.

It was as if an electric wire had been put in the water.
Valeri got to his feet and pressed his ear against the rough
wood of the door.

"Who is there?" he called, also in English.

He heard a faint splashing of water. "Are you Russian?"
the voice called.

"Yes."

"Are you of the new ones who came this morning? Are
you being punished? You cannot be a spy. There is nothing
on which to spy in here."

"I did not know they were here," Valeri said. "I brought
Nadia back. I was a friend of Colonel Okulov." He could
hear more splashing. There were others here.

"How are you called?" another voice asked. He too sounded
weak, and his English also held an odd, formal note.

"Valeri Kostikov."

"How can we know you are this Colonel Okulov's friend?"

"Nadia had the notebook with your names, and numbers. I have given it to an American intelligence officer. The information is now certainly in Washington, D.C. Do you understand?"

"Oh, thank God!" the first one cried.

"Shut up, you silly bastard," the other one snapped. "If the information is out, then why has he brought Nadia back? Why have the other soldiers shown up? And who is this Kostikov to be here in the isolator with us?"

"There were gunshots earlier," still another voice said.

"I heard them," a fourth man called out in the darkness.

"They murdered my aircraft crew," Valeri said.

"We'll all get our nine grams soon," one of them said. It was prison slang for a bullet in the back of the head.

"Your government knows about you, I swear it," Valeri said. He turned away from the door and hunched down again, his knees wedged against the opposite wall. He was sick to his stomach again. He was seeing bright red flashes in the darkness. He thought he might have a concussion.

"Then what are you doing here?" the skeptic asked.

"I came to get more information to take to the United States." Valeri wondered where Nadia had been taken.

"Why?"

"To prove that you are here."

"They don't believe it?"

"I don't think so," Valeri said.

"And you are a traitor?"

"Yes."

"They mean to kill you, then," the skeptic said. "And us. That's why the new guards."

"In the morning," Valeri said.

Except for the wind moaning outside, it was very quiet for a long time. Valeri found that he had to fight to keep awake. It was his injuries, he figured, combined with the nervous tension and the air inside his cell, rotten from the charcoal heater.

"Where are we?" one of them asked timidly.

Valeri raised his head. "Karaginskiy Island. It is in the Bering Sea."

"Near Alaska?" another asked hopefully.

"Northwest of your Aleutian Islands. I think a thousand kilometers, perhaps a little more."

Again the Americans fell silent.

"How long have you been here?" Valeri asked.

"Most of us were brought here in '64 and '65. A few came earlier, and one or two in the next year."

"Do you know what year this is?"

"Yes," the skeptic said. "We're prisoners, not lunatics who cannot tell time."

"I'm sorry, I didn't mean anything . . ."

"That's all right," one of the other Americans said. "Who is President of our country?"

"Ronald Reagan."

"He's a cowboy star," one of them said.

Valeri held his peace.

"It's a different Reagan, stupid. What about the war? In Vietnam, I mean?"

"It's over," Valeri said.

"We beat the bastards?"

What to say, Valeri asked himself. The truth? Didn't the condemned man deserve that much? "Saigon fell in 1975. In the spring."

"Fuck you!" the skeptic shouted.

"There were riots in your country. Some of your young men fled to Canada instead of submitting to your draft. Your President Nixon resigned. It was a very difficult time for your country."

"You're a lying bastard."

"No. I swear it. I am here with you now. What reason would I have to lie to you?"

Valeri could hear that someone was crying softly, but the sound carried.

"What else?" one of them asked. "What else happened?"

Valeri smiled. "In 1969 your country put astronauts on the moon."

"We made it?" the skeptic shouted. "We did it? It happened?"

"Yes. It was a triumph," Valeri said.

"Is there fighting now?" another asked. His voice was soft. It sounded Irish.

Valeri sighed deeply. "Yes," he said. "Not like Vietnam. But young men are dying."

"Where?"

"My country is fighting in Afghanistan. Your Marines

have been killed in Lebanon. But you invaded Grenada and kicked out the socialist workers there.''

"In Spain?" someone asked.

"No," Valeri said. "It is an island in the Caribbean."

"An island?"

"Near Venezuela."

"Christ."

Again a stillness descended upon the isolator. It was a lot for them to assimilate. And he had merely scratched the surface. There was so much more.

"You have families here," Valeri said. "Can you tell me about them?"

The silence stretched.

"Nadia said you would not leave without them. Are they still here on the island?"

The wind seemed to intensify, the air thicken.

"How many are there? Are there a dozen wives? Two dozen? Are there many children?"

"Can you describe the new cars for me?" an American asked.


The red flashes in his blinded vision seemed to move left to right of their own volition, as if he were scanning a distant horizon. Sometimes he could look away, in his mind, and disconnect himself from the images. As the night deepened, however, so did the shapes: evil portents that finally began to metamorphose into the devil itself.

How life ended seemed more important than when.

# 25

A light rain was falling when the Military Air Transport Service KC-135 touched down at Pope Air Force Base outside Fayetteville, North Carolina. Lieutenant Hill and Sergeant Monahan had slept during the brief flight down from Andrews. Besides the crew, they were the only three on the big transport jet.

Bertonelli hunched up his coat collar as they hurried across the ramp to a civilian station wagon. The ground crew servicing the plane ignored them. Monahan drove.

Lieutenant Hill checked his watch. "It's after midnight. We're going to have to hustle." He turned to Bertonelli in the back. "I'm sorry, sir, but you're going to have to catch whatever sleep you can on the run."

"Are you people serious about this?"

Hill was surprised. "Yes, sir, of course. We've been going over the scenario now ever since you returned from Moscow."

Bertonelli sat forward. "You're telling me that Delta Force is planning on making a strike on Karaginskiy Island?"

"Yes, sir. It is a hostage situation, after all."

"Karaginskiy is in the Soviet Union."

"Yes, sir, it sure is," Sergeant Monahan said, looking at Bertonelli's reflection in the rearview mirror.

They came to a back gate and the Air Policeman on duty waved them through. The night closed in on them. Fort Bragg, where Delta was headquartered, was nearby. Bertonelli thought about the Iranian hostage debacle.

"The Russian air force might offer objections."

"We're going in under their radar," Hill said as if he were discussing the weather. "Navy has put a sub out there to

344

check on Soviet naval activity. By the time they know what
has hit them we'll be gone.''

"Why wasn't I told about this earlier?''

"I couldn't say. But General Canfield has been working
pretty closely with us.''

"Admiral Taylor?''

"He's pulled a lot of strings, sir. We've been moving
pretty fast here.''

"I can appreciate that, Lieutenant. But don't you people
understand the ramifications—''

"Excuse me, Mr. Bertonelli, but there isn't a politician
among us. We just do our jobs, nothing more.''

Bertonelli sat back. "Why was I invited along?''

Sergeant Monahan grinned. "You speak Russian, and from
what we're told you're a pretty fair shot.''

"You brought us the bacon in the first place,'' Lieutenant
Hill added. "And you've been leaning hard on a lot of people
these past few weeks.''

They were kids. Bertonelli didn't think either of them
could be thirty. They probably didn't even shave, yet they
were calmly discussing invading a foreign country . . . a
nuclear power. *The* nuclear power. Christ.

There was very little traffic on the main highway, and
absolutely none when they turned down a narrow road. They
could have been in another world. Bertonelli felt a great sense
of isolation.

"It is awesome when you stop to think about it,'' Lieutenant Hill told Bertonelli.

"How are we getting there?''

"We have a pair of Hercules—C-130s—standing by for us
at Pope. We're scheduled out of here by oh-five hundred.
We'll fly direct to Malmstrom Air Force Base at Great Falls,
Montana, refuel, and then fly up to Elmendorf outside of
Anchorage. We'll refuel there again and then make the hop
out to Adak Naval Station in the Aleutians. Just a little over
eight hundred miles to Karaginskiy. Two and a half hours in,
one hour groundtime, and two and a half hours home free.''

"There is an airstrip on the island?''

"Oh, yes, sir. A big one. They've had some heavy aircraft
in there at one time or another. Only problem for us is that
the strip is five klicks up from the camp. Not so bad for our

people, but it'll be tough getting our customers moved to the aircraft.''

"Thirty hours from now, Mr. Bertonelli," Sergeant Monahan said. "We'll be drinking beers on Adak." He chuckled. "Plop plop, fizz fizz, oh, what a relief it is."

"What?"

Hill had a big grin on his face. "Haven't you ever heard the song? The TV commercial?"

"Alka-Seltzer?"

"Yes, sir," Sergeant Monahan said. "It's our mission code name."

They came onto the Fort Bragg Military Reservation through a side gate. The stockade was a large complex that housed Delta. Very few lights shone from any of the windows. From the outside no one would know that a major operation was on its final countdown.

The rain made the streets glisten and the trees shine in the car's headlights as if they had been brushed by silver. There was no going back now, Bertonelli thought. Even if he wanted it. That option had been closed on the night he had met with Colonel Okulov in the Moscow Zoo. Had Valeri Kostikov not shown up that night, he felt certain that he would still be at this spot at this moment. It had been inevitable from the beginning.

But a strike on the Soviet Union?

He felt as if his life was comng to one of those junctions you always read about. No matter what happened he would be different afterward. They all would be forever changed.

They were passed through the gate and drove around to a side entrance of the large complex. Inside, Lieutenant Hill led them along a series of corridors and finally up to the second floor where they entered a large, very busy room. At least a dozen men, dressed in battle fatigues, small arms at their hips, were busy at work checking backpacks, talking on telephones, poring over maps and charts spread out over a large table on which a three-dimensional contour map of the northern tip of Karaginskiy Island had been constructed.

There was a definite sense of urgency here, like a high voltage in the air that seemed to emanate from a single man who was a little taller, a little more intense than the others. Bertonelli recognized him from the congressional hearing.

Colonel Kraus turned as they approached. His face was animated. He'd apparently been arguing a point with his staff. "Welcome to Delta," he said, his voice surprisingly soft.

Bertonelli let his eyes roam around the room. "Looks like you're getting ready for war games here."

"You don't approve?"

"I think it's insanity, if you ask me."

"I am asking you," Kraus said. His eyes were narrow now. There was no anger in them, only a watchfulness, as if he were a high-flying hawk waiting for his prey to make a mistake.

"We stand a very good chance of not only losing the MIAs, but of losing your people as well."

"If that happened, Mr. Bertonelli, there'd be one hell of a big splash, beause we'd take out a lot of them on the way down. They wouldn't be so successful in hiding what they've been doing after that."

Bertonelli looked at him. A purely diplomatic solution could not have been overlooked by Washington. But how to approach the Russians, who themselves were seriously divided on the issue? It was a trait, a particularly Russian trait, that would have muddied the waters of negotiation. Russians could not accept losing face. Not in private talks, and certainly not in the world arena. That fact alone almost precluded any normal means of repatriating the MIAs. But God, Bertonelli thought, the risks of using force were frightening.

Another man came around from behind the map table. Like Kraus he was well built. There was a no-nonsense air about him. Kraus made the introductions.

"My chief of staff, Bill Dennison."

He and Bertonelli shook hands.

'I understand you ran around Moscow in a Soviet Militia uniform," Dennison said. He wore a major's gold oak leaves on his shoulders.

"I only had myself to worry about."

Kraus nodded. "You did throw us quite a curve when you brought up that business about civilians."

"Goddamnit, Colonel, that's the point. Whether you want to believe it or not, there are women and children on that island. I'll be damned if I'll see their lives jeopardized—"

"We know that," Kraus broke in. He was a man of great patience.

"What?" `

"There were a few anomalies on the satellite recon photos we couldn't quite explain," Dennison said. "We had your list of MIAs. We know what it takes to house them. The camp was too big by a third."

"We didn't really think they'd have a two-to-three ratio of guards to prisoners," Kraus put in.

"We're going to get our people off that island, Mr. Bertonelli. That includes their wives and children," Dennison said.

Bertonelli wondered then if he wanted to go along with them. Perhaps he was getting too old to be putting his life on the line like this. Maybe he was beginning to grow up in the fashion JoAnn had wanted. There was something missing inside of him, according to her. Some genetic code that would make the proper connections for operating in a civilized society had gone wrong, or had never formed in him. The bogeymen were outside in the night; best to leave them there and remain inside where it was bright and warm.

It hadn't worked for him then, of course. Nor would it work for him now. He missed his wife and his daughter, but not so much that he would give up his life simply for their approval.

Colonel Okulov had promised that night in the zoo that if anything went wrong, the prisoners would be killed, their bodies destroyed. That had haunted Bertonelli's thoughts ever since because he knew the man had been telling the truth. After more than twenty years, what condition would they be in? Like the Jews in the Nazi concentration camps? The parallels were inescapable. These days the Russians were the acknowledged world experts in that sort of thing.

The fact of the matter was, he told himself, the politicians on both sides of the fence were frightened out of their minds by the entire idea. The Americans because they feared the information wasn't true, and they would end up looking very foolish if they ran off half-cocked. And the Soviets because they knew their names would be vilified for years if not decades to come once it got out.

In the long run, then, it would be easier for the Russians to destroy them, and for the Americans to forget them. That made his gorge rise. He found himself shivering.

"I'll need a kit," he said.

Dennison grinned.

Kraus drew him closer to the three-dimensional map. "We need some information from you—"

"It'll save a lot of shit if you drop the mister and start calling me Tony."

Visibility at Elmendorf Air Force Base just north of Anchorage was nearly zero in a dense ice fog. It was shockingly cold after North Carolina, and even Malmstrom in Montana. They were allowed off the C-130s to stretch their legs, but there was nothing to see. Four huge fuel trucks came out of the mist, and their crews silently connected the hoses.

Major Dennison came up. He was square-jawed, with thick eyebrows and blue, honest eyes. He reminded Bertonelli of a police recruiting poster; here was a face you could trust.

"Got a cigarette, Tony?"

"While we're refueling . . .?" Bertonelli started to ask, but then he shrugged and pulled out his pack.

"Can you smell it?" Dennison asked, taking a cigarette. He lit it.

"The fuel?"

"The Arctic. We're barely three hundred miles south of the Circle." He grinned. He was nervous.

"Where are you from?"

Dennison looked surprised. "You mean originally?"

Bertonelli nodded.

"International Falls, Minnesota. About as far north as you can live and still be in the CONUS . . . continental United States."

The big four-engine planes were lined up one behind the other. The Delta Force troops (they called themselves operators) were dressed in arctic camouflage whites over their battle fatigues. They were nearly invisible in the fog.

They had left Pope at five that morning. It had taken them eleven hours to get this far, including a one-hour fuel stop at Malmstrom outside of Great Falls. Most of them had slept on the two legs, but Bertonelli had found sleep nearly impossible though he had dozed. His adrenaline was pumping. Now it felt as if someone had poured hot sand in his eyes.

"You okay?" Dennison asked. He was a sensitive man.

"A little tired."

"Can't sleep?"

Bertonelli shook his head.

"You want something for it? I can give you a couple of bennies to keep you going. We're a third of the way through this."

Bertonelli looked sharply at him. "You're telling me that your people use drugs? Uppers? That kind of shit?"

"No need for it, Tony. We know how to sleep. Doc gave this to me in case you needed it."

Bertonelli was relieved. The Army had been having its share of drug problems. He couldn't imagine it had spread to a unit such as Delta. But he had to ask.

"I'll get some sleep on the way out to Adak. It's the excitement."

Dennison looked relieved. "It affects everyone differently. You'll be all right." He turned to leave. Bertonelli stopped him.

"What do you think our chances are?"

Dennison turned back. "Too many variables, but hell, we've got a shot."

"What about the Pentagon? What do they think up there?"

Dennison smiled. "You've got to understand something, Tony. We don't have the green light on this one. We never had, nor will we ever get it. We're on our own, you see. We were handed a theoretical problem, and we were given the complete cooperation of your Agency: intelligence, the satellite photos, the notebook, your testimony, that sort of thing. But no one has ever told us to actually go ahead with it."

"If we go belly up, we're on our own. Is that what you're saying?"

"Make you nervous.?"

"Damned right. But I want to know what I'm up against."

"The Navy will be standing by off the Soviet coast. Nuclear submarine."

"We'd have to get out to her."

"If it came to that, we'd make it," Dennison said, a hard light coming into his eyes. "Believe it." He turned and disappeared into the fog.

A light breeze sprang up. It moved the fog in swirls. The odor of aviation fuel was strong at times, and almost gone at other times.

Bertonelli flicked the hot ash from his cigarette and pocketed his butt. He walked back to the big hatch forward of the portside wing and climbed up into the aircraft. A few of the operators had remained aboard. They were still strapped into their canvas seats, asleep. Colonel Kraus was speaking on the radio up on the flight deck.

In the rear of the Hercules where their equipment was stowed, someone had made a pot of coffee. Bertonelli poured himself a cup and leaned up against one of the bulkheads near the open aft hatch.

An aluminum ladder was propped up against the wing. A pair of Air Force technicians were doing the refueling. One of them glanced down at Bertonelli, then turned away. It was an odd, bothersome gesture.

One of the young lieutenants Bertonelli had seen back at Fort Bragg came down from the flight deck. He was one of their intelligence evaluators. Dennison had identified him as David Gardner.

"We'll be out of here shortly," he said, joining Bertonelli.

"Who is Kraus talking to?"

"Weather. There's a bit of a blow out there."

"What if we're grounded?"

"The storm will provide us cover. We're going."

The young man was shivering. Bertonelli could not remember seeing anyone so intense. His instinct was to step away in case the man exploded.

"Do you want a cup of coffee?"

Gardner shook his head. "Makes me nervous."

For just a moment Bertonelli didn't know if he had heard right. But Gardner cracked a smile. Bertonelli laughed, shaking his head.

"You get any tighter, and you're going to bust your gut."

Gardner shrugged. "My dad is out there."

"Out where?"

"Karaginskiy."

Bertonelli almost dropped his coffee cup. "Your father is an MIA? On the list?"

Gardner nodded, then looked away. He could hardly contain himself. "A-1E pilot. He got himself shot down over Pleiku in August of '64. Hadn't been in 'Nam for more than five weeks. I was just a kid."

"I'm sorry," Bertonelli mumbled.

Gardner turned back. "No, sir, don't be. You brought him back to me. Wasn't for you, we'd have never known. He'd be dead and buried on some stinking Siberian island. They'd all be.''

''Do you remember him?''

''Sorta. My mother used to talk a lot about him, so I don't know how much is my memory and how much is just what she said. But I think I can see him at the lake. We had a cabin. He was swimming with my mother. They were fooling around while I was sitting on the beach.''

Bertonelli didn't know what to say. He thought about DeMille who wanted to drop the entire thing, and Valeri Kostikov who had probably given his life for them.

''I have all of his letters to my mother. Some pictures. One tape recording. Not much.''

''Has your mother been told—'' Bertonelli began, but he cut it off. He could see in Gardner's eyes that she was no longer there.

''She got remarried a couple of years ago. That's when she gave me all the letters. They're living out in California.''

''Shit,'' Bertonelli said softly.

''Yeah,'' the young man said, a crooked smile on his lips. ''It's a bitch.'' He went outside.

Moscow City Zoo was a long way off in time and in distance. But so then was everything else.

In the long view nothing really mattered. The earth would continue to spin, the sun to shine.

JoAnn would not understand this any more than she had understood anything else he had ever done. At the beginning of their relationship she had pretended for the sake of the first blush of love. She'd done them both an injustice.

Men were talking quietly in the fog. Bertonelli never felt lonelier.

''He was too good to leave behind,'' Kraus said, coming aft.

Bertonelli turned around to him. ''Coffee?''

''Sure.''

Bertonelli poured him a cup. ''He told me there was some weather brewing out there.''

''Blizzard over Karaginskiy right now. It'll provide cover. We've got some pretty good pilots.''

''There is fuel for us at Adak?''

''Navy dropped some off a month ago,'' Kraus said. ''Nervous?''

"Scared shitless," Bertonelli admitted. "The middle of a revolution in Chile is easier than this. Even Moscow was safer."

"You can stick with me, you'll be all right."

"That's not what I mean."

Kraus just looked at him.

"I'm talking about our boys. Their Russian families."

"We'll take care of them. We're not going to leave them behind."

"What if they don't want to come?"

"We thought about it."

"It's been more than twenty years."

"We know about the hostage syndrome. It's our business."

"The hostage syndrome, made more intense by the fact that at least some of them have wives and children."

Kraus went to the open hatch and looked out. The fog seemed to be thinning. It looked as if the refueling operation was going well. A lot of the men were already starting to drift back.

"Geoff Hill is in charge of the Red element, picking up the MIAs. I'll talk to him." Kraus looked back. "How sure are you about any of this, Tony? Did someone tell you they wouldn't cooperate?"

"I have nightmares about them."

"I know."

"Twenty years."

Kraus sighed deeply. "Incredible. Fucking incredible."

There were ninety-seven Delta Force operators including Colonel Kraus on this mission. They had been divided into three elements: Red, which was charged with securing the MIAs; White, which would take and hold the airstrip; and Blue, which would take out the Russian guards. Bertonelli's primary job was to aid the Blue element in interrogating the gulag commandant or his officers, and getting answers to the top-priority questions: the exact number and location of all live American prisoners; the location of any radio links with the Russian mainland, especially military links; the extent of coast defense measures, especially those targeting Karaginskiy; and the locations of the dozen graves containing the remains of the MIAs who had already died on the island.

"I'll stay with my assignment, if you don't mind," Bertonelli said.

"Right," Kraus said heavily.

"I just wanted you to know what we might be up against."

Kraus turned back. "I appreciate it, Tony, I really do." He shook his head, his jaw tight. "There are going to be a lot of sorry, dead sonsofbitches on that island tonight. I can guarantee it."

Afternoon tinged the edges of the clouds with pink and salmon. Darkness still came early at this latitude. Before long the summer sun would shine late into the night. For now, however, the impending night seemed fraught with terror and uncertainty. From ten thousand feet the islands of the Aleutian chain seemed devoid of life; the Pacific Ocean to the south and the Bering Sea to the north seemed inhospitable. The world below could have been Mars.

They fixed a hot meal in the aircraft's galley. No one slept the last hour into Adak Naval Station.

Lieutenant Gardner came aft. "Do you think my father is still alive?"

"I'd suspect there was a good chance of it," Bertonelli said.

Gardner kept fingering the safety catch on his .22-caliber suppressed automatic. "I don't know what I'll do if he isn't."

"Your job."

Gardner was sheepish. "You're right."

The sun was setting in the west, filling the airplane with a bloodred light when they touched down at the remote naval station. To the northwest out across the Bering Sea, a huge bank of thick, black clouds rolled angrily across the horizon. They would be flying into that in the next hour or two. Bertonelli thought about Washington and Moscow; he'd been a misfit in both places. Maybe here was his proper milieu after all.

Kraus and Dennison went off across a stony field to speak with the station commander while the troops brought the aviation gas back to the airplanes in fifty-five gallon drums from a depot at the end of the runway.

There was a sense of quiet urgency now. The nearer they

got to their objective, the more subdued they became. Their
mood was infectious, and Bertonelli found himself ordering
his thoughts, making ready for whatever might come their
way.

It wasn't until long after dark before the refueling was done
and Kraus and Dennison returned.

"The storm is showing no signs of letting up, at least for
the moment," Kraus told his people on the runway next to
the lead aircraft. "But it's not getting any worse. With luck
we'll be back here in six hours. We'll refuel and continue
back to Elmendorf where we will drop off our customers, at
which time our mission will be completed."

Kraus was a conductor, and his men the finely tuned
orchestra. To a man they were music lovers, and this would
be their finest symphony.

Every one of them knew it.

The Hercules's engines seemed louder; the props bit deeper
into the thick air. The sound was unnatural. Labored. They
were well below Russian coastal radar, which meant they
flew at barely fifty feet, just above some of the larger waves.

There had been no lights outside or inside the aircraft.
Occasionally someone lit a cigarette, but they cupped the
flame and the ash. There was little or no talking in the
darkness.

At times the blizzard tossed them around like a toy in a
maelstrom. At other times the air was smooth. Nothing could
be seen out the windows except for the black night and the
horizontal streaks of snow.

On a mission like this, life was reduced to its essentials.
Choices became simple. Food, warmth, firepower. Nothing
else mattered.

There was no future in thinking about mortality at a time
like this. Bertonelli felt he had become soft. Like Gardner
before, he began to play with the safety catch on his weapon.
He had to consciously stop himself.

The interior of the main cabin was suddenly bathed in red
light. Everyone looked up. It was the signal they were five
minutes out. For a long moment or two no one moved, until
Steve Monahan jumped up and clicked a toy clicker twice. He

was in charge of the White element. They'd be the first off the first plane.

On his signal twenty operators donned their balaclavas, their silk gloves (which provided warmth yet allowed dexterity), and lastly their night vision infrared goggles. The advantage this night would be theirs.

The plane banked to the left. They had found the exact location of the airstrip with a sophisticated satellite navigation system. They would make one pass to drop ground flares, then come in steeply for a quick landing.

Monahan clicked his clicker twice again. This time his operators brought out their weapons, worked the ejector slides several times in rapid succession, then reloaded the clips and cycled live rounds into the firing chambers. Two of the men each carried a pair of disposable LAW rockets, which were light antitank weapons. Recon photos had shown no evidence of any type of armored vehicle on the island, but there was so much natural foliage that half a division could have been hidden down there.

The C-130 climbed steeply, its engines screaming at full power, then it banked sharply to the right. For several long seconds they seemed to hang at an extreme angle, but then the Hercules's nose dropped and it seemed as if they were falling out of control.

Monahan was hanging on to the overhead straps, nothing of his face visible behind the balaclava and the goggles. He looked like a man from a fifties science-fiction movie.

Bertonelli's bowels felt loose.

They touched down very hard with a savage bark of tires. Instantly the big props were reversed, and the pilot laid on the brakes. The second C-130 would circle once to make sure the runway was secured, and then would make its landing approach and touch down.

Even before the big plane came to a halt, Monahan went to the aft hatch and undogged it. He held it in place with one hand. With his other he clicked his clicker again.

His twenty operators jumped to their feet and, weapons at the ready, lined up at the door. The two men with the LAW rockets pulled the firing pins and extended the firing tubes.

The plane came to a complete halt, the red lights flicked twice, and Monahan slammed open the hatch. The interior of the main cabin was suddenly filled with the howling blizzard.

A strange orange light flickered outside from the runway flares they had dropped. The White element was out of the plane in five seconds flat.

Kraus came down from the flight deck as Dennison jumped up and went to the hatch. The rest of the men lined up behind him. They were the Blue element who would be first into the gulag itself. They would neutralize the guards.

Kraus was forward with a walkie-talkie. Bertonelli was aft, just opposite the main hatch. He was sweating beneath his face mask.

Over the shrieking blizzard and the deep-throated roar of the aircraft engines, they could hear the sounds of small arms fire just outside. A second later one of the LAW rockets exploded with a tremendous white flash.

Kraus raised the walkie-talkie. Dennison was looking over his shoulder. Gardner was in his group. He wasn't shivering. Now that the operation had actually begun, he looked as steady as a rock.

Bertonelli checked his automatic.

Kraus looked up and nodded.

Dennison and his operators literally exploded out of the airplane. They would run flat out in two columns the five kilometers down to the Gulag. Any unfriendly in their path wouldn't stand a chance.

Kraus shouted something up to the aircraft's crew.

Bertonelli went to the hatch. Back along the runway several flares still provided some light. Straight ahead, at the edge of the access road, which recon showed led down to the gulag, some sort of a half-track vehicle was furiously burning. In the flickering lights he could see the ghostly figures of the Delta operators moving through the horizontally driven snow.

"Get out!" Kraus shouted, starting aft. "The other plane is coming in."

Bertonelli scrambled out of the airplane into the howling wind. Even before Kraus joined him and they started away, their C-130's engines revved up and the plane was moving to the extreme end of the runway where it would turn around.

Monahan appeared out of the darkness at the side of the airstrip. He flipped his night vision goggles up. "There is a Tupolev recon aircraft at the end of the runway."

"Crew?"

"Deserted. Main hatch open. Looks like blood in the cockpit."

"Christ, have they started moving out our people?" Bertonelli asked.

"No way of telling," Monahan said.

"Put a torch to it," Kraus said. "What about Blue?"

"They're on their way."

Powerful landing lights appeared above the end of the runway as the second C-130 came in for a landing. Aboard was the Red element in charge of securing the MIAs and their families. They carried with them clothing and first aid gear. None of them knew what shape the prisoners would be in. Bertonelli was getting worried about what they might find.

"Send Red down on the double!" Kraus shouted. "Tony and I are going to head down to the encampment."

"Watch yourself. They have this place staffed with KGB Border Guard-troops. Maybe Viktor units. We neutralized four just at the road."

"Any casualties?"

"Howard and Todd. They'll be okay."

"No matter what happens, I want this airstrip kept open."

"You got it, boss," Monahan said.

"Let's hit it, then," Kraus said tersely.

Bertonelli fell in alongside him as they scrambled over the snowbank at the side of the runway and skirted the still burning half-track. Behind them the C-130 that had just landed was slowing down in gusts of wind and swirls of snow.

They started down the access road that cut through the tall pine trees. In places the road made sharp curves around gigantic black boulders and rock outcroppings. The airstrip was atop a flat hill. The road dropped steadily down toward the northern coast. The elevation was something of a surprise. The satellite photos didn't show much in the way of contour.

A dark figure came charging out of the trees behind Kraus. Bertonelli caught the movement out of the corner of his eye. He spun around, brought up his weapon, hesitated only a split second, and then squeezed off three shots in quick succession the moment he realized the man was not wearing white camouflage. The Russian went down in a bloody heap.

Kraus had turned back, his suppressed .22 automatic at arm's length. He looked up.

"You all right, Tony?"

"Yeah."

Several shots from unsilenced rifles came from farther down the road. Kraus jumped up. The firing only lasted a second or two and then stopped. Blue had evidently run into some resistance.

"Keep on the move—you'll be harder to hit!" Kraus shouted over his shoulder as he started down the hill.

Bertonelli fell in behind him, his heart hammering. KGB Border Guard Viktor units were execution squads. They'd been sent here to kill the prisoners. Three months, he kept telling himself. He'd taken too long. He was too late.

He caught up with Kraus a few hundred yards down the road as they encountered the first of the bodies. There had been a fierce fire fight here. Eight KGB Border Guard troops were down. There was a lot of blood in the snow. Most of them had been shot only once in the head. One had taken three hits in the chest. There was no doubt they were all dead.

This low, protected by the rocks and the trees, the wind and snow weren't so intense. Above, they could faintly hear the C-130s. Below, there was no noise. Straight overhead the wind worked in the treetops.

Kraus had stopped just past the last body. He raised the walkie-talkie. "Blue, K-one."

An explosion rumbled up the hill from below.

"Come," the walkie-talkie blared.

Two more Russians were lying beside the road fifty yards farther on; both of them had been shot in the face at close range. There was a lot of blood in their eyes. It was clearly visible. Everything suddenly was.

Bertonelli stepped back, his stomach suddenly twisting into a knot. He raised his gun. Everything seemed wrong, somehow. He couldn't understand what it was, though. The light was disturbing. He looked up.

"Aurora borealis," Kraus shouted from the other side of the corpses.

Bertonelli looked at him. For just a moment he did not know where he was. He'd never been affected like this . . . or had he, he asked himself.

"Move it, mister!" Kraus shouted.

Bertonelli took another half step back. He thought he might have seen horses farther down the road. Mountains in the distance. The air was suddenly high and very thin. Up the road would be the women and children. Dozens of them lying there carved up in the snow, their bodies violated, mutilated. No one was safe now. Especially not the women and children. The women and children. . . .

Kraus came back. He could not understand. Christ, how could anyone understand. Not unless you had been there. . . .

"This isn't Afghanistan!" Kraus shouted. "We've got a job to do. Now! They're depending on us."

Bertonelli stared at him. He knew. Kraus knew it all. The merry-go-round was beginning to slow. The snow was suddenly cold and real on his face. The wind was here, in the trees, not in the mountain passes.

"These aren't prison guards," Bertonelli said, looking at the Russians.

"They're Viktor troops. The execution squad."

"Christ."

"Are you all right now?"

Bertonelli looked up. "We can't leave anyone behind."

"We won't," Kraus promised. "Ready?"

"Sure," Bertonelli said. He stepped over the bodies of the two Russian executioners, walked a few feet, then stopped and went back. He raised his pistol and fired the rest of his fourteen-shot clip into the two bodies.

When he was finished he ejected the spent clip, pocketed it, and inserted a fresh clip. He released the ejector slide.

Kraus was waiting for him a few yards farther down the hill. "Now we have lives to save."

Bertonelli felt better. A certain clarity had come to the night. He felt good. Elated, now. Heady. He had finally struck a blow at his own personal demons. When the Russian army came here to pick up the pieces, to bury their dead, they would see the condition of these two bodies. In Moscow the old men would know what happened here, and why. They would feel his outrage all the way to the Kremlin.

Kraus started down the hill. Bertonelli fell in behind him. At the bottom, the road flattened out where it curved through a dense stand of trees and then came out into the open snowstorm. They could hear the waves pounding the rocky coast very near. A fire burned ahead, and off to the right, a red glow seemed to light a part of the night. The aurora borealis lent a ghostly, unreal light to everything. The odor of

charring wood was everywhere. Dante could have written this
scene, Bertonelli thought.

"K-one, at the edge of the woods," Kraus spoke into the
walkie-talkie.

"Straight ahead about five hundred meters. Keep your
head down." The speaker was Dennison.

They started across the open ground. They could see the
tracks of Blue element in the snow. Several shots were fired
from ahead. They sounded like they had come from a rifle.
Probably a Kalashnikov, Bertonelli figured. The Russian assault rifle. To their left they heard three soft pops from a
silenced .22. Dennison appeared out of the storm.

"Four of them in the main building about fifty meters
straight ahead," Dennison said. "Including the commandant,
we think."

"How about the others?" Kraus asked.

Bertonelli couldn't see very much. But it was hard to
imagine the MIAs being stuck here for more than twenty
years. There had been live sightings of Americans in Vietnam
and Cambodia and Laos. There, it would have been hell for
them. But here there was no reason for their captivity. There
had never been a reason.

"Dead," Dennison said.

"We take any casualties?"

"Dave Gardner. He's dead."

"His dad was here."

"Yeah."

"How about the MIAs?" Kraus asked.

Bertonelli held his breath.

"They're here, Jerry," Dennison said grimly. He shook his
head. "You're not going to believe it when you see them."

"Bad?"

"From what we've seen so far, we're going to have to
carry a lot of them."

"Have you talked to any of them?"

"They don't know who we are. They're distrustful."

"Families? Did you find them?"

"Not as many of them as we thought. Tom and Rodriguez
are up there now. They're all in a big hut back toward the
charcoal kilns. Probably a dozen women, maybe fourteen or
fifteen kids. They're scared out of their minds."

"How about the grave sites? Any word?"

Dennison lowered his night vision goggles. His eyes were moist. "We found the graves, Jerry. They've all been opened. And emptied. No bodies."

"What happened?" Bertonelli asked. "What the hell did they do?"

"The charcoal kilns, Tony. They cremated the bodies. Probably dumped the ashes in the sea so there wouldn't be any evidence."

Bertonelli's stomach heaved. Dennison had more to say. Kraus motioned for him to continue.

"That's how they were going to kill the rest of them. In the kilns. They had the place set up like a production-line crematorium with steel body racks on skids."

A couple of shots were fired from the main building. They ducked down.

"We got here first," Kraus said harshly. "Let's take the main hut. But I want their C.O. alive if at all possible. I'd like to have a few words with the sonofabitch."

"How about communications?" Bertonelli asked.

"In the main hut, but we took out their antenna almost immediately." Dennison looked worried, though. "They had plenty of time to send a message, Jerry. At least thirty seconds, maybe even a lot longer."

Kraus raised his walkie-talkie. "Red element, K-one."

"On our way," Lieutenant Hill radioed. They could hear he was puffing. They were running down the hill.

"Pick up the pace. Half hour ground time. We may be getting some company. The main hut is the only hot spot for the moment. Everything else is home free."

"Roger."

"Lets get it over with," Kraus said.

They ran forward. Three more shots were fired at random from the main hut, followed by a half dozen from the Delta's silenced .22s.

Kraus flopped face down in the snow, Dennison and Bertonelli on either side of him barely thirty feet away from a large, rough-hewn log building. Smoke poured from one chimney. The two windows they could see in front were dark. It looked to Bertonelli as if they wre covered from inside.

One of Dennison's men crawled over from the left. "We got four dead Russians this side of the building. Not Viktors."

"Who the hell are they?" Dennison asked.

"Don't know. But they look like flyboys to me. Dressed in flight suits. One of them has been shot in the head at close range."

"There is a Tupolev at the end of the airstrip. They must have brought it in," Kraus said.

"That probably explains the Russian in the punishment cells, then."

Bertonelli looked at the kid. "Did he give you his name?"

"No, sir. But Smitty thought he was talking in English."

"He's not dead, is he?"

"We left him there. None of the prisoners have been touched."

"Do you know who he is?" Kraus asked.

"I think so," Bertonelli said. "I want to pull him out of there."

Kraus thought about it for a moment. He looked up at the main hut. "Let's get this situation stabilized first."

"What do you want me to do?"

"Just hold here for a bit," Kraus said. He motioned for Dennison to go ahead. A half-dozen Delta operators had moved up into position on either side of the main hut. Dennison gave them the thumbs-up, barely visible through the blowing snow, except for the night vision goggles they were wearing. They moved in closer to the front door, then crouched down.

A Delta operator came up from behind and Dennison moved out of the way for him. The young man carried a LAW rocket.

"Ready?" Dennison asked softly.

The kid grinned and raised the rocket-launching tube to his shoulder. He sighted on the front door of the main hut.

"Now," Dennison said.

The rocket fired. A split second later the front of the main hut erupted in a brilliant flash. Even before the debris stopped flying, the six Delta operators who had crouched on either side of the door leaped up and charged into the building. Two unsilenced shots were fired from inside and then there was nothing, the sounds of the suppressed .22s too faint to be heard at this distance.

One of the Delta operators appeared at the front door a few seconds later and waved. It was over that quickly.

Kraus got to his feet. "Go ahead and get your man," he

said to Bertonelli. "But if he's not who you think he is, shoot him."

"With pleasure," Bertonelli said, jumping up. He glanced at the main hut, then followed Dennison's man through the eerily lit storm. They reached a low, very long concrete-block building without windows or vents, and only one small door in the front as a short burst of rifle fire sounded from somewhere up the hill, then was silenced.

"Just in here." The kid pulled open the door. "Red element should be along momentarily to release them."

Even in the arctic cold the stench coming out of the isolator was intense. Bertonelli was almost bowled over backward by it. He fought with everything he had not to vomit, and to force himself to go inside.

"I don't know which cell, sir. They're all occupied."

There was another burst of unsilenced small arms fire from somewhere outside. In here it seemed distant. Bertonelli stood just within the doorway for several long seconds trying to get himself accustomed to the stench and the lack of light. In his heart he knew he could never get used to it, though. He would not have survived twenty years. He would have been one of the ones already dead.

What chance would anyone have in here?

The thought of what had already happened, and of what had almost happened up at the charcoal kilns was impossible for him to believe. He was actually here, yet he couldn't believe it.

What would happen when they got home? Who would accept them? Where would they fit?

"Kostikov?" he called out. "Valeri Kostikov?"

How many people had died in this stinking hole? It made him dizzy to think about it.

He stepped a little farther into the low, narrow corridor off which short wooden doors were barred with metal angle irons.

The shooting outside stopped completely. Bertonelli turned his head to listen.

"Bertonelli?" Valeri called.

"Kostikov?" Bertonelli shouted, crossing to one of the doors. He pounded on it with the butt of his gun.

"Here," Valeri called from the next cell.

Bertonelli hurriedly pulled the angle iron off its brackets, tossed it aside, and yanked open the door. The room was incredibly small: barely four feet tall, five feet deep, and two feet wide. Valeri wore no coat. The collar of his KGB uniform tunic was pulled up around his neck and ears. It was freezing in the cell; his nose and eyes were running. He was squatting, his arms around his chest for warmth, his back against one wall, his knees wedged against the opposite wall.

"It is incredible," Valeri croaked, squinting up.

"I brought the cavalry."

"Cavalry?" Valeri asked, pushing himself up. "Horses?"

Bertonelli stifled a laugh. He helped Valeri up and out of the cell. Even the dim lights from the fires and the aurora were too much at first for him after the total darkness of the cell.

The isolator was extremely quiet. There were other prisoners there. Americans. They heard the English, but they were keeping still. Bertonelli thought it ironic that the first man he had released from the gulag was a Russian. And KGB, at that.

"Nadia is here somewhere," Valeri said. "She must go with you."

"We're taking you all."

"I can't," Valeri said, stiffening in Bertonelli's helping hand.

"Bullshit. They're not exactly going to welcome you with open arms in Moscow for this, you know."

"I will go to my father."

"You'll come with us until this business is sorted out. Afterward, if you still want to return, you have my word you'll be free to go."

Bertonelli had to help him to the outside door. The Delta operator, his weapon in hand, looked at Valeri's KGB uniform. He raised his gun, the hammer was back.

"He's one of us," Bertonelli said.

The kid was shaking. "Step aside, sir."

Behind them a half dozen of Geoff Hill's Red element hurried by, leading a group of at least two dozen barely human figures, most of them dressed in filthy rags, white arctic parkas thrown over their frail shoulders.

The kid glanced over his shoulder at them. "That's the third group. They look a whole hell of a lot better than the first two."

"He didn't do this! He helped stop it!"

"He's a fucking Russian!" the kid shouted, stepping forward.

Bertonelli braced himself for the bullet, his left hand on Valeri's arm, the .22 automatic in his right. He would not raise his gun against the kid, whose reflexes in any event would be much quicker. The young man was just as nervous as he was outraged. He had probably never seen a Russian before this night.

It seemed to take forever.

"The colonel is in the main hut." The kid finally lowered his gun. "He'll want to talk to you about this one."

"Get someone to let our boys out of here right now," Bertonelli said tiredly.

"Get him something different to wear," the kid said. "Someone is bound to shoot him dead."

The main hut's front door, a part of the front wall, and a section of the roof was gone. Valeri wore Bertonelli's camouflage white outer cover over his KGB tunic. Even so, several American shock troops did double takes as they hurried past. There seemed to be activity everywhere. The gulag was definitely being liberated. Valeri couldn't figure out how they had gotten there. A steady stream of Delta operators and MIAs hurried through the storm to the road that led up to the airstrip. Up the hill, to the left, the charcoal kilns had been set afire, the wind-whipped flames dancing crazily in the night, sparks rising hundreds of feet into the arctic sky like ten trillion fireflies finally set free after a lifetime of darkness and servitude. They would see it in Moscow.

A Russian flag had flown in front of the main building. It was gone now, the halyard whipped straight out about halfway up the pole.

Other buildings around the gulag had been set afire, and were furiously burning in the fifty-to sixty-kilometer-per-hour winds off the Bering Sea.

Thirty-six hours in the cell with only one meal of cold gruel, stale black bread, and weak tea had sapped his strength. But then, Valeri had not expected to be alive this long.

The Russian has three principles, his father used to say: perhaps, somehow, and never mind. The last had stayed the colonel's hand.

Had the Americans somehow managed to manufacture the storm as well? Anything was possible, he thought, on a night such as this.

A major came out of the main hut. He stopped short when he spotted Bertonelli and Valeri.

"Is this Kostikov?" Dennison asked.

"Yes," Bertonelli said.

"Have you found a girl?" Valeri asked. "Her name is Nadia Burdine." From where he stood he could see into the big hut. Colonel Yezhov was alive. He stood in front of the table, his hands over his head. A half-dozen Americans surrounded him. A tall, thickly built man said something, then reached out and backhanded Yezhov in the mouth.

"We haven't really identified anyone yet, Major," Dennison said.

"How about the families?"

"We're getting them. But I want to tell you that many of them do not want to leave."

"They must!" Valeri said. "Anyone left here will be killed!"

"We know that. They will come with us."

"There will be a place for them in the United States?"

Dennison took a moment to answer. He nodded. "Yes."

"The families, I mean." Valeri wanted to make his English crystal clear.

"The families," Dennison said.

Valeri looked up then, and he saw her. Nadia, bundled up in an arctic camouflage coat, her feet and legs bare, was being led from the rear of the main hut by one of the Americans. Blood trickled down from her nose.

"Nadia!" Valeri shouted to her.

She was looking at Yezhov. She turned when she heard her name. So did everyone else.

Valeri pushed Dennison aside and jumped over the still smoldering debris. Yezhov stepped back in fear when he saw who it was.

"Who the hell . . ." the thick-necked colonel who had been interrogating Yezhov shouted.

Nadia broke away. "Valerik!" she cried.

They flew into each other's arms. Her coat opened. She was nude. It was very cold in the destroyed building and everyone was watching them, but they did not care.

"I thought you were dead," she said in Russian.

"They came to take us away. We are safe now."

"I am afraid, Valerik."

"Yezhov and his men were planning on killing all of you . . . and me too. They were going to burn our bodies in the charcoal fires. But we're safe now."

"Will they take all of us?"

"Yes. And I will come with you to make sure everything is right."

She pulled away from him and looked deeply into his eyes. "Valerik, you will stay with me?"

Valeri shook his head. "Not in America, Nadia. Not there. I am not a traitor to my country."

"Your country did this!"

"No. Only some men who were crazy, and later other men who were afraid. Not the *Rodina*."

"You cannot go back."

"No," Valeri said softly. "Not that either."

"Then Finland, or Norway or Sweden. My father says these are good places like Russia. Better. Free."

Valeri nodded tiredly. He had no fight left.

Bertonelli had come into the hut. As Nadia stood by, in total fatigue, her coat still open, Valeri saw that her body was covered with bruises. Her breasts and her thighs were marked with cigarette burns. Some of her hair had been pulled out of her head. Two of her teeth were missing; blood trickled from her mouth as well as her nose. Tears welled up in her eyes.

Yezhov had done it. He had tortured her. *Used* her.

"Find the girl some clothes, and then get them both up to the airstrip," the bull-necked colonel said. His name tag read Kraus.

Again, incongruously, Valeri thought back to his sad Tanya and her poetry. *What reasons can there be for my life/so oddly shaped/so like the visage of some terrible apparition./ Looking out the window across the plane of my past/what hint of future/what harbinger of fates yet unknown.*

"Kostikov . . . ?" Bertonelli was saying.

As a young boy at home with his mother and father and his sister Lara, his future had been crystal clear. Only after his mother died and after he got older did his vision become muddied. For a while there, married to Tanya—after the happiness had gone out of their relationship—his eyes were so blinded he sometimes didn't know what would happen week to week.

Now, however, at this moment he fully understood who he was and what he would have to do. He smiled.

He stepped around Nadia, and before anyone had a chance to react, he grabbed Bertonelli's .22 automatic, raised it, and fired four shots into Yezhov's face, one taking the man's cheek, the second exploding in an eye socket, the third shattering his teeth, and the last entering his forehead and exiting the back of his head with a mushroom explosion of blood, bone, and brain tissue. Yezhov crashed backward onto the table, which collapsed beneath him.

Kraus, Dennison, and the other Delta operators had dropped into shooter's stances, their weapons trained on Valeri, who very slowly lowered the automatic, then let it drop to the floor.

Nadia came to him again, and he put his arm around her.

"Now we will go," he said.

# EPILOGUE

The spring wind off the Gulf of Finland was still very cold, though not nearly so cold as Siberia. Valeri Kostikov, his coat collar hunched up, his hands stuffed deeply into the sheepskin-lined pockets, stood on the rocks at the water's edge looking at a distant point of land to the northeast.

It was Russia.

He had come a long way, the thought occurred to him. Much farther than he could ever have predicted, and certainly much farther than he had ever wanted. It was a one-way road. There was no way back. Not for any of them. With Uncle Gennadi dead and his father implicated in the escape of the MIAs, Mikhail murdered, Lipasov dead, and Tanya gone, there was truly nothing left there for him.

Nor could it be much better for the MIAs. He shuddered to think of them. Colonel Kraus, Bertonelli, and the others knew it too. Certainly it would take months and years for many of them to return to a normal life. Some of them would never heal, of course; their wounds were too deep. There were other problems as well. Many of the MIAs had left families at home when they had gone off to war. Now some of them were bringing Siberian families home. How that could work was impossible to imagine. There would be heartaches. Finally there was the problem of the relationship between the United States and the Soviet Union. If it could not survive, neither could the world.

Valeri closed his eyes and tried to imagine his past. It seemed important to him at the moment. His mother was there. His father and sister too. They were happy and it was summer. They were dancing around and around for the sheer joy of it. A family together. . . .

"Valerik," Nadia called from the road.

Valeri opened his eyes and turned as she made her way down the rocks from where their car was parked. Her hair streamed out behind her as she ran and jumped. It was a joy to watch her.

"Be careful you don't fall," he called out.

She laughed, finally reaching the spot where he stood. He took her into his arms and they kissed for a long time. When they parted she glanced across the bay toward the Russian border less than three kilometers away, then looked up into his eyes.

"Do you miss it already?" she asked.

"I'll always miss it," he said softly. "I'm a Russian. I'm proud of it. Even now."

"I know," Nadia said with great feeling. She touched his cheek with her fingertips. "I know, Valerik," she said again. Then she took his arm and together they slowly made their way back up to the road.

Bertonelli showed his pass at the main gate of Andrews Air Force Base outside Washington, D.C., then hurried down to the flight line.

There was a lot of traffic today. Crowd control barriers and ribbons had been put up. Even so, people seemed to be everywhere. Near the Military Air Transport Service's main hangars, a dozen Greyhound buses were parked.

The day was bright and warm, in the eighties, with a light breeze from the river that ruffled the huge banner draped across the front of the east hangar. WELCOME HOME, it said. It gave Bertonelli a chill. The problems were just beginning.

He parked his car behind base operations after going through three more security checks. At the base of the outside stairs that led up to the observation platform on the roof, he was stopped again, and this time he was searched for weapons before he was allowed to pass.

The DCI, Admiral Taylor, broke away from his retinue at the roof's edge. He and Bertonelli shook hands. There were at least two dozen people here. Most of them high-ranking military and civilians who did not choose to be a part of the public reception.

"They should be touching down at any moment now," the director said.

"I was afraid I was going to miss them," Bertonelli said. "Traffic . . ." Actually he had no real reason for being here other than curiosity. He'd been told that the medicos and the psychologists had worked wonders in the past three months. He came to see for himself.

Taylor took his arm and led him back to the edge of the observation deck. Across the flight line were at least ten thousand people. The television networks had set up towers for their camera equipment, and a large section of bleachers had been erected for the print media.

"They're getting the story they want, Anthony, in a large measure because of your efforts."

"It looks like a circus, sir."

"They're heroes," Taylor said, smiling.

In the distance, to the southeast, Bertonelli suddenly could see the two Air Force KC-135 transport jets coming in on their approach, supposedly from Bangkok, Thailand, where their repatriation had occurred. Neither the government of Vietnam nor the Soviets had made any response to the story. But it would not hold up for long, Bertonelli thought. It could not.

"Do you really think the public will buy it?" he asked.

Taylor's smile spread wider. "Who would believe they were in Siberia. All these years." He shook his head. "Of course they'll buy it."

Then they could hear the crowd beginning to roar, the sound rising and rolling across the flight line, applause building and cascading over the cheers, somewhere car horns tooting, and finally the jet sounds of the incoming KC-135s.

# Tales of International Intrigue and Riveting Suspense from

# SEAN FLANNERY

# Bestselling Thrillers—
# action-packed for a great read